Steal the

Thieves, Book 3

Lexi Blake

Steal the Moon
Thieves, Book 3
Lexi Blake

Published by DLZ Entertainment, LLC
Copyright 2014 DLZ Entertainment, LLC
Edited by Chloe Vale and Kasi Alexander
ISBN: 978-1-937608-25-5

Acknowledgments

Thanks as always to my editorial team – Chloe Vale and Kasi Alexander and my amazing beta readers, Riane Holt and Stormy Pate. As always, I thank Liz Berry who cheers me on when I think I can't edit another word and has a glass of wine waiting for me when I cross the finish line. I want to thank my husband and my mom who keep things going at home when I can't be there. And I want to thank my kids for always understanding.

This book is for Dylan who will likely never read this, but who should know that I love him always. My baby started out as a boy, but I'm deeply proud of the man he's becoming.

Chapter One

It isn't the easiest thing in the world to ditch one bodyguard, much less two. The task is made infinitely harder when said bodyguards are also werewolves. They don't tend to fall for the whole pointing one way as you run the other way "made you look" ruse. Even if you manage to arrange a small diversion, say a minor pixie invasion, once they handle the problem, they're right on your ass again. A werewolf bodyguard will track you through a crowded club, across an enormous mall, and they'll follow you into the ladies room if you take too long.

If, and I give this just as an example, you manage to dodge them long enough to catch a bus, at least one of those suckers will race after you. When you get off the bus you thought was your ticket to freedom, you get to face a wolf who's had to hang on for dear life more than twenty city blocks. He's breathed in enough exhaust fumes to make him one truly angry puppy, and you can kiss any goodwill you previously earned bye-bye.

When saddled with two men dedicated to curtailing your fun and freedom, you have to get creative. They don't understand your need for alone time. Your privacy is not their concern.

Unfortunately, I really needed a little privacy.

I grinned at Zack Owens. Zack was my main tormentor, er, bodyguard. His brother, Lee, preferred to take whichever duty allowed him to prowl around in search of a threat. He claimed to have attention deficit disorder and an extreme dislike for staying put. Zack had drawn the short straw and got to be my main baby-sitter. From his constant taciturn expression, I don't think he liked his job much. He looked at me across the table we were sitting at in Ether, my boyfriend's nightclub, and got that "shit, what are you up to" look.

"Zoey, I swear to god, I have exactly one hour left on my shift." Zack pointed an accusatory finger at me. I'd seen that well-manicured finger turn into a really dangerous claw on more than one occasion. "If you try to run off somewhere, I'll lock you up for a week. I'll write a report that will terrify Quinn and Donovan so much they'll put another two guards on you."

"That's mean." He wasn't above doing just that. He would write a gleeful fiction, and the truth was it would probably be believed without question. I crossed my arms defensively. "And should you really be talking to your employer that way?"

Zack rolled his chocolate brown eyes. "You're not my employer, Zoey. You're my trial. You're my tribulation. You're my fucking headache at least eight hours a day. Your husband is my master. Your boyfriend is my boss. For some reason, they don't want you dead, although I swear to god after that trick you pulled with the bus, I just might be the one who does you in."

Maybe it was a little more than an example, but I stand by the attempt. Zack was more tenacious than I could have dreamed.

I'd met young Zack the previous year in Las Vegas when Danny, Dev, and I attended a vampire convention. It had been awful and wonderful. I died and met Hell's big boss. That part had been crappy. The wonderful part had been finally sorting out my relationships. I'm that insane woman who's madly in love with two men. I'm that insanely lucky woman who gets to keep them both. After Vegas, the boys decided to try alternative lifestyles. Given the boys in question were an earthbound faery prince and a vampire king, alternative is fitting.

I married Daniel Donovan through a sacred ceremony that ties a vampire to his companion. I'm his nightly meal, his best friend, and his true love, though lately I was replaced in the best friend role by my boyfriend, the other tip to our triangle.

Devinshea Quinn is the second in line for the *Daoine Sidhe* throne, not that he would last long on it. He's mortal, a fact his people couldn't accept. He left his home to make his way in the human world after he got sick of his mother's manipulations. His twin brother was the heir, and I'd already promised his family a good thrashing if I ever had the chance to meet them.

Dev met me on a blind date, found he had an appetite for my personal brand of destruction, and our little triangle was formed. It was hard at first. There'd been jealousy and guilty tears and lots of heavy objects tossed about, but in the end, we settled into our happy ménage à trois. At least the boys seemed happy. I was fine with everything except their adamantly united front concerning the bodyguards.

"But Zack, it's my birthday." I was twenty-seven years old, but if I kept taking Daniel's blood, I would be forever twenty-six. My husband is way better than Botox.

Zack shook his head and softened slightly. Despite his rough talk, I knew he had a certain fondness for me. It had been my friendliness that convinced him vampire kind wasn't all bad. "I know it is, Zoey. Mr. Quinn has been running himself ragged trying to get your present. He's taking it seriously."

It didn't surprise me that Dev was making a big deal out of the occasion. He's the kind of man who enjoys the mundane rituals of everyday life. Dev is more than happy to follow convention because it gives him a sense of belonging. We might be an odd family, but we're his family. "How about Danny?"

Zack's face finally broke into a small smile. "I think he went to the comic book store yesterday."

And that sounded like my Danny. Danny is the one who swoops in and saves me from all the evils of the world. I need saving more often than I liked to admit. Danny is the guy who can sweep me off my feet when he wants to. I mean that literally because he can fly. He's also the guy who would buy my birthday present at a comic book store.

"So you aren't patrolling my dad's house during the party tonight?" I glanced around the club looking for tonight's desperate plot to walk in the room. I had a meeting that I didn't need prying werewolf ears to listen in on. It wasn't really the listening part that bothered me. It was Zack's propensity for tattling that made me insane. He just loved to file reports on me.

"Lee and I have the night off. The big guy can handle one little party."

I waved as Sarah Day and her husband, Felix, entered the club. Sarah's electric blue hair made her stand out in the crowd, but one really couldn't help but look at Felix, too. His serene masculine beauty turned many a head as the couple made their way to the bar area. Felix looked like he might have been painted by Michelangelo on the ceiling of the Sistine Chapel. Radiance just rolled off him. It's possible he'd been the actual inspiration for that bit of art. Felix Day is a fallen angel. He'd found himself deeply in love with his former charge, Sarah, and decided to experience life on the Earth plane.

"Hey!" Sarah greeted me with a big hug.

"Hello, little cousin," Felix said, smiling indulgently. "I understand it's your birthday. Congratulations."

"Thanks, Felix." I noticed my distraction for the evening had just walked through Ether's double doors. It was time to get rid of my bodyguard. "Zack, Sarah and I want Cosmos."

"I'll have the bartender bring you some," Zack said, getting ready to motion a waitress over.

I shook my head and made a sour face. "It's Tom tonight. Tom always puts too much Triple Sec in. It tastes too orangey."

Sarah picked up my cues. "That's right. His Cosmos are awful."

"Zack's are like heaven," I told Sarah and then we both turned on the werewolf with feminine sighs and big doe eyes.

"I'm not a bartender anymore," Zack groused.

"With talent like yours, Zack, you'll always be my bartender." Before Zack signed on for the hazardous duty of protecting me, he'd been a bartender in one of Dev's clubs. He was a genius when it came to vodka. I still manage to talk him into making me drinks from time to time.

Zack sighed. "Fine, but only because it's your birthday. I'm going to teach Tom how to make them. But Zoey, if you aren't sitting here when I get back, I'm writing that report. You have no idea how creative I can get. I lie awake at night thinking of all the ways you could be killed."

Sarah slapped the table as he walked away. "He's very unfriendly. You should talk to Dev about that."

She didn't mention talking to Daniel. Dev was the one who might be moved by tears and feminine cajoling. Daniel was that rock someone shoved against a hard place. Unfortunately, unlike many things I could talk Devinshea into, he was in complete agreement with Danny on this one. It was getting harder and harder to get my way. The longer we all lived together, the more they realized to survive me they had to stand together. It was a lesson I wish they'd never learned.

"Won't work," I replied. "The boys love Zack and Lee. They

never let me do anything."

"Until Daniel hunts down Lucas Halfer, I doubt you're going to get anywhere on that front," Felix pointed out.

Lucas Halfer was the dumbass demon who'd gotten the jump on me six months ago and managed to pretty much kill me. He'd also killed Dev, but we'd been surrounded by vampires, and their blood brought us back. I'd gotten Halfer tossed out of Hell, and apparently he was holding a grudge.

"Watch this," I said in a whisper as a lovely young woman walked past our table with a wink in my direction. She was dressed to kill in a halter top and jeans that made her golden skin shine and showed off her toned body. I kept my voice as low as possible. The music was thumping all around me and there was the loud chatter of the crowd, so if I kept it down, even Zack's super hearing wouldn't be able to make out what I was saying.

"Who is she?" Sarah didn't take her eyes off the woman as she made her way toward the bar.

Zack was working the cocktail shaker when he caught her scent. One minute he was pouring out pink Cosmos and the next he was spilling said drink all over the place. I smiled as he lost his perfect control.

"She's Lisa Hernandez." I answered Sarah's question with great satisfaction. "She's Angelina's older sister. You remember Justin's girlfriend?"

"Yes." Sarah had become well acquainted with Daniel's vamps.

There were six of them, not including Chad, who we'd sent to spy on the Council. The Council didn't know the rest of them even existed. Daniel found them and turned them. They were loyal to Daniel instead of the all-powerful Vampire Council. Angelina was a werewolf who'd come to Daniel for protection last year when her pack leader tried to force her to mate with someone she didn't even like. Daniel had matched Justin and Angelina, and now they were happily living in my house since I'd agreed to move into Ether with Dev and Daniel. They shared my house in the country with a vampire/shapeshifter couple.

When I'd needed this particular favor, Lisa had been more than happy to oblige. "She's a wolf, of course, and she's also…in season."

Sarah's mouth dropped open. "That is so mean and evil and kind of brilliant."

"I think Zack is going to drool," Felix pointed out. "Yes, he is."

The well-dressed wolf fumbled to dry off his sleeves and tried to straighten his jacket. Though Zack had taken a blood oath to my husband and was his official animal servant, he modeled himself after Dev. Daniel might be all strength and power and brooding intensity, but Dev is silky and smooth. He was always immaculately dressed and polished. You wouldn't catch Devinshea Quinn wearing a wrinkled Spiderman T-shirt and jeans that might or might not have seen a washing machine lately. That was Danny's territory.

A few weeks into his gig, I noticed that Zack started to emulate his boss. He'd traded his flannel shirts for silk and the jeans became cashmere slacks. He started a meticulous grooming routine and even joined my weekly mani-pedis. He claimed it was all part of his job, but he didn't join me for the waxing portion of my spa day. All this had transformed the former bartender into a total big city hottie. Unfortunately, the nature of his job left him with little time for the ladies. I was just giving him an opportunity.

I watched as Zack smiled. It wasn't quite that intimate, sexy smile of Dev's that always set my heart racing, but he was trying. It isn't easy emulating a man who would have been worshipped as an actual sex god in the olden days, but the werewolf gave it a go. Lisa smiled up at him, and I thought I saw Zack skip a couple of breaths. He looked down at his watch and his face fell a little when he realized how much of his last hour was left. He re-poured our drinks and added a third for that vixen Lisa, who accepted it with a sultry smile. Zack moved quickly to bring Sarah and me our orders.

"Here you go, girls." He left a shaker on the table. "This is full so just pour some more if you need it." Zack gave Felix a manly handshake. "Felix, since you're here, I thought I'd just go hang out at the bar. I don't want to get in the way of all the girl talk, you understand."

"Absolutely," Felix replied smoothly. "I'm sure I can handle the women."

He couldn't, but I wasn't about to say that. Felix was absolutely the least scary thing at that table. Sarah and I were way scarier than Felix ever thought of being. Felix was a freaking pacifist. I liked guns and blowing things up. Sarah was a witch who had a way with dark magic. But if it made Zack feel safe leaving us in Felix's incapable hands, I was willing to go with it.

Zack practically tripped over his expensive loafers trying to get back to the luscious Lisa.

"Poor Zack," Sarah said with sympathy as she took a sip of her drink. "Damn, he's good. He missed his true calling. Oh, well, when Lisa dumps him later, he can mix his own drinks."

"I'm not that cruel. Lisa has no intention of dumping him. She's had her eye on him for a month. She just hasn't been able to get too close because he's always working. I think our horny little wolf is going to be satisfied with tonight's outcome. See, I'm nice. It's just too bad I can't use it more to my advantage."

Sarah glanced around. "Where is she?"

I gave her a "don't give up the game" look and she settled back down. Sarah's recent sojourn on the Hell plane may have netted her one hot husband, but it had done nothing to keep her subterfuge skills sharp. "She'll be here. When she walks up to us, we need to pretend she's an old friend."

Shaking his golden curls, Felix sighed. "Do I need to point out how upset the boys are going to be when they inevitably discover this plot of yours?"

I didn't need that lecture. "They aren't going to find out. Why do you think I went to so much trouble playing wolf pimpette? Daniel and Dev both told me they don't want to talk about this particular problem. I'm just following orders. Besides, they're so busy getting ready for this big werewolf meeting they don't have time to follow my little plots."

"And you aren't going to say anything," Sarah warned him.

Felix held up his hands in complete surrender. "I just thought I would point out the obvious. The relationship Zoey finds herself in is dependent on trust between the three of them. I wouldn't want her to screw everything up just because she wants to avoid a fight."

But I really, really wanted to avoid this particular fight. They were completely unreasonable, and I wasn't going to let their male pride and bravado get in the way of doing what was right. They should have known me well enough to figure out I wouldn't let the subject drop. If they weren't going to help me, I would find someone who would.

"Here she comes," I whispered out the side of my mouth as Jane Nichols walked off the dance floor in her mini skirt and tank top. She looked super cute and young. On the surface, she looked like the girl you went to college with and wished you still saw on a regular basis because she was so much fun. She didn't look like a badass werewolf private detective.

"Oh, my god, Zoey Wharton!" She practically squealed my name. She jumped up and down and pulled me into the girliest hug ever. I glanced back and saw Zack was comfortable the *Legally Blonde* reject wasn't a threat. Even in the werewolf world, a female like Jane is considered soft and sweet right up to the point when she takes your head off. Her blonde Barbie look is one of her greatest assets.

"Jane, it's been so long," I said with a sorority sister sincerity. It hadn't been that long. I'd been talking to her almost daily on my cell.

Jane seated herself and we chatted lightly, as though we were catching up. When I was satisfied that Zack was paying attention to Lisa and nothing else, I looked at Jane and asked the question I'd been asking every single day for the last six months.

"So where is Neil?"

Chapter Two

I missed Neil Roberts every second we were apart. He was my best friend and official gay husband. He'd been my bodyguard and my playmate. Everything that had gone on in the last six months didn't quite seem real because I had yet to share it with him. I might have been able to handle the separation if I knew he was off somewhere having a good time and enjoying his life, but he was in trouble.

Neil had been Daniel's servant for several years. He was a crucial member of the crew I worked with. Before Daniel had come clean about his status as the Council's *Nex Apparatus*—a really pretentious way of saying he was their assassin—we made our money the old-fashioned way. We stole things. We specialized in arcane objects no human thief would touch.

Neil was the muscle. Sarah was our witch. Daniel handled everything we needed a broody vampire for, and I held us all together and took care of anything that required a deft touch. Over the years, we'd become close.

That all changed six months ago when Daniel had forced his will on his servant.

Danny had been riding a high from feeding off some supercharged sexual energy and discovered his new power over his preferred animal, the wolf. Neil was angry because his lover had been the one chosen for sacrificial lamb duty. Back then I sided with Neil, causing a rift between myself and Danny that led to my untimely death and Daniel's refusal to even hear Neil's name spoken.

I didn't blame Neil. Maybe he should have hung around and fought it out with Danny, but I understood the impulse to run. I also understood how stubbornness could put a person into a corner it was hard to get out of. I wanted to reach out to my friend to let him know I was still here for him. I just needed to find his ass first.

"He's been really hard to track." All the bimbo act had been erased from Jane's demeanor. "I started in Vegas where Sarah saw him last."

Sarah nodded and shared a look with Felix. "I wasn't very helpful, I'm afraid. He hugged me. He told me to ask you to forgive him. Then he changed and he ran off."

The minute Felix had picked up Neil, he'd come out from under Daniel's influence and been able to act on his own again. He fled Las Vegas that night with nothing but the fur on his back. I made sure to put money in his bank account, but as far as I could tell, he hadn't touched it. He was alone with no money, no cell phone, and no friends.

"I suspect he spent most of the winter in wolf form. I have reports of a white wolf wandering the Sangre de Cristo mountains in Colorado. Most of the wolves in the area are gray or brown, so he stands out," Jane explained. "I tracked him for a while in my wolf form, and I spent a couple of days running with him, but I couldn't get him to change into his human form."

I took a long breath. At least he was alive. "How did he seem?"

Jane frowned. "He seemed weak. It's surprising because staying in his animal form for that long should have made his wolf incredibly strong. It makes it harder when you're in human form, but his wolf should be solid. Do you have any idea why he was weak? He was thin despite the fact there was ample game in those woods."

I had a theory, but I suspected Jane wouldn't like it. "Do you know who my husband is?"

Jane nodded, but her expression was blank as though she didn't want to give away her real opinions on the subject. Daniel was a controversial figure even in the vampire world. Jane was a wolf, and wolves rarely trusted vampires. What I was about to tell her wouldn't make that trust any easier. "I know who Daniel Donovan is. Everyone in our world is aware of him. Your faery made sure of that."

The last bit was said with a hint of salacious question. Lots of people were interested in our living arrangements. I had learned to ignore it. "Neil was Daniel's servant."

Her eyes tensed slightly. "So it's true. Donovan can call wolves."

There was no point in lying about it. Daniel didn't. "Yes, he can. Neil took a blood oath to serve my husband several years ago. When he made the oath, Daniel's control of this particular power was nominal. Since then he's grown and his power grew with him. When Neil attempted to break his oath, Daniel was able to control him physically."

Jane shuddered. "I've heard of this power, but it's been many generations since a vampire's shown mastery of it. You have to understand how this will affect my people's view of him. They'll fear him."

Making inroads with the werewolves had proven difficult despite the fact that he couldn't control a wolf without the wolf making a blood oath to him. It almost would have been easier if his animal to call had been the panther or the tiger. For sheer numbers, the wolf reigned supreme. "That's neither here nor there. Our problem is Neil. Neil was justifiably upset by the turn of events. He felt betrayed by Daniel. In my husband's defense, we were going into an incredibly dangerous situation and Neil was our only backup."

"I'm not judging anyone, Zoey," Jane said. "I'm just trying to do my job, and I don't see how any of this makes him weak."

"Part of the oath is an exchange of blood. Neil took Daniel's blood once a week. It made him unnaturally strong. Without the blood, he would become weak, possibly weaker than he was before." I knew how addictive Daniel's blood could be.

"None of us knew Neil before he made his arrangement with Daniel," Sarah said quietly. "We don't know what he was like before. All I know is how freaking strong he was with the blood. He could control the change down to a single finger, and he wouldn't break a sweat."

The blonde wolf tapped a finger against the table. "I can see where that kind of power would be tempting. It certainly seems to have tempted Zack over there. Tell me, Mrs. Donovan, does it make you stronger?"

I smiled wryly because I wasn't about to let that phase me. I was married to a vampire. What did she expect? "It tends to make me heal, and after some of the damage I've taken, I appreciate that. Look, I understand you might not like my husband. Perhaps you don't approve of my lifestyle. It doesn't matter. I just want to find my friend. If you can't do that for me, please let me know so I can find someone who can."

The private investigator studied me carefully. "Do you really care for Neil?"

That was the easiest question she'd asked. "I love him very much."

"So this isn't about revenge," Jane said as though she had suspected all the while it might be.

I laughed long and hard at that thought. "No. I don't want revenge. I want to find my friend. I want to let him know I still love him with my whole heart. I want him to come home."

Her brows met in a *V* over her eyes. "You're not at all like I thought you would be. You'll have to forgive my prejudices. Vampires are a little like bogeymen. We're suspicious of your husband because vampire kind has tried to enslave us more than once, so when a king comes calling, we have to wonder why. I would have thought his queen would be cruel. I wouldn't have thought she could love a servant."

"He isn't my servant. He's my friend." I didn't explain that I hated the title of queen. I loved Daniel, but there were many times I wished he was just a regular guy because the queen crap got in the way of my life all too often.

Jane nodded, her mind obviously made up. "I'll go back out and try to talk to him again. If I can arrange a meeting, I will. If I can get him to come back with me, that would be best, but I think a meeting is more likely."

Hope lit in me. It was the closest I'd gotten in six months. "I'll take it." Jane got up to leave but I held her back. "If he needs anything, please provide it for him. I'll pay for whatever. Just put it on my bill."

The detective nodded and promised to update me soon.

When she was gone, I sat back and Sarah reached out to squeeze my hand. "We're going to find him."

I gave her a watery smile, then cursed foully as I saw Lee Owens standing not two feet away, bulky arms crossed with an amused expression on his bearded face. I had managed to keep Zack out of it, but now I got to deal with Lee. He normally didn't spend a lot of time with me, but he was loyal to his brother.

He looked from me to the bar where Zack had his tongue about halfway down Lisa's throat. "Nice, Zoey."

I shrugged and started coming up with roughly a thousand different excuses.

"So you're looking for Donovan's first wolf," Lee surmised.

Lee wasn't exactly a fool. I simply nodded.

"I don't think he wants his first wolf back," Lee pointed out. "But then this isn't about Donovan, is it? This is about you."

"Yes, it is and I…"

Lee held his hand up to stop me. "It can stay between us, Zoey. He's my boss not my master." Lee refused to make an oath to Daniel, preferring to simply be an employee. I often thought Lee had only taken the job to make sure Zack didn't get himself killed. "I think it's nice you want to find your friend. I also think I'll deeply enjoy the creative ways you keep Zack's nose out of your business. I have to say, Zoey, watching you make him crazy is the best part of this job."

Relief flooded my system. I was just about to thank Lee when I noticed the door to Dev's office open.

Dev walked out followed by Daniel. Dev was mouthwateringly sexy in black slacks, an olive dress shirt, and a sport coat. He made sure the door was locked behind him, and then his eyes searched the floor until he found me. He smiled and my heart fluttered. Daniel was already halfway down the stairs. He'd dressed for the occasion as well. The jeans were at least a dark wash and his shirt had a collar. I still sighed over his broad shoulders and those dimples he got when he grinned.

"Girl, you're just a goner," Sarah laughed. "I don't know how you keep up with that."

"It can be really tiring," I admitted.

"Hey, Z." Daniel greeted me for the first time that day. He'd been asleep when I left earlier. He pulled me off my stool and wrapped those strong arms around me. "Happy birthday, baby."

His lips met mine and suddenly I didn't care about anything but the fact that they were here with me. I let go of my frustrations with Zack and the situation with Neil for the time being. I wanted to enjoy my time with my guys. I let my arms wrap around Daniel's neck as he held me tight.

He set me on my feet and while he greeted the Days, Dev leaned over and kissed me as well. "Good evening, Felix, Sarah. Lee, I appreciate the work. We'll take it from here."

My bodyguard bid us farewell and I turned to Daniel. "Hey, don't you need to eat before we go?"

While this was my traditional birthday dinner with my dad, Daniel wouldn't be enjoying whatever my father had catered in.

Daniel gave me a slightly sheepish look. "I kinda already did."

Dev held up his left wrist which sported two neat fang marks. "We were in a Halo match and I was kicking his ass. He whined that he was hungry and couldn't concentrate."

"Well, I was," Daniel replied. "You had a substantial advantage."

"Yeah, the advantage is I'm way better than you," Dev shot back with a laugh. "Stick to chess, egghead. Anyway, I had to find some way to shut him up."

"Yeah and what happened after I had a little snack?"

Dev pointed. "Do you have any idea how much that hurts, asshole? Those aren't girlie fangs you got there. My wrist still aches. This is my firing hand."

"Oh, maybe mommy will kiss it better," Daniel returned. "I killed him like forty-two times after I ate. I'll give you your rematch tomorrow because I'll enjoy killing you again."

I punched Daniel in the arm. "You hurt him? You're supposed to make that nice for him."

Both boys backed off with hands held up.

"Not going to happen, Z," Daniel said.

"I'm with Dan on this one," Dev agreed. "It's all fine and dandy if you're there, but if you're otherwise disposed, there's going to be some manly pain involved. It's okay. I punched him in the face after he was done."

A grin lit Daniel's normally somber face. "He did. It tickled."

Sarah and I looked at each other and shook our heads. Boys. I would never completely understand the male friendship that was blossoming between Danny and Dev. It involved playing a lot of video games, calling each other all sorts of vulgar names, and trying to hurt each other on a regular basis. I'd caught Dev shooting Daniel in the leg just to see how long it took him to heal. They had a bet.

I glanced up at the clock. "We should get going. I don't want to keep Dad waiting."

Sarah and Felix took their own car. They were going clubbing after the party so Dev, Daniel, and I found ourselves happily alone in the limo as we drove through the Dallas night.

"So tell me, baby, how did you make poor Zack's life hell today?" Daniel asked as the limo pulled away from the club. His eyes held an expectant gleam.

"I was perfectly well behaved today." I lied because I wasn't about to tell the truth.

"I seriously doubt that." Dev pulled me into his lap. "I like the skirt, sweetheart."

He didn't really give a crap about the skirt, but he enjoyed having easy access to what he did like. He slid his hand up my leg, squeezing my thigh and making me lean against him as I tried to breathe. We had some time before we got to my dad's and I had to deal with the intricate social situation we were in. Maybe if my guys were satisfied, they would be a wee bit more tolerant when they realized I hadn't exactly done what they asked me to. I'd promised them I would have a conversation with my dad about our living arrangements. Yeah, I hadn't exactly gotten around to that.

"I like what's under the skirt," Daniel said. He sat across from us, his body relaxed as he watched.

Dev started to pull my skirt up, revealing my legs. "I think the vampire wants a show, sweetheart. Spread those legs for him."

I did as he asked, letting him arrange my legs so Daniel got a good view.

"That is a gorgeous sight, baby," Daniel said. "It's the perfect end to a damn fine day."

Dev's hand slid up my leg, and I could already feel his cock pressed against my back. I had to hope they had asked the driver not to stop until they told him to or my dad might find out some things he didn't want to know about my love life.

"Why was it a perfect day?" My skin was already heating up.

Daniel's lips quirked up slightly. "We got invited to the Gathering today."

I sat up, a little shocked. Dev huffed and pulled me back, obviously peeved at the interruption.

21

"The wolves are going to let you come?" The Gathering had been this spring's big project.

Once a year there was a gathering of wolves held in Colorado, where the strongest pack in the country resided. The alpha of the pack was a man named John McKenzie. The alpha had been adamant in his refusal to meet with Daniel. Dev had spent the spring playing the king's ambassador, attempting to find a way to convince the alpha it was in his best interest to hear us out. The Gathering was coming up in a few weeks, and they were beginning to believe their attempts would prove futile.

"Can't we talk about this later?" Dev asked as his long fingers teased their way around my underwear. "I'm off the clock, Your Highness, and would seriously like to concentrate on fucking our queen."

Daniel smiled ruefully. "Yes, I got that. I just thought you might want to tell her she's the centerpiece of your successful proposal."

"And I will," Dev replied as my back arched when he gently pinched my clitoris, and I felt that slow build starting. I shuddered in anticipation of what I knew was going to be a nice couple of minutes. "After I make her come a couple of times."

Dev was insistently trying to build me toward what he thought of as a starter orgasm. He used his thumb to apply sweet pressure and worked two fingers into my pussy.

"Hello, gorgeous," he whispered against my ear. "I missed you all day. His Highness over there kept me in meeting after meeting while he slept the day away, but all I wanted to do was find you and fuck you."

Daniel frowned. "Well, it wasn't like I was really sleeping, Dev. We agreed I couldn't let anyone know about the daywalking thing. That means you have to handle daytime meetings and I only get to listen in. Otherwise, we might not be having this discussion."

It ran through my mind that they were really having a whole conversation I should probably be a part of, but I wasn't listening. How could I when Dev was so expertly driving me toward pleasure? His thumb pressed on my clit while he and Daniel argued about something. I just tried to breathe. My vision went soft and fuzzy as Dev spread my legs further and worked a third finger in. He curled them inside, tickling some magic place he always found, and I let my head fall back against his chest as I sort of exploded in a daze of pleasure. No one can get you off as fast and well as a fertility god.

I looked at Daniel as I caught my breath and saw the episode had definitely heightened his interest. His jeans were full and my hands itched to cup that heaviness. I had been questioning the wisdom of going to my dad's, but now I really just wanted to stay in the limo forever.

"Beautiful, lover," Dev was saying behind me. "Let's switch positions and see if I can make that happen with my tongue. Who am I kidding? We both know I can."

I was just about to do whatever he said when Daniel's previous words managed to punch through the haze of lust. I sat straight up and moved away from Dev's clever hands because if he got them on me, I would be a puddle of submissive pleasure again.

"How am I involved in this particular plot of yours?" I tried in vain to straighten out my skirt, but it was hard to look respectable after an experience like that. My every muscle was a little limp, and I had to force myself to focus. They'd been working on this operation for months, and not once had they really talked about it with me. So I was surprised to discover I was the centerpiece.

Daniel frowned. "I told you we should tell her."

"And I was going to," Dev replied curtly as he reached for a bottle of champagne he had chilling. He popped the cork expertly and poured two glasses. "At the appropriate time."

He passed me a glass, and I downed it just to get some of my composure back. "When is the appropriate time, Dev?"

"There's a time and a place for everything, lover." Dev sat back, not attempting to hide the fact that he had a massive erection. He was the very picture of decadent beauty. "Tonight is not for business. Tonight is the time and place to have your lovely legs wrapped around my head. Tomorrow we can discuss business, but Dan over there just can't stand the pressure."

Daniel stared at Dev from across the limo. "Trust me. We should get it out of the way. She can blow up and scream at us for a while and then you can do that thing you do where you talk to her and rub her and she'll come around and then we can get freaky. She's going to be ten times more pissed if we do the freaky stuff first and then tell her."

He really did know me well. I was getting anxious because the last time they decided something without talking to me about it, I got saddled with Zack and Lee. "Somebody better tell me right now or I swear there won't be anything freaky happening to either one of you for a long time."

"It's not a big deal, Zoey." Dev's voice went all smooth and silky. "We just had to use our assets to get us into the meeting, and you know I consider you our greatest asset."

I rolled my eyes because I wasn't about to let him "handle" me. "Cut the bullshit, Dev. What am I supposed to do?"

He shrugged and refilled his glass. "You do it almost every day, lover. All you have to do is fuck me."

I raised my eyebrows because there had to be more to this. "And John McKenzie cares that you get laid why?"

"It's a fertility ritual, Z," Daniel explained. "The wolves are willing to pay handsomely for a high priest of Faery to perform a fertility ritual, and one of the methods of their payment is to let me in. That and a million dollars."

"A million dollars?"

Daniel leaned forward. "Their birth numbers have been low the last couple of decades. Dev's magic is rare on this plane. Even in Faery he's rare. The fact that he lives here and is willing to provide the service is an opportunity the alpha can't pass up. McKenzie is viewing this as a way to truly consolidate his power. If he can provide fertility for the packs, they'll follow him. It does nothing but help me to have a strong leader for the wolves. I would really prefer to only have to deal with one alpha instead of fifty. It also provides excellent cover. If the Council finds out I'm there, it's a cash-making enterprise."

Dev, Danny, and I had performed our first ritual together in Las Vegas, though I hadn't really known that was what we were doing at the time. It had been a happy accident, but since then, Dev had been thrilled to regain his power. His hold on the magic had gotten impressive. Since it involved sex, Dev liked to practice at every given opportunity. Daniel was able to feed off sexual energy as readily as blood, so it had given him a boost as well. The more he fed off that magic, the earlier he woke and the more sun he was able to handle.

Daniel's ability to daywalk was a secret we guarded zealously. Besides Dev and me, only Zack knew, and he'd been told to keep the secret even from his brother. The only vampire who knew was Daniel's patron, Marcus Vorenus, who also had the ability.

A sense of relief came over me. I wasn't sure why they had thought this would be a big deal. We kind of did it a lot. "I don't have a problem with the ritual. Let's go to Colorado and help some wolves make puppies."

"Good. Now let's get some practice in." Dev reached out to haul me back into his lap.

Daniel cleared his throat. "It's a public ritual, Z."

"What?" Now they definitely had my attention.

"Again," Dev began, gritting his teeth as he glared at Daniel. "That was something to bring up later. We have to ease her into the situation."

"You expect me to do that with the two of you in public? That's not going to happen. Do you know how fast that will end up on YouTube? How could you agree to that?" I asked Dev, but then rolled my eyes because I was talking to the wrong boy. "I know why he agreed. He's a pervert. But you? How can you be willing to do that with a hundred wolves watching?"

"I won't actually be there," Daniel clarified. "This is an experience for just the two of you."

"You see, sweetheart, Daniel is a greedy bastard," Dev explained, his voice soft and cajoling. "If he's there, he'll suck up all the energy and then there won't be enough left for the wolves. If we were talking about fifty or sixty couples it might be fine, but this is a big gathering. We need as much of the magic to disperse in the crowd as possible. It's just me and my goddess. That's you, lover. You're my goddess."

"Don't you 'goddess' me. How could you have thought I would be all right with this, Devinshea Conlan Quinn?"

"Now you're in trouble." Daniel chuckled under his breath.

I pointed at him. "You stay out of it."

Dev sat forward and reached for my hand, taking it in both of his. "This is important to me, Zoey. This is far more than just a way to get into the Gathering. I was going to ask you to be my goddess anyway. Please believe that. Daniel and I have discussed it, and he's agreed that it's time. Our relationship has settled and we're all happy."

"So I get to be a porn star because we're all happy?" I might have a crazy sex life, but I hadn't gone that far despite Dev's multiple attempts to convince me that cameras were fun.

Daniel glanced out the window, obviously leaving this conversation to us.

Dev squeezed my hand, moving closer. "No, you get to be my goddess. I want it to be real, Zoey. There are rituals involved. I gave up my priesthood when I left Faery. I can call myself a high priest all day long, but no one will really recognize me without my ascension and my goddess. When I left the *sithein*, I never thought I would be able to do this again. This is sacred to me. This is who I am. I am a priest, and this is what I was born to do."

"Dev, I'm sorry." I just couldn't envision myself allowing such a private act to be public. I'd played his "goddess" on several occasions, though he'd never used the term before. Those had been intimate situations where the magic had been just for us. I knew that many fertility rituals were public, but I couldn't see myself performing one. "I just can't. I hope you understand. I want to help, but not like that."

Dev let go of my hand, sat back, and took a deep breath. He looked like a man who just had something important taken from him. He sat back and took a long drink of champagne. When he was done, he smiled at me. "Of course I understand, sweetheart. It won't be a problem. I'll figure something else out that will satisfy McKenzie. Now, it's your birthday. Let's have some fun."

A grim expression settled on Daniel's face, and I knew I'd really done something bad. Dev was talking about how much he was looking forward to this weekend and our plans for the three of us to go to the movies. He chatted on but his smile didn't reach his eyes. Daniel kept looking at me like I'd kicked Dev and needed to apologize. I wished Dev would just get mad and scream at me. I could fight, but I hated this feeling that I'd let him down.

"Devinshea, can we talk about this?" I asked quietly.

He took a negligent drink. "There is nothing to say, sweetheart."

"There is. You're obviously upset."

"I'll get over it. It makes things a bit more difficult on the political front, but I'll figure it out. It's why I get paid the big bucks." His cavalier attitude was bullshit. He didn't get paid crap, obviously. He worked because he believed in the cause. "I'm looking forward to your party, sweetheart." He frowned suddenly. "I'm afraid I have to disappoint you a little bit, lover. I wasn't able to have your present delivered tonight. You'll get it in the morning. How would you like a candy-apple-red Porsche?"

If Dev had meant to buy me a Porsche, it would have been sitting in my father's driveway with a big bow around it. Dev didn't forget or put things off. In all our time together, Dev had never forgotten a birthday or anniversary or holiday.

"Why can't you give me my real gift? It has something to do with the ritual, doesn't it?"

He shook his head. "It's nothing, Zoey."

"Then give it to me," I requested softly.

Dev pulled a small box out of his pocket and sat it on my lap. "It isn't the real one. I sent a request to the *sithein* for the real one. They refused me. This is a facsimile, but the jeweler did a good job. You may have it if you want it, of course."

I opened the box, and my eyes widened at the lovely gold medallion. It was delicate and feminine. There was a raised sun symbol, and the entire medallion was circled with a foreign writing. I suspected it was Gaelic. "What does it say?"

"It says 'you are my goddess, maker of my magic, keeper of my power.'" Dev read, his voice too steady. "Like I said, it's not the original."

Tears burned in my eyes. How much was my modesty worth to me? Dev had given me everything he had, and I was willing to let him down because I didn't want strangers getting a glimpse of me? Dev had grown up in an entirely different world from Daniel and me. Dev was the one who so often had to adapt to fit into our culture and respect our customs. Perhaps it was time for me to mold myself to his needs. We were a threesome though, and I had to make sure we were all on the same page.

"Daniel, how do you feel about the ritual?"

He took a long breath, releasing it with a sigh. "We've been talking about it for months. If this is what Dev needs and you're okay with it, then so am I. Z, this could be something big for us, but

I don't want to use either one of you like that."

Dev groaned, a sure sign that this was a well-worn argument. "You're not using us, Daniel. We're in this together. I want this. I want it very much. This is a chance to prove myself. If it also gets us the loyalty of the wolf pack, then I don't see why it's bad."

He was right. And, hey, if I was going to be a porn star, at least I'd be a highly paid one. I leaned into him. "I love you both. Yes, I'll perform the ritual with you, Dev. I'll be proud to be your goddess."

Dev smiled, the world around me lighting up. He unclasped the necklace and put it around my neck, his hand touching where the disc lay against my skin. "That looks perfect. I love you so much, Zoey."

"Now aren't you happy we got through that?" Daniel said, relaxing as the tension left the space.

Dev winked at me. "I am."

Daniel pulled me into his lap, cuddling me close. "Good, then it's my turn." Daniel pulled out a similar box and handed it to me.

I looked down at it. "Did you shop together? Zack told me you got my present at the comic book store."

Daniel's hand tightened around my waist. "No, yesterday was just new comic day. I got this a while back. I was just waiting for the right time to give it to you. I hope you like it. I...would really like for you to wear it. I mean, only if you want to."

I opened the box and there was a polished golden band. "A wedding ring?"

He held up his left hand. There was a matching masculine band on his finger. He hadn't been wearing it earlier, so I assumed he'd slipped it on when I wasn't looking. "I know we didn't have a traditional ceremony, but I like the idea of wearing rings. You can wear Dev's necklace and my ring."

It was times like this that made the rest of the crap worthwhile. I let the sweetness of the moment wash over me because I would remember it for the rest of my life. I gave the ring to Daniel and let him slip the band on my ring finger. He brought my wrist to his lips and laid a tender kiss there. I hugged him for the longest time because I was finally wearing my Danny's ring.

The car pulled to a stop and I realized we had reached our destination, and several problems suddenly occurred to me. My father would probably make no comment on the necklace, but he was damn straight going to notice the wedding ring I was suddenly sporting.

"Danny," I said carefully, "I love my ring but I'm going to put it back in the box just for tonight." I slipped it off my hand and placed it back in the little velvet box.

A long moment passed as both my men stared at me.

"Would you like to explain why, Zoey?" Dev's voice was practically arctic.

Daniel moved me off his lap. I was pretty sure it was so he could properly glare at me. "Damn it, Zoey. You didn't tell him."

Dev frowned at me, too. "You promised me you would talk to your father about us. He hates me, Zoey. He thinks I wrecked your marriage. I was looking forward to actually making some headway with your father tonight of all nights."

I cringed just a little because I had promised the boys I would talk to my dad, but my dad could be really hard to talk to. I'm his only child, and he stills treats me like a princess. It was not an easy conversation to have. What was I supposed to say? "Hey, Daddy. I'm shacked up with two men and I really love them both and I sleep with them sometimes at the same time." It just isn't a thing you share with your dad. I had been sure I could get through one little dinner. "I just need more time. I promise I'll tell him soon. Let's just get through tonight."

Daniel shook his head as the driver opened the car door. "I'm not doing it, Zoey. I'm not lying to him. If he asks, I'm going to tell him."

Daniel got out of the car and stalked up to the front door, where my father was waiting with a hug for his son-in-law.

Dev moved to the sidewalk but turned back to help me out. Though he was courteous, it was easy to see he was pissed. He offered me his arm, and we started up the driveway. "One has to wonder what you're ashamed of, Zoey. Given the fact that Harry loves Daniel like a son, I have to assume it's me."

"Devinshea," I sighed.

"I'm sure it will be a lovely evening, darling," Dev murmured as my father was giving him the evil eye.

This was why I memorized the earlier sweetness. Loving two

29

men is twice the joy, but when it goes wrong, it really goes wrong. I'd made a terrible mistake because I had the feeling my father was going to find out exactly what had been going on, and I wouldn't like the way my messengers delivered this news.

Chapter Three

I was surprised to see Ingrid standing in the living room. She wore a designer dress and was beyond gorgeous with her perfect ice-blonde hair and lithe figure. It was a glamour, but I'd never seen her any other way. I wouldn't recognize her troll form. I rushed into the room and was greeted with a bright smile.

"My little Zoey," Ingrid said with only a hint of Scandinavian accent. She looked me over and took in the sight of the medallion around my neck, her eyes widening. She smiled as she touched it. "It's good to see you. You're practically glowing. This is beautiful on you."

Yes, I was thrilled the see Ingrid, but I was also more than happy for the distraction. Dev had dropped me off at the door and then walked back to deal with the driver. Daniel was practically ignoring me. It was nice someone was happy with me. "Dev gave it to me."

"Yes, I know," she explained, studying it. "They did a good job on it. It's a shame his brother refused to give him the real one. It belongs to Devinshea. It's his to give to his goddess. I have no idea what his brother is thinking of keeping it from him."

"His brother's a jerk." From everything I knew about Declan Quinn, I was convinced the heir to Faery was an asshole.

Ingrid chuckled at my descriptive language. "I'm certain the future king would disagree. You know there are always two sides to a story, Zoey. You've only heard one. Now, where is our Devinshea?"

"He should be here in a minute," I replied.

I kind of hoped by the time Dev walked in, my dad would be passing out the drinks, but he hadn't made his way into the living room yet. It was a bad sign. I didn't think my father was ever going to like Dev, but the situation might have been better if I had talked to my dad about our living situation. Dad still thought Dev was some temper tantrum I was having. Once he realized I was serious about him, he was going to have to calm down.

"What is your father's objection to Devinshea?" Ingrid asked, looking genuinely confused. "He is an excellent catch in both worlds. He's of royal blood and well placed. In the human world, he's wealthy and successful. He's kind and loving toward you. I don't understand the animosity."

I understood it all too well. "Dad thinks that if Dev were out of the picture, I would settle down and do what Daniel tells me to."

She sighed. "Your father doesn't know you at all."

My father wanted me safe, and he believed Daniel was the best bet. We'd been careful not to bring my father into our political games. Dad didn't know Daniel's status as the Council's official assassin, and we agreed to keep it that way. I was just now realizing that Dev was the one who took the brunt of this particular ruse. Dev hated to be the outsider. He'd left his own family seven years before, and though he almost never spoke of them, I knew he missed them. Perhaps what he really missed was a sense of belonging. Well, he wasn't going to get that tonight.

"Where is Halle?" I glanced around, trying to find Ingrid's husband. I loved Halle the Loyal. The trolls had been my surrogate family for most of my childhood.

She gestured around the room. "It's too much for Halle, too much artificialness. He sends his best and wishes you would visit soon."

It's difficult for many Fae creatures to be surrounded by metal and even walls. Halle was the weaker of the two. I wasn't quite sure when I would be able to visit with the man who had helped to raise me, though. I doubted my bodyguards were going to be hip to checking bridges until I found the right one. The limits on my freedom were beginning to chafe.

"Ingrid." Daniel greeted her with a happy smile. He walked up to the troll and pulled her into a hug. "I'm so happy to see you. It's been too long."

Ingrid looked at me, her eyes wide. When Daniel let her go, she studied him for a moment. Like me, Daniel had spent a lot of his human life walking the bridges with the trolls. We'd spent every summer with them even after we graduated from high school and went to college.

She brought her hands up to touch his face, a maternal gesture. "I don't understand this face, Daniel. Your lips are turned up. It's strange. What has happened to our brooding vampire?"

Daniel laughed, the sound filling the room. "I'm only allowed to brood two hours a day now. Dev put me on a schedule. He gets bitchy if I don't follow it."

"What have you been doing, Zoey?" A look of satisfaction crossed her face. She'd been the one to introduce me to Dev. I knew she was fond of the faery prince. She also loved Daniel. If she had a hand in making all three of us happy, she would be satisfied with her meddling.

Sarah rushed into the room before I had to answer the question. "Seriously, Z, I think Dev is going to punch your dad. Felix is trying to talk them down, but they're not listening."

My father stalked into the room, his face flushed. "You're the one who ruined everything."

"Oh, that's rich, Harry." Dev followed my father into the room. I knew I was in trouble the minute I heard Dev's bad-boy drawl. It told me my dad had pushed the button that always brought out vulgar, rebellious Dev. "Please tell me how I screwed up your daughter's perfect marriage. It was all going so well until I popped into the picture. Daniel and Zoey were happy together except that they weren't together when I met her. She wasn't married when I started dating her. I don't see how you can blame me. You know she seduced me, Harry, not the other way around."

I groaned and let myself fall onto the couch. This wasn't going to go well, and I had no one to blame but myself.

"Now, Dev, perhaps we should sit down and really use this time to talk about the situation." Felix was studying to be a therapist. It was a fitting occupation for a former guardian angel.

"I don't think this is the time for a fucking therapy session, Felix," Dev replied.

"That's the way to talk to one of God's pure creatures," my father shot back, his Irish accent so much worse for his emotional state. Every muscle in my father's body seemed to be tense and ready to fight. "I've got no idea what me daughter sees in you."

"Oh, I can think of a few things," Dev began.

I knew whatever came out of his mouth next was going to be

awful. Daniel watched the scene with a sort of interested expectation. I suspected he was enjoying not being the object of Dev's vitriol for once. Usually it was Daniel who managed to push those buttons.

Daniel winked at me. "This is going to be good."

I shot him a dirty look and thought seriously about punching him.

Dev continued with his tirade. "What could Zoey possibly see in me? Let's see… I'm filthy rich, have a ten-inch cock, and no sense of shame. What the hell else does she need?"

"Dude, you measured?" Daniel asked, finding the whole thing way more amusing than he should have.

"It's an estimation," Dev said between clenched teeth.

"Well, you are known for your generosity." Daniel sat down on the couch beside me. He tossed an arm around my shoulders. "Hope you're happy, Z. This is your fault. You could have handled this without an audience."

My father's girlfriend entered the room, a tray of drinks balanced in her hands. Christine shook her head at the scene in front of her and wisely set the tray down. "Have we already made it to the brawl portion of the evening?" She picked up two cocktail glasses and handed one to me. "I'm sure you're at the center of it, Zoey, so you'll need this."

I took a long swig of vodka and set the drink back down. Dev and my father were screaming at each other now. The insults were flying as my father questioned Dev's parentage and Dev questioned my father's sanity. It was time to own up to everything. I'd made a mess, and it was my responsibility to clean it up.

"Wish me luck. I'm going in."

"You're braver than I am." Daniel saluted me sarcastically as I got up.

"Stop it, both of you." I had to move between them to make sure this didn't turn physical. I looked to my father. "Dad, you're going to have to accept that Dev is in my life. If you want me to come over here, you have to stop screaming at my boyfriend."

Dad reeled around on Daniel. "What I don't understand is why you put up with this. Why haven't you killed the faery? I believe you have the right, Danny. No one in the vampire world is going to question his death. They'd help you."

"I'm a lover, not a fighter, Harry." Daniel managed to look as innocent as a guy with fangs can look. I rolled my eyes and heard Dev laugh sarcastically behind me. We'd both seen Daniel fight. "Besides, I don't think killing Dev is going to make Zoey love me more. I think it would just piss her off."

"I know that, Danny." My father softened as he considered the man he thought of as his son. "I know how hard this is on you. I apologize for my daughter. I thought I raised her better. I don't know where I went wrong. It isn't fair, but then your life hasn't been fair, has it? Your dad dies, and then…I just don't know how such a gentle soul handles becoming a vampire."

Dev practically fell on the floor laughing. "Gentle soul? Who the hell is he talking about? Has he met you?"

"I'm talking about my son-in-law, you vulgar piece of trash," Dad spat. He'd always put Daniel on a pedestal. Daniel's father had been his best friend, and when George Donovan died, Dad took Daniel into our home. "I'm talking about the kindest boy I've ever known. He wouldn't hurt a fly. Zoey was always getting him into trouble, and he always tried to take the blame for her. She was a wild one growing up, but Danny took care of her, he did. I'm sure he's a good husband, or he would be if she would just let him. Danny was always too good for her, but she can't see it."

Yeah, Dad knew how to push my buttons, too. As he went on and on about how I was lucky to have Daniel, I felt all that old childhood anger start to rise. I'd put up with this crap while I was growing up. It was just enough to make me feel like I was fifteen again and getting blamed for everything. Daniel got better grades in school. Daniel was so smart. If I was just a little more like Daniel, maybe I could have a future. Really, it was a miracle I still loved Danny.

Daniel sat up. His look of amusement changed to one of horrified expectation. He held a hand out. "Baby, I want you to think about whatever is going through that head of yours."

But I wasn't about to listen to Daniel. "Oh, Dad, Daniel is perfect, isn't he? Do you have any idea how hard it was to live up to his perfection?"

"Now, girl, I love you," Dad backpedaled. "I didn't mean to say

35

I don't love you very much. I was happy to be your dad all these years. You're a good girl and a good professional. No one can crack a safe like you, love. I'm just disappointed you haven't treated Danny with the respect he deserves."

"I waited years for Danny to get over his 'I died and rose a freaking vampire' angst. I stood by him all that time. It wasn't until I started dating Dev that Daniel suddenly had an interest in me again. I'm so sick of how you kiss his ass, Dad. Daniel's had such a hard time with the whole big, scary vampire thing," I said, sarcasm dripping because I was tired of being the bad guy while Daniel polished his halo. "Do you want to know why Danny hasn't killed Dev yet?"

"Zoey, let's talk this through. Maybe Felix is right." Dev sounded far too reasonable for me.

"He hasn't killed Dev because Dev feeds him." I reached around and pulled up Dev's hand, exposing the fang marks. "He doesn't kill Dev because he's living with him. Daniel doesn't kill Dev because they sleep together."

"Nice, Zoey," Dev ground out, pulling his hand back. He smoothed down his jacket and frowned at me like I'd planned this out. "That's going to make things so much easier."

Daniel had his head in his hands. "Of all the ways you could have told him, this is how you go?"

My father just stopped. He was still as a statue, standing there with his mouth open as his mind tried to process what I had told him. He slowly turned and stared past me at Dev. "You bastard. You stole my daughter's husband."

"I give up," Dev said, throwing his hands in the air.

Daniel groaned and stood, his face a nice shade of pink. "He didn't steal me, Harry. I don't sleep with Dev. I mean, I do sleep in the same bed, but Z is firmly between us. Unless she gets up first, of course, but then we stay on our own sides of the bed. There was that one time when he thought I was her, but we got that settled really quickly and there have been no further incidents. None. Dev decided he wanted to keep all his limbs intact."

"I was half awake, dude. You've gotta get over that," Dev explained. "I can't help it. I like to cuddle."

My anger dissipated, and I could easily see that I'd screwed up.

It was time to make things clear. "Dad, I'm living with Dev and Daniel. I love them. They love me. You wanted me to get back together with Danny, and the good news is I have. We're together, and we take those vows we never got around to making seriously. Well, all except for the forsaking all others part. We're forsaking all others except Dev."

My father shook his head and walked out of the room.

"Great, Zoey," Christine said, giving me a harsh look as she walked after him. "I think you broke him."

I wished I could take it back, but it was done, and now I had to deal with the fallout. Daniel was shaking his head like he'd known this would happen. Dev just stared after my dad. Sarah covered her mouth, trying hard not to laugh. It wasn't the first time she'd witnessed one of my knock-down, drag-outs. Ingrid appeared serene and somewhat pleased. Felix just shook his head.

"When I get my practice up and running, I'll give you a group discount," he promised.

****

"All right. So someone is going to have to explain to me how the hell this thing between the three of you works." My father spoke for the first time in an hour. Dinner had been served and my father had taken his place at the head of the table, but he hadn't touched the excellent *osso buco* or said a single word since I made my announcement. "Do you have a schedule? Do you see Dev on certain days and Daniel on others? I'm just not sure how something like this functions."

"Well, Harry, when two boys love one girl very much…" Dev began.

"Devinshea, you hush." Ingrid sent him a quelling look. To her credit, he actually shut up. "Harry, it's a common thing in the Fae world. It's a committed relationship, much like a marriage. Zoey is at the center. She's beloved by both of them, and they take care of her. Can't you see how happy they seem? I'm thrilled for the three of them."

"We don't live in the Fae world, Ingrid. We live in this world where marriage means one man and one woman—at least in the state of Texas it does," my father replied. "If Dev wanted a Fae marriage, he should be with a Fae girl."

"Harry, give Dev a break." Daniel sat back in his chair, the only one without a plate in front of him. "He's not a bad guy. He's trying to make Z happy."

My father took Danny's reasoning seriously. "What about you, Danny? Is this…relationship making you happy?"

"It's working." Daniel leaned forward and rested his hands on the table. "In a perfect world, I wouldn't be a vampire and Z wouldn't be a companion. We would have gotten married after college and started giving you a ton of grandkids. That ain't happening. In this world, our current situation works. You have no idea how much trouble she can cause. It takes two of us just to keep her alive."

"And satisfied," Dev added needlessly with a salacious grin.

I let my head drop and just prayed the evening would be over soon. My father already knew too much about my sex life. If the night kept going like this, I should just send him a video.

"Dev and I can switch off duties," Daniel explained, warming up to the subject. "I can handle all the dangerous stuff, and Dev can take her shopping. Don't forget those pedicures he gets with her, either. Apparently it's important his toes are pretty."

"Laugh it up, Dan, with your hobbit feet. I have no idea why Zoey lets those hairy things anywhere near her," Dev cracked. "And I enjoy shopping with Zoey. I especially enjoy all the time we spend in dressing rooms."

Daniel sighed. "Man, I should have known there was a reason you did that. I'm going next time."

"I'm sure Zack will be thrilled to get the day off. Zack is one of the bodyguards I provide for your daughter," Dev explained my father's way. "Daniel can't protect her during the day. She's precious to me, and I try to give her everything she needs."

My father watched the byplay with a shocked look on his face. "The two of you get along?"

Daniel shrugged a little, relaxing again. "Once we stopped trying to kill each other, we realized we had a lot in common."

"We both survive Zoey on a daily basis," Dev agreed. "It builds camaraderie."

"Well, I think it's perverted." Christine watched the scene with a judgmental look on her face. I thought it was nice that I got judged by a woman who practiced black magic and slept with a man more than twice her age.

"It often is perverted," Dev said with a big smile. "As often as I can convince Zoey."

"Zoey, it isn't normal," Christine continued, wagging her finger at me and pursing her lips. "You should pick one and be miserable with your choice just like the rest of us."

"Christine, if you'll get on board, I promise I'll speak to your witch's support group about the time I met Lucifer Morningstar." I knew how to handle her. Even though I sometimes couldn't stand her, it would help if she was on my side. It didn't look like she was going anywhere soon.

Christine sat up straight and patted my father's hand. She was interested in a little social climbing. Bringing in guests might get her on that committee she'd been angling for. "Honey, I think we should support your daughter's lifestyle choices no matter how counterculture they are. She's your daughter, and we can't really ignore her because we don't agree with her living arrangements. Maybe I could start a support group."

"Does Heaven want to weigh in on this?" Dad looked to Felix for advice.

"They love each other, Harry. It might not be conventional, but it is love," Felix stated sagely. "Now, the thievery on the other hand is something we should talk about."

My father immediately disregarded Heaven's opinion. "Are you happy, girl?"

I stared at him across the table. There was a tired cast to his eyes, the lines deeper than I remembered, and I realized how old my dad was getting. I nodded. "I am, Dad. I really hope you can accept it."

My father nodded and picked up his fork.

Daniel leaned over and kissed my cheek. "See, I told you it wouldn't be so bad."

****

An hour later, I made my way up the stairs and out to the balcony. I closed the door quietly behind me and took a deep breath. The heat of the June night rushed over my skin, but it couldn't possibly be more oppressive than where I'd just come from.

The night had settled into a sort of awkward therapy session. My dad asked an awful lot of questions and Daniel and Dev and Ingrid answered them. I'd been much discussed but my voice wasn't needed. I had no doubt the people in that room loved me, but they didn't seem to want my opinion.

It was a lot like the months since Dev and Daniel had made their agreement.

When I left, Daniel and Dev had been discussing my security situation with Dad. Suddenly my father had been interested in what the boys had to say. I'd neglected to mention to him that Lucas Halfer had pledged bloody revenge on me and he was taking it seriously. Dad wanted to know everything about both of my guards and the protocols Dev had put into place concerning my security.

I was breaking those sacred protocols by coming out to the balcony. I was supposed to be in the bathroom, but I just had to get away for a minute. It had been months since I'd been on my own even for a few moments. I wasn't even alone in the condo. Daniel or Dev were always there, or Zack and Lee were on duty.

It was a hard place to be for a woman who was used to being on her own. I'd been alone for years after Daniel died. Even when he'd come back from his Council training, we lived apart.

The pool light was on, making a silvery glow against the dark of the night. I needed to work. That was the real problem. Daniel had a job. He spent his time training the vampires he found and turned. He educated them in what it meant to walk the night. He taught them how to hunt and how to remain undercover. It took up a lot of his time. He was providing for them out of his funds and the money we made from our last job. It was imperative that those vampires remained a secret to the Council. In addition to caring for his charges, Daniel had work to do as the Council's go-to guy for executions and other horrible acts. It wasn't easy being the vampires' own bogeyman.

Dev ran five nightclubs and was always thinking about expanding. He was a shrewd businessman, and though he'd ceded much of the day-to-day operations to his second in command, Roman, he still kept up to date. He was much more involved in Daniel's politics now. Dev had become convinced that Daniel should be on the throne and the Council should be disbanded.

Both of my men had valuable things to do with their time. I shopped. I made my bodyguards regret that they had ever been born. I had an awful lot of sex. It was everything I'd been afraid of when Daniel and Dev made their proposal. I was a plaything to them; precious and beloved, yes, but also marginalized in a way. They coddled me and spoiled me, but they rarely treated me like a partner anymore.

I was a pleasure to be had. I was a problem to be handled.

I leaned over the secure railing and the lights of the pool made the night seem serene. It was humid, but the quiet made up for the heat. In the distance, I heard a bird calling a playful little cry. "Tik-tik," it sung, but it seemed to be moving away. That bird had the freedom to just fly away when it wanted. I didn't want to fly away from Dev or Daniel. I loved them, but I needed some space.

I couldn't really blame the guys. I'd allowed myself to get to this place. I knew how domineering each was, and I'd let them have their way the last six months. It had been far easier to give myself over to the pleasure they offered than to fight for the relationship I really wanted. It was simple to just lay back and let them handle everything, but my laziness was coming home to roost now.

I shook my head ruefully as the bird continued to "tik-tik." When I was running a crew, I'd had to be a badass or no one took the little human seriously. I hadn't picked up a freaking gun in months. What the hell was happening to me?

Out of the corner of my eye, I caught something moving in the trees. A large black bird sat on one of the lower limbs, its big body perched delicately. It opened its beak and the sound came out again. I leaned forward to try to get a better look at it because something was wrong with this picture. That sound was coming from far away, yet I knew it was the bird making it. It was almost as though the big black bird was throwing its voice.

I was concentrating so much on the freaky bird, I almost missed the woman who moved silently from the trees. She was small, her body slight. Her hair was pitch black, long and disheveled. Dressed

41

in dark clothes, she blended in with the night. I almost called out, but my eyes caught on something that was deeply wrong. As she moved closer to the pool, I could tell that her feet were on backward. She wasn't wearing shoes, so it was easy to see her toes moving across the deck. In the wrong direction.

That good old adrenaline started pumping through my body because whatever the crazy bitch with the dark hair was, she wasn't human. I wished I hadn't seen all those Japanese horror films. She could have starred in one. I kept my eyes on her, not willing to turn my back as I moved toward the door.

She changed so quickly it almost didn't register. One moment she was a freaky-ass chick who had her feet on wrong, and the next there was a big black bat hovering in front of me. I couldn't help but stare. Big mistake.

The wings moved slowly, hypnotically. I was caught for a moment, unable to do more than watch those wings and look into her eyes. Obsidian eyes peered at me, like giant holes I could easily fall into. This was not a living creature. This was a dead thing. It might move and change form, but there was no spark of true life in those eyes.

The black bird had joined the bat and I watched, horror coursing through me as they opened their mouths.

The bat's tongue slithered out, far longer and stronger than I could imagine. It was like a thin arm, and it wrapped itself around my waist. I finally came out of my stupor, struggling as I was pulled toward the edge. It gripped me so tightly I could barely breathe. I shoved at the wet muscle hauling me toward the bat. It was slippery, and my hands just got coated in goo. I could see fangs now, and they were so much larger than Daniel's. Daniel's fangs were large but were meant to feed and leave the victim alive for another meal. These had no such function. These teeth were meant to tear and rip and get at soft, sweet insides.

The black bird's tongue didn't look at all like a tongue. It was more delicate and rounded. As it came closer to me, I could see it was actually a little mouth, a circular tube, and at the end were tiny, sharp teeth. The mouth knew exactly where it wanted to go.

As the bat hauled me into the air, I lost all footing and any way to fight. I was pulled from the safety of the balcony and hovered over the pool lights. My sense of balance shattered as I fought, trying to punch out as the bird's mouth sought a place under my right breast, just below the rib cage. It struggled with the layers of fabric. I was lucky that wide belts were in this season.

The tongue tightened around my waist to the point of real pain. I pushed at it, but it just kept going. I couldn't breathe, couldn't move, couldn't fight. My eyesight started to fade, my arms feeling like useless, flailing things.

Just when I was starting to lose consciousness, I heard a whooshing sound and the bat jerked. The large animal convulsed forward and the black bird retracted that mouth and squawked off. The bat's tongue released its hold and for the barest minute, I was relieved.

Unfortunately, that freaking tongue was the only thing holding me up, and I found myself in midair without the ability to fly. I dropped, my head hitting the railing as I made my way to the pool. I didn't even feel myself hit the water.

Chapter Four

I woke up completely drenched, my head pounding in a nauseating rhythm. The world seemed too quiet, but then I felt a gentle press against my lips. I forced my eyes open.

Dev held me gently in his arms, his lips caressing mine. Despite the pain, I couldn't help but think of the old stories where the prince woke the princess with a kiss. He pulled back, staring down at me, his eyes like jewels gleaming in the hazy light.

I shivered despite the heat of the night. Dev's clothes were as wet as mine, and his hair was slicked back. It looked so much longer when it was wet. It flowed down his back. My eyes weren't completely focused, and I realized it must be a trick of the light because Dev's hair was short. I'd been damn lucky he found me. I could easily have drowned.

"Thanks for the rescue, baby." The words came out in a croak. I could taste the pool water and wondered if he'd had to give me mouth to mouth.

Dev touched my face, a gentle brush of his skin to mine before he lowered his head and kissed me again. It was odd. Perhaps it was the pain I felt, but I missed the passion that normally flared up between the two of us the minute he got his mouth on mine. I pulled him closer, trying to find that bond we had. It was a nice kiss, but it felt flat to me. Dev's hands found my breasts, and he cupped them through my wet shirt but it felt more curious than passionate. I finally pulled away.

"Stop, Dev. What are you doing? I think I need to lie down."

He grinned over me and put a finger to his lips. "Shhhh." He winked and laid me back down on the deck. He was gone before I could push myself up.

The minute my head was down again, darkness threatened. The world went hazy once more and I lost some time. I had no idea how long I was there, lying by the pool, but a sound finally woke me again.

"Jesus, Zoey." I heard Daniel curse from above. He leapt over the balcony and hit the deck with a resounding thud. "What the hell happened?"

I pushed the wet hair out of my face and glanced around, trying to see where Dev had gone. Why hadn't he stayed with me? My head was so foggy. Daniel hauled me into his arms, his blue eyes glowing in the dark as he stretched his senses outward. He stilled, a sure sign that he was trying to catch a scent or a sound that would lead him to his prey. It wasn't hard to figure out that he was looking for any evidence that Lucas Halfer had surfaced, but I knew he wouldn't find any.

He shook his head. "I'm getting a bunch of small animals and Dev. When was Dev out here?"

I let Daniel cradle me, loving how safe I always felt in his arms. I tried to force myself to focus. "He saved me. There was this bird and then this chick with weird feet and she turned into a bat with a freaky tongue and then the bird had this mouth and it tried to eat me, but Michael Kors saved me."

At least his well-designed black leather belt with metal grommets had been wide enough to protect my midsection. If I hadn't had it on, the bird likely would have punctured my middle and I would have been a nighttime snack.

Daniel looked down at me like I was crazy. I probably sounded like I was. I was slurring my words slightly, and he was still out of focus. "How much did you drink tonight?"

"I am not wasted," I protested, except that I was a little bit. The evening had been crappy, and Christine was always generous with the good vodka. But I was pretty sure my pounding head had to do with the fact that I'd bounced it off the side of the deck. "It happened and when the bat thingee dropped me, I fell in the pool. Dev must have pulled me out. When I woke up, he was holding me and trying to get into my pants."

Daniel didn't look convinced. "Dev's been inside talking to Ingrid for the last thirty minutes. They're going over the ceremony and all the things you have to do to prepare yourself. There's a whole purification process."

I shook my head to try to clear it. It didn't work. It just throbbed more. "That's not possible. I know what happened, Danny. Dev

45

kissed me and felt me up and then he was gone."

"What's going on?" Dev walked through the French doors that led from the kitchen to the back porch. His clothes were dry, and I had to admit that maybe I'd hit my head harder than I thought I had. "Where the hell have you been, Zoey? I checked the bathroom and you weren't there. Halfer is out there just waiting to get his claws into you. You had to know how disappearing would scare the crap out of us."

"Apparently Zoey decided to take a little swim," Daniel said with an obnoxious smile.

"I didn't jump in the pool, Daniel Donovan." He was treating me like an obnoxious kid, and I'd had about enough of it. I knew what I'd seen. "Put me down."

He acquiesced, and I immediately felt my knees buckle. Daniel cursed and helped me back up. I watched as he and Dev shared a look.

Dev shook his head, his eyes deeply disappointed. "I'll go tell everyone we're heading out."

"I'm not drunk," I protested, but my skull felt like it was going to split open and I bit off a cry.

Dev held my head in his palms, gently inspecting my scalp. "She has a bump on her head."

"I hit it when I fell in the pool," I explained.

Dev's eyes went wide as he thought about the implications. "You fell in the pool? You could have killed yourself. I realize we pushed you tonight, lover, but that's not an excuse to get so drunk you can't walk. I can't believe I didn't see this. She was all right earlier."

Daniel's mouth was grim. "This wouldn't have happened if we'd brought Zack."

"He has to have the night off sometime, Dan," Dev replied.

"Screw Zack," I said, needing to rebel. I could see exactly what was coming since neither one of them seemed willing to believe I wasn't drunk off my ass. "What's he going to do? Monitor my alcohol intake?"

Dev frowned. "If necessary, yes. At least he would have been here to catch you. I'll start looking for some more muscle because she needs twenty-four-hour surveillance. Somebody should be with her even when she's out with us."

"But you were here, Dev." I teared up because my head really hurt and I didn't understand what was going on. It was all a jumble in my mind, and now they were talking about more restrictions. I couldn't take it. "You saved me."

Dev looked at Daniel for explanation. "She thinks the two of you got it on out here after she nearly drowned herself."

Dev shook his head. "God, she's out of it. I should never have come. I should have just let her have her way. It's not like it worked anyway. Harry still hates me, and now he blames me for corrupting the both of you. What a clusterfuck."

"Dev, I wanted you to come." I tried to explain as I sought to make things stop spinning. "He'll come around."

"Not when he sees the condition I let you get into, sweetheart," Dev said bitterly. "He's going to think I'm turning you into an alcoholic."

"Once and for all I am not drunk." And that was the moment my gut decided to completely betray me. "Oh, god, I'm going to be sick."

I pulled away from Daniel and managed to make it to the grass before emptying the contents of my stomach.

Dev was behind me, trying to hold my hair and making sure I didn't fall over. When my insides stopped clenching, I sat back up. I was so miserable and it wasn't all about the concussion I was pretty sure I had now. There was no way I was going to be able to make them believe me, and it really pissed me off. I was willing to ponder the idea that Dev had been a hallucination. The hit to my head was obviously more serious than I'd first thought. I must have managed to get myself out of the pool. But the weird bat and bird were no hallucinations. They'd been very real, and I needed to figure out what the hell had happened tonight. It looked like I was going to be doing the research on my own, though.

"Can you get up, sweetheart?" Dev asked. "Daniel's gone to get a cool towel. We're going to move you into the limo and then see how well vampire blood works on a hangover."

"It's not a fucking hangover." I was forced to let him help me up because my legs weren't exactly listening to commands. I would have to take that blood, too, because while I wasn't certain it would help a hangover, I was pretty damn sure it would work on my concussion. My stubborn nature told me to tell the boys to screw themselves, but I didn't want to end up in the hospital. At this point, they would take the concussion as a symptom and not the cause.

Dev sighed. "All right, sweetheart. We can call it anything you like."

"Don't you condescend to me, Dev," I managed to get out. Daniel was back, and he pressed a cold rag to my forehead.

I found myself in the limo before I could say anything vaguely like good-bye. I was an embarrassment to be dealt with, and Dev was good at smoothing over a difficult situation. I was hustled out with all haste and scooped into the limo, still shivering in wet clothes.

The car pulled away as Daniel pulled his shirt over his head. Dev was attempting to get me out of the wet clothes, but I slapped his hands away.

"Zoey, don't be difficult," he said with a huff.

"I haven't been difficult enough, Dev." I'd been accommodating for months, never questioning them or asking to be let in on their plans. I'd allowed them to maneuver me to a place where I was nothing but ornamental. I had no one but myself to blame. "I'll take the blood but these clothes stay on until I get home."

"You're going to be uncomfortable," he pointed out as though that was the absolute worst thing a person could be.

"Maybe I've gotten too comfortable," I muttered more to myself than anyone else.

Daniel tossed his shirt aside and leaned back. He pulled me into his lap, not complaining about the wet clothes. He quickly popped a claw out of his right hand, the change as elegant and quick as any alpha. He drew the claw across his chest in a short deep stroke. The blood welled up, and I put my mouth to it.

It tasted like a dark, slightly metallic chocolate, rich and thicker than a human's. It healed and brought youth. It brought Daniel great pleasure. He held my head to his chest and encouraged me to drink my fill as I felt the pressure building in him. After a minute or two, I licked the wound. It closed quickly once I was no longer sucking at it.

Desire was plain in Daniel's eyes, but I pushed away to the

other side of the limo—the side the boys were not on. I knew what Daniel wanted. He wanted me to ride him hard and fast until he came. He wanted to feed and make me scream.

I wasn't ready to do any of those things. My head was clear now and those pesky twitches were gone. My stomach felt infinitely better and a pleasant, healthy warmth was infusing my entire body. Unfortunately, now that I was able to think again, I was getting really angry. Had they told me the same story, I would have believed them until facts proved me otherwise. I would have given them the benefit of the doubt. I would have been out there trying to hunt down the things that had attacked my men.

"Thank you, Daniel." The events of the night were weighing on me. They didn't trust me. I didn't really have a place in their lives besides the bedroom. "I feel better now."

"Glad to help, Z." His jaw clenched as he dealt with the sexual frustration. In the normal course of our lives, I would be riding him by now and Dev would be cheering me on, waiting for his turn.

I stared out the window as we moved back into the downtown area where Ether was located. I could feel the tension in the car, but I wasn't ready to talk yet. Dev tried to initiate a conversation, but he fell back into silence when I said nothing and refused to look at either one of them.

We pulled into the parking garage, and the three of us walked silently to the elevator. One of the reasons Dev had decided Ether was the best place for us to live was the labyrinthine path we had to take to get up to the penthouse. We had to go all the way down to the club and then up to Dev's office, which was protected. There was an elevator in the office that only went to the penthouse. It was controlled with a keycard and could be locked down. It was great for security purposes. It sucked because it meant I got to parade past much of the supernatural world looking like a drowned cat.

I crossed my arms over my chest because everyone could tell I was cold. Dev tried to give me his jacket, but I was stubborn enough to ignore it. He tried to argue but Daniel sent him one of those man-to-man looks and Dev backed off. We walked by the long line of patrons waiting to get in, and every one of them stared as we strode past.

When we entered the club, I realized there was one person who

Lexi Blake

might be willing to help me. At the very least, he would tell me if
what I'd seen had any possibility of being real. I looked around and
quickly found the large male I was seeking. Albert, Dev's butler and
sort of personal assistant, was sitting at the bar talking to the
bartender with a cup in front of him. No highball glasses for Albert.
He was strictly a tea drinker. Albert was a seven-foot-tall, red-
skinned half demon. Only his personality and his blue eyes were
even vaguely human. He'd also forgotten more about the
supernatural world than most people ever knew.

I started to walk off, but Dev's hand came out, catching my arm
and pulling me back.

"Where do you think you're going, Zoey?" he asked in a voice
that told me he'd had enough of my antics for one evening.

I pulled away from that warm, tingly feeling I always got when
Dev touched me. I didn't want to feel good right now. I wanted
answers. "I'm going to talk to Albert about my hallucinations, Dev. I
would like to know what it is my alcoholic's brain managed to pull
out of thin air. So back off."

His jaw tightened, and a long sigh came out of his mouth as
though he was struggling to keep his patience. "Zoey, you need to go
upstairs and rest."

His condescending tone pushed me over the edge. I might have
been able to handle that from Daniel. Fighting had always been a
part of our relationship, but it was new with Dev. The fact that Dev
was beginning to see me as a problem to be handled really cut to the
quick, and following true to form, I struck out as hard as I could.

"I'm not five, Dev," I pointed out, hearing the cruelty in my
voice but not quite able to stop it. "Contrary to what you might
think, you don't own me. We're not even married. If providing for
me means I suddenly have to obey you, then I can sure as hell
provide for myself. I'm going to talk to Albert. If you think you can
stop me, feel free to try, but you have to sleep sometime. You can let
me get the information I need now or I can get it later when you least
expect it."

I saw the hurt register on his face before that careful mask fell
into place. This was the king's advisor, not my love. "Of course.
Feel free to speak to Albert. As I am not your husband, I will leave
your care to him. I'm going out for a while. I'll sleep in the office

50

tonight. I wouldn't want to disrupt your marriage bed."

Dev walked off, loosening his tie, his posture and movement a testament to his anger.

"Damn it, Z," Daniel growled, getting into my space. "That was just fucking mean. You got anything you want to say to me? You want to try to run me off? Give it your best, baby, because if your plan is to alienate the people who love you, you've done a fantastic job tonight."

I didn't say anything because I was worried if I started talking, I would start crying. I needed to be hard and cold. I needed every bit of my inner bitch or I would be upstairs with both of them making me feel like a spoiled child. "Are you done?"

Daniel rolled his eyes. "For god's sake, don't let me keep you. Go talk to Albert. You've already fucked up the evening, so what's another ten minutes of waiting on you?"

"If you don't have the time to wait, the door is that way, buddy." I made my way to the bar.

Albert turned his eyes to me and an amused curiosity lit his face. Since I'd moved in with Dev and Daniel had joined us, Albert's attitude had distinctly softened toward me. Apparently, while the demon had trouble with adultery, he didn't mind a little bigamy. Once I was in a committed relationship with his master that included my husband, he started treating me with fondness.

"Mistress," Albert acknowledged with a slight bow of his head. He considered himself a servant to the three of us. We'd adopted him through our relationship with Dev. "Your birthday evening has gone awry?"

I pushed myself up onto the barstool. "Tom, can I get some coffee?" I asked, though the perverse side of my nature goaded me to order a martini and make sure Daniel saw me drink it. I was still chilly though, and my stubbornness wasn't going to warm me up. "It's been past awful, Al. It might make my top ten crappy nights of all time."

"Master Daniel seems more angry than usual," Albert commented, looking across the club. Daniel was staring at me, arms crossed, foot tapping.

"Well, if you think he's upset, you should see Devinshea." I wrapped my hands around the mug Tom passed me, letting the coffee warm my skin.

"It was inevitable," Albert said with a sympathetic stare.

"Why? Because the whole threesome thing can't work?" I took a gulp of the excellent coffee. "Let me tell you, Al, if the whole threesome thing doesn't work out, I think you'll be surprised who gets kicked to the curb. I think Dev and Daniel are much happier with each other than they are with me right now."

The delicate cup looked fragile in his huge hands, but he held it with the infinite gentleness of one who truly knew his own strength. "Oh, I believe your relationship can work. I just don't think you're the same girl who went into the relationship."

I took a deep breath and couldn't quite meet his eyes. "Maybe I've changed, but I did it for them. I've done everything they've asked me to for the past six months. I've tried to be what they need me to be."

"What if they need you to be Zoey? I've talked to my master on several occasions, and I believe he needs you now more than ever. The experiences he had in Las Vegas have put him into a sort of shock. I think it affected all three of you. I believe you are the only one who is strong enough to break the three of you out of the state you find yourselves in."

"I don't think they want to be broken out of anything." It was my greatest fear, that they were truly happy with the status quo and wouldn't accept anything less than a docile, submissive me. "I think they enjoy the way things are going."

"Master Daniel does not seem to be enjoying himself," Albert said, shaking his horns. "And if Master Dev has sought other entertainments on tonight of all nights, he is unhappy as well. He gave you the chain of the goddess, did he not? Have you refused him?"

I touched the gold at my neck, pulling it out from under my shirt and showing it off. "No, I didn't refuse him. I'll perform the ritual with him. That's not what our fight was about. Something happened earlier tonight and they don't believe me. I was attacked and ended up with a concussion. They preferred to believe I was just drunk. I won't bore you with the sad details of our fight, but I need some info, and you're my go-to guy."

Albert's eyes went wide. "You were attacked by the demon?

Should we place the club in lock-down?"

"It wasn't Halfer. It was a woman and a bird. The bird was black and it had a…I don't know what to call it. When it opened its mouth, a long tubular thing came out and it had teeth."

"Proboscis," Albert said thoughtfully. "It's a type of mouth. It elongates and aids the creature in piercing flesh and sucking out the sustenance it needs."

I shivered and not from the cold. It had been trying to get at my flesh. "Okay, that makes sense. It was going for my middle, which is softer, so it probably eats viscera. Eww. The woman turned into a bat."

Albert thought for a long moment. "Many hags can shapeshift, and they often have familiars. I would begin the search by looking into this plane's various witches. I would also check on the corporeal undead. There are several species that might be able to do the things you've described."

"Oh, and it was the weirdest thing." There was one fact about the creature that stood out. "Her feet were on backward. What was that about?"

A slow smile crossed Albert's face. "Oh, Zoey. That's important indeed. What did the bird sound like? Did it sound far away though the creature was close?"

"Yes," I said, getting excited because it looked like he knew what I was talking about. Maybe I wasn't going crazy.

"Did it sound like 'tik-tik'?" Albert asked. I put my forefinger on my nose and pointed at Albert, who laughed. "You certainly can attract the deadliest of creatures. The bird is a familiar to a deeply insidious creature. The female is an aswang. It is an undead creature. It is a long way from home, though. They're concentrated in the Philippines."

I shrugged. "Hey, the faeries immigrated. Why not the undead? Dallas is hopping lately. Where do I start looking for this bitch?"

"They typically work in villages as a butcher or some form of meat processor," Albert explained. "I believe if you look on the Internet, you'll find everything you need. Though they're rare here, the stories are plentiful."

I hopped off the barstool and planted a quick kiss on his cheek. I was certain if he hadn't already been red, he would have blushed.

"Thanks, Al. I really appreciate it."

"You're welcome, mistress," he said solemnly. "Think on my advice. You might want to push this issue before it breaks the three of you. My master loves you, but make sure his need to see you safe doesn't turn you into something you don't wish to be."

I promised I would consider what he'd said and knew I would think about it far too much. For now, I just wanted to get upstairs and start my search. It was easier than thinking about my problems with Dev and Danny. The truth was I was invigorated at the thought of the hunt. I was already thinking of how I could track this bad girl and find out who sent her. It had my adrenaline up. Since returning from Vegas, the most adrenaline I had was picking a new nail color at my mani-pedis. I missed working. I missed being me.

Things had to change.

"Can we go upstairs now?" Daniel asked, irritation flavoring every word.

"We can go upstairs but just so you know, you might as well grab a pillow and cuddle up with Dev on the couch because if you think I'm getting into bed with you, you are so wrong." I passed him and started toward the door.

I heard him curse as I ran up the stairs.

Chapter Five

I didn't find my boys cuddled together on the couch in Dev's office when I woke up the next morning. Daniel was safe in the interior room we used for visiting vampires and Dev was up and out before I woke up. The only person waiting to greet me after I showered and got ready was Zack. Though he was perfectly dressed, there was a puffiness to his eyes that let me know he hadn't slept much the night before. I guessed Lisa had kept him up.

"Good morning, Zack." For the first time in a long time, I felt a thrum of excitement at the coming day. I had some adrenaline pumping, and I was looking forward to needing it. I had a job— hunting down the aswang.

Zack grumbled something that may or may not have been a hello.

"Where's Lee?" Zack might be a hard-ass, but Lee was the one who loved the hunt. If I could talk just one of them into going with me, I could get started. Lee was a much better bet than Zack. Lee was reasonable and didn't have his head up Dev's ass.

I'd stayed up late reading everything I could about the awful, baby-eating aswang and her familiar, the Tik-Tik bird. What I read hadn't made me feel kindly toward my attackers. That freaking bird had been after my liver, damn it. I needed my liver.

I was certainly intrigued because I wasn't their normal prey. Someone had sent that bad girl after me, and I was going to find out whom.

Zack yawned and shuffled through some papers. "Lee's at the restaurant."

"What restaurant?"

Zack handed me a single sheet of paper. It was my daily itinerary. Once Dev had taken over Daniel's bid for the crown, we'd become extremely organized. Dev believed in efficiency when it came to running a royal household. "He's at the restaurant where you're meeting Kelly. Mr. Quinn says you need a new summer wardrobe. He doesn't want you attending the Gathering in cutoffs and a tank top. He's also banned flip-flops."

I rolled my eyes. I was getting awfully tired of shopping and besides, I looked damn good in shorts and a tank top. What the hell was Dev expecting at this gathering? Wolf society isn't as formal as vampire society. I was pretty sure most of the wolves would be wearing as little as possible, when they weren't showing off the fur god gave them. "I need to reschedule that. I'll call Kelly and move it to next week. We have a couple of errands I need to run, and I could really use that sniffer of yours."

It would come in handy. I wouldn't be able to tell the difference between the aswang and her living co-workers from a distance, but the wolves could. If I had to find her by my lonesome, I was going to spend the day looking like a complete idiot.

Zack shook his head firmly. "No way, Zoey. You're following that schedule. I heard all about last night and until the new bodyguards are vetted, I'm on twenty-four-freaking-hour call. I had to cancel a date. I'm not in a good mood. If you have a problem with it, take it up with Mr. Quinn."

"Fine. Where is he?" I didn't need another bodyguard. I couldn't handle the ones I already had. This was getting completely out of hand. I would be on house arrest if it kept up. It was time to deal with the problem.

Zack's smile held no humor whatsoever. "He left early this morning. I think he wanted to avoid you. He's out at the farm. My master has a new vampire, and Mr. Quinn is making arrangements to move him into the third bedroom of your old house. I'm sure he'll be back sometime tonight. You can yell at him all you like then. Until that time, you're going to follow the schedule. So are you ready to go?"

"I'm not going, Zack." I meant it right up until he tossed me over his shoulder and started walking to the elevator. "Put me down."

"I'll put you down when we get to the restaurant," he promised. "And, Zoey, if you try to run, I will catch you."

Thirty minutes later, I was sullenly shown to a nicely decorated table. I managed to convince Zack to allow me the dignity of walking into the restaurant, but his eyes hadn't left me once. Lee tried to hide a grin as I cursed his brother with every vulgar name I knew. The early afternoon sun lit the small café with soft light, and I ordered a drink while I waited on the stylist.

Dev and I were going to have it out tonight, and he was either going to see things my way or…I didn't know what I was going to do. The thought of walking out made me sick to my stomach. I just couldn't imagine my life without Devinshea in it, but he had to see that I was suffocating. I was just going to yell until he gave in and that was that.

I glanced up, expecting to see the waiter with my iced tea, but I was met with seriously green eyes. Dev stood over me, smiling down.

"I thought you were at the farm." I hated the breathy sound that came out of my mouth. His six-foot-five-inch sinfully gorgeous body always made my heart skip a beat even when I wanted to throttle him. The fact that I wanted to molest him right there on the table didn't help me fight with him. Dev and I had very few fights. I usually started to fight and somehow ended up on my back, agreeing to do whatever he wanted.

"I finished early, lover," he said, gracefully taking the seat next to me. He pulled my hand to his lips and kissed each finger. The tender gesture softened my heart. It was something he did often, and it never failed to make me smile. "I thought I could have lunch with you. It would be nice to have you all to myself for a change."

"What about Kelly? I thought you wanted me to plan a whole freaking wardrobe." I didn't attempt to hide my lack of enthusiasm.

"I've rearranged things with Kelly. You can meet with her later." He inspected the menu. His eyes caught mine over the daily specials and he winked. "I prefer you without any clothes at all, lover. If you like, we can skip lunch altogether and I'll just eat you."

I laughed because if he was being filthy, he couldn't be too angry with me. Dev became rigidly polite when he was pissed at me. In this case, his horniness might work to my advantage. If I could convince him to spend the afternoon with me tracking down the aswang, it might go a long way to healing the rift that was opening between us. I wasn't worried about Daniel. Daniel and I fought and made up all the time. What I had with Dev was much newer and infinitely more fragile. It was the first time I really realized how delicate the balance between the three of us had become.

The waiter brought Dev a beer and set my tea down. He took a moment to take our orders. I let him know I wanted the grilled fish as Dev's hand played tantalizingly with my knees under the table. I wondered what he really had planned. It wouldn't be the first time he hauled me into the bathroom of a fancy restaurant, paid off the attendant to keep it private, and had his wicked way with me.

"So you're not mad at me anymore?" I wanted to get everything on the table. I'd been pretty rough on him the night before, but I had my reasons. If we could both apologize, I was willing to start completely fresh this afternoon.

His lips quirked playfully. "I can't stay mad at my sweetheart. You know I wish only to please you. Let's put this fight from our minds and enjoy the afternoon together."

It was nice to have him to myself for a change. Daniel and Dev had both been busy with their plans and rarely found time to do anything like taking me out for a leisurely lunch. The last several months had found endless visitations and boring dinners where I entertained the women as Dev and Daniel discussed business with the men.

I found myself talking to him about inconsequential things as he held my hand, his fingers tangling with mine the way they so often did. This was what Devinshea did best. He could make me feel like I was the only woman on the planet. After a long while of enjoying his attention, I finally found myself broaching the subject of the night before.

"I am entirely at fault for any misunderstanding, lover," Dev admitted earnestly. "I should have listened. I am ready to listen to you now. Please tell me about the undead creature and that odd bird of hers."

"Well, it's called an aswang." I felt myself smiling because I was relieved. The hunt would be so much better with Dev at my side. He always had enjoyed a bit of adventure. "It's from the Philippines and…" I stared at my lover and shivered suddenly but not from the air conditioner. His words rang in my head. "How did you know she was undead, Dev? I didn't tell you anything. I told Danny, but you didn't want to hear about it."

He smiled at the accusation, settling back in his chair. "Well, sweetheart, I talked to Danny about it later. We do live together. It only makes sense that we would discuss what happened last night."

Perhaps nothing about the previous night had been a hallucination. I had never once heard Dev call Daniel Danny. He used Dan but never Danny.

I decided to try something. I smiled brightly, my best bimbo look, which would have sent the real Dev into suspicious mode. This version just smiled. Yes, something was wrong and I knew how to figure this out.

"You're right, baby. I don't think sometimes." I leaned across the table and planted a kiss on his lips. He opened his mouth willingly and curved a hand around the back of my head to pull me in closer. Just like last night it was nice but not my Dev. I pulled away from whoever the hell was currently kissing me and sat back. "All right. Who are you?"

He leaned back and studied me. "Is my game up, then? Well, I was hoping for more time, but I will take what I can get. Do not bother calling the bodyguards. I sent them back to the club. I explained to the younger one that I wished to care for you myself. He took the other one with him. So much for the superiority of wolf senses. It is just you and me, Mrs. Donovan. That is the name you go by? You are married to the vampire? Tell me, Mrs. Donovan, do you mind my brother fucking your husband?"

"Declan." I should have freaking thought about him last night. When your boyfriend has a twin brother, you should probably expect him to show up sometime.

"I see my brother remembers my name," Declan Quinn, heir to the *Daoine Sidhe* throne, said, his face taking on an arrogant expression. "Too bad he does not remember his obligations."

"He has no obligations to you, you cowardly piece of shit." How dare he walk into Dev's life and accuse him of neglecting his responsibilities? Dev had fled the *sithein* to get away from his family's manipulations. "What do you want with him after all these years?"

"Years?" Declan asked, confusion temporarily clouding his face. "Devinshea left only eighteen months ago. How long has it been on this plane?"

"Seven years." Time moved differently in a *sithein*, as once you were in the *sithein*, you were no longer on the Earth plane. Each faery mound housed a piece of Faeryland, with its own moon and sun and its own distinct clock.

Declan nodded and the lordly look was back. Now I could plainly see he wasn't my boyfriend. He wasn't as vibrant as Dev. His eyes, while just as green, didn't have that sparkle. "That explains much. I wondered how Devinshea had managed to accumulate such wealth in so short a time. He seems to be living exceptionally well, though that should not surprise me. He always found a way to make himself comfortable. I assumed it belonged to his vampire lover."

"It's all Dev's, asshole," I tossed back at him, not liking the assumption. Dev might like his comfort but he wasn't afraid of hard work. "He's an amazing businessman. He owns five nightclubs, and they're all popular. He's also good with investments. He's thriving on this plane and needs nothing from you. Daniel isn't his lover. I'm the only one he has sex with. He's a faithful boyfriend in a committed relationship."

Declan threw back his head and laughed. It made me really wish I could punch him, but I didn't trust someone to not call the cops. "My brother has never been monogamous in his life. It is against his nature. I would be quicker to believe he had ten women in his bed at once than he was faithful to one. Do not get me wrong. He has certainly kept women before, but while they might have served as his main lover, they were never alone. When he sent word to the *sithein* that he wanted the Goddess Chain, I had to come and see for myself what game he was playing. I see that you are the pawn. That thing you are wearing isn't real and it means nothing. If you think it will help you gain some access into Fae society, I promise you it will not. Whatever arrangement he has made with you requires royal consent, and I will not be giving it."

"It means something to me and it means something to Dev," I said, my hand going to the medallion. "As for your consent, you can stick it, Declan."

"I would prefer Your Highness."

"And I have no desire to have anything to do with Fae society." I'd had it up to here with the societies on this plane. I didn't need to go looking for more.

Declan was quiet for a moment as he studied me with interested eyes. "Well, I must say, my brother always had good taste in women. I am afraid we share that. We grew up surrounded by fair, lithe women, so we perversely loved small, curved ones. You look like a fertility goddess, you know. I watched you last night and could not take my eyes off that body of yours. And that hair. We do not have that color in our world. I can certainly see where Devinshea would be amused with you for a while, but I assure you he is not faithful. If he is not screwing the vampire, then he is finding variety elsewhere."

"You don't know anything about us, Declan." I pushed the chair back and rose. "I don't care what you think. Dev is faithful, and it doesn't matter if this chain is real or not. The feeling behind it is real. That's all I need. Good-bye."

His hand shot out and held me firmly. This was not a man used to having people walk out on him. "Not yet, I think. As I said, I sent your bodyguards away but mine are still here. Please sit, Mrs. Donovan. They will not allow you to leave and will only cause trouble for the humans in this place. I am afraid they care only for performing their duties and not a whit for who gets hurt in the process."

I sat back, scanning the crowd. Declan chuckled. "You will not be able to see them," he explained. "They are hidden, but I assure you I have a small army with me. I am a future king and never without my servants."

"Why are you here?" I wanted to get away from him as soon as possible. I was going to go out to the farm myself and let Dev know his brother was in town.

The waiter showed up, and Declan dug into his prime rib. He liked it rare. I pushed my plate away. Declan shrugged, my appetite obviously none of his concern. "I told you, I wanted to see my brother's chosen goddess. I wanted to see the female who tempted him from his obligations."

I held my hands out. "Here I am, buddy. Now you can go home."

Declan shook his head. "I find myself unwilling to do that. I miss my brother. I wish for him to return home. His fit of temper has lasted long enough. He will return to the *sithein* with me and resume his duties. His priestesses have missed him. They petition daily for his return, and I am, quite frankly, sick of dealing with his women."

"Priestesses?" Dev was a priest, but it wasn't like a Catholic priest. He performed fertility rites and sex magic. There was nothing celibate about Dev. I was pretty certain these priestesses wouldn't be anything like nuns.

The faery prince seemed amused with my jealousy. "Yes, little human, he has six priestesses. He has six lovely Fae women dedicated to providing him with pleasure so he can perform his duties. Two of the women are even Unseelie. They have extra…bits Devinshea finds amusing. His magic must be practiced or it gets rusty. My brother is dedicated to his magic. He kept those women so satisfied they weep his loss, Mrs. Donovan."

I was feeling mighty insecure now. This was a part of his life Dev had never spoken of to me, and Dev was open about his past sexual partners. I knew they included most of the phone book, but this was the first I'd heard about an actual harem. "He isn't going to leave me."

Declan stared at me, and I really hated the pity on his handsome face. "Zoey, why do you think it took so long for you to realize I was not your lover? I am excellent at mimicking my brother. I had years to practice. Why did I call you sweetheart and lover? How did I know to kiss your fingers and constantly have my hands somewhere on you? I knew because this is how he treats all of his mistresses. You might be very sweet, Zoey, and the fact that you are a companion was probably a challenge that Devinshea could not pass up. Only my brother could place himself between a vampire and his obsession. It is yet another thing to check off that list of his."

Declan was rubbing an old wound raw. When Dev and I started dating, I worried this was his reason for being attracted to me. Dev even admitted a part of him enjoyed the forbidden nature of our liaison. What if that was still his chief interest in me? I wasn't so secure that I hadn't looked in the mirror and wondered just what the hell a man like Devinshea Quinn could see in me. I knew about his list. It was a constant joke between the two of us—all the places he wanted to have sex in so he could check it off his list. What if I was the butt of this particular joke? A companion is not a common thing. It would be just like Dev to want that checked off.

"I have hurt you." Declan actually appeared a little apologetic about it. He sighed and leaned forward. "I did not mean to. I can see you have feelings for my brother. This is unfortunate. I can only apologize for my behavior. I believed you to be a fortune hunter. Though you are a companion, I understand a vampire master can be cruel. Perhaps you thought Devinshea would save you from your husband. Perhaps you believed life in a *sithein* would be preferable to serving the vampire. When my brother asked for the chain, I thought you had ensnared him in some way. I wondered if he had gotten you pregnant."

"No." I didn't like the awful feeling welling up inside me. I really didn't like the careful way Declan was treating me. I hated to be an object of pity. I preferred his bile.

"I understand, Zoey," he said quietly, and I saw another side to the man who would be king. "If your heart has been engaged, then I am sorry. My brother always did this with his mistresses. He makes them dependent on him and then, inevitably, he loses interest. He is simply a romantic always looking for that one woman who will complete him. It is a foolish notion. If it helps, he is always most generous when he breaks off a relationship. He does not mean to hurt his women. They just cannot help but fall in love with him." Declan stood now and pulled cash out of his wallet. "I apologize if I have caused you distress. I thought you were somewhat different from the other women my brother has kept in the past. I can see now that you are sweet and soft and more than likely submissive sexually. It is what he likes. I am sorry to have injured your feelings. Tell Devinshea I will be calling on him."

He was looking at me like he'd kicked a puppy, and something inside me just broke. There's nothing I hate more than being treated like I don't have a brain in my head. I'm more than willing to use the male population's belief that anything as curvy as me couldn't possibly be dangerous, but this was too much. I was sick of every man in my life treating me like a pathetic little toy.

It had taken me six months, but I was back with a vengeance.

"Listen here, motherfucker," I hissed between clenched teeth. Declan had the good sense to be taken aback. "I'm not submissive. Maybe sometimes it's fun, but I assure you that I don't submit on a regular basis. You want to get to know the woman your brother's been screwing, then let's get to know each other. We'll need to head back to Ether. I have to accessorize."

I walked straight up to him and took a fistful of silk shirt. I pulled him down and his eyes softened, his mouth opening slightly as though ready for a kiss. I stopped just short of his lips. "And, Your Highness, if you wish to survive the experience, I suggest you stay behind me."

I let him go and walked out the door. I wasn't surprised when he came running after me.

Chapter Six

I walked into Ether hopeful that Declan would be able to keep up his end of the bargain. I needed him to be Dev in order to get past my bodyguards. Since I moved into the grotto, I had access to everything in the penthouse, but no one had given me the key to the small armory Dev kept in the club. It was tightly locked down and only Dev, Daniel, Zack, and the head of security had a keycard. That was just one of the things that was going to change if I stayed here, but for now, I needed a ruse to get in.

Looking up at Declan, I could see he'd already turned on his Dev face. He looked less arrogant, his smile decadent and smooth.

The club was quiet during the day, with only a minimal staff taking care of restocking, cleaning, and maintenance. I let my hand find his. "You need to look like you want to sleep with me."

That was a requirement for anyone trying to pass as Dev.

"Not a problem, lover," he replied, sounding exactly like his brother. "As I stated before, I find you attractive. If you would prefer to spend the afternoon in coitus, I would be more than happy to oblige. It would not be the first time my brother and I have shared a woman. Devinshea can be generous with his lovers. Perhaps I will allow him to bring you back to the *sithein* when we leave, and then we could share you in all ways. Would you like a future king in your bed, Zoey?"

"I think I'll take a pass on the offer, but thanks." I already had enough kings in my bed. Between my vampire king and my personal faery prince, my royal dance card was full. Declan sounded far too much like Dev for my sanity.

Zack and Lee were sitting at a table when we reached the bar area. They were having lunch and going over reports. They looked up and Zack frowned. "Mr. Quinn, I thought you were going to call us when you were ready to go."

"Ah, Zack," Declan said in Dev's smooth tones. "There are some things that require privacy." He let his hand drop mine and pulled me into a more intimate embrace. He gave me a smile that told the wolves I had probably done something naughty. His arm was around my shoulders, and he used his free hand to nudge my chin up for a kiss. I had to play along, allowing Declan to explore my mouth briefly, but I promised myself I would get him back. He nodded to Zack, who had completely bought the act. "My girl here would like to go to the shooting range and practice this afternoon. Would you be so good as to escort her to the armory? She would like to select her own weapon."

Zack sighed heavily, like escorting me into the armory was the last thing he wanted to do. It probably was. I was sure the thought of an armed Zoey was not a pleasant one for my bodyguard, but then I had given him no reason to believe me competent. He would have no such impression of me after today.

"Of course, Mr. Quinn," Zack said in his best professional voice. I thought it made him sound like a kiss ass. He pulled the card out of his pants, and I allowed him to lead the way.

As I walked past Lee, he stared at me, brown eyes searching mine, looking for something. I gave him an encouraging smile and he relaxed slightly, but I saw him staring at Declan as I turned the corner. Lee was going to be far worse trouble than Zack.

Zack let his keycard slide into the door to the armory, and he held it open for me. The odor of gun oil washed over me, the sweet scent of home. I smiled at the thought of being well armed again. Today there would be nothing between me and whatever came my way but my own skills and a happy gun. And Declan, since if anything tried to take a shot at me, I firmly intended to jump behind him. He deserved it and he would heal.

"Let's see, Zoey." Zack looked around, probably trying to find the smallest caliber possible. "I'm sure I can find something for you."

I rolled my eyes and went for the specialized Ruger Daniel had modified for me years before. Why I had ever let myself be parted from it, I had no idea. Somehow it wound up in here when Daniel and I moved in with Dev. I opened the box and took a moment to balance the weight. It felt good in my hands. It belonged to me. It meant something to me.

Sighing, I pulled out the second box that contained the exotic rounds the Ruger had been altered to handle. There were silver bullets, cold iron bullets, wooden bullets, bullets that sent salt through the victim's body, bullets that injected colloidal silver, and the one I was looking for—tranquilizers.

"Zoey, that's Donovan's gun. I don't think you should play with that," Zack said like the big brother I never wanted.

"That's where you're wrong, Zack." I loaded the gun quickly and efficiently. "It's not Danny's gun. It's mine, and I'm not playing with you anymore."

I twisted around and shot him squarely in the chest. I have to say I grinned as he went down with a really surprised look on his face. I didn't move though because I knew exactly what was coming next. The gun might be quiet but there was no getting past those wolf ears. I firmed my stance and waited.

Lee kicked open the door and had a semiautomatic in his hand. His eyes first went to his brother and then to me. "Zoey, what the hell is going on?"

"He's fine, Lee." I kept my aim level with his chest. "It was a tranquilizer dart. He's just going to take a little nap."

"Who the hell is that out there, and don't try to tell me that it's Quinn because I know it's not," Lee said, proving his senses were better than any of us suspected. I always thought he had the look of an alpha but this proved it. Not even Daniel had been able to sense the difference between Dev and his twin.

"It's his twin brother, Declan," I explained, not quite able to keep the vindication from my voice. "I'm sorry for having to take Zack out, but it was necessary. He can be entirely unreasonable. The boys told you about last night?"

Lee nodded. He still had his gun trained on me. It was a nice little standoff. "I take it they were wrong. I thought we should check into it, but this is Zack's gig. I let him make the decisions. So the twin was there last night."

"Yep. We're going to hunt down the thing that tried to kill me. I would prefer if you came with us but understand this, Lee, this is my mission and I won't be bossed around."

He sighed. "Zoey, that's not…"

The minute I heard the negative, I shot him. I had a distinct advantage on him and I used it. He didn't want to harm me. It made him slow to act. Like his brother, he went down, though his eyes stayed open longer. I leaned over him. He was in a really uncomfortable position. If I left him like that, he would be sore and while I had no problem with Zack having back spasms for days, I would feel bad about Lee. He was just trying to look out for his brother. I kicked the gun out of his hand and helped him down to a more suitable position to lie unconscious in for several hours.

"Zoey." Lee managed to speak even as his eyes were getting heavy. He should have been out, but he fought it. "Don't get yourself killed."

"I promise. I'll bring you back a head or something, Lee. You'll wish you had gone with me."

"I probably will, you crazy bitch," he said with a smile as the drug finally took effect.

"Night, night, Lee."

I stood up and looked around my own little candy store. I would love to have been able to take one of those cool looking P90s, but they were really hard to conceal under a skirt. I would have to rely on handguns and knives. I could probably fit a couple of grenades and flashbangs in my really big bag. Kelly had sworn it was the handbag of the season. At the time it seemed like a bit much for a girl who only carried a wallet, a cell, and some lip gloss, but now I saw the advantages.

"You took out the wolves." Declan stepped gingerly over my now defunct bodyguards.

"I told you I would." I steadied my foot on a shelf and hiked my skirt up to mid-thigh. I efficiently strapped on the leather piece designed to hold knives. I selected two, turning them slowly in my hands to test their weight before securing them against my leg.

"I admit I was skeptical." Declan carefully watched every move I made. He frowned when I smoothed the skirt down. Looking around the room, his eyes widened as he took in the weaponry. "Why does my brother need such an armory? You said this was a club. If I know my brother, he declared it a place of peace. He never did like to take sides, or rather he never liked to appear to take sides."

I shrugged as I placed the Ruger in my bag. I would have preferred to have it in a handy holster, but it was summer in Texas. I was wearing a skirt and one of those recently outlawed tank tops. I could conceal the knives but not the bulky gun. "He sometimes has security problems. Even a place of peace has to have a security team."

My logic was sound even as I lied through my teeth. Since Dev had thrown his lot in with me and Daniel, the armory had grown exponentially.

"This is not for simple security. Someone is planning a war. What has my brother gotten himself into this time?"

"I don't know," I replied, unwilling to get into that argument. "I'm just a soft, sweet girl. He wouldn't tell his little mistress about his plans. Now drop the glamour."

"What?"

I gestured up and down at his perfect facsimile of Dev. "I'm talking about the glamour you're using to look exactly like your brother. You've been apart for a long time. I seriously doubt you tracked down his hair stylist and asked for 'the Dev.' You were watching us the other night and you copied him. I want to see the real you."

The prince nodded and dropped his perfect glamour. I gasped at the quick change. His hold on the magic was damn near perfect. I saw the real Declan for the first time and couldn't help but stare. Declan still looked exactly like Dev with a major exception. His hair was really long. It created a midnight black waterfall around his handsome face. It reached halfway down his back. It strangely didn't make him look feminine. It made him look slightly savage, as did the gold circlet that sat on his head. In the center of his forehead was the same sun symbol that adorned my necklace.

"When did Dev cut his hair?" I made no effort to hide my fascination. Even in the awful florescent light, Declan's hair shone. I found myself thinking about what Dev would look like with all that hair. It would cover me like a blanket when he laid on top of me. I would get tangled in it when we cuddled together. It was so black it almost looked blue.

"He used a knife to butcher it before he left the *sithein*." Declan lowered his head silently, giving his assent for me to touch him. I let my fingers run through the thick, silky fall of his hair. It was truly his crowning glory. "It was then I knew he meant to leave."

69

"You're beautiful, Declan," I said because he was and it was polite in Fae society to compliment someone on their looks. "Your hair is the sexiest thing I've seen in a long time."

He gave me an arrogant grin, bowing slightly. "Thank you, Zoey. And I think your breasts are completely succulent. If I had found myself with more time the other night when I shot the undead creature, I had planned on getting them in my mouth."

"Nice," I replied with a shake of my head because faeries were also big on the over sharing. "How many guns do you want? I always try to carry at least two."

He shook his head. "I do not carry such weapons. They are not honorable."

He turned and showed me that he wore a long, ornate bow on his back along with a quiver containing arrows—a traditional Fae weapon. It was also pretty much crap in the urban field. A longbow worked well when you had the high ground against an army, but I preferred bullets. They were quick, did their job, and I didn't have to notch one every time I needed to fire. There were other reasons I didn't like the bow as a weapon.

"You know what's not honorable? Shooting a hostage in the belly with an arrow. It hurts like hell going in and that is nothing compared to the way the sucker feels when you have to shove it out through the back. I'll take a bullet wound any day of the week. That weapon there isn't honorable. It's barbaric."

"You have had this happen to you?"

"Oh, yeah," I assured him. "Just ask your brother about it. He was tied up at the time, but I'm sure he remembers the experience. He was quite impressed that I managed to shove the whole arrow out the back and I only passed out once." To be honest, I was pretty hopped up on vamp blood at the time or I would have been dead, but I didn't need to tell Declan that. I suddenly remembered we were alone, and I had some unfinished business to take care of. "Declan, this is for Dev."

I hauled my fist back and put every bit of strength I had into breaking his nose.

The Gaelic started flying, and I suspected it was not a flurry of polite words. There was an odd rush of energy against my skin, and I suddenly found myself shoved against a row of shelves with a knife at my throat. I was held firmly in place by a large male with long white hair who had not been in the room thirty seconds before. Declan had been serious about the fact that I couldn't see his guard. The new guy's pale eyes told me he would slit my throat in an instant and probably enjoy the experience. So this was what passed for a bodyguard in the Fae world. I was suddenly glad for Zack.

"Padric, release her," Declan ordered, holding his nose.

I'd drawn blood. That made me happy.

"She attacked you, Your Highness." Padric proved he had an excellent talent for stating the obvious. I stayed really still because that knife was starting to cut into my throat just the tiniest bit. "I cannot allow the insult to pass."

"You can and will obey me," Declan ordered, his temper on a short leash. "Do you think I cannot handle one small female on my own? I am a warrior of the *sidhe*. Now let her go. This is my brother's mistress, for the goddess's sake. If you harm her, he will never come back with us. You know how he is about his females."

Padric looked me up and down, and I could tell he found me wanting. "I do not understand your perverse interest in human females. They seem so breakable and short."

I was, compared to Padric. He had to lean down to hold the knife to my throat. I hoped it caused a crick in his neck. Of course at barely five foot four, I was short, period. If Dev didn't like me to wear four-and-a-half-inch heels, I would reach the middle of his chest. I only barely made it to Daniel's shoulders. That day I was wearing flats, and Padric loomed over me.

"I do not require your understanding," Declan declared, and Padric finally let me loose. "You are ordered to remain hidden until such time as I call you. Is that understood?"

Padric nodded and was suddenly gone. I looked around but there was no sign of the big scary Fae and his knife that I could still feel at my throat. I would love to have known how he pulled the invisible trick though. Something like that would come in handy when running a job.

"You will explain." Declan had managed to wipe himself clean of the blood, and I could see now his nose wasn't actually broken.

I didn't pretend to misunderstand. I remembered the episode Dev and I had experienced on the Hell plane like it was yesterday.

Dev and his brother had been barely seventeen when they were sent to the Unseelie *sithein* for a bit of torture their mother had decided should be part of their education. Dev was the mortal of the two but he had handled it so much better than his immortal brother. "You left him. You left him to the mercy of those Unseelie monsters to save your own hide, and I promised him I would beat the crap out of you if I ever met you."

Declan laughed. "Now I see why my brother finds you so amusing. He would enjoy the idea of a woman defending his honor." His eyes turned serious. "I remember that day well. I was ashamed of my fears, and I lashed out at the brother who had sacrificed to save me pain. I have not forgiven myself for that day, so if you choose to hit me again, I assure you it will be a drop in the bucket compared to what I owe him."

It meant something to me that he was willing to own up to what he'd done. Ingrid had said there was always two sides to the story. I was willing to listen to Declan.

"I'll keep that in mind," I said. "I have one more thing I need. It's in the kitchens and then we hunt down this bitch."

Chapter Seven

Declan turned out to be a complete baby when it came to mass transit.

He whined about the people, the smell, the metal. I wasn't sure what he thought a train should be made of, but he really didn't like the metal. In the end, I had to get off the train and hail a cab because I was sick of his whining. It made me wish Dev had bought me that Porsche. I'd left my own crappy car on the farm for Justin and Angelina to use. I could have used the limo, but I thought that might be conspicuous in the neighborhoods where I was going.

I settled into the cab, and Declan quickly opened the window, pressing his face out of the vehicle. He sat as close to the fresh air as he possibly could. I gave the driver the first address on my list and was happy to learn he didn't speak a whole heck of a lot of English. That would make it easier to talk to Declan freely without the cabbie calling the loony bin on me. I'd done all my research the night before and found ten possible locations for the aswang's workplace. There were a couple of Filipino markets, six restaurants, and two butchers. I was going to try the butchers first as all the legends claimed this was the aswang's chosen profession during the daylight hours.

"Why would the undead creature wish you harm?" Declan asked as though he was trying to get his mind off the fact that he was encased in two tons of steel.

"I tend to piss people off." I rifled through my printouts. "I think someone hired the aswang. I'm not its normal prey. It tends to feed off of corpses or newborn babies. It leaves an effigy behind to take the place of its victim."

"What have you done to anger people? Did you refuse their suits?" Declan asked because he probably couldn't think of any other reason someone could be angry with a female.

"Well, I've narrowed it down to a couple of people. It could be the local werewolf alpha. I shot his balls off a few months back.

They've probably grown back by now, and he could be looking for some revenge. There's always Lucas Halfer. He's a demon. I managed to get his dumb ass kicked off the Hell plane. I've killed any number of people whose relatives could be out for revenge. I even considered Cecilia, that vampire Dev slept with. She was hot to get him back, and I don't doubt for one instant she might try to take me out to clear the way."

Declan smiled with the memory. "Yes, I remember her. She was quite terrifying. I still cannot believe he got into bed with that. He had nightmares about it for weeks. I was surprised to discover him in another vampire's bed."

"Well, Daniel's bite is quite the experience." I looked out the window, wondering briefly if I would ever get to watch that sight again. I really loved to watch the two of them together. They were so freaking hot. Maybe it made me perverse, but I wanted to watch them, craved it kind of. I had some very specific fantasies. "It's totally different from Cecilia. It was Danny's bite that brought Dev's magic back."

Declan's whole face flushed. "You told me he did not fornicate with the vampire."

"He feeds Daniel on occasion," I clarified. Despite my best efforts, I hadn't managed to get them to do more than have Daniel suck on Dev's neck. I had pointed out that there were other veins he could draw from. "Other than that, they share me. Why would you care even if he did?" I had to ask because the Fae weren't known for their homophobia.

"If the vampire has forced himself on my brother, then I will be honor bound to kill him."

I laughed a long time at that one. I was going to have to tell Danny, and he'd have a laugh, too. "Well, let me spare you an ugly death, Declan. I assure you that apart from high-fiving at basketball games, the boys don't exactly get physical."

"I can handle one small vampire," Declan assured me with a snooty arrogance.

Daniel Donovan had once killed twelve vampires in the course of an hour in the arena, and he hadn't been full of companion blood at the time. He was the first vampire in more than a millennium to earn the title of Death Machine. I once watched him decapitate a vampire with one hand as he flew through the air, and he'd managed to catch the head before it hit the ground. If Declan thought he could take Daniel out with his little bow and arrow, I was willing to buy a ticket to that show.

"I bet you can," I offered as the cab stopped at our first destination.

I asked the driver to wait as we hustled out of the cab. Declan was back in his Dev glamour as I'd decided that running about town with a character from *Lord of the Rings* was bound to attract attention.

"I can kill the vampire for you if that is your wish, Zoey," Declan said confidently as he strode beside me. "If he is cruel, then I will slay him and you, my brother, and I will return to the *sithein* together."

I rolled my eyes and kept walking. "He isn't cruel. I'm not using Dev to try to escape Daniel. I love my husband. I love your brother, too. We're happy together."

Well, we had been until I'd shot my bodyguards and defied both their orders.

I opened the door to the small meat market. There were signs in both English and Filipino in the window. The store was neat and clean, but a butchery still smells like meat.

"Ah, it is a ménage?" Declan asked. "I always thought Devinshea would be happy in this sort of arrangement. I rather thought he would be at the center, however."

I glanced around the shop. There were only three customers, and I disregarded them. I was more interested in the woman behind the counter. She was a small woman with tired eyes. Weariness was stamped on the lines of her face, but if I had to guess her age, I would put her in her early thirties. It was the tired look that made me suspicious. The aswang was always weary during the day from all the prowling it did at night.

This was the part where one of my werewolf bodyguards would have really come in handy. If Lee had just come with me, I wouldn't have had to look like a complete idiot. He would have been able to smell the decay that hung about the corporeal undead and I wouldn't have to identify the fucker myself. There are many creatures in the supernatural world that can perfectly mimic the human form. It's one

75

of those Darwinian traits that makes a species successful. Werewolves are successful because they can pass for human most of the time. Vampires can pass. Dragons got their asses slain because they were scary. They were no longer on this plane because they couldn't hide what they were. Humans tend to hunt down and kill what frightens them.

My point is, when dealing with supernaturals passing for humans, there are always tricks to identify your prey. Hunters wrote entire books about it, passing these tomes from generation to generation. In the human world, they're called superstitions, but in my world, it's called a good defense.

There were a couple of tricks I'd discovered for identifying the aswang. I could find an elder to mix a special concoction of coconut oil and herbs and leave it on the suspect's porch. When the aswang walked by it, the oil would boil, thereby unmasking the creature. As I didn't know any Filipino elders who wouldn't laugh me out of their homes, nor did I have any suspects, I had to go with option two, which I did, much to everyone's surprise.

Right there in the middle of the butcher's shop, I turned my back to the suspect, hiked my skirt up as modestly as I could, and bent over to view the possible ghoul through my legs.

Like I said before, I was going to spend the day looking like an idiot.

"We are doing this for what reason?" Declan asked from beside me. He had taken up the same position, and I was glad I wasn't the only one looking foolish. "Are we trying to anger the creature by…what is the human term…mooning it?"

I sighed because the chick behind the counter was still human. Just to be sure, I checked out the customers because as long as I was down there, I might as well.

"It would only be mooning if our asses were bare," I corrected Declan as I stood back up and smoothed down my skirt. That had been a waste of time.

Declan gave me a sly smile. "If your ass had been bare, I would not have mimicked you. I would have stood back and enjoyed the sight."

"The two of you were hell on your mother, weren't you?" Everyone was staring at us with looks ranging from disbelief to anger at our disrespect. I gave the crowd a little salute. "Thanks for the cooperation, folks. Carry on."

I walked out, already pulling out the next address. I glanced up and down the street but the cab was gone. I was never going to find another freaking cab in this part of town. The next address was only a block over, but then they started to spread out. Declan was just going to have to suck it up and get on a bus or walk his ass around town.

"Miss," I heard a soft voice call from behind me.

I turned to see the woman from behind the counter trying to get my attention. She was slightly shorter than me and up close, she seemed extremely fragile. She was thin to the point of worry, and her eyes hadn't seen sleep for many days. I immediately felt sympathy for her because it was so easy to see she was in pain.

"I apologize for disrupting your business." It certainly wasn't her fault something was out to get me. I was just some crazy white chick making an ass of herself. It was rude so I tried to make up for it. "I won't bother you again. I promise."

I began to go, but she caught my arm.

"You are looking for her?" There was hopeful expectation in her quiet voice, and I knew I had caught a break.

"I am hunting her," I corrected.

"She came only weeks ago," the woman explained in a haunted voice. "She opened a shop, and I went to welcome her. We are a small community here, and I was looking for news from home. I thought perhaps since we did the same work, we could be friends. She told me how beautiful my baby was…"

Her eyes were glassy with tears, and I understood why she had not slept.

"This creature took your infant?" Declan stood tall, his whole body becoming tense as though he'd finally found a reason to be serious. It hit me that he was responsible for his people's welfare. Dev had been the priest but Declan was the warrior. He would be the king one day. It was a heavy mantle of responsibility to wear.

She looked at Declan and nodded. "The authorities said she died in her sleep, but I know that body I held was not my child. She took my baby and she…I know my child is gone. I know I will not hold her again, and I know beyond a shadow of doubt that she was responsible. There have been two more infants dead, and I know it was the creature. No one will believe me."

What she had not said, what she could not say, was that her child had been a meal for the creature. It was too horrible to comprehend. "Do you know where she is?"

She didn't answer, simply pointed. I followed the arm and saw a small, rundown shop with a hand-drawn sign in the window. Grime coated the storefront and the windows were dark. Everything inside me that had hunted or stolen before told me this was the right place. This was the creature's home.

"Will you kill her?" the woman asked.

I stared down at her and hoped she felt the depth of my vow. This went beyond my own concerns. This was suddenly about more than just finding a creature that had tried to hurt me. This was about protection for people who wouldn't find it from the police. This was about justice. "I promise you that she will take no more children. She will feed no more after this day."

She smiled, though it was a sad one. There was a glimmer of tears in her brown eyes. "I thank you."

I turned back to the small shop as she returned to her customers, steeling myself for the work ahead. I was going to kill her, but not until I had my questions answered. The neighborhood was quiet during the heat of the day, but I noticed even the few people out crossed the street to avoid the shop. Though they might not know what the creature was, these people instinctively knew to avoid her.

"You are a warrior," Declan said, and I found him staring as though he was reconsidering me.

I started to walk down the street. I had to case the place before I went in. I might have considered a full-out assault if I had Lee with me, but I didn't know how Declan would handle himself, so I had to be careful.

"I'm not really a warrior. I'm a thief by trade." I didn't mention that some in our world called me queen. That wasn't a title I'd earned. It had come through marriage to Daniel.

"No," Declan said thoughtfully. "You are truly a warrior. The woman knew this. She recognized one who would protect her."

"Then she should have been looking at you," I pointed out. "Didn't you say you were a warrior of the *sidhe*?"

He nodded. "I am, but first I am a prince who will be a king. A king does not necessarily consider the needs of one person. A king protects a kingdom. It is a practical thing to be a king. It is more honorable to be a warrior."

I smiled at him. "That's nice, Declan. Does this mean you're going to take me seriously and stop trying to see me naked?"

He grimaced as though trying to understand me. "I can take you seriously and still wish to see you naked."

I rolled my eyes and prayed for patience. We reached the door of the shop. It appeared to be closed. There was a sign that stated the owner was out and would return at 4:00 pm. I checked my watch. We had about forty minutes. The shop was on a corner, and the side of the building curved into an alley. I glanced around and walked to the rear of the building. The back entrance was locked up tight. I cursed when I realized I hadn't brought my lock-picking kit. I was really getting rusty if I'd forgotten something so basic.

"Let's walk around a bit and see if she reopens when she says she will," I said to Declan. He nodded his assent and followed me.

I was spared conversation by the sudden trill of my cell. I took a deep breath and considered not answering it because it could only be one of two people. Glancing down at the screen, I saw there was a nice picture of Dev. He was smiling and looking smoking hot in the picture. I also noticed that he'd called about ten times before. My phone had been at the bottom of my endless bag and I hadn't noticed with all the noise going on around me.

I hit the green answer button and prepared for some screaming. "Hey, baby. How's it going?"

"Where the fuck are you, Zoey?" he yelled into the phone. "I'm out on the farm trying to handle things when I get a call from Albert that both your bodyguards have been taken down and you're missing. I had every single member of my staff searching for over an hour before we finally managed to get Lee up and on his feet. Zack is still asleep. I thought Lucas Halfer had you."

Panic was plain in his voice. I know how I would have felt if I thought Dev was in trouble. "Halfer has nothing to do with this. I'm fine, Dev. I promise you I'm safe, and I'll be home soon."

"You'll be home right fucking now, Zoey," he snarled in my ear. "Tell me where you are. I noticed you turned off the locator service on your phone."

Oh, I wasn't stupid. I'd shut that off the minute I realized I was going on the run. If I told him where I was, I would likely find myself in not-fun bondage and being dragged back to the condo. "I wasn't crazy or drunk last night. What happened was real, and I'm taking care of it."

"Alone? You're alone running around the city? Why not just make a date with Halfer? Just call him up and tell him you want to be murdered."

"For your information, I am not alone," I explained patiently. I hit the button to put it on speaker. "Say hello, Declan."

Declan leaned toward the phone. "Hello, brother. I assure you I am taking care of your female. I will meet any needs she has. It will be my pleasure to ensure she is satisfied with my services."

There was a long pause. "Declan? What the fuck are you doing here?"

I shrugged at the future king of Faery who was staring at the phone like it was a snake that might bite him. "You'll have to excuse him. He gets a terrible potty mouth when he's upset."

"I have come to speak with you, Devinshea. It is time for you to return. I have decided to allow you to bring your female with you. She is extremely entertaining," Declan offered. "And her body looks like it will be a joy to fornicate with."

"I need this today," Dev said and I could see him standing there with his head in his hands. He was quiet for a moment. "I will deal with you later, brother, after I have dealt with my mistress. I am going to ignore the fact that you have acted like a spoiled child today, Zoey. Give me your address, and I will pick you up myself."

"Have you listened to anything I've said?" Frustration was starting to well. I wasn't a child, but I'd let them treat me like one for far too long. "You were wrong about last night. Something really did try to kill me."

"Then Daniel will handle it," Dev said and I imagined that perfectly shaped jaw grinding in frustration.

"I'm done playing these games, Dev." Albert was right. I had to punch through this or it was going to break us. "I'm safe. I'll be home later."

Over his vigorous protests, I hung up and switched off the

ringer. I was going to pay for that later, but I needed to deal with the creature now.

"My brother spoke to you cruelly," Declan said with no small amount of surprise in his voice.

"I pissed him off. What did you expect?"

He considered this for a moment. "I expected him to sweetly ask for your return. He does not speak with his females the way he just spoke to you. He does not get angry with them."

"Never?"

"I suppose if he got angry with one he would gently end the relationship," Declan reasoned.

I laughed, but there was no humor behind it. Spending the day with his brother had made me think Devinshea would tire of me. Perhaps he already had. "Well, he gets angry with me a lot lately, so maybe I should start packing."

I would have gone on but I was suddenly caught by an odd sound. It was a weird, rhythmic thudding, like the sound of a locomotive moving at enormous speed. Fear flared and for a moment I wondered if I'd made a terrible mistake and Halfer had found me.

I backed off and heard Declan curse as we looked down the alley. I caught sight of a man running so fast, he was almost a blur. He had a strange looking gait, as if he wasn't exactly on his feet. He was moving on all fours, his limbs in perfect harmony, making what should be awkward a veritable dance of grace and power. It was the hat that gave him away. Only one person in my life wore a trucker hat. Unless Halfer had given up his perfect suits, there was no question who was coming for me.

I heard Declan notch an arrow and pull back his bow, and I quickly moved my hand to stop him.

"Don't. He won't hurt me," I said with more certainty than I really felt. He was probably pretty pissed off.

He barely slowed down as he hit me. Even with the full force of our bodies slamming together, he held me carefully, pulling me into his arms. As we tumbled to the concrete, he made sure he took the brunt of our fall. When we stopped tumbling, he glared down at me and his eyes were all wolf.

"Hey there, Lee," I said with what I hoped was an ingratiating smile.

"You shot me," he snarled. I'd never seen Lee's wolf. He'd never changed in front of me before, and I found myself utterly fascinated with the way he looked. His canines were long, his eyes large in his head as though he could find a halfway between his human and wolf forms.

"Yeah," I admitted. "Sorry about that."

Lee stared for a moment and then laughed. "No, you're not, Zoey. Have you enjoyed yourself today?" He got off of me and gave me a hand getting up.

"It's been a nice change," I admitted.

The wolf crossed his arms over his chest, his face back to perfectly normal. "I was wondering when you were going to show up. Zack thinks you're just some sweet piece of ass Donovan and Quinn pass between them, but I could see the crazy bitch hiding in there. You handled yourself well today. You certainly got the jump on my brother."

"Hey, you went down, too," I pointed out.

He shook his head. "Don't try it again, Zoey. I wasn't going to make the first move because I didn't want to hurt you. I won't make the same mistake again. I've decided you can probably handle a little pain. Now, have you found this thing you're looking for?"

"You're not here to haul me back to Ether?" I asked because I pretty much figured that was exactly what he was going to do.

Declan stepped forward, bow still in hand. "I will not allow him to take you."

"Yeah? You're going to stop me?" Lee was probably thinking that Declan was like his brother, and Lee wouldn't consider Dev a threat. "You and what army?" He stopped and was suddenly still. Lee took a deep whiff of the air around him and his superior grin became a self-deprecating grimace. "Forgive me. That army, of course. How many are there? I think I count eight, but there are two I can't identify."

"There are ten," Declan acknowledged. "Two are Unseelie, and I doubt you have ever come across any such as them. The wild hunt has been gone from this plane for many centuries, and they were a part of it. I am surprised you can sense them. Why did you not sense them before this?"

I'd been wondering the same thing. Lee answered with a shrug.

"If I kept my senses wide open all the time, I'd go crazy. Your men are subtle. A lesser wolf would miss it entirely."

I was beginning to get the idea that pretty much all the wolves I had met before were less than Lee. It was a little hard to believe he'd been able to track me. I was a long way from Ether and I'd taken both a bus and a cab. I'd never seen a wolf run like that without the change. Neil had been quick and strong but not nearly as fast as Lee.

"As to your question, Zoey, I was ordered to find you as quickly as possible." Lee confirmed my fears. "Quinn is out of his mind upset, and your husband won't be awake for several hours. Quinn panicked. He really thought you were dead somewhere. I'm supposed to track you, find you, and hold you until Quinn can collect you himself. I would expect a fight out of this, Zoey. I swear he was ready to beat you when he realized you'd run off."

"My brother would never beat a woman," Declan replied, obviously horrified at the thought. "My brother is a priest. He is not a man of violence."

Lee and I both laughed at that.

"It's been a long time since you saw Dev last." I didn't know what Dev had been like in the *sithein*, but in this world he didn't shrink from violence. I turned my attention back to my bodyguard. "So you're just going to throw me over your shoulder and haul me back to Ether like a recalcitrant child? Let me tell you something, Lee. I get the distinct feeling that Devinshea is about to wash his hands of me." The thought made me sick to my stomach, but Declan had really gotten to me. Why would Dev stay here and deal with all my shit when he had six women back home willing to do anything he asked? I was betting he didn't yell at them. Of course, they probably didn't cause as much trouble as I did. I looked at Lee with my hands on my hips, hoping to keep my pride intact. "If he's going to turn me out then at least let me finish what I came out here to do."

The wolf considered this for a moment. When I saw his eyes soften, I knew I was in. "Fine, we'll do this your way. You're wrong about Quinn if you think he's going to let you go. He might seem softer than the vampire, but he isn't where you're concerned. He's just as obsessed and he doesn't even need your blood to survive. He might lock you up, but he won't ever let you go."

"That does not sound like my brother, either." Declan huffed a little. "I need to speak with him because I feel there is something wrong. Let us hunt this creature so that I may assure myself my brother has not been possessed. I do not like this plane. It is filled with dangerous creatures."

One of those creatures was opening his senses. Lee became still as he allowed the world around him to settle into different sounds and smells. Neil had described this process to me once. He said it was a lot like sorting through the mail. You went through it once and then separated the important stuff from the junk. After a long moment, he walked straight to the building I'd identified as the aswang's home and stopped. He put his hands on the bricks and then laid his head against it, listening.

When he spun back to me, his eyes were distinctly wolflike. "It's in there and it's not alone. There's another creature, a bird perhaps? I smell death. There's an enormous amount of death in this building."

"She's undead," I confirmed.

"I believe she's hurt as well. I smell something like blood," Lee added.

Declan's shoulders squared and he nodded briefly. "Yes. I shot the creature last night. I would have pursued it had I not been distracted by Zoey's breasts. Her shirt was wet and her nipples puckered so sweetly, I forgot about the beast."

"Donovan's going to love him," Lee said sarcastically. "Seriously, he's not going to be happy there are two of him."

I let that go for the moment. Daniel knew Dev had a twin, but I don't think it really registered that he would be so like Dev when it came to his libido. "I need information from the creature, Lee. I have questions for her and I may have to get nasty to get my answers. If this disturbs you, I'll understand if you choose to remain behind."

"Yes," Lee said, sarcasm dripping. "I can't stand violence. Just point me to the kill, sister. My only regret is there won't be flesh or blood. I'm hungry, damn it, but I like my meat living when I begin to eat it. The bird thing smells pretty tasty, to tell you the truth."

"Okay, ewww," I said with a grimace. "Good to know. How about you, Your Highness? Are you up for a bit of ultra-violence?"

Declan bowed, a courtly gesture. "I am at your service. I will assist you in extracting the information you need from the creature and then, if the violence places you in a state of sexual need, I will aid with that as well. I will fight the wolf for the privilege if that would please you."

Lee rolled his eyes. "Yeah, I'm not interested in hitting that, so feel free."

"Some bodyguard you are," I groused.

"Well, you shot me," he returned lightly, but I could see his body tense with anticipation. He pulled a semi from its hiding place in the small of his back. I reached in my bag and pulled out my Ruger. Lee waited for my nod and then kicked in the door.

We rushed in and our assault had begun.

Chapter Eight

The aswang's nest reeked of death. The building was utterly silent as we moved through the door, but there was nothing peaceful about the quiet. This was the silence that came with absence—absence of life, of hope, of love. This place was devoid of joy. I'd read that the aswang was considered by certain scholars of the arcane to be the Pacific Rim's version of the vampire. Walking into its lair, it was clear those scholars had never actually met a vampire.

Even the oldest of vampires surround themselves with life. They're obsessed with the vitality of humans, and while they might break their toys on occasion, they would never be able to live like this. The aswang was truly undead. Unlike the vampire, whose body merely survived the process of death, the aswang had no spark of life in it. Vampires lived. They had ambitions and made plans. They sought out entertainments and diversions. They had a multitude of desires and for the most part, sought pleasure.

The aswang was different. It existed only to feed, to turn life into death.

Lee entered first because his senses were far better than any Declan or I possessed. He moved with the odd grace of a wolf stalking its prey. His head was down and it swept the area, moving from side to side. He silently pointed up and I nodded. She was on the second floor.

It was dark though the sun was bright outside. The windows were coated with filth, allowing little of the day's glow inside the gloom of the building. Lee stalked down the hall and into the storefront. Declan was at my back, moving as silently as a warrior of the *sidhe* could move.

I had the Ruger in a double-fisted hold. Being a somewhat small female, I had to worry about kick back, and I'd discovered I was better able to handle the recoil with two hands. I was sure Lee could do *The Matrix*, shoot-with-two-guns-blazing thing that Daniel and Dev could do, but I didn't have preternatural strength. I also didn't have the strongest of stomachs I learned as Lee led us into the part of the building where the aswang should have been doing her work. My stomach rolled at the stench of death in the kitchen.

I must have gagged a little because Lee gave me a look. It silently asked what the hell I was doing hunting undead crap if I couldn't stand a little decomp. I sucked it up and forced the bile down. It was nice to know Lee wasn't the type who was going to coddle me and try to hide me from the nasty parts of the world. He silently asked if I could proceed, and even without the use of his voice, I could hear the sarcastic "princess" he added at the end. I gave him my unfriendly middle finger and he was satisfied.

I found myself in the middle of the butchery. It was a good thing most of the people around here avoided this place like the plague. If this bitch did get customers, I wasn't sure what she was going to sell them. Though it looked like there was a side of rotting beef hanging in the corner, the rest of the place was filled with nothing that vaguely resembled a cut of meat from a grocery store.

The scent of formaldehyde assaulted my nose, and I saw the pale flesh of a corpse on one of the tables. I shuddered, but forced myself to study it. The corpse was that of an elderly man still wearing the top half of his suit while the pants had been removed. I wasn't terribly surprised to find that his legs had been chewed on. This was the aswang's way. She was an eater of the dead. As the corpse was still mostly together, I had to assume she hadn't liked her meal. Modern funeral home practices had to be hell on the aswang. It might have been the reason she'd been taking so many babies.

I almost tripped over something, my feet skidding across the floor. When I glanced down, I saw a pile of what appeared to be small dolls. Even in the gloom I could see they were effigies. I leaned down and touched one. It was made from plants and without magic looked like a primitive doll, the kind that didn't have a face. The aswang had made them. This was what she left behind when she took the babies. A doll like this was what the poor woman had been left with when she lost her child. She'd known what it was, her intuition telling her what her eyes could not. Once the aswang had the child, the doll she left behind would be a perfect copy. Only her mother had known it was an empty reflection of her lost baby.

"Hit the deck!" Lee growled.

Behind me I heard Declan move, but I did as I was ordered and hit the floor just before I felt a mighty *whoosh* fly past my body. There was a loud squawking as the bird was frustrated in its attempt to take off my head. I flipped over and tried to get a sight line on the sucker. I laid on my back as close to the floor as I could and held the Ruger, ready to take my shot.

Lee prowled over to me, keeping low.

"Are you all right?" he asked quietly, but the words were garbled. I was startled to see that his face looked like it was caught mid-change. I had seen many strong wolves who could change parts of their bodies. It was one of the ways to determine an alpha but by no means a sure thing. Zack and Neil had both mastered the power but only had it because of Daniel's blood, and they could change an arm or a hand when they needed it. Lee's snout was out and his teeth were long. His hands were indeed ugly claws, but the rest of his body maintained its shape.

He shoved my head down, taking care with his claws as the bird made a second pass. After it swooped past, Declan was on his feet, an arrow notched and tracking the bird as it flew. He cursed as it disappeared from view.

Lee shoved me under one of the tables, and I had to stop myself from shrinking back. There was another corpse under this table, but the aswang had gotten to this one before the undertaker had done his damage. This corpse was chewed on thoroughly but had enough flesh left hanging to make me really not want to be up against it.

"Protect her," Lee ordered.

Declan kneeled in front of me, weapon in his hands. He smiled down, and I noticed he'd dropped the glamour. He wasn't concentrating on anything so silly as maintaining his Dev illusion now that we were fighting for our lives. His hair hit the floor as he crouched. He seemed calm and unruffled by the experience. "I will protect her. You kill the bird, and I will save the girl."

Lee rolled his wolf eyes and then moved to the center of the room where he knelt down, that long snout scenting the air. He quickly found the bird's perch but made no move to get it. He was waiting and it was a strangely active thing. Lee was patient and still, but I knew there was nothing complacent in him. The bird watched him with black, dead eyes. I held my breath for the longest moment, waiting to see who would break the stalemate first.

The bird gave a great cry, and a rush of wings filled the room. As the bird soared Lee leapt, his great mouth open, and caught the bird midair in his teeth. A loud crunch and the sickening sound of bones breaking cracked through the space. The wolf and the bird hit the ground again, and I knew the fight was over when Lee growled and got that meal he'd been hoping for.

He was back to normal and spitting feathers out when he looked down at me and Declan. The faery got up, helping me to my feet.

I gave my bodyguard a questioning look because I wasn't sure he should have handled things the way he had. "Do you have any idea where that thing's been? It's dirty and what do you do? You eat it. Don't you come to me later when you get a tummy ache."

Lee grinned, and it made him look younger than his thirty-five years. "Tastes like chicken."

I laughed, but my relief didn't last long as I tripped and hit the floor face first. My gun shot out of my hands and tumbled away as I groaned with pain. I was about to look back and see what I had tripped on when something closed around my ankle and started pulling me under the table. My stomach was rolling again as I realized the freaking Internet hadn't mentioned a damn thing about the aswang having control over corpses. Sure enough, a bony hand was pulling me inexorably toward fleshless teeth.

The people who had seen this particular power were probably all freaking dead.

Scrambling to get away, I tried to kick at my assailant. I glanced back and saw the corpse trying to get on its bony knees. Though its eyes were long dead, they seemed to look my way more out of habit than anything…unless the freaking thing could see through the corpse's eyes.

This is why I don't hunt. I steal. In all my years as a thief, I've seen some freaky things, but not once was I assaulted by rotting corpses, and it was a credit to my profession, if you ask me.

Declan hauled me up, and I heard the satisfying pop of those undead joints coming off. "I believe the creature has awakened the dead."

"Ya think?" I was only slightly hysterical as I realized there was still a hand attached to my ankle. I reached down and forcibly removed the offensive, still twitching, limb. I tossed it across the room and wasn't thrilled to see it start to move my way again.

Lee walked up to the hand and crushed it under his boots. "Zoey, behind you."

I swiveled around quickly just as the corpse began to crawl out from under the table. It was missing an arm but it managed to slither along. I kicked out, catching it on the jaw which cracked under the force of my supercute J. Reneé jeweled ladybug sandals. I was really going to have to think about proper footwear the next time I went hunting. Living with Dev had made me soft.

Declan stepped on the corpse's spine and the weight of his big body stopped all forward motion. The bones still twitched and pulsed with the need to follow orders, but it no longer was capable.

Shuddering, I reached down to pick up my lost gun. I had it in my hand when I heard that horribly now-familiar zombie groan and brought my eyes up just as three more corpses entered the room. They moved slowly, as though every motion was deliberate and required great thought, but these corpses were more flesh than bone. They also had stopped to get weapons. Two held long butcher knives and the third held an axe.

Lee sprang away from the zombies and across the room to join Declan and me. Even Lee shuddered a little when he stared at the creatures facing us. Declan notched an arrow and shot the one closest to him in the eye. It didn't actually stop the zombie. It just gave the zombie a nice place for birds to perch.

"See, Dec," I said with a frown at his cute little bow and arrow, "this is why we bring guns."

Lee smiled and we both took aim. "Take off the head."

The world was suddenly filled with the sounds of bullets cracking through the air. It took more than a couple of tries because we weren't carrying the right kind of weapons, but then we hadn't known we were going to be dealing with freaking zombies in the middle of Dallas. When killing zombies, the movies really do have it right. A shotgun is the only way to go. You have to take off the head, not just leave a neat little hole in it.

Usually.

I say usually because this time was the exception. I suspect it was because these weren't true zombies. These were reanimated dead being controlled directly by another creature. For whatever reason, even after I had successfully blown my opponent's head to smithereens, it just kept coming. Lee was having the same trouble and finally cursed and tossed his semi aside. His hands became long claws and despite the knife about to come down on his head, he leapt into the fray and began tearing the body apart.

Declan sent me a regal frown even as the other two zombies shuffled our way. "Yes, Zoey, your guns have been entirely effective at splattering brain tissue across the room. Now, if you will allow me?" He snapped a finger and Padric showed up as though twisting reality around him. He emerged from wherever he hid and handed Declan a long silver sword. The prince nodded and Padric was gone again.

"Hey, we could use some backup here." He had a whole army hidden in some weird pocket world.

Declan hefted the sword easily. "We don't need Padric for this. I can handle a few undead."

I pulled the knives out of their sheaths and sighed because I hate wet work. I would way rather shoot something from a distance than have to get up close and personal. It usually gets gory and my clothes get crap on them. Not to mention the fact that I almost always get hurt.

One knife in each hand, I followed Declan into the fray. He wielded the sword with the grace of a master and blocked the knife the zombie held.

I kicked out, trying to get my guy off balance. He went down with a satisfying thud, and I put my weight into breaking his spine.

The truth is zombies, while creepy and nasty, aren't really all that hard to deal with. They tend to be slow and spend an enormous amount of time groaning. They really will eat your brains but then they'll pretty much eat whatever part of you they can get their mouths on. As I had blown this bad boy's mouth off, I just needed to avoid that freaking axe and cut off enough pieces to make it stop moving.

Lee was busy tearing his zombie apart with his bare hands. Declan had split his in half with a single sword stroke, and I brought my knife straight down on the corpse's shoulder. I chose the one that moved the arm holding the axe because I didn't want to get anything chopped off. I was pretty sure if I survived this that Danny and Dev would be taking a piece of my hide, so I wanted to keep it intact.

I kicked the arm along with the axe to the other side of the room. The body was convulsing as though whoever was animating it was in definite distress. I let one of the knives drop and held the longer one directly over my head. I leapt over the body, straddling it, and brought the knife down onto the sternum with every bit of strength I had in an attempt to split the body in two. The bones cracked and finally an eerie silence came over the room.

Declan surveyed the battlefield with a satisfied smile. "It was a good exercise. It has my spirits up, along with other things."

Declan was annoying, but he'd been fairly good in a fight.

"Well, put those other things down for now, boy, because the job isn't done." I wiped a chunk of…something off my shoulder. This is where a true hunter reveled in the blood and the kill and I just wanted a freaking shower. I put aside my need to unleash a girlie squeal and picked up my bag, replacing my knives. I switched the rounds from silver to salt in the Ruger and pulled out my secret weapon: a really big-ass jar of minced garlic from Ether's kitchens. I tossed it to Declan, who looked at me like I was crazy but held it anyway.

"Zoey, I'll go first," Lee offered.

"No, this is my gig, Lee." I took the stairs at a run. I didn't intend to give her time to wake the local graveyard. The second floor was simple, three doors all on the right side. The first was a bathroom that could have doubled as a horror movie set. I found what I was looking for in the second.

The aswang was in human form, her cadaverous body in the middle of a filthy mattress. Her skin had transformed from white to a sickly yellow and there was an arrow protruding from her belly. A foul stench hit my nose, and I fought not to gag. I probably should have felt some bit of sympathy. I knew what it felt like to get an arrow stuck in my gut, but then I hadn't eaten any babies lately so I figured the bitch deserved it.

She stared at me, and I saw it in her eyes. She was done. She was completely spent. In her state, it had probably cost her every bit of energy she'd had left to control the corpses the way she had. So she wasn't going to fight me. I still had questions to ask. "Who hired you?"

"Help me." The plea came out in a reedy voice. Her eyes were black, but even in the dim light I could see their dullness. Now that I was close, I could see the paper quality to her skin. Though she had no real blood in her body, the wound still puckered and appeared filled with some sort of puss.

"I will help you die after you tell me what I want to know," I stated firmly and with no sympathy.

"I will tell you if you help me live." She panted the words out as though the very act of speech was painful.

I shot her in the leg, the dead flesh flying apart like tissue paper. Though the flesh was dead, the creature howled in pain. "I need the garlic, Declan."

"Over the wound?" he asked and I nodded. He took a handful of the herb and slapped it on the crevasse I'd created. The minute the garlic hit her open flesh, the aswang screamed, her agony a palpable thing in the room.

When she stopped screaming and her wailing ground down to a low sob, I leaned in. "Who hired you? I can do this all night long or I can take your head quickly. It's up to you."

Lee was watching the scene before him with a frown on his face. I couldn't tell if it was merely the seriousness of the situation or if he was disappointed in me. I couldn't care. If he walked away from this thinking I was a stone-cold bitch, then that was how it was going to have to be. After today, he probably wouldn't be my bodyguard anyway. If Dev left with Declan because he was sick of me, then I certainly wouldn't be able to pay him. Despite what Declan thought, I wasn't about to be bought off. Dev might throw me out, but I wouldn't be taking anything with me.

When the creature was silent I reached down, took her stick-like arm in my hands and twisted as hard as I could until the arm began to tear off. She was extremely vulnerable without her familiar, without flesh to feed upon, with that arrow poisoning her. I wasn't about to let go of my advantage. I nodded at Declan, who covered the sinew in sticky garlic.

"Please," the creature begged after she became too tired to wail further. "It was a demon or what once was a demon."

Lee cursed. "I told Zack this was about Halfer."

Lucas Halfer was a never-ending pain in my ass. "What did he want from you?"

She shook, her entire body trembling, and I wondered what death was going to be like for the undead. Was there some other plane they fled to when the body they inhabited was gone?

Finally, she began to talk. "He came to me. He promised me many corpses. He told me he knew a place where there were so many babies, I could feast forever."

"He lied." It was kind of what demons did.

She smiled, a ghastly thing. "Oh, but he did not. At least not at first. No one believes here. No one sees me here. They do nothing to protect themselves, and I had many babies. Their blood is so sweet I thought I had found paradise. Then he gave me his price."

I waited but let her see the gun. She needed to know she was far from anything like paradise now.

"He told me I must kill you," she whispered. "I did not want trouble with the vampire, but Halfer threatened to out me. He said you had to die before the Strong Arm of Remus got here."

Lee gasped, his eyes widening. "That's a legend."

It wasn't one I'd heard of. "What's the Strong Arm of Remus?"

Lee shook his head. "It's a story wolves tell their pups when they want to scare the crap out of them. It's nothing, Zoey."

"The demon does not think so." The aswang shuddered. "He says it is hidden, and he wants it. He wants to control the wolves. I was to kill you before the fifteenth of July. He said you would get the object if I did not kill you."

"I don't even know what the object is," I admitted.

"He was paranoid. He was sure the vampire was always behind him. He is…not right in his mind." She moved her attention to Lee. "She is cruel. Will you be kind? Please kill me. I no longer wish to play these games."

"He won't help you." I couldn't give in now. "Where is Halfer?"

"I do not know," she replied, and I watched as she tensed for more pain. She truly believed it was coming and yet she held out. "He always sought me. I did not follow him. I just wanted to be left alone to feast."

I held my hand out to Declan, who tried to pass me the garlic.

The aswang's eyes had closed, her mouth tightening as she waited for more torture. And that's exactly what it would be if I continued. "No, she's done. She doesn't know anything else. I need the sword now."

"This is the sword of a warrior. This is the sword of a king." Declan twisted the handle my way. "You wish to use it? What do I get in return?"

"I won't punch you in the face again," I offered.

He held the sword out, hilt first. "That is not what I would have chosen, but it will do. You actually have quite a powerful punch. Do not damage it."

"I'll try." I gripped the sword with two hands. This was my job to do.

I turned back to the pitiful thing on the bed and actually managed to feel the slightest stir of something resembling sympathy. I raised the sword and brought it quickly down, separating her head from her neck. I tossed Declan back his precious sword which was quickly and efficiently taken by Padric. "We have to find an incinerator. We can burn the body here, but I'd rather the head was done elsewhere."

It's always a good idea to keep the head separate from the body when dealing with the undead. They have a pesky habit of putting themselves back together.

Lee tossed the head my way and wrapped the body up in the dirty sheet. Declan went to make a nice fire in the butchery, and Lee turned his brown eyes to me.

"Did you enjoy that, Your Highness?" His voice was neutral. It was the first time in my memory that he'd used my title. I got the feeling Lee wasn't really into the whole royalty thing.

I thought about it for a moment and answered him honestly. "I didn't. I thought I would, but in the end it's all just death, and there is nothing joyful or fulfilling about it. It was necessary, Lee. It had to be done."

He considered me for a moment before finally allowing himself to crack a small smile. "I'll take over the duty of guarding you, Your Highness. Zack isn't strong enough. Even if Quinn refuses you, and I don't believe that will be the case, I'll stay on until the demon is found. I'll protect you, and other than a situation that I feel completely compromises your safety, I'll follow your lead."

"No more itineraries?" I asked with a half-smile because it sounded a little like heaven.

"None beyond the ones you set."

I sighed with relief. "Thank you, Lee."

We joined Declan and proceeded to make sure the aswang troubled us no more.

Chapter Nine

The sun was just beginning to set when Lee, Declan, and I sat back in my favorite park and enjoyed tacos from the local street vendor. We'd managed to clean up enough that we didn't cause comment. The butcher who had shown us where the aswang nested had been kind enough to give us a place to clean up and a fire to roast the aswang's head. Though she could never replace her precious child, I could see a burden had been lifted off her shoulders.

I was procrastinating. I knew I should head home, but I'd used Lee's grumbling tummy as an excuse. It was kind of good to be back in my old neighborhood. I'd kept my apartment for a long time even after I bought my little house in the country. It had been important to still have a place in the city, but Dev convinced me to give it up after Danny and I moved in with him.

As I breathed in the early evening air, I wondered if my apartment was still available. There had been no voice mails on my cell when I checked after we burned the aswang. I'd expected Dev to leave a flurry of angry "get your ass home" messages, but there was absolutely nothing.

The silence said a lot.

"You are not enjoying your cat?" Declan asked, his voice not unkind.

"It's great. I'm just worried about going home. What the hell do you mean cat?" I sat straight up and looked down at my beef soft taco with sour cream and guacamole.

Lee took a big bite of his fourth taco. Werewolves can really pack it away. "It's definitely cat. You were right about this place. This is some damn fine cat. I'll have to bring Zack here."

"It can't be cat, guys." They had to be playing a joke on me. "People in the regular world don't eat cat."

"Trolls do." Declan gestured toward the taco stand. I stared back at the perfectly human-looking husband and wife team who'd sold me tacos for the last five years. They bowed when Declan looked their way. I'd been surprised that they refused to allow Declan to pay them. "See, they know their future king."

Declan got up and excused himself to get another lemonade, which he thought was the greatest invention ever.

I set my taco down. I really hoped Taco Bell wasn't run by trolls because I was going to have to stop somewhere on my way home. I was still really hungry.

The ground in front of me shook as Daniel landed on the lawn. He was wearing a Superman T-shirt, which I found ironic, and those dimples came out as he smiled down at me.

"Hello, Z," he said, his drawl satisfying something deep in my soul. "You've been a very bad girl. Dev has pulled out a good portion of that hair of his. If I don't get you home soon, he's going to be bald, and I don't think any of us wants that. What's he going to do with his spare time if he's not fixing his hair?"

I frowned. "I don't know if I want to face Dev, even though I was totally in the right on this one. I killed the creature and got the info I needed. Lucas Halfer sent her, by the way. He's sending out the troops apparently."

Daniel cursed and sat down beside me, his hand sliding over mine. It felt so good to have him next to me. "Damn it. I'm sorry, Z. It didn't seem like a big deal last night. It's been quiet, and I guess I didn't want to admit that anything could be wrong. Are you okay?"

I nodded, enjoying being close to him. Danny and I had fought a lot, but we always put it behind us. "With the singular exception of really needing a shower, I'm fine." I twisted around to put my feet in his lap. "And these are now my official zombie-killing shoes."

"Zombies?" Daniel asked with an expectant smile.

"That was some fucked up shit," Lee admitted as he got up and shook the grass off his jeans. "Zoey, I'll be in the club at noon tomorrow. If you need me before then, just call. Don't go running off on your own, okay?"

I saluted my new BFF.

Daniel shook his head, his face going grave. "Sorry, Lee. Dev fired you. He was adamant. You didn't follow direct orders. No more bodyguards for her without a blood oath to me."

"Quinn can fuck himself," Lee said with an arrogant grin. "I take orders from Zoey. As for the oath to you, you can fuck yourself, too. You haven't given me any reason to tie myself to you, Donovan. I'll make an oath when I find the leader I want to dedicate myself to. I don't think it's going to be you."

Daniel looked up at the wolf, and there was only the slightest hint of anger in his eyes. "Understood, Lee. Feel free to remove yourself."

I rolled my eyes at the alpha-boy fight. "I'm happy with Lee, Danny. If you put Zack on my ass, I'll just tranq him again and run off on my own. Lee and I made a deal. If he's my bodyguard, I promise not to try to give him the slip."

Shaking his sandy head, Daniel gave the wolf a hard look. "If you get my wife hurt, I swear I'll kill you myself."

"I'm sure you'll try," Lee muttered. "I think I'll be going before the real fight starts." Lee gave me a nod and I heard him say, "Good evening, Your Highness," as he walked away.

Declan walked up, giving the wolf a regal nod of his head as he exited the park. He stared down at Daniel, whose face flushed at the sight of the future king of Faery.

"There's two of him?" Daniel's eyes widened.

"He told you he had a twin," I pointed out.

"I thought it was a fraternal thing." Daniel stood up. He stared at Declan like he really didn't want to believe it. I probably should have mentioned it. I'd seen Dev's twin before in a Hell plane vision, but Dev didn't really like to talk about him. I'd kept it to myself, figuring if Dev wanted to talk to Daniel about his brother, he would.

"Nope, they're identical." I joined him, scrambling up. "He's the one who saved me last night. It's why I thought I was with Dev."

Declan bowed slightly as he introduced himself. "Vampire, I am Prince Declan Quinn, future king of Faery. I did indeed save the fair Zoey from the beast, though she has yet to offer any real payment for the deed. I have had to steal kisses from her all day as she selfishly refuses to give them."

"And they have the same taste in women," I pointed out with a sigh.

I thought Daniel would laugh and have a good joke about me having to put up with not one but two horny faeries. I kind of thought he would roll his eyes and treat the prince like an obnoxious child. I'd gotten used to my husband being somewhat good natured about other men sometimes looking at me. Dev had helped him get over the crazy maniac vampire jealousy thing.

It had been a long time since Danny had gone a little crazy, so I didn't expect his fangs to pop out to violent lengths as he reared his fist back and sent the prince flying through the air. His completely over-the-top reaction reminded me that the extremely possessive nature of Daniel Donovan was not something to be messed with.

Declan hit a tree with a nasty crack, but he popped back up, weapon in hand. Before we could move, he'd notched the arrow, drawn it back, and released it. There was a whizzing sound and then a *thunk* as it slammed into Daniel's leg.

"Guards," Declan yelled. "The vampire only. Do not harm my brother's mistress."

Suddenly the park was filled with warriors and weapons, and a couple of freaky flying things with big teeth. I stared at the flying creatures because they greatly resembled manta rays with their long spiked tails. They didn't need water though. They moved through the air with a menacing grace that took my breath away. Those tails slapped around with audible cracks and came at Daniel even as two large Fae bore down on him with broadswords.

Declan stood in the back of the fray with Padric in front of him, and he managed to slam several more arrows into my husband's body.

I found a place away from the fray because the truth of the matter was this wasn't a fair fight. So I made myself comfortable. There were only eleven of them, including Declan, and they didn't even have guns. Daniel moved faster than my eyes could track, but I was able to see how the Fae fell one by one under his claws and teeth. He reached up and pulled the Unseelie creatures straight out of the air, slamming the two into each other with a mighty crunch before kicking them against a tree.

I just sat and watched, comfortable with the fact that Daniel wouldn't really kill Declan. He would enjoy the fight, but unlike my boyfriend, these Fae were immortal. Danny could take out all of his frustration on them and other than a nice long healing process, they would turn out okay. I thought about tossing Danny one of the knives I had strapped to my thigh, but just as I was mustering the will to get up and do it, I noted that he'd wrestled one of the long swords away. He used it to skewer a tall faery with blond hair. He'd already incapacitated half the small army.

While Danny was working through his problems, I was still worried about Dev. I pulled out my phone and checked my e-mail. Other than some Nigerian prince who really wanted me to help him smuggle money out of the country, there was nothing. Dev hadn't even written me a single freaking e-mail, and I usually got five or six from him a day. There was at least one every day with an attached photo that I couldn't open in public, but today I got nothing. How pissed off would Daniel be with me if his chief advisor left us because he was so sick of dealing with my crap? I found myself hoping the fight would last a little longer so I could avoid Dev.

There was no such luck as Danny stuck the sword into the last fighting Fae and began to move on Padric and Declan.

Declan watched Daniel with serious eyes even as Padric gave a great shout and leapt forward to protect his king. He looked pretty scary to me as he sprang through the air with a warrior's cry and an upraised sword, but Daniel just punched him in the face with all of his might and the Fae flew backward. When he hit the ground, he didn't get back up.

Daniel's eyes were stark, his claws long as he stalked the faery prince, who now had the good sense to realize he was in real danger. Still, even with death staring at him, he was curious.

"What are you?" Declan asked, no longer bothering with his weapon. "You're not a simple vampire."

Daniel took him by the neck and hauled him up. His voice was deep as he talked around his fangs. "I'm a king, Your Highness, and not because my mother spat me from her womb. I am a king because I kill everything between me and my crown. Do you think I will not guard what is mine? She is my queen, my wife, my companion, my precious blood, and my property. I will kill you if you so much as think about touching her again. Do I make myself clear?"

"I believe I fully understand you," Declan agreed, surprisingly calm. He didn't fight Daniel's hold, didn't kick out. He merely waited.

Daniel dropped Declan, turning from him and starting toward me. "And don't think your brother will be returning with you. He has work to do here. Take your ass back to Faeryland."

Daniel stalked across his small battlefield, not caring that he stepped over various groaning bodies. He was completely ignoring the fact that he had three arrows sticking out of his body. He'd taken more, but the ones that had hit his chest had come out and the wounds were already healing. It was the three that had hit his legs and gone through to the other side he was struggling with. His body couldn't figure out which way to push the foreign object out and he seemed reluctant to deal with them himself. He reached down and pulled me off the ground. His arms went around my back and under my knees.

"Property?" I wound my arms around his neck. It was the only thing on his list of words to describe me that I had issue with.

"Well, he pissed me off," Daniel said as he leveled one last scowl at Dev's brother. His eyes moved down toward me as we started to float. "And you were right. Arrows fucking hurt."

Our flight through the city was far too short for my liking. Danny didn't speak, but he held me tight and kissed my cheek. Even as we approached the balcony of the penthouse, I could see Dev pacing and watching the sky. It was no use because Daniel shielded himself when he flew. No one could see us as we made our way through downtown Dallas. The lights were beginning to flicker around us, but I couldn't see anything but Dev and the emotion playing on his face.

Daniel landed on the balcony. Dev turned, his eyes finding mine, and I saw a momentary relief that was quickly replaced with anger. His eyes flared when he took in Daniel.

"Dude, what the hell happened to you?" he asked as Daniel set me on my feet.

Daniel gestured to the arrows sticking out of his body. "Your brother happened to me. He got handsy with Z, and I took offense. He brought out his little bodyguards and after I took them out, we came to an agreement. He won't touch her again, and I won't hack him into small pieces."

"You took out Padric?" Dev's mouth was slightly open in surprise. He dropped to his knees in front of Daniel, inspecting the wounds.

"I don't know who that is," Daniel admitted. "If he was with your brother, I assure you he got his ass handed to him. Now will someone go get a knife and cut these things out of me? I know it would be easier to shove them through but the wood hurts way more than whatever they used on the tips."

"It's made from a rock found in Faeryland." Dev glanced up at me with little expression on his handsome face. I noticed he hadn't shaved. There was a sexy five-o'clock shadow across his jaw. "Give me a knife, Zoey. I know you have at least two. I inventoried the armory."

I pulled out the knives and handed them over. Now that I was standing in the same room with him, I really wanted to say whatever it took to get through this. "Dev, I think…"

"Not now, Zoey." He dismissed me as he started to slice through the denim of Daniel's jeans. "I'll handle this while you go take a shower. You smell like you waded through corpses. When you're presentable, we can discuss how this is going to work from now on."

"Ultimatums, Dev?" I'd told myself I would be calm, but he was starting to push my buttons.

He didn't even look back. "Oh, yes, my mistress. There will likely be several of them. After what you put me through today, I will give you ultimatums all night long."

Daniel grunted as Dev widened the hole on his leg made by the arrow and with a jerk pulled it out as fast as he could. The hole immediately started to heal. "Baby, calm down. We need to talk, but it isn't going to get us anywhere if we start yelling at each other."

But I wanted to yell. They'd been wrong. They'd spent months and months putting me in a corner, and I was so tired of being stuck. "I think I'd like to hear what Dev really has to say."

"I don't think you do." Dev started on the next arrow sticking out of Daniel's leg. "I don't think you want to know what I think. Daniel and I have done our level best to protect you and you turn right around and make it hard on us. Do you honestly think this is the way to prove you give a shit about us?"

"Dev." Daniel made his name an admonition.

Dev pulled the next arrow out, making Daniel groan. "I'm speaking the truth. She walked out on us. She did that."

"Yes, and she's got the pussy, dude. Maybe you can get pussy wherever you want, but I'm a dude who's only wanted one pussy his whole life. You gotta deal with the pussy in a certain way." A low groan came from Danny's mouth. "Fuck. Don't twist it, asshole."

There was no headway to be made with him. I walked away through the grotto, making my way past the bedroom we shared and into the master bathroom, already planning my exit strategy. Dev didn't need me. He had a whole harem. And Daniel had Dev now. Neither one of them needed me.

Anger thrummed through my system. Everything I'd gone through during the day served to feed my anger. He'd ignored my very real problems and then thought he could give me ultimatums.

Tossing off my clothes, I turned on the shower without bothering to wait for it to heat up. With short angry strokes, I washed every inch of my skin and then started in on my hair. I had to hold on to my anger or I would cry, and I really didn't want to cry. As I rubbed the shampoo in, I made plans.

Staying with Sarah was an option, but that might be hard on her brand new marriage. The last thing a newlywed couple needed was a crying, depressed friend turning their couch into her own personal mourning space. I could stay with Dad, but the idea of listening to "I told you so" twenty-four seven was unpleasant. As I finished with my hair, I switched the shower off and knew I would do what I had always done when I was really lost. I would walk the bridges and hope I could forget them.

Adrenaline was still pumping through my system as I wrapped the fuzzy towel around me and walked out of the shower, already planning what I would pack. I didn't need much, just some clothes and my gun. Halfer was still out there, and he wouldn't care that Dev didn't want me anymore.

"You look ready to run, my mistress." Dev stood by the sink, his arms crossed over his chest. "Just who are you planning to run to?"

"I thought I'd spend some time with Ingrid and Halle."

"Did you now?" He moved away from the sink, his whole being stern and authoritarian. "You thought you would just walk away and nothing else mattered except what you wanted."

"You think I wanted to almost get my ass kicked by an undead piece of crap? You think I wanted to spend the day with your brother trying to get in my pants? You can go to hell, Dev. Oh, wait, we've already been there."

I tried not to think about how much I loved him. Weariness was stamped on his face, and I wanted to smooth his hair down and kiss him until he smiled at me again. Instead, I walked past him and into the bedroom.

He followed close behind me. Daniel was stepping into sweats as I entered the room, his strong body showing no evidence of the damage it had taken. Declan hadn't done anything Daniel couldn't fix in a couple of minutes.

Dev gave him a caustic smile. "You win that bet, Dan. She thinks she's running."

Danny looked over at me, his lips a flat line. "Baby, don't do this. You're digging a hole."

But it was my damn hole and there weren't any bodyguards or people who wanted to hold me back down in my hole.

Dev didn't seem to want to listen to Daniel any more than I did. "Before you attempt to leave, Zoey, I would like to ask you a few questions."

Taking a deep breath, I moved to face him. "Fine, Dev, ask away."

"What did you think you would gain by walking away today?"

That was an easy one. "I thought I would figure out what was happening to me. You didn't seem to give a crap."

"I will admit I mishandled the situation last night. I am very sorry about it. I should have listened to you. I can only say that dealing with your father put me in a bad mood. This morning however, is a completely different matter. You didn't call me. Didn't think to talk to me."

"Oh, I did. I talked to you. You just turned out to be Declan."

He shook his head. "And you should have called me. The minute you realized what had happened, you should have called me or Daniel."

"Because you would have believed me." They wouldn't have. They would have come up with twelve different ways I'd done the wrong thing, and I was so tired of being treated like an idiot.

Dev looked to me, his face a polite mask. "Please tell me what I have done to earn this. What have I failed to provide you with? I've given you a home. There's an entire staff to wait on you. You need only ask for something and it's provided."

"You wanted me to move in here, Dev. It wasn't like I didn't have a place of my own," I shot back because I'd been called property one too many times already. "I can certainly get another. I stopped working because the two of you wanted me to."

Daniel sat down on the bed, watching Dev and I circle each other. "Zoey, that was for the best. We've got to concentrate on taking over the Council. We're close to being able to do it."

"That's not the point, Dan," Dev said, his emerald eyes on me. "Zoey broke trust with us today. We agreed to this arrangement. She agreed to her bodyguards, and the first time she finds it inconvenient, she takes off on her own without leaving so much as a note to let us know she's still alive."

Anger welled in my gut. He wanted to do this now? Oh, I could do this. He had no idea what it meant to be followed every minute of every day. "The first time? I assure you, Devinshea, I've found Zack to be entirely inconvenient from the day you hired him."

"Well, you get your wish on that one, sweetheart, because I fired them both," Dev said smoothly. "Zack will continue to work with Daniel, but I'll be supplying Lee with a one-way ticket back to Nevada in the morning."

"Don't. I like Lee." And I hated the fact that I'd gotten him in trouble.

Dev's face went stony and stubborn. "He was supposed to bring you home. I will not be defied like that. I've already hired a security firm to handle you from here on out. You'll have four guards on you at all times and three others watching from a distance. I doubt you'll be able to shoot them all."

It was everything I'd dreaded. And everything I couldn't accept. I couldn't live like that. I'd hated the last several months where I was never alone, always watched. It made me insane. I couldn't work, couldn't breathe.

"I'm not going to be a prisoner." I walked over to my closet and pulled out a backpack. I threw it on the bed. "You and Daniel can come and go as you please, but I have to give up everything I am so the two of you can play your little games with the Council."

Taking my arm in his hand, Dev whirled me around, and I was shocked at the anger I saw there. It made me try to take a step back. He crowded me, using every inch of his six and a half feet to invade my space. "This has nothing to do with the Council, Zoey, and

106

everything to do with the killer who's stalking you. I apologize that you've been forced to give up the more impulsive portions of your personality in order to stay alive. And don't you dare say I've given up nothing for you. You have no idea the sacrifices I've made in order to continue to remain at your side."

"Oh, I have some idea," I spat back, warming to my topic now. He'd kept a few things from me. "There was something about six priestesses. What's wrong, Dev? You couldn't find a seventh so you could screw a different girl every day of the week?"

"I knew she was going to find out about that one day," Daniel said, staring at us with his arms crossed.

I was just about to ask how Danny knew about it when Dev's demeanor changed, and I knew I'd pushed him past politeness. "Oh, sweetheart, I didn't have one lover for each day of the week. I fucked all six of them every day of the week. I assure you, I took their pleasure seriously. It was my job, and I always do my job."

"And the mistresses?" I asked because I just wanted it all out there. If we were going to break up, I wanted to know every minute detail. "I seem to remember you saying I was your only serious girlfriend. Guess that was a lie."

"My brother was a busy boy today," Dev pointed out. "He's been telling tales. Let's clear this up, then. I haven't had any human girlfriends except you, and I've been absolutely monogamous since the moment we began dating, even when you returned to Daniel. I apologize for having a life before you, Zoey. We can't all be as pure as Daniel over there."

"Don't you bring me into this, Dev," Daniel warned. "I told you we were pushing her too hard. I told you she was going to wake up and want to be herself again and we would have to deal with it."

Dev frowned Daniel's way. "Well, of course. You know everything, Dan. I'm sure you're planning on leaving with her."

"I was planning on not letting her leave at all," Daniel replied, looking fed up with both of us.

"You're avoiding the point." I wanted to get back to the fight. "Did you or did you not keep a bunch of women? I want to know if I'm just the latest in a long line of women Devinshea Quinn paid for and got rid of when he got bored."

"You should know I was extremely generous with each of them

when I was done," Dev drawled with a bad-boy smile that didn't reach his eyes. "My mother once asked if I planned to empty the royal coffers with payouts to my women. If it makes you feel better, lover, you're absolutely the most expensive woman I've ever paid to fuck."

My hand shot out, instinct leading me, and I slapped him with everything I had. I couldn't stop my face from flushing with rage.

Dev shook his head to let me know my little attempt at violence had been somewhat pathetic. "You're also the most trouble I've ever gone to for a piece of ass."

"Stop it." Daniel stood up, his voice stern. "Damn it, Dev. If I ever want to get rid of you, all I have to do is wait and let you do the work for me. Do you ever think about the shit that comes out of that mouth of yours? You don't mean a word of it but it just keeps coming."

Backing away from me, Dev sat down on the bed and let his head fall into his hands. "I was good at this once. I was good at handling women. I never yelled at a female until I met Zoey. I certainly never pushed one to strike me."

"You never loved one before, man," Daniel said quietly, and I knew this wasn't the first conversation they'd had about me. It caught me off guard as I'd never considered they discussed me in anything more than a casual way. I knew they spent time together working and playing video games but not talking about their lives. Daniel obviously knew things about Dev he'd never chosen to discuss with me.

Dev was silent on the subject, and all those doubts Declan had placed in me came raging back to the surface. I looked down at Dev, who was obviously trying to get himself under control, and gave him an out. "If you're tired of me, Dev, all you have to do is say so. I won't cause you any trouble. I'll just leave."

"Tire of you?" His head came up, and I saw the tears he was trying hard not to shed. "I could never tire of you. I can love you. I can hate you sometimes. I can miss you when you leave the room for as little as five minutes. I can worship you. I can curse you because my life was easier before you invaded every inch of my soul, but I will never tire of you."

I knelt between his legs and stared up at his face, touching the roughness of his dark beard. I wasn't exactly innocent in this fight. "I am so sorry about last night. I should never have said that to you. It was awful, and I didn't mean a word of it. I'm also sorry about today. I didn't do it to hurt you. I love you, Dev. I love you and Danny, but I can't live like this. I need you to trust me. I need to be more than just your mistress."

"You died," Dev whispered, leaning into my hand. "I still see it when I close my eyes. I fell to the floor and knew I was going to die and it hadn't meant a damn thing because I could hear him killing you. Daniel can protect you. What the hell can I do? I'm utterly useless when it comes to Halfer. The only thing I can do is pay a phalanx of stronger men to keep you safe. Do you have any idea how that feels?"

"No," I admitted. "Though I have nightmares about that night, too, and I know Danny does. We have to get past it. What does keeping me alive mean if I'm not me anymore?"

"I just wish I wasn't so soft sometimes," he said quietly.

"That's why we train," Daniel said, sitting down beside Dev. "You're much stronger than you were before. It didn't feel soft when you pulled me into the ground last year with all those freaking plants. We were on the Hell plane. There was nothing alive for you to work with. You have to forgive yourself. We have to move on. I've loved Z most of my life, and let me tell you, this is not the last time she's going to pull this crap."

"It's not," I agreed because Danny was right. I wished I was a different person sometimes. I wished I was simpler because most of the time when I got into real trouble, there was no one to blame but myself, but I knew I wasn't going to be changing.

"She's complicated and obnoxious, and she'll make you completely insane," Daniel explained. "And we'll never get bored. We had a good six months of pretending to be in charge of this relationship. Well, the boss is back."

Dev laughed and finally kissed me. "I have missed her."

I pushed myself up against his lips, so happy to have them pressed to mine. They could complain about me all they liked as long as they kept me. I needed them so much.

"I really missed you, Z," Daniel said with a sarcastic sigh. "I can't tell you how happy I was you finally broke out of your funk.

It's been damn hard being the only guy in this relationship."

"Danny," I scolded him because the last thing Dev needed was that kind of teasing. He really could be sensitive about it.

"Oh, no, Daniel. I disagree." Dev's eyes took in the fact that I was only wearing a towel. "I don't think anyone could look at those tits of hers and think boy. If being properly organized and giving a crap about the way I present myself to the world makes me feminine in your eyes, then so be it. But let me assure you, if I'm female, I'll be coming out of the closet because I'm definitely a lesbian."

Dev reached out and suddenly I was no longer wearing that towel. Cool air caressed my skin, but I was heating up because of the way they were both staring. He tossed the towel aside and took a moment to let his eyes roam my body. "I believe we had an arrangement before, lover. Do you remember it? I was more than willing to concede the reins of our relationship to you as long as I maintained a certain level of dominance in one very specific place."

Dev liked to be in control in the bedroom. He liked to play certain games, and we hadn't done anything like that since bringing my husband into the relationship. I have to admit everything female in me tightened at the thought of Dev taking control again. Sex had been good the last six months, but Dev had allowed Daniel and me to explore what we were willing to do together. The boundaries had yet to really be pushed. As I gazed into those green eyes, I realized he was done with going with the flow.

Dev was going to take charge.

Dev stood up and before I could protest, I was in his arms. He tossed me on the bed. I tried to scramble up but found myself tangled in green vines that shot out from the walls to hold my arms. Another pair of snaking vines appeared at the end of the bed, wrapping themselves around my ankles. The lush ivy held me tight, and I couldn't stop the startled cry that sprang from my lips as I was spread in a wanton fashion across the bed.

"Now, my goddess," Dev drawled as he and Daniel looked down at my body. Dev's eyes were hot, and there was no mistaking the erection he sported. "You were a bad girl today. You caused an enormous amount of trouble. Did you think you could get away with it? It's time to discuss your punishment."

Chapter Ten

"God, she looks hot." An expectant grin lit Daniel's face as he stared down at me.

"She does indeed." Dev watched me struggle against the bonds. They caused me absolutely no pain but held me tightly. I wouldn't be going anywhere. My skin was already getting hot under the boys' scrutiny.

My arms were held over my head. Cool green ivy rolled over my skin, gently forcing my hands toward the headboard of our enormous bed. Vines had sprouted from somewhere under the bed and wrapped themselves around my ankles, spreading my legs wide.

"I've always liked this room." Daniel winked down at me. "Now I know why."

I knew why. Because we shared it. Because it was ours. All of ours. The last seven months had been the best of my life in some ways. In others ways it had been difficult, but I knew now that I wouldn't have really walked out the door. I couldn't have. I loved these men. I would fight for myself, but I didn't think I could leave them for any reason.

From my right side, a marigold snaked its way across the bed. It was gold and yellow, the bloom as big as my palm. Dev's control had grown over the last year. Since that night in Vegas, his control of his magic had grown in leaps and bounds. The marigold was from the front hall. Dev had drawn it in, pulling the flower from the pots that lined the entryway. Soft petals caressed my skin. Dev flicked his hand and the marigold brushed across my breast.

"We should talk about the new protocols," Dev said. The silk from the bloom trailed to my other breast, lighting up my skin. Already I could feel Dev's magic beginning to flow like a warm wave of lust.

My pussy was getting wet and he wanted to talk security protocols? Maybe we weren't done fighting yet. "If you think you can get me hot and bothered enough that I'll agree to anything you say, you're probably right, Mr. Sex God."

A sexy smile curled his lips up, and he reached out to tweak my nipple. After the softness of the bloom, his fingers were a little flare of sensation that went straight to my pussy and had me gasping. "I'm glad that you admit how good it can be, but I wasn't going to force you to agree to anything."

Daniel's eyes were watching the marigold as it started down my torso. "He's smart enough to know that after the sex you would start yelling. Well, I'm smart enough to know it and he's decided to listen to me. Are you going to set that thing on her pussy?"

Dev's hand moved again, and he proved that he could turn a perfectly innocent flower into a sex toy. The bloom skimmed against the tenderest part of my flesh, making me squirm. "I'm going to tease her with it. We're both going to make sure she can't wait a second longer to have a cock inside her. I think I would like to hear her beg, but first we should get a few things straight. I don't like Lee."

Damn it. That little flower was tapping on my clit. "I do like Lee. I'm not getting rid of Lee."

Daniel got to his knees next to me with a little laugh. "This should be a fun business meeting. Dev, I'm going to make a royal decree. All of our business should be done while Z here is naked and fornicating with plants."

He leaned over and his deeply talented tongue licked at my nipple.

I groaned as he sucked it inside. "I'm still not giving up Lee."

"I'm not asking you to, but I am asking that you tell me where you're going and you let him do his job. Halfer is out there." Dev sat down on the bed. "Everything we've done has been because we're worried about you."

"I love you both. I'm sorry about today, but I can't live like this. I'll keep Lee with me whenever I leave the building. I promise."

Dev pouted a little, his gorgeous face staring down at mine. "I'm going to miss giving you your daily schedule. I like knowing where you are. I like scheduling your appointments."

Because it made him feel useful. It made him feel important. I knew he liked handling all of the same things for Daniel as well. We'd formed an odd little family, and I could see now that Dev was trying to make a solid place for himself in it.

"You can still make my appointments for all the social stuff, but you two have to let me have a life outside all the politics. I'm not good at them. It's making me miserable." I hated the whole "be quiet and look pretty" crap I had to go through whenever Danny and Dev had their meetings.

The marigold slid up my torso and seemed to give me a little kiss on the lips before it zipped away, likely back to its place in the foyer. Dev replaced the blossom with his fingertips. As he stood, he slid his fingers down my body until he reached the juncture of my widespread legs. He ran a single finger through my pussy, testing it. I sighed against the light pressure, wanting so much more. My faery prince smiled down at me, obviously satisfied I was already responding. I gasped a little as he pressed in, spreading my labia and lightly delving inside. He drew the saturated finger directly into his mouth and sucked the cream off. Daniel gave my nipple a final tweak and stood. There was a large tent in those sweats of his.

"I have never had a lover get so fucking wet so fast. It's intoxicating," Dev commented, shaking his head.

My vampire smiled. "I spent most of my youth with my face in her pussy, so I have to agree with you. It's my happy place."

"I'm sorry, sweetheart," Dev said as though suddenly noticing I was writhing on the bed. He gave me a slow, sexy grin. "Was there something you needed, my mistress?"

I held my head up so I could look at them. "You know what I want, Dev."

He sighed. It was the sound of true contentment, and I knew he meant business. If I had busted out of my funk today then Dev was right behind me. "I know exactly what you want. I know what he wants, too. I also know it will be a while before either one of you gets it."

"What does that mean?" Daniel was used to getting straight to the fun.

Cupping my breast, Dev sat on the edge of the bed. I was truly trapped, a toy bound for their pleasure. Yeah, it did something for me. It did a lot for me. I might prefer to be in charge when it came to work, but it had been so long since Dev had truly taken charge of me in the bedroom. I'd forgotten how much I needed it, how much I could let go and enjoy when they took the lead. Dev played lightly with my nipples, allowing the tips of his fingers to dance softly across the peaks. They hardened again and I tried to press up, needing a much firmer touch. I would have preferred his mouth there, but I was going to have to take what I could get.

Dev turned to Daniel. "It means that I'm ready to move this relationship forward. It means I'm done with merely participating. You've trained me to be a better fighter. I've listened to your advice and allowed you to be the master. In this room, I'm the master. Up until now, our sex has been what I can only call somewhat circumspect."

Daniel's head shook, his eyes narrowing. "Dude, we fuck the same girl in the same bed. How much freakier can it get?"

Dev laughed. "You have no idea, Daniel. Until tonight, I've been content for the most part to wait my turn and allow you to have yours. We've watched as the other pleasured our lover. This is not true sharing. Tonight we're going to play a little game, and I'm going to take us places you haven't even thought of yet."

"Oh, I've thought of it, Dev," Daniel admitted, his voice tight so I knew his fangs were out. "Are you kidding me? It's all I've been able to think about for months. I just don't know if Z's ready."

"She isn't, yet. But she will be." Dev's face was perfectly serene even as I knew mine was tight with need. "Do you trust me, sweetheart? Will you let me lead you?"

"You know I trust you, Dev." I trusted him implicitly. "Please, please fuck me."

I was already going crazy. I was worried this little game of his just might kill me with wanting, and he hadn't really touched me yet.

"Your Highness?" Dev asked, looking at Daniel expectantly.

Danny nodded. "I'm willing to let you lead in this."

"Why don't you find your happy place then," Dev ordered softly, looking at my husband. "But Daniel, long slow strokes of the tongue. This is meant to tease, to torture in the most exquisite fashion. We don't want her to come too soon. There should be some work behind a truly good orgasm. Make her beg for it."

"Dev, that's not fair," I managed to say before Daniel took my breath away with that first sweep of his tongue. It ran the length of my pussy, and I could feel every inch of that stroke. Daniel's big hands spread my legs even farther as he settled in and started to torment me with light caresses. I tried to push up, to force him to fuck me with his mouth, but the bonds held too firmly.

"Will it help if I promise you'll be completely satisfied with the experience?" Dev asked as he rolled a nipple between his thumb and forefinger. He leaned down and touched the puckered flesh with the tip of his tongue. Teasing the nipple to a hard point, he finally pulled it into his mouth. He lightly sucked on it, the sensation making me want so much more. I nearly came off the bed when he gave me just the slightest edge of his teeth. I wanted to cry, to beg, to plead with him to give me more.

"Dev, please." I gave in to the need.

His emerald green eyes held mine. "Yes, tonight we will please Dev. I can be your lapdog outside this room. I can spend my whole life fetching for you. I really don't mind. In fact, I prefer for you to depend on me. But here, when we're intimate, I'm the boss, Zoey."

He needed to be in control and I'd finally figured out why last year when we'd walked through the Hell plane together. I'd discovered just how often he'd been forced to give up control during his life in the *sithein*, especially in sexual situations. Dev was a Green Man, part fertility god, and his sexuality had always been his greatest bargaining chip. He needed to know that I would submit to his wishes. As they'd never hurt me, never taken me any place besides pure pleasure and loving affection, I was more than willing to go down this path with him.

With both of them.

"Yes, Dev."

"That's what I like to hear. Now thank your husband. He seems to do an excellent job at eating that sweet pussy."

I felt Daniel chuckle against my flesh. "It's my favorite food."

Dev tweaked my nipple again, a little bit of pleasure/pain. "Zoey, thank him."

"Thank you, Daniel. It feels so good." One of the things Dev loved to do was talk about sex. He'd allowed Danny and me to enjoy ourselves without putting too much pressure on us, but I realized how much he'd restrained himself. And he was right. What was wrong with telling Danny I loved how his mouth felt on me? What was wrong with talking about what I needed?

Oh, and this was exactly what I needed. The hurt was slipping away because we were together and we were finally being honest with each other.

"Daniel, I believe she's ready to move on. Let's see how her little pussy handles your finger. Only one."

I felt Daniel chuckle against my swollen, saturated flesh as he lightly dipped a finger into my heat, stretching me gently. He worked his long finger into my passage and rotated it in a tantalizing fashion. It wasn't anywhere close to enough and Dev knew it. Both of my men were a hell of a lot thicker than that scrawny finger, and yet I still fought to shove it in deeper, to get it to that place where it would do the most good.

"Danny." I was panting, trying to get some oxygen into my lungs. "Baby, you really should fuck me now. I need it. Please. I don't want your finger. I need your cock." I went after the weak link. Danny had never played this particular game before. He'd never denied me anything when it came to sex. He had always just leapt in and did whatever he could to please me.

I nearly jumped out of my skin as his tongue delicately lapped at my desperate clitoris. It was just enough to make it swell but not so much that it sent me over that blissful edge I was so damned close to. Daniel didn't look up at me. He stared straight at the flesh he was working. "Sorry, Z. I can't disobey the teacher. You know how that goes."

"It's going to go poorly for her if she tries to get around me again." Dev tweaked my nipple a little harder this time. "Do you really want to prolong this with a nice spanking?"

I shook my head because he wasn't above doing it. Dev was a total deviant, and he liked to experiment. If I gave him a shot, he would torture me all night, and I really wanted to avoid that. "I'll be good. Please."

Daniel continued his slow tongue lashing. "I really like hearing you beg, baby. It's making me forget how scared I was earlier. I think I'll spank that pretty ass of yours if you disappear without any protection again."

Dev moved on to my other breast, satisfied with the hardness of the first nipple. "You will find this is an excellent way to vent our frustrations when Zoey does something to make us insane. We need to go shopping, Daniel. There are a couple of stores that might have certain toys we would find amusing. I think these gorgeous tits would look pretty in nipple clamps."

"Clamps?" I wasn't sure it was a good idea to let the sex god loose in an adult store.

"Light pressure only, my lover," Dev promised. "You'll find you like the sensation. I'll like the way it looks. Emeralds, I think. They would glow against your porcelain skin." He ran a hand down to my navel. "And I think I have to insist on a belly button ring."

Daniel groaned against my clit. "Oh, god, yes."

"Daniel and I will choose something pretty," Dev offered, running his hands over my curves. "Your body is our temple, lover, and we would like to decorate it."

"I'll do it." I was willing to give them pretty much anything as long as they gave me what I needed. My body had been Dev's temple since the first night we had sex. He genuinely enjoyed brushing my hair and even painting my toenails on occasion. I realized for the first time why he enjoyed selecting my clothes and pampering me. It went far beyond pleasure. This was Dev's version of possessiveness. I was his—his to dress, to adorn, to please. He would select a navel ring, and every time he caught sight of it, he would feel a sense of satisfaction that I wore it to please him. Others could look at it and admire it, but he would know it was only there for him.

Daniel looked up, his eyes as desperate as I felt. "Dev, man, I'm dying here. I'm so fucking hard I think my balls are going to explode. She tastes so sweet, but if I don't get my dick in her soon, I'm going to die."

"Wimp," Dev said through clenched teeth though there was no lack of affection. "We're going to have to work on delayed gratification. I suppose since you're not the one I'm attempting to punish, I should allow your release. Zoey, would you like to take your husband's cock in your mouth?"

"Yes," I said quickly, just wanting to participate. I really wanted out of those bonds so I could get my hands on them. "I'll be a very obedient girl, Devinshea. I promise I'll play your game if you just let me touch the two of you."

Dev's gorgeous face loomed over mine. "You know I find it

difficult to deny you anything, my goddess. Especially when you ask so sweetly." He leaned down and ran his tongue across my lips. I opened eagerly, letting him explore my mouth. This was the difference between Dev and his brother. When Declan had kissed me, it had been pleasant but nothing to write home about. When Dev kissed me, I felt it in my womb. Everything in me sparked to life when his lips met mine. When he was satisfied, he sat back up and flicked his hand. The vines recoiled back to their place. "Behave yourself, lover. I can always tie you down again. Now get up on your knees."

When I'd done as he asked, I noticed Daniel, who was standing at the end of the bed, his sweat pants tossed to the floor. He stroked that glorious cock of his as he waited for me to welcome him. Danny was six foot three inches of pure muscle, and I never seemed to get over just how hot he was. His cock was long and thick, reaching almost to his belly button.

I felt Dev shift off the bed and heard him begin to undress. I smiled at Daniel, knowing it wouldn't be long now before Devinshea gave in and I had them both.

"Go on, sweetheart." Dev's voice lost a bit of his control as he upped the level of lust in the room. He was naked now, and I could feel his magic starting to pulse through his body. He was still in control at this point but before long, he would let it roll over us like a warm wave. "Give him a taste."

I leaned forward and licked the drop of salty heaven that was already seeping from the sensitive slit on Daniel's cock. He hissed at the sensation. I twirled my tongue around the purple head of his engorged penis and was satisfied with his groan. Daniel's eyes were a deep blue, looking down at me, taking in the sight of his cock pushing into my mouth.

"Fuck yeah, baby. Suck me," he said, tangling his fingers in my hair. He guided me, showing me exactly what he wanted as his hips pumped forward. "Take me, all of me."

I sucked him into my mouth, glorying in the way he filled me, in the pleasure I could give this man I loved so much. I wasn't able to take all of him, but I gave it my best shot. His skin was soft, the cock beneath it hard as a rock. My tongue played around him, feeling him pulse, and I steadied myself on the bed so I could balance on one hand, leaving the other free to cup his heavy, tight balls in my palm. Even as I played gently with them they tightened further, getting ready to release. Over and over I let my tongue play on his cock, sucking him deep and pulling back out. Daniel moaned over me and I knew he was close.

I heard Dev curse and then the sound of a condom wrapper tearing open. My whole body tightened at what I knew was going to happen next. I shoved my ass up as high as I could get it to give him the best possible angle of entry.

Dev moved behind me, his hands firmly gripping my hips. "You're going to be the death of me, lover. Just like our vampire, I am going to have to work on discipline. I'm afraid I just can't resist." He started to fill me, working to get every inch in me just as Daniel's head fell back.

"Oh, I'm gonna come, baby," he warned just before I sucked him hard and he filled my mouth with his release. I drank him down and licked the last bit off as Daniel stroked my hair and Dev started to fuck me seriously.

"I love you, Zoey," Daniel said. "I love you so fucking much."

Without losing a single stroke, Dev leaned back and pulled me with him. I was up on my knees with his cock stroking into me from behind. I moaned as he glided over my G-spot, teasing it with every stroke. The tension built, strumming through my body.

"Daniel," Dev commanded, his voice harsh as he worked inside me. "Stroke her clit. Make her scream, man."

Daniel kneeled on the bed and he had the most decadent look on his face as he reached down and rubbed two fingers firmly against my oh-so-ready-for-it clitoris. He kissed me hard, his tongue mimicking Dev's actions. I was caught between his fingers and Dev's cock as I exploded and did exactly what Dev had planned. I didn't hold back an instant. I moaned and screamed my pleasure and fought for every second of it. I felt Dev pick up the pace as I tightened everything I had around him, and he gave himself over. He plunged mindlessly into my pussy, holding my hips and pumping out every ounce of come he had.

He fell back, pulling me with him. Daniel followed and we ended up in a warm tangle of flesh. Dev kissed my neck and stroked my breasts because he was never one to finish and turn over to sleep.

It would take much more than that to satisfy a sex god.

"Don't think I'm done yet," he whispered against my skin. "We haven't even started."

I smiled as Danny kissed my breasts and rubbed himself against me, letting me know he was already hard again. I would definitely have to misbehave more often.

* * * *

It was a long, long time later when we cuddled down together, and I thought about what Dev had said. Up until tonight, besides the first night we'd been together, he and Daniel had been content to take turns and watch. This was so much more intimate. This was real sharing, and I felt a bone-deep satisfaction that went far beyond the multiple orgasms the boys had wrung out of me.

Daniel licked my neck from behind, cradling my body to his, and I realized he hadn't even fed yet. We'd been so involved in the sex he'd forgotten about blood. Dev kissed me lightly, our mouths just playing. I loved this part, and it was so much better because I was between them. I was surrounded by them, warm and happy.

"Did you enjoy yourself, my goddess?" Dev asked, a smile in his voice. He sounded entirely satisfied with the way the evening had gone.

"You know I did." I let my tongue tangle playfully with his as Daniel bit down gently and began to suck. "Oh, god, that feels so good, Danny."

This was a gentle feeding. Daniel had been well fed on the sex magic that flowed from Dev. Vampires feed on blood and sexual energy, and the sexual energy had been off the scale. He was more than likely full, and I was just a little snack. Sure enough, he released the vein quickly and was back to long, luxurious strokes of his tongue to help close the little wounds.

"I truly hate to interrupt an intimate moment, Mr. Donovan." A deep voice with a thick French accent shattered our intimacy and any feeling of safety I had. "But I fear the three of you are never going to tire of each other, and Marcus is going to expire from sheer frustration if he has to watch much more."

Daniel was on his feet, claws out and fangs long, looking for the intruder. Dev shoved me behind his body, dragging his sheet up.

"All right, Marini," Daniel growled. He stopped and stared at a place in front of the bedroom door. "I know you're there."

"Mr. Thomas, you may release the illusion." Louis Marini chuckled as though he'd been watching something amusing and not becoming the vampire Peeping Tom.

One moment we were seemingly alone, and the next there were three vampires standing in front of our bedroom door. Louis Marini was the head of the Council. Marcus Vorenus was a handsome Italian and Daniel's patron. The third vampire made my heart hurt a little. Chad Thomas was Neil's lover. Six months before, we'd sent him to the Council in Paris to cover up our activities and gain a spy.

Dev relaxed and leaned back against me, drawing my arms around his chest and my legs around his waist. His body covered mine completely, but he seemed negligent. Dev was excellent at playing the lovely, insignificant lover. His fingers tangled with mine, begging me to play along. I tried to relax and pretend I was comfortable, but my heart was pounding and not in a good way. I didn't like Marini. I really didn't like the covetous expression he had as he stared at me and Dev. I wasn't sure who he was more interested in since he'd propositioned both of us the year before.

"Would you care to explain why you come into my home and insult me like this?" Daniel's voice came out in a low growl as he pulled gray sweatpants over his hips. He didn't bother with a shirt.

"Daniel, we meant no harm," Marcus tried to explain.

"It was a small test, Mr. Donovan." Marini took in the bedroom, walking around, examining the contents. "I thought it fitting we try it out on you. You were responsible for finding the talented Mr. Thomas. He's quite the savant."

"He turns out to be a master illusionist. It's a rare talent." Marcus watched as Dev brought my fingers to his lips and pretended to be far more interested in playing with me than listening in on vampire talk. I knew he was processing everything they said to figure out exactly how much Marini knew. The only reason we were still on the bed and not trying to fight our way out was the fact that Marini was outnumbered. Marcus and Chad were on our side.

"Criss Angel's got nothing on me," Chad said, giving me a little wink.

"I thought if anyone could sense the unseen it would be our *Nex Apparatus*, though I fear it wasn't a fair test. Your senses were involved in other things. This home is impressive, Daniel," Marini said, taking in the lushness of the surroundings. Dev sprang for the best of everything. "It's far better than anything the Council could provide for you. The security is excellent. If we hadn't brought along Mr. Thomas, we would have been unable to reach you without much advanced warning. The club downstairs is yours as well?"

Daniel watched the head of the Council with his arms crossed. "It belongs to Devinshea, who belongs to me."

Marini's eyebrow arched at that. "You claim much for one so young. Mr. Quinn is not some mere companion. He's a prince of Faery and a powerful man in his own right."

"Are you questioning my right?" Daniel's voice hardened and I winced a little because his possessive nature was coming out again. "I assure you I can defend my blood."

"Daniel," Dev said, a certain pout to his voice. "When are you going to be through with business? You promised us no business tonight, only pleasure. I haven't even been bitten yet and Zoey hasn't passed out, so we couldn't possibly be done."

I realized what Dev was trying to avoid. Daniel had been dangerously close to pushing Marini. It didn't take much to cause Danny to lose his temper when it came to what he considered his, and Marini had crossed a line. We weren't ready for this fight yet. I followed Dev's lead. I watched Daniel even as I playfully nipped Dev's neck. "You did promise us, Danny. You said you would stay in bed with us until I let you go. I'm not tired yet."

Marini's face went from stirring anger to amusement. "Are they always so insatiable?"

A slight smile crossed Daniel's face, and I knew we'd defused the situation. "You have no idea. There's a reason it takes two of us to please her. I won't even go into his appetites. I assure you what they require of me might kill a lesser vampire."

"I am afraid, Mrs. Donovan, that your husband will have to reschedule his little orgy," the Frenchman said dismissively. "The Council is on its way to Los Angeles where we have business. We decided to stop here for the night and check in on our *Nex Apparatus*. We require updates on your progress."

"Of course," Daniel replied, his anger pushed down in favor of a businesslike demeanor. "I will brief you at your earliest convenience. I think you'll be happy with what I've accomplished."

"I'm sure we will," Louis murmured. "We're having a small party at the club. You will be there in an hour."

"Yes, sir. I'll have everything ready." Daniel nodded and gestured for the door.

Marini moved to leave and Chad followed him. Marcus glanced reluctantly back at us as though he didn't want to go.

Marini looked back at Dev and me, taking a moment to watch our play. "And bring your lovely blood, Mr. Donovan. They'll bring much-needed life to our otherwise dull evening."

"Sir," Daniel began.

"That's an order, Daniel," Marini said shortly. "Come, Marcus, you can drool over the girl at the club. We'll expect you in an hour, Donovan."

Everything stopped as the vampires left. Daniel stood in the middle of the room, his body so still it could have been made of marble. Dev kept perfectly quiet, listening for the moment he heard the elevator close and begin to move down toward his office.

"We're supposed to be safe here," Daniel said, not looking our way. He was keeping his face hidden, and I was sure his beast was close to the surface.

"I'll call Albert and find out what happened." Dev climbed off the bed and reached for his pants. He gave me a look that said "deal with him."

I nodded because when it came to Daniel's temper, I was the only one who could handle him. It was a testament to his control that he wasn't tossing furniture around. It hadn't been so long ago that he would have been doing just that.

Dev left the room without a backward glance, and I slid out of bed and ran my hands along my vampire's back. Every muscle was bunched with potential violence. I let my arms wind around his waist and pressed my skin to his.

"It's all right, Daniel." I let my hands slide along his waist and then up his chest. Oftentimes our connection could help calm Danny's beast. "If Marini had found anything, Chad and Marcus would have handled it. He was just showing off. Everything's okay.

Dev will have twelve security experts in here tomorrow installing motion detectors and all manner of crazy, paranoid safety equipment."

"He sure as hell better, Z." His voice was still rough, but his hands came up to cover mine, holding them against his skin. "He promised me you would be safe here."

I kissed the smooth skin of his back, feeling him begin to relax under my ministrations. "Don't blame Dev. It fooled you, too, and you have supersenses."

"I was concentrating on other things," he admitted quietly. "I wonder if they're going to ruin every good minute I have, Z. Tonight was…god, tonight might have made the whole vampire thing worth it."

"It just might have."

"And now I have to hold a piece of myself apart when we make love because the fuckers can get me wherever I am," he said bitterly. "I always have to listen because they could be anywhere."

"It won't be forever," I said, hoping I was right.

Dev walked in, cell phone pressed to his ear. "Yes, that's what I want. I want the entire place wired with motion detectors and whatever the hell can detect heat signatures. I don't care what it costs, Albert. We also need to change the keycards to thumbprints and voice recognition. Get them in here tomorrow."

Daniel shifted and leaned over, kissing me softly. "I'm sorry to drag you into this, Z. I've got to get some stuff together. You get dressed. It'll be okay."

Dev was issuing further edicts on new security protocols and I looked sadly at our bed. I wanted to be back in it where we'd been safe and secure and loved. Now we had to worry about safety and subterfuge, and my stomach was already rumbling because I skipped dinner. I was betting they didn't have a dining room at Daniel's club, at least not one where I wasn't on the menu.

Chapter Eleven

In every major city where there is even a small vampire presence, one can find a vampire club. It's usually in an out-of-the-way part of the city housed in a neat, unassuming building that does nothing to attract unwanted attention. The club provides the vampires with anything they require. It serves much the same function as an old-world gentlemen's club. This is the place a vampire comes for a meal, companionship, or a game of cards. In addition to serving the local vampires, the club is capable of housing visitors and is the place to entertain.

I'd never been in this inner sanctum. After we began living together, Daniel stopped going. When we'd been apart, he spent a good amount of time in the club, but once Dev and I became his regular meals, he no longer required it.

I looked the place over with more than a little bit of curiosity as the limo pulled up in front of the small three-story building. It was a townhouse, and a Victorian one at that. I could see the lights from the windows, but they were dim as though lit by candles rather than modern light bulbs.

Daniel took my hand and helped me out of the limo. "Stay close to Dev. I'll be in a meeting with Marini and the rest of the Council, so I think you'll be fairly safe. Michael and Alexander are probably here. I know you can handle them."

"Perhaps she can, but Michael is always looking for a way to righteously kill me," Dev said with a jaunty smile. I could tell he was hoping for a fight. He'd been tense ever since the vampires showed up in our room. He'd dressed in a three-piece suit and had forced me into something designer. Daniel looked slick and sexy in his suit.

"Michael knows our situation," Daniel replied, picking up the briefcase he'd loaded his laptop into. Michael House was Daniel's friend and ally. Though he had a problem with Dev, he wouldn't cause trouble here. "Just try to stay inconspicuous."

I didn't laugh, but it wasn't easy. I might be the kind of girl who doesn't get a second glance in a bar or a club, but when I walk into a room full of vampires, all eyes are going to be on me whether I like it or not. I'm a companion. I can't hide the shine I have for those who walk the night. I glow for them, and they know my blood will make them strong. I would give pretty much anything to be able to be inconspicuous, but that wasn't going to happen on this particular night.

Dev's hand went to the small of my back as he guided me up the steps to the house. Daniel pulled out a keycard and the door opened for us. He held his hand out and Dev moved me to Daniel's side. He took a step back and allowed us to enter before him. This is what I hated about so called "society." I hated the little games we were forced to play whenever we left the confines of our home.

"Good evening, Daniel," a husky female voice said. A woman in a killer dress stood in the lobby. A brilliant smile crossed her face as she rushed forward to greet my husband. "It's been so long I wondered if you would ever visit here again."

And bitch was not happy to see me. The tall, lithe female had murder in her eyes as she took me in. She was pretty with short, blonde hair and light-blue eyes.

"It's nice to see you, Stacy." Daniel nodded casually to the woman as if her eyes weren't completely filled with desire for him and animosity for me. He was totally oblivious as he smiled at her and pulled me forward. "I got married. You know how it goes. You get married and just want to stay in. I only came tonight because Marini's in town and ordered me to. This is my wife, Zoey Donovan. Z, this is Stacy Sears. She runs the club. She was really nice to me after I turned."

I just bet she'd been nice to Daniel. I wondered just how many times she'd offered to be especially nice to him. As far as I could tell, she was human and the humans in a place like this were good for the dinner table or the bedroom, sometimes both. "Nice to meet you."

"So she's a companion." She looked me up and down, letting me know she didn't see anything special.

"She's my wife," Daniel corrected, apparently not noticing she refused to speak directly to me. I heard Dev chuckle behind me.

"We've been together since we were kids, but we just got married about two years ago. Gosh, I guess I haven't been in here in a really long time."

"Yes." Her mouth tightened with displeasure. "You just stopped coming."

Daniel shrugged, looking past the foyer into the hallway beyond, searching for something. "I guess you could say I prefer to eat at home. Do I need to sign Zoey and our friend in?"

Stacy shook her head as though trying to shake something off. "Your companion is already on the books, but your friend will have to sign in. Your name is Quinn, right?"

"Yes, Devinshea Quinn, Prince of Faery, at your service." He bowed at the waist but not before I saw the amusement in his eyes.

Stacy produced a leather-bound book and Daniel signed it. While he handled the formalities, I took a moment to look around the place that had been a mystery for so long. There had been a time when I would have given anything to follow Danny in here as his companion. Now I just wanted to go home.

The carpet beneath my feet was lush and ran the length of the foyer. It looked expensive and old. The room was lit with candles and gas lamps. I could have been on the set of a Victorian film. Music thudded softly from somewhere in the building. It was a sexy hip-hop beat, much like the stuff that played at Ether, and I wondered just how the Council partied. I'd attended a ball last year but that had been a formal occasion. This was a more casual affair, and there was a small part of me that was fascinated by seeing vampires in their element.

"I'll need the conference room," Daniel was saying to the blonde, who nodded vigorously and promised she would do anything she could to help him. "Are they in the parlor?"

"Yes, they are." Stacy began to lead us down the hallway. She smiled back at Daniel. "You should know that I don't believe any of those rumors about you. I know you, Danny. You aren't like that."

"Like what?" Daniel asked, not sounding like he really cared.

I cared. She said "Danny" in an intimate way. Danny was my husband. Danny was the boy I grew up with. Daniel was a badass vampire. Everyone called him Daniel except me. She might as well have called him "baby" or "lover."

Stacy turned and she almost touched him. Her hands came out to reach for him before she caught herself. "I know you aren't really living with him. You're not the type." She glanced back at Dev and was the first woman I'd ever met who didn't melt at the sight of him. She glared at him like he was a bit distasteful. "Did the Council force you to take a companion? It makes sense. They need you to be strong for the important work you do. You don't have to pretend with me. I can keep your secrets. The faery can have her. You can come back to me and no one is going to think less of you."

Daniel looked to Dev, a confused light in his eyes.

Dev laughed outright. "Seriously, Dan, you're screwed now. Don't you know to handle your ex-lovers before introducing them to the wife? The preference, of course, is to never introduce them to the wife."

"Lover?" The question came out of my mouth as a little screech.

Daniel went the slightest bit pale. "Z, baby, I swear to you. I never…"

Stacy put her hands on her almost nonexistent hips. "I was his favorite. I fed him for years. He'll come back to me. He only keeps you because of that blood you have."

Dev's arms went around my waist just in time to keep me from launching myself at the woman and snatching that bleached blonde hair straight out of her head. "Don't, sweetheart. She isn't worth messing up that dress. It's Versace, and you'll ruin the line if you tumble around on the floor."

"Z, I never slept with her." Daniel was talking as fast as he could. "I swear I never touched her except to feed. I had to eat. That's what this place is for, but I didn't even feel her up or anything. There was no funny business going on."

"He was a gentleman because he loves me," Stacy continued. "Tell her about all the nights we sat up talking, Danny. Did you know he used to take me with him when he went on assignments?"

"You did what?" I growled at my husband and tried to bring my heel down on Dev's toe. He was far too used to my moves as he avoided the four-and-a-half-inch stiletto with ease.

My husband had the good sense to stay a couple of feet away from me. "It was only a couple of times, baby. I had to go kill some people in really rural places. It was easier to pack a lunch than find one in the field." He frowned at Dev. "You don't have to look so damned amused."

"Oh, I assure you it is entirely necessary," Dev returned. "I've dreamed of this day, Dan."

"You never take me on assignment." I tried to push Dev's arms down. It was no use.

Stacy had the audacity to put her hand on Daniel's shoulder.

Daniel stepped away quickly. "I don't take you with me because it's dangerous, baby. I love you so much. I'd never put you in harm's way like that. God, I do everything I can to keep you safe."

Stacy rolled her eyes. "That's not you talking, Danny. That's the addiction. You fought it off once before and I'll help you do it again. You don't need her. She's been nothing but trouble from what I've heard. She isn't even a good companion. I was good for you. I took care of you. She gets you in trouble. And she's far too short for you. I certainly didn't expect her to be so pudgy."

"Let me go, Dev," I snarled.

"Oh, thank the heavens." Marcus's rich voice was filled with amusement as he leaned against the wall and watched—which apparently is something he really likes to do. "I worried after the earlier events of the evening that Zoey would be far too embarrassed to misbehave. I see I was mistaken. Don't listen to her, *cara*. You're stunning and she knows it. Daniel might be attracted to your shine above that body of yours, but I believe Mr. Quinn will attest to the fact that there is nothing pudgy about you."

"Zoey knows how I feel about her body." Dev loosened his grip.

"I'm pretty damn attached to her body," Daniel corrected. "I think I proved that earlier tonight."

Marcus shifted his stare to Stacy, and the affectionate look on his face vanished. "As for you, Miss Sears, if you ever treat Mrs. Donovan in that fashion again, I will see you turned out. She is your mistress yet you insult her. You'll remember your place or I'll be forced to show you. Make your apologies."

Her head was down now and her eyes averted. "I'm sorry, master."

"Not to me. To her." Marcus gestured my way.

"Please accept my apologies, Mrs. Donovan," she said quietly, and I realized this wasn't the first time she had been forced to humble herself.

"Of course," I returned, and Dev finally let me loose.

"Miss Sears, try to stay out of Mrs. Donovan's way for the rest of the night. And you should definitely keep your distance from her husband," Marcus ordered.

The blonde walked away, a sheen of tears in her eyes.

I turned on my husband and pointed at him. "You have a lot of explaining to do. I believe that you didn't sleep with her, but that girl is obviously in love with you. She was hurt. You should have told me about her and don't throw Dev in my face because I never hid him from you."

"How can you hide him from me when he's always on top of you?" Daniel asked, still seemingly confused by the entire episode.

"I'm not always on top," Dev replied. "I often enjoy being on bottom. I like the view."

Daniel had gotten good at ignoring Dev. "Z, I had no idea she thought that about us. I swear I just needed someone to talk to, and she was a good listener. Hell, most of the time I was talking about you. I never said anything to make her believe she was more than a friend."

"I'll have her reassigned," Marcus said with an imperious wave. "I won't have her causing trouble. The last thing we need is our slaves wreaking havoc. I warned you about getting too friendly with them, Daniel."

"Slaves?" I asked, my voice tight.

Daniel grinned at his patron. "I'll leave you to the explanations. I have to set up." He kissed me hard and quick. "Stay out of trouble, Z."

As I watched him disappear down the hall, I had a feeling that wasn't going to be easy.

"Come, *cara*." Marcus offered me his arm. "You can rail at the injustices of our world in the parlor."

"So slaves?" I let Marcus lead me down the hall.

Marcus shrugged. "Of course. Did you expect vampires to run the club? We have human slaves to do menial labor."

"By menial labor he means all labor," Dev pointed out helpfully.

"How exactly does one become a slave?" I was pretty sure I

didn't want to hear the answer, but it was like a car accident.

Marcus stopped and looked at me like I was the most naïve of children. "One is born a slave, Zoey. It isn't difficult. The slaves mate and create new slaves. I believe the modern term is 'renewable resource.'"

I felt my blood pressure rise. "Marcus Vorenus, that is the most horrible thing I have ever heard. Are you telling me you've enslaved entire generations of humans so you don't have to worry about payroll?"

"Well, not me personally," Marcus replied. "It's the way of our world."

I made the horrible mistake of looking into one of the rooms we were standing near. It was small, but there were two females and one male sitting on a leather couch. They were wearing little in the way of clothing. There was a desk where a man sat with a large book in front of him. Alexander Sharpe stood in front of the desk.

"I'll take the blonde," he said in his crisp British accent. The man at the desk signed out Alexander's dinner and the poor blonde found herself on the creepy vamp's arm. Alexander nodded at me. "Good evening, Mrs. Donovan. I'm surprised Daniel brought you here. He always swore he would never bring his precious blood to a place like this."

"Sharpe." Marcus acknowledged the Brit. "Mrs. Donovan is here at Louis's pleasure. Daniel isn't happy about it. I would advise you to make her stay as pleasant as possible or he'll be unhappy with you, too."

"We couldn't have that now, could we?" Alexander said enigmatically as he ushered his dinner up the stairs.

I shook off the need to shower again. I felt that way every time I found myself in the same room as Alexander. "So that girl—who may or may not survive the night—is a slave, and her parents were slaves before that."

Marcus nodded. "Yes, Zoey. How did you think we filled positions? Did you think we held a job fair? All the humans here are slaves in one form or another. They were either born into slavery or chose to enter it because they wished to serve Vampire. Ms. Sears was born a slave. She grew up in a vampire household and proved to be intelligent and organized. She was trained to run a business and was promoted to manager of this club. Now she will be demoted to blood slave. I warned Daniel he should feed from all of them so as not to show favoritism."

"Please don't, Marcus." I didn't want to give a crap about her but an unwanted sympathy was creeping in. "Don't demote her. It's Danny's fault. I don't really blame her. If I had to live like she does, I would have fallen for the first decent man to come my way, too."

"You're too kindhearted, *cara*," Marcus said. "She'll cause trouble."

"Maybe she'll start a slave uprising and I can join in," I replied tartly.

Marcus shook his head Dev's way. "Who does she think runs her household? Who does she think cooks her meals and cleans the rooms of her home?"

I slowly turned to look at Dev, who was doing the running-two-fingers-across-his-throat thing to tell Marcus to cut it out.

I smiled up sweetly at my lover. "You pay Albert, right?"

"Of course," Dev replied, lying straight through those perfect teeth.

"Albert's a slave?"

"Not at all, my love." Dev took one of my hands in his. "Albert is family. Just because I bought him at an auction doesn't make him any less a member of our little family."

My mouth fell open, and I just stared at the two of them.

"Fae society is full of slaves," Marcus pointed out.

"That is a complete lie," Dev returned. "We don't consider them slaves. They're serfs and vassals. It's a completely different thing."

"Yes," Marcus murmured. "It is different because you use different words. The result is the same. Zoey, you're surrounded by slaves. It's a fact of the world you live in."

I poked Dev in the chest. "You're going to free Albert the second we get home. You're going to offer him a generous salary, medical and dental, and a 401k."

Dev smiled smoothly. "Of course, darling. I'll throw in some vacation time as well."

"Do you always just give in like that?" Marcus asked.

Dev shrugged. "Absolutely. It's so much easier than arguing. I'd spend hours with her pissed at me and I'd only give in anyway, so I make my life simpler and just lay down in the beginning. When I first met Zoey, I promised I would lay down for her anytime she liked. I keep my promises."

Just as I was about to start walking again, Chad came down the stairs. He looked nothing like the sweet, smart lawyer I'd met a year before. He was like sin on two legs. His hair was longer, framing his handsome face. He wore tight black leather pants that showed off his lean physique to spectacular advantage. His white shirt was half opened, revealing his sculpted chest. This Chad was a rock and roll god.

"I'd like to speak to Zoey for a moment, Marcus," Chad requested with a slight smile.

Marcus glanced around to see if anyone else was noticing the exchange. "All right, but be careful. You're not supposed to know her."

Chad took my hand and led me quickly up the stairs and to a bedroom. He shut the door behind us and sighed. "How are you doing, Zoey?"

"I'm all right." I waited for him to ask me the question I didn't want to answer. "Are you okay?"

He shrugged. "It's nothing I can't handle. I'm turning out to be quite the spy. I've gotten close to Marini. He's taken with my talents. It's about to get bad, Zoey. You have to warn my master. Marini is doing things behind his back that Marcus doesn't even know about. In the last few months, he's ordered the executions of three powerful werewolf alphas in Europe. He's intensely interested in subjugating the wolves as they were when the vampires were powerful. He believes he can do this by putting Daniel in a corner. He'll work on the wolves in Europe and then force Daniel to bring the American wolves in line."

"Daniel will never allow that to happen." We'd known Marini had plans, but I'd hoped they were years away. Vampires were known for taking their time.

"Ah, but Marini believes he knows the key to forcing the *Nex Apparatus* to do anything he wishes," Chad said quietly, looking at me.

I let my shoulders slump forward. I hated the fact that I was Daniel's only real weakness. "I'll let him know."

The vampire nodded. "He has plans for you, Zoey. He has plans that you can't imagine. Watch your back around him. Marini believes Daniel's love for you will be his downfall, and what he saw tonight didn't change his mind about it."

I felt my face go beet red. "God, Chad, please tell me you were only there for a few minutes."

He grinned. "That would be a lie. I'm afraid I'm back to envying you your men. When did they get so friendly? When I left, Daniel still growled every time Dev walked in the room."

"Vegas," I admitted. "We've been living together for about seven months. Just how long were you there watching us?"

"Long enough. Seriously, Zoey, that was the hottest thing I've ever seen. I would have given just about anything to take your place in the middle of that sandwich. I really did think Marcus was going to lose control. He's crazy about you. That magic of Dev's is pretty amazing. It felt like I was feeding, but I didn't need blood."

Well, at least now I could participate in Dev's ceremony knowing I'd already performed in public. I shook my head.

"Now I can get to the real reason I needed to see you." Chad gestured toward the small door that probably led to the bathroom. "You can come out now, baby."

The door opened, and Neil walked out looking perfect and healthy and whole. He smiled at me, and I immediately teared up.

"Neil," I said, my voice catching. He grinned and held his arms open. I ran into them and caught only air as my body passed through the illusion. I searched around and then back at Chad, who was frowning at me. It was just a trick. "That was mean, Chad."

"That was necessary to find out just how bad the situation is," Chad replied, his voice hard. "I wanted to know if you've turned on him. He isn't answering his phone. Marcus told me what happened. My master used his power to make Neil a slave."

"Daniel was trying to protect us all. Neil was beyond upset when he found out you were the spy. Please understand, Chad. We were going onto the Hell plane with only Neil as backup, and he threatened to walk." He'd been halfway out the door when Daniel turned on that power for the first time. "Daniel was desperate. He would never hurt Neil."

"I doubt that, Zoey." Chad sat down on the bed and studied me for a moment. "You don't see the ruthless streak in Daniel. You never have. How did Neil get away—because I assume he got away. He isn't dead, is he?" The last question was asked calmly, with Chad's voice perfectly controlled as though he was only interested in the answer in an academic fashion.

"I let him go. I went behind Daniel's back and freed him." I neglected to add the part about Neil's absence leaving me and Dev vulnerable to Halfer's attack. "He ran. I tracked him down, but I can't get him to meet with me, yet. I'll get him back, Chad."

"See that you do, Zoey," Chad said. "I didn't sacrifice myself to have my lover treated this way. I expect him to be happy and whole when I return."

"I promise." I was a little afraid of this Chad. He was colder, infinitely harder. I hugged my arms to my chest because the room seemed chilly. "I love him, too. I want him back."

Chad shook his head, and suddenly he was himself again. He stood and pulled me into a hug. "I know you do, Zoey. I knew you would be the one looking for him. Tell him I love him when you succeed in finding him. Now let's get you back down to Dev. Stay close to him. Marini would just love to get you alone. He's been talking about how sweet you taste ever since the ball."

I frowned but let Chad open the door. I exited, leaving the vampire behind, my mind filled with doubts and worries.

135

Chapter Twelve

Marcus and Dev were waiting for me when I returned. Dev looked at me curiously, as though sensing my mood. He helped me down the last two steps, but I knew we wouldn't be talking about what had happened with Chad until we were alone again. I liked Marcus, but preferred to let the boys decide when and if to tell him anything. I'm not a spy. They tend to know when to talk and when to keep their mouths closed. Those are two lessons I never learned.

Marcus led us into a room that looked nothing like a parlor. It reminded me of the VIP section of a gentlemen's club complete with half-dressed attendants. The lights were low, creating a decadent atmosphere.

I immediately spotted Louis Marini holding court in the center of the room. He lounged back on a chaise, and when he caught sight of me, he gestured us over with an imperious wave of his hand.

I caught my breath as Marcus led me to the head of the Council. Louis Marini was the oldest vampire who lived in society. There were rumors that older vampires still existed, but they no longer lived among the humans. In vampire society, Louis Marini was practically a king. Unfortunately, he lacked the DNA necessary to crown himself. He would have been a handsome man, but there was a hardness to him that left me cold. His hair was dark brown, his eyes nearly black, and there was something vaguely reptilian about them. He was dressed in slacks and a black T-shirt that hugged his well-formed chest. As we approached, I realized there was a girl huddled next to him.

"Mrs. Donovan, I see Marcus has already sought you out," he said in a deep voice that sounded amused and annoyed at the same time. "I swear when you're around he becomes a sad little lapdog begging for your affection. Did he wait by the door so he could catch you as you entered?"

"I can't help but follow a beautiful woman around. When I no longer wish to I shall stake myself, for there will be no reason to walk the night," Marcus replied gallantly, pulling me down with him onto the opposite chaise. It was large and plush, and Dev settled himself on the other side of me, his arm going negligently around my waist.

"Prince." Louis acknowledged Dev with a satisfied nod. He took in every inch of Dev's well-dressed form. "I was pleased to see you again. I feared after the events of the ball, you would return to your *sithein*. It's good to see our *Nex Apparatus* hasn't frightened you away from vampire society."

"Oh, I think you'll find I don't scare so easily. It takes more than a couple of stab wounds to the gut to deter me from a lover I'm enjoying. I find Daniel to be a perfectly pleasant reason to stay in your society," Dev replied smoothly.

"Obviously," Marini said with an intimate smile, and I wondered which of the numerous sex acts he'd witnessed he was thinking of. It made me want to turn away, but I forced myself to remain calm. "Our Mr. Donovan seems to think he's your master."

Dev arched an eyebrow at the thought. "I'm content to play the minion as long as it suits me. I like variety, and this ménage of ours meets my needs. Daniel is very aggressive. He's everything one could want from a male. Zoey is a heavenly bit of femininity. I enjoy both, and I'm unwilling to deny myself either. Zoey and Daniel are somewhat liberated in their sexual thinking. I don't have to hide one from the other."

"I agree with you. I'm of the same persuasion. I admire males and females equally." Marini took in the low cut of my dress. "You're right about Mrs. Donovan, though she pretends to be demure and retiring when I'm around. Do I frighten you? I rather think not. I think you're behaving yourself, Mrs. Donovan, for your husband's sake. You can keep your mouth shut all you like, but your eyes tell a different tale. Your eyes flash fire, *chère*. In different times, you would have been a great courtesan holding court with the kings and nobles of the age."

"Is that a prostitute?" I was pretty damn sure it was. Dev's hand tightened slightly, a small warning about my temper.

"I suppose you would think so, *cara*," Marcus said with a smile as he reminisced. "But in my day, a great courtesan was practically a queen. When she reached a certain level, she was a maker of fashions, ruling her own salon with an iron fist. She was highly intelligent, beautiful and clever. Her conversation was as important and delightful as her skills in the bedroom. Unlike a wife in those days, one needed her permission to be welcomed to her bed. She chose her lovers with great care."

"Ahh," Marini said with great satisfaction, as though he had finally ferreted something out. "She reminds you of Elizabeth. I wondered if that was the fascination. She does have her stubborn will and her lovely body. Females in this age are far too thin. If I want a boy, I'll take a boy. When I want a woman, I want breasts and hips and curves."

Marcus's lips curled up in a chagrined expression. "I suppose she does remind me of her. Certainly she is similar in her demeanor. Elizabeth was a courtesan in Venice during my much younger years. She was also a companion."

"Your companion?" I knew so little about the Italian's long history.

"Oh, yes. I've had three over the years," Marcus confided. "Unlike Louis, I don't keep one at all times."

"Bah," Marini said dismissively. "I don't like the withdrawals. Why should I get sick because I'm immortal and a companion dies? I prefer to stay strong. Marcus simply becomes too attached and must mourn his loves. He's had several chances over the last hundred years or so to purchase a companion, but they're never perfect enough for him. He's far too picky."

"And you're not picky enough." Marcus pointed at the girl cowering on the chaise next to Marini. So young. I knew she was over eighteen or they wouldn't have taken her out of the Paris stronghold, but she looked younger. She reminded me of a little mouse with her large, frightened eyes. "How is she a companion to you? She can barely speak when you're around."

Marini rolled his eyes. "Her blood is good. That's what matters. It pales in comparison to Mrs. Donovan, but then she's rare. Of course, Rose also cries when I fuck her, so perhaps you're right, Marcus, and I should choose them with more care. Mrs. Donovan doesn't seem to mind a little rough sex."

Dev reached over and pulled me down to recline on his chest. I was grateful for his strong arms around me. He dropped a kiss on my ear. "I'm right here, sweetheart."

Without thinking, I brought my lips to his because I needed something sweet. When I looked back, Marini was staring at us.

"Donovan allows the two of you to play when he's not around?" There was a hard edge to the question. It reminded me that Vampire kind is jealous of what they consider theirs. Technically, Marini could kill Dev for even touching me like this, not to mention what he'd witnessed the two of us doing earlier. Only Daniel's permission saved us from a righteous kill.

Pulling me now firmly in his lap, Dev chuckled, and I could tell he'd decided to push through brazenly. I wrapped my arms around his neck and let his hand slide onto my knee. "As you said before, Mr. Marini, I'm a royal and a priest. I'm a powerful man in my own right. Daniel and I have an arrangement. I've placed my wealth and influence at his disposal, and in return, I have full rights to our lover. I tend to play by the rules at formal occasions. I assumed this was more informal. If I'm offending you by showing my affection, then I can certainly act in a more proper fashion."

"I believe after what we've seen tonight, Prince, that I'm aware of your affection for the girl. I think it would be difficult for you to behave in a proper fashion. Her master doesn't mind, so why should I? Please feel free to enjoy her. You make a lovely couple," Marini offered. "I very much enjoyed watching the two of you make love. I'm merely surprised that our *Nex Apparatus* is practical. He seems obsessed with his wife."

"I like Dev." I kept my voice calm, trying to follow Dev's lead. It was difficult because what I wanted to do was smack that nasty vampire across the face and then shove a stake in his heart. My life had been infinitely easier before Daniel had decided to change the whole freaking supernatural world. "And Danny likes him, too. They get along well. They're friends."

Marcus leaned toward his mentor. "She and Daniel were together before Daniel's turn."

"Yes, that explains much." Marini nodded. "Poor sap. The connection is much stronger when there was a human relationship before. It tends to give the companion the upper hand. You wouldn't find another vampire master so easy to handle."

"I don't intend to have another vampire master," I replied,

settling myself in Dev's arms. "I'm content with the one I have."

Marini pinned me with his black eyes. "You never can tell when your whole world can change. Don't worry your lovely head. The Council will always take care of their beautiful companions." He switched his stare to Dev. "We would also take care of our good friends. You might not mind belonging to a vampire, Prince."

I felt Dev stiffen behind me, but his voice remained casual. "Oh, I rather like belonging to myself. It's for the best, really. My brother already doesn't approve of my lifestyle. He's indulgent, of course. Just today he had lunch with my darling girl here."

I nodded, and that was easy because it was true. Marini didn't have to know that little meeting had eventually ended in a bloodbath. "I found the future king entertaining."

Especially when Daniel was attempting to kill him.

Dev continued. "He would prefer I settled down and performed my duties, but he is my brother. I'm afraid if he found out I had actually made myself some vampire's slave, you would be looking at a war with Faery. That might not be such a huge deal if it were just the Seelie, but I'm beloved by the Unseelie as well. I fit in with them better than my brother. I shall do what I've always done and seek my pleasure while it lasts and then move on."

I wish he didn't say that with such complete conviction. Sometimes Dev's acting skills scared me. I could never lie as well as he did, and I had to believe he was lying. Despite what Declan said, that necklace he'd given me felt like a commitment, and I was planning on holding him to it. If he tried to get bored with me, I would just have to liven up his life, and if he thought he could hide in some *sithein*, he would be surprised when I showed up to drag his ass back home.

Marcus stood up and offered me his hand. "Louis, I beg leave to dance with Mrs. Donovan. Daniel is probably close to ready for us and I haven't gotten my hands on her all evening."

Louis waved his hand dismissively. "Go. Paw the girl while her husband is gone. I'll stay here and talk further with the prince. He's an intriguing gentleman."

Marcus pulled me up, and Dev gave me an encouraging smile. I found myself on a small dance floor. The music was slower now and had a sultry beat. We were the only ones on the floor and many eyes were on us. Marcus pulled me close.

"I'm sorry for earlier, *cara*," he whispered against my ear. I could barely make out what he was saying. "I tried to talk Marini out of it, but he was most insistent. To tell you the truth, I believe he wanted to spy. The three of you together was a welcome distraction. I believe if you'd been doing something less entertaining, he might have looked into places we would have regretted."

"Well, at least it was for a good cause," I said sarcastically. I didn't like the thought that Marini was getting suspicious. If he'd spent any time at all in Dev's office, he would have found the laptop. Dev had it password protected, but that was anything but foolproof. There were also some interesting files in his safe. I was proof positive that his safe was not the most secure of locations. "He won't be able to try that again. Dev will make sure of it. He'll be a hell of a lot more careful now. I just wish you had coughed or something to give me a damn heads up."

Marcus smiled down at me, a devilish little look. "I'm afraid that I'm not a gentleman when it comes to you. I enjoyed the show far too much to allow it to end prematurely. It also pointed out some rather ugly truths to me. Devinshea isn't some whim on your part. He isn't a third indulging some perversity. You're in love with him as you love your husband."

"I do love him," I admitted freely. "He's as important to me as Daniel."

"I fear I shall have to love you from afar, *cara*," Marcus said wistfully. "It's probably better that way. I'm too much a man of my time."

"Which time is that, Marcus?" I let my voice get slightly louder. We could talk about this in the open.

"Long ago. I was born in Rome when there was still a senate."

"Ancient Rome." Something teased at the surface of my brain. There was something playing around there that I couldn't quite catch.

"I remember the bread and the circuses, and I certainly remember the coliseum," he mused with a smile. "Rome was fading somewhat by the time I was born. Its hidden history is fascinating. You wouldn't believe the wolves who ruled Rome. At one point, it was a werewolf stronghold."

"The Strong Arm of Remus," I whispered, figuring it out. I knew from mythology that Romulus and Remus were brothers and wolves. The legend was they had founded Rome. "Have you ever heard of an object called by that name?"

"Of course," Marcus said as though it should be self-evident. "It's a great legend."

"Halfer doesn't think so." I briefly gave him an overview of the way I spent my day. "The creature said he wanted me dead before July the fifteenth. I don't know what any of it means."

"Nor do I, *cara*. I'll think on it." His face fell as the other Council members began to leave. "Daniel is apparently ready for us. It's time for me to go. I'll call on you in the morning and tell you all I know about this object. For tonight, you and your Lancelot should leave. I'll attempt to make the meeting last as long as possible so Louis doesn't come looking for you again."

Marcus kissed my wrist and left the dance floor. I glanced around the parlor but somehow I'd gotten turned around. The vampire club was one of those odd places that seemed larger after a while. It was a type of magic some supernatural species use to confuse humans, and now standing there without Dev or Daniel, I was feeling mighty human. I was lost and I didn't recognize anyone. I took a deep breath and tried not to panic. It was all just an illusion. I found the bar and walked straight up to the man behind it. I only hoped he was human.

"How can I help you, mistress?" he asked.

"I'm a little turned around, I'm afraid," I admitted.

He nodded. "Yeah, that will happen to you. You're new?"

"It's my first time. My husband doesn't really like me spending a lot of time around other vamps."

"Well, ma'am, you should really stay close to a vampire until you're used to the place. If you have a physical connection to one of the vampires, then the place makes sense. If you're on your own, it can get confusing."

What he didn't have to say was why the place was confusing. If a human happened to find her way in, it would be difficult for her to get back out. She would be an easy meal. The club was a trap.

Someone could have mentioned that to me. It might have been nice for Marcus to deliver me to someone who could have helped me follow that advice of his. I decided to just stay put and sit myself on a barstool until Danny could come and lead me out. I glanced around, a little worried. I hoped the magic didn't work on faeries. Dev would look for me, and I didn't want him to get lost.

Suddenly there was a tap on my shoulder. I twisted the stool around to see Stacy Sears looking at me with a frown on her face.

"Mistress," she acknowledged.

I felt an unwelcome surge of sympathy for the girl. She was in a bad position, and Danny had placed her in an even worse one. He'd always been oblivious when it came to women who were interested in him. Danny had only ever been in love with me, and it apparently hadn't occurred to him that someone else could fall for him. It was ridiculous because he was gorgeous and kind, but it was just who he was. I didn't blame her at all for falling for him.

"How can I help you?" I asked politely, hoping we could both forget that I had almost smacked her for looking at my man. I needed to work on my anger issues.

"Marcus asked me to come find you." Stacy didn't quite meet my eyes. "He realized he left you. He forgets sometimes that you're human like the rest of us." There was the tiniest bitterness in that last statement, but I let it go. I would be bitter, too. "I was the only one without a duty. I can try to find someone else if I displease you."

I shook my head because that just seemed silly. "Can you take me to Mr. Quinn?"

"Yes, mistress," she replied. "Those are my orders. If you will follow me, he's waiting for you. Don't let your eyes stray too far. Things can fool you in here. The building itself wants you to stay. It will do what it can to trap you."

Jumping down from the barstool, I began to follow the blonde, not taking my eyes off her back. "How do you manage it?"

She glanced behind at me. "After a while, the magic recognizes you and stops trying to trap you. It's there for humans who wander in and could cause trouble. If you wander in uninvited, you really should expect to never leave. It's our way."

It wasn't my way. I thought some helpful bouncers might be just as effective, or maybe a well-placed exit sign. Several times a year, some adventurous human found their way down to Ether, but the club certainly didn't try to catch them and hope a club member needed some dinner. Our bouncers politely told the humans to go away. If they showed up more than once, one of the witches put the whammy on them and they forgot all about the experience. And though some of the plants in the grotto might shoot out from the walls and hold me down, it was always a nice experience. I doubted getting caught up in this strange place would ever end nicely.

It was difficult to keep my eyes straight because things kept happening just out of my peripheral vision. Little flashes of color or movement would try to catch my eye. Little whispers bid me to leave the path. A silky voice in my head promised great pleasure if I just snuck behind one of the doors.

Stacy took my hand and pulled firmly. "Ignore it."

I held on because I didn't dare let her leave me behind. I was going to kick some vampire ass when I got out of this place because I really didn't like being as scared I was in that moment.

Stacy smiled at me, and I didn't like the way her lips curved up. It looked a little like victory, and I hadn't realized we were playing a game. It was another mistake on my part. She opened a door and pushed me in.

"Here she is, master," she said. "Just as you ordered."

"Excellent." Louis Marini sat in a wing-backed chair.

The door closed behind me, and I suddenly wasn't worried about what the house would do to me anymore.

Chapter Thirteen

The problem with covert operations is the fact that everything is so damn secretive. It can be almost impossible to tell who knows what and how to react properly to a situation. The last thing you want to do is give away valuable information when the mark is really only trying to size you up a little.

There are three ways to handle a situation like the one I found myself in after nasty bitch Stacy led me into the lion's den. I could cry and beg and hope Marini didn't really know anything and was just looking for a forbidden snack. I could assume the bastard knew everything and I was about to get my ass drained. That scenario called for me to find the nearest available piece of wood and try to get it really pointy. The third method was to be patient and try to figure out what the hell was going on. While I actually preferred method number two, I settled for a restless patience.

"Mr. Marini, you wanted something from me?" I asked, keeping my voice somewhat steady but letting a little of my fear seep through. Louis Marini struck me as the kind of vampire who liked to be feared. When dealing with a man such as this, it's always best to provide him with what he wants or he tends to give you something to be afraid of.

Marini sat down on a plush sofa and offered me the seat next to him. I smoothed down the skirt of my dress and tried to sit in as ladylike a fashion as I could while also giving me an opportunity to run should the need arise. I was already thinking of how I could ditch my shoes. Jimmy Choo doesn't design with speed in mind. One of these days I was going to force the boys to run a mile in my stilettos and see if they still found them sexy.

Marini gave them a glance that told me he approved. "There are many things I would like from you, Mrs. Donovan. I'll settle for a little conversation."

"I thought we already had a little conversation this evening."

Marini regarded me thoughtfully. "No, we had a small exchange in which your lover controlled the dialogue. The men in your life are carefully controlling you around me. I noticed how the prince brought the conversation back to himself whenever you seemed to be ready to show any kind of personality."

"Perhaps the prince is simply extremely self-centered."

"Perhaps," Marini allowed with a frown that said he didn't believe it. "Royals tend to believe the world revolves around them, but I think he's protecting something. I don't know what that is, but I would like to. It occurred to me last year that you're in a powerful position, Mrs. Donovan."

I couldn't stop my sharp, somewhat bitter laugh. There was little about a companion that screamed power. We were to be pretty and feed our masters. We were not to cause trouble. "I assure you, Mr. Marini, I understand my place. It's been made clear to me that I'm property. If this is a chastisement then consider me chastened."

"And what would I be calling you to account for, Mrs. Donovan? Would it be the demon contract you signed?"

"That was an oral contract," I pointed out quickly. "I never actually signed anything."

"Or perhaps using our demon hosts to steal onto the Hell plane and release an angel from a powerful ally's palace?" His litany came out as an accusation, and I found myself getting defensive.

"Halfer was a crappy ally. He tried to steal your precious *Nex Apparatus*. I doubt he was going to have Daniel teach him arts and crafts. Daniel is a vampire killer. Halfer wanted to take out some vamps. And as for the accusations about setting the angel free, no one can prove that. But I have it on the highest authority that if I had pulled that job, Lucifer himself would have thanked me." He hadn't actually said anything vaguely resembling a thank you, but he also hadn't murdered me. Coming from him, it was practically a hug.

"Do you know the name Donna Johnson?" Marini asked, his tone telling me he already knew the answer.

"I might have heard of her." It was an alias I used from time to time.

"From what I understand, she's wanted for questioning in a multiple homicide in a small county in Arkansas. There's a police sketch of her. She bears a remarkable resemblance to you, though the police can find no actual record of her arrest or that of her strikingly attractive partner. Daniel was forced to call in a clean-up crew after the fact. Daniel did an excellent job on the sheriff, but one of the deputies remembered you. He wanted to call in the FBI. You won't have any problems now. The cleaners are very thorough. We don't usually have to send them in to clean up after a companion." Marini seemed merely curious, but there was an undercurrent to this conversation I obviously didn't understand yet. "Was your accomplice the prince?"

"Yes." I replied honestly because he seemed to know everything already. I only lied when I was damn sure I could get away with it. I also needed to protect Chad. He had been the one putting the whammy on the authorities, not Daniel. "I'm sure the Council vetted me before I married Daniel. I'm a thief, Mr. Marini. This is the twenty-first century. A woman tends to keep her career even after she's married. And just to set the record straight, I didn't kill those witches. That was another demon. I've been completely demon free for seven months. That twelve-step program is working."

"See, if your prince were here I would not be having this amusing conversation with you," Marini said. "He would have pulled you or pushed you, and your charming mouth would have closed. Perhaps I would have believed Daniel and the prince were enamored of your mere beauty, but then we come to the problem of Marcus. I've known Marcus for almost two thousand years, and not once has he lost his head over a beauty with no brain. Marcus likes the clever ones. Marcus loves the difficult ones. Your husband can try to present you as a lovable piece of fluff, but I think any woman with a criminal record like yours has to have a backbone."

"I believe you'll find I don't have a record of any kind." I'd worked hard to not have a record. The only time I'd been caught by the cops was in Arkansas and that was because I refused to leave Dev behind.

"I assure you, you have a long record with the Council, and we count far more than any human authorities." Marini leaned forward. "When Daniel Donovan turned, he was an unassuming college student with a flawless academic record. He might have ambled through school, but he was certainly not planning a life of crime. That happened after he reconnected with you."

"Or maybe it happened after you turned him into a freaking assassin." My patience was wearing thin. I stood up and glared down at the head of the Council. "Where is the holier-than-thou attitude coming from, Marini? Are you legit? I'm betting that little girl you chew on every night wasn't legal when you started gnawing. What's your record like? Let's start with murder because I'm betting you've gone there and I'm thinking it wasn't just self-defense. There's kidnapping and forced prostitution."

"Prostitutes tend to get paid, Mrs. Donovan. We do not pay our companions."

"Then let's call it what it is—slavery. Have you read a history book in the last couple of centuries? That was outlawed a long time ago. I might have a record somewhere, but I'm sure it pales in comparison to the atrocities you've committed over the years."

"You assume I am displeased with you," Marini said, completely nonplussed with my show of temper. "That's not the case. I've spent the last several months wondering what to do about you, Mrs. Donovan. I thought about arranging for a convenient accident, but I decided against it. I think it might make Daniel difficult to control. You're the best measure we have against his threat. Any other method requires us to kill him. You alone have the power to force him to comply. I've decided to bring you into the fold, so to say."

Now I was really scared. I didn't think I would like being in the fold. I was damn sure I didn't want to get pulled any further into the Council's machinations. Unfortunately, I didn't think this was going to be the kind of job you get to turn down.

"It occurs to me that you could be an asset. There are certain items I'm interested in acquiring, and I believe you're the only one who can do the job. You'll be allowed into places a vampire cannot go."

"You want me to steal from Faery," I said flatly. Vampires had been forbidden to enter the mounds centuries before. It was the only place I could think of where I would be more effective than a vampire.

"See, I knew you were a smart girl," he said, looking satisfied. "I was pleased to hear the prince's brother is attempting reconciliation. It will make it much easier on you. Tell the prince you wish to see his home. Tell him you need a vacation. I don't care how you do it, but get him to take you to his mother's palace. I'll send my emissary to you with the full details in a few weeks."

148

"Why the hell would I do this for you?" I asked more to myself than him.

"You will do it because if you don't, I'll kill your husband." Marini's tone was flat, and he shrugged a little as though he didn't really care either way.

"You and what army?" The Council hadn't had a hell of a lot of luck hurting Danny before.

The head of the Council pulled out a small, palm-sized box, and I knew deep in my heart that he was about to change the game. "This is the only army I need. I'm no fool. I remember how hard it was to kill the last king who rose. That was a long time ago, but modern technology has made it so much easier. I'm going to tell you something that no one else knows. While your husband was with the Council during his training, I realized how dangerous he could be to me. I had a small device surgically attached to his heart during a medical examination. Daniel doesn't remember it. He was placed under a strong spell for the procedure and, of course, he heals quickly. If I push this little button, a lethal dose of colloidal silver enters his heart and then I no longer have to worry about another king. I prefer to use Mr. Donovan's talents for as long as possible, but when he becomes troublesome, I will push this button."

"You could be lying. Vampire bodies expel foreign objects." My hands were shaking at the thought of Marini holding Daniel's life in his hands.

"Not if they're placed there with very strong black magic. I've been working with a group of witches for years, preparing for a time when one like Daniel would rise. You can call me a liar all day, but are you willing to test it? I don't think so. I think you love your husband. If I have read the situation incorrectly, I'm more than happy to get rid of Daniel. I can find another way to force you to do my bidding." A smug smile crossed his face as he replaced the box in his pocket. "You have a father, I believe. There's always the prince."

"You know I'll do it," I admitted quietly because I didn't doubt Louis Marini would do exactly what he said he would.

"Excellent. I'll send you the information in a few weeks. Use that time to get the prince to agree to grant you access to his *sithein*. I don't buy his 'I belong to me' crap. Nor do I believe he belongs to

Daniel. That prince belongs to you as Daniel belongs to you. I'm not such a fool that I can't see who my real opponent is. I've certainly lived long enough to know it would be an enormous mistake to underestimate you merely because you're female. Most of the deadliest creatures I've encountered were women."

I found myself unwilling to praise him for his liberated attitude. I was far too busy wondering if I could get that little box out of his hand. It had been a while since I played the pickpocket, but I figured I could still do it.

Marini laughed, easily discerning my intentions. "Don't even try it. It's not the only one tuned to the proper frequency. I would advise you not to try to remove the device either. It will only cause it to engage. Do the job."

"And then what?"

"And then you will do the next job and the one after that," Marini answered. "Would you prefer I lie and tell you I'll give you the box after you do this one little job? I doubt you would believe me. I promise you I'll treat you fairly, Zoey. I'll call you Zoey from now on because I think we're past formalities. Make yourself useful to me, Zoey, and we will get on well. You can keep your husband and your lover and other than the occasional job, you'll be left in peace."

I doubted that, but what was I supposed to do? I needed to survive the interview first and foremost. When I got out of this room intact, I could start worrying about how I was going to get that thing out of Daniel's body. Then I could figure out how I was going to kill Marini. I nodded my reluctant consent. One minute Marini was on the couch and the next he was invading every inch of my space.

"Then we have a deal." His face was so close to mine I heard the light snap of his fangs as they popped out. I tried to take a step back but the wall was against me, and there was nowhere to go. "We should seal the deal, little thief. In your world you would do it with a handshake. We're not in your world."

I held myself still as he rubbed his face against my neck, breathing in the scent. I felt the sharpness of his fangs graze my vulnerable flesh and shrank back. He chuckled and pulled his head away, his body still pinning mine against the wall. He obviously enjoyed my discomfort on a base level.

Still laughing, he pulled my left wrist to his mouth and there was a short, sharp sting before his tongue licked the blood he had spilled. When he was done, he let me go.

"You are so sweet. It's truly intoxicating. You should run away now, Zoey," he said softly. "Before I change my mind and decide your blood is worth more than your talents."

I was out of the room before he could say anything else. As I shut the door behind me, I ran directly into Chad.

"Are you all right?" He had to hold on to my shoulders because I was anything but steady.

"Where's Dev?" I didn't really want to answer his question. I was so past all right it was ridiculous. I was shaking and my wrist hurt. I wanted to go home and forget the evening ever happened.

"He's waiting in the limo," Chad explained, taking my hand and leading me down the hall. "I had to convince him not to tear up the place looking for you. He wants to have a few words with Marcus about leaving you."

I would have a few choice words for Marcus when I saw him tomorrow as well. "Did you know Marini was going to corner me?"

Chad's face was blank as he decided how to answer me. "I did. I thought it best you went in cold. I have to play things close to the vest when I'm around him and I'm almost always around him. I've become valuable to the Council," Chad said, helping me down the stairs. "Until everything is ready, I would suggest you play along with whatever Marini wants. I'll do what I can from this side to help you."

"He's sending someone with some information for me in a few weeks," I told him. "If there's any way…"

"I'll try, Zoey," he agreed. "I think he trusts me enough. Watch your back and find my boy."

I nodded and then we were in the lobby. I practically ran out of the club, slamming the door behind me. The heat of the night should have been oppressive, but I let it fill my lungs as I took my first deep breath in hours. In a second, Dev was out of the limo and wrapping his arms around me. He took me back to the car and securely locked the doors but made no move to tell the driver to leave. It was comforting to know I didn't have to ask. He would rather wait all night than leave Daniel here.

I sat in Dev's lap, feeling safer than I had in hours, and told him everything. I didn't leave out a thing, even the fact that I was supposed to steal something from his mother's kingdom. I told him about the tiny bomb on Daniel's heart. It was such a relief to talk to Dev because I knew he would immediately start working on the problems and I could concentrate on what I do best.

I was half asleep, resting on the limo's plush seat, when Daniel finally opened the door. The minute he was seated, the car pulled away, and I heard the two talking softly. Daniel tried to keep his voice down so as not to wake me, but there was no mistaking his fury.

"Give me one good reason, Dev," he said in a low growl. "Give me one reason I don't go back there and kill that son of a bitch right now."

"Well, for one, he'll press a button and your heart will explode," Dev pointed out. "We should probably come up with a way around that before you go berserker on him."

"I'll do it during the day. After the way I fed tonight, I'll be up by noon."

"Even if you could find his resting place—and I think he'll probably hide—we have no idea what safeties he's put in place with that device. He could have any number of ways to kill you if he's suddenly gone. Then there's the fact that if we take out the Council now, we run the risk of all-out war that would risk the human population. Get your alliances in place and then we can move. Get the wolves and I'll get Faery and then we can kill them all."

Daniel cursed and sat back, but he knew Dev was right.

"I'll contact Declan tonight," Dev said. "I'll talk to him in the morning. We meet with the wolves in a few weeks. It could all be over by the end of summer."

"Dev, you know what to do if he uses that thing," Daniel said.

"She'll be protected," Dev assured him. "I'll make my brother understand. I'll get consent one way or another, and then we won't have to worry about it. If they try to come for her, they can fight all of Faery."

I watched, my sleepy eyes loving every bit of them, and I knew I would do whatever it took to protect my men. I would play Marini's game, but I was going to find a way to change the rules.

Chapter Fourteen

Zack was on me before I even closed the door to the office the next morning.

"You want another shot, Zoey? You want to try to take me out this morning?" Zack gave his chest a masculine thump as he advanced toward me. "Let's try it again and see who ends up unconscious on the floor."

I grinned down at my former bodyguard because I found the situation entirely amusing. "Wow, Zack. That little nap did nothing to help your disposition. Maybe I should tranq you again."

Zack growled and seemed just about to change and chase me down when Lee pulled him away from the stairs. "Now, Zack, you should be thanking Zoey. You no longer have to spend every minute of the day following her around the mall. I thought you'd be happy to get reassigned to Quinn. Now you can worship him from up close."

Zack gave his brother a shit-eating grin as I joined them. "We'll see how you like having to follow Zoey. You won't be able to prowl around like you prefer, brother. Not when you're her primary baby-sitter. You have to keep eyes on her every minute because she's like a two-year-old following the first shiny object that catches her attention."

I rolled my eyes. "That's not true."

"Is, too."

"Is not."

"Both of you stop it." Lee got in between us and turned his attention to me. "Zoey, hold still." He walked around me, lifting his head and breathing in long passes, filling his lungs up. "I need to get your scent."

Werewolves make a big deal about scents. They're connoisseurs of smells. What smells awful to a human is merely different to a wolf. They don't make judgments or play favorites. Scent is simply a way to view the world or, in Lee's case, a way to do his job.

Zack crossed his arms over his chest and watched with glee as

Lee invaded my space. He rubbed his nose in my hair and across my neck, causing me to get goose bumps wherever he ran his sniffer. He held his arms tightly to his sides, not allowing himself to touch me at all.

Pure amusement lit Zack's eyes. "You want Lee, you get a serious wolf. I swear he's more wolf than human sometimes. He'll smell you like this three times a day."

"You would, too, if you wanted to be serious about your freaking job, Zack," Lee grumbled. "She's my responsibility. Her scent should be around me all the time. I should know it like I know the smell of my own home. I should be able to track her for miles because I know every nuance of her. You rely on that damn vamp blood, but it can't replace memorizing every goddamn inch of her body. Now be quiet. I'm concentrating."

I stood there and let Lee sniff me, feeling only vaguely uncomfortable as he ran his nose down my arms and into my arm pits. I'd cleaned up and used all the products a hygienic female should use, so I tried to be tolerant. I tried not to let Zack know how weird it all felt until, damn it, Lee just had to drop to his knees and go there. He put his damn nose right in my girl parts. I slapped his curly brown head.

He frowned up at me as Zack laughed out loud, practically bending in half. Lee's eyes were impatient, and he looked at me like I was an idiot. "It's the place where your scent's the strongest. Why do you think dogs try to get their noses there?"

"It's private," I said, blushing.

"Not if I'm guarding you, it isn't," Lee replied, now starting on my legs. "Don't you think I'm trying anything funny, sister. I assure you I don't have any designs on you. The last thing I need in my life is some high-maintenance princess with a criminal mind and two damn husbands."

I chose not to mention that I only had one husband. Dev was just my boyfriend. Lee continued on his quest to embarrass me to the fullest extent possible.

He sniffed my feet and then glanced over at Zack. "You should try it sometime. You would be able to tell all kinds of things about the client. It's harder for them to lie when you really know their scent."

"Please try it on Dev." I would really love to see how my green-eyed boy handled a sniffing wolf.

"So what's the report on the brat?" Zack ignored me completely.

"Well, there's citrus, both soap and body lotion. She used something minty on her teeth. Shampoo, conditioner, and some other product but not hair spray. There's the faint hint of sandalwood, but I bet that's from Quinn. She likes her coffee black. She had something for breakfast with maple syrup. Her clothes were washed with soap, not dry-cleaned." Lee was just warming up. "She had sex with Quinn this morning, probably in the shower, but she was with Donovan last night, maybe both. She isn't completely human, by the way."

Zack looked interested in that last bit. I was trying to deal with the fact that my bodyguard was always going to know when I had sex. I hadn't really minded when it was Neil because I would have talked about it with him, but Lee wasn't my gay husband.

"She's a companion." Zack leaned in now and I tried to pull back. He took a deep whiff. "You're right. I've smelled that before. She smells a little like…"

"Felix Day," Lee pronounced, and the brothers nodded at each other, obviously satisfied at solving that mystery. I chose to try to move past the morning's embarrassing incident. There was a reason I smelled like Felix Day. A companion has strong angelic DNA, but I didn't want to hear a bunch of crap about how unangelic I acted, so I kept my mouth shut.

"Well, I'm glad for you, Zack," I said. "I think you and Dev will be very happy together. Now you can kiss his ass all you like."

"I'd rather have you kiss my ass, lover," Dev announced, walking into the club. He was followed closely by himself. Declan was in full-on Dev mode, appearing to be wearing the same suit, with the same shortish hair. "I'll just let Zack save it on occasion, but I assure you, your lips are the only ones allowed to touch me there."

I walked across the room and faced him with my hands on my hips. God, my heart beat harder the minute he walked in the room, and something fell in place for me. I needed him the way I needed Daniel. But I wasn't going to let him know that. There were things that had gotten lost in the craziness of the previous evening. "What about those six priestesses your brother kept going on about? Are they not allowed to kiss your assets?"

"I have been informed I was horribly mistaken about those priestesses," Declan said smoothly. "Please forgive me for the mistake. Devinshea left them behind when he left his temple. He has only one goddess now and intends to keep it that way."

So the boys had their stories straight now. I wouldn't be able to break them up. "He better keep it that way because he doesn't want to piss me off. I consider it cheating even if it's part of a religious ceremony. Those priestesses are going to have to find another priest."

"Of course, my mistress," Dev said with a smile. "Consider thousands of years of Fae tradition tossed aside."

"See that it is," I replied before turning to the other one. "What did I tell you about the glamour, Declan? I can't handle two of him."

Declan smiled as he dropped the illusion. "I don't believe it for a moment, Zoey. From what I've heard, you handle two men with great efficiency."

"And flexibility," Dev offered. He turned to the wolves and regarded Zack with a businesslike demeanor. "Zack, we're having some meetings today. I'm lunching with my brother and then we have club business to attend to. At dusk, we need to head out to the farm."

Zack pulled his professional persona around him the minute Dev stepped into the room. He held his phone in his hand, his fingers moving across the screen. "Yes, I downloaded the schedule, sir. I made arrangements with Albert to have lunch delivered from your favorite restaurant. It will be served in the private dining room in twenty minutes. I have a bottle of wine chilling."

I looked back at Lee. His brother was the consummate professional in his expensive suit and silk tie. Zack's haircut had cost at least two hundred dollars. Lee was in old jeans and a wrinkled T-shirt with some sort of beer ad on the front. His hair needed a trim and his boots were worn. I smiled back at my wolf and let the sarcasm flow. "What are our luncheon arrangements today, Lee? Have you called The Mansion to have it catered in?"

"I don't know what that is, Zoey," Lee admitted, his low voice a rumble. "If you want some lunch, I think I saw some peanut butter and bread in the kitchen. While you're at it, make me a couple of sandwiches, too. I can always eat." Lee punctuated his statement by reaching behind his ear and scratching quickly back and forth. He sighed when he was satisfied he'd taken care of the itch. Zack was right. He was more wolf than man.

"You see, this is why I fired him." Dev shuddered a bit. "He's insubordinate and won't take care of you the way he should. He's fine as straight-on muscle, but you need an assistant as well. Let me hire someone who knows how to dress, sweetheart."

"I'm her bodyguard, Quinn, not her nanny." Lee didn't sound like he cared about the man who paid his salary. "How the hell am I supposed to make sure she doesn't get killed if I'm always running her errands or making sure her hair appointments are scheduled? I'll leave that to you. You're the one who treats her like your damn Barbie doll."

Dev looked the wolf over seriously and then regarded me. "Are you sure this is what you want, Zoey? I can have more reasonable guards here in an hour. They'll take care of you the way you deserve."

Lee frowned, an extremely taciturn expression. He wasn't going to give Dev an inch, and he certainly wasn't about to do anything so energetic as defend himself.

"Lee is fine, Dev." I had to fight for my wolf because he definitely wouldn't fight for his own ass. "I'm good with him. He promises not to let me get horribly murdered, and I promise not to shoot him."

"I told you that won't work a second time, Zoey," Lee shot back. "I'll take you out first."

"If you lay one fucking hand on her I swear…" Dev started, and I pushed him back, getting between the two.

I rolled my eyes at Lee, who was not one bit impressed with my lover's show of temper. "You could give me something to work with here."

Lee shrugged. "Donovan already gave me the whole 'death and dismemberment' spiel. I get it." He cast his brown eyes at Declan. "I'm actually surprised to see you in one piece. I figured after the way you pawed his wife that Donovan would kick your ass back to Faery. Guess he's more patient than I thought."

"Not at all." Declan's hair flowed down his chest in a midnight waterfall. "He did indeed kick my ass, as you say. He took out my entire retinue. It was quite impressive. He threatened to kill me if I ever so much as glance his lovely wife's way again. I believe the vampire thinks I am no longer a threat. He should know that I am made of sterner stuff than that."

"We Quinns never allow something like death to deter us when it comes to sex," Dev admitted.

"Not at all," his brother agreed. "There are some things worth dying over. I took everything the vampire king said to heart. I then sent for reinforcements and bought better weaponry. I shall be ready to meet the vampire at his earliest convenience, and this time I shall be victorious. I shall reap my reward."

"He's talking about you, lover," Dev pointed out. I was staring at Declan. I really couldn't help it because his hair was so beautiful. I was thinking about how lovely his hair was and how good it would look on Dev. Dev's eyes suddenly went wide. "You're staring at his hair."

"It's pretty," I offered lamely.

"Oh, *cara*," Marcus said from the doorway. He had a damn good sense of timing. "Now you've done it. Don't you know how faeries prize their hair? It's a man's crowning glory and something a lover would appreciate about him. Your Lancelot must feel insecure with his short hair when in the presence of his brother's beauty."

I frowned at the vampire, who always knew how to make an entrance. "Dev's hair is beautiful. I didn't know I wasn't supposed to admire Declan's. It's just really pretty and very soft."

"You touched it?" Dev practically screamed the question.

Declan sighed with obvious satisfaction. "She stroked me with her little hands. It was pleasurable. Her hands are almost as soft as her lips."

Dev bore down on me, every bit as enraged as Daniel could get. "You want to talk about cheating, lover? That was cheating. You do not touch his hair. You do not kiss him. Just because he looks like me doesn't make him a freebie. You stay out of his bed."

I looked up at him, my eyes wide because Dev never got jealous. "I didn't know touching his hair was a big deal. And I didn't kiss him. He kissed me. It was how I knew he wasn't you."

Dev stared down at me for a minute and then his lips quirked up. "Just how was my brother's kiss different from mine?" He asked the question with the certainty of a man who knew he was going to like the answer.

I smiled up at him because I had him now. How could the man be insecure after what I'd done to him in the shower not an hour before? I wrapped my arms around his neck and pushed myself up on my toes to get as close as I could. "Well, Declan's kiss was fine, but it didn't make me melt and it didn't make me want to lock myself around him and do anything he asked of me."

He ran his hand along my neck, palming the nape, pulling me close until his mouth hovered above mine. I could feel the heat from his body. It always made me warm. "See that your fingers stay out of my brother's hair. I'll begin growing mine immediately."

I nodded and then Dev was back at his brother's side as though nothing had happened.

"I did not try very hard," Declan admitted. "The next time, I shall attempt to make her melt as well. She is lovely, brother. I do envy you. Her body reminds me of that woman we shared in Paris when we snuck away to the human brothel."

Dev smiled wistfully. "She had beautiful breasts as well. They bounced, but not as nicely as Zoey's do. Come, brother. We'll have lunch and I'll regale you with stories of my amorous adventures with my mistress."

They walked out with Zack trailing behind, and I shook my head at Marcus. "I know we're supposed to talk this morning, but I think I should go and monitor that little discussion. Afterward, we need to talk about what happens when you leave me alone in a damn vampire club."

"I am sorry about that, *cara*. I didn't think." Marcus held up a newspaper advertisement. "But I can make up for my mistake. I think you'll find what I have for you to be even more compelling than Devinshea's conversation with his brother."

The ad was half a page and invited all of the Metroplex to come to the Kimbell Art Museum starting on July fifteenth for the opening of a new exhibition. "Treasures of Ancient Rome" promised to be spectacular.

So Halfer thought the Strong Arm of Remus was going to be on display and he planned to steal it. There was only thing to do—steal it first myself.

I sighed and looked back at Lee. "We'll have to get that lunch to go. We're going to Fort Worth."

Lee watched as Dev and the others left the room. When he was sure we were alone, he turned on Marcus. He moved forward in two quick steps and his hands were on Marcus's lapels. He picked up the vampire, lifting him high into the air and slammed him onto one of the tables with a violent force. I was surprised the table held up under the pressure. He pressed Marcus against the wood with one hand and the other became a wickedly sharp claw right above Marcus's heart.

"Lee, what the hell is going on?" The suddenness of his violence shocked me. He'd moved almost faster than I could see, and Marcus had no chance at avoiding him.

"Yes, I would rather like to know myself," Marcus added blandly, though his fangs were out and his body tense. "Are you a hunter or an assassin?"

Lee's eyes were dark as he stared at the vampire. "Like I said to my brother, I'm responsible for her now. I want to know if you're the vamp who left the marks on her wrist. Healing skin smells different even when the process is shortened because the victim is on vamp blood. Those marks might not be visible, but I know they're there. She can't hide them from me."

"She's married to a vampire," Marcus pointed out logically. "He does feed from her."

"Not from her wrist he doesn't," Lee snarled. "Donovan likes it from the neck or the groin on his wife. It's the neck or the wrist from the faery. I know my employer's habits. Zoey's a good girl despite the whole bigamy thing. She doesn't cheat on her boys. So if it wasn't Donovan then some vamp forced himself on her. If that was you, then we're going to see what you look like with your heart on the other side of your chest."

"It wasn't Marcus, Lee." I wished his senses weren't so damn good. There was no way Zack would have caught that. I'd told Dev everything, but we'd decided to leave that part out when discussing the night with Daniel. I was afraid no amount of good sense would have stopped Daniel from marching back into the club and confronting Marini if he knew. The sight of that little box in Marini's hand made me keep my mouth closed. "Daniel was called to the club last night. While he was in a meeting, one of the vampires cornered me and had a little snack. It was no big deal. It's nothing I can't handle."

"Name, Zoey," Lee said through clenched teeth as he took his hands off Marcus.

Marcus sat up and straightened his clothes. "I believe you will find it was Louis Marini. I wondered why he was thirty minutes late. He said he was with his companion. I should have been more suspicious since he'd obviously showered and changed clothes. He didn't want Daniel to smell Zoey on him."

"Where will I find him?" Lee asked, his voice tight.

I shook my head. "You can't kill him, Lee. He's the head of the Council, and if you kill him, it brings hell down on all of our heads. We aren't ready for that yet. We just need another couple of months and then he won't bother us anymore."

"I don't like politics, Zoey," Lee growled. "I don't want my hands tied because your husband would rather let you get assaulted than handle his business."

"Daniel doesn't know and he's not going to," I stated implacably. "I understand that it's your job to protect me, but this is not negotiable. If you can't allow me to handle this then you need to go back to Nevada. You won't have to worry about politics again. I'll find someone else to guard me."

Marcus watched the two of us. "I believe, wolf, that if you had been with her Marini would have found it difficult to assault her. They made a mistake sending her in without a dedicated guard. It's too easy to separate her from Devinshea. He must play the political game. And Zoey is right to keep this from Daniel. He would likely behave poorly. Daniel might not be ready for this fight, but neither is Louis. If you stay at her side Louis may still corner her, but he will find it difficult to force himself on her."

Lee stared, obviously unhappy with his choices, but he finally relented. "Fine. You don't go into a place like that again without me. He gets anywhere near you and you give me a 9-1-1. I'll be there before he can sink his fangs in. Is that understood?"

I nodded. "I'll call you, but Lee, you have to understand that this is the nature of the game we're playing. It's too important. It's not like we're doing this for fun. Our lives are on the line and so is the freedom of every wolf you know. If I need to sacrifice to keep us all free then that's what I'll do."

"I believe you, and that's why I'll protect you," Lee replied. "Now go make us some sandwiches because it's thirty damn miles to Fort Worth and I'm hungry."

I started toward the kitchen. "You're a crappy employee, Lee."

"Yeah," he admitted. "But I'll be damn good at keeping you alive."

Chapter Fifteen

Having really good intelligence is important to any job but crucial when it comes to being a thief. While a guy robbing a random house might be comfortable picking up anything that catches his eye, the real professionals want to know exactly where the object of their desire is kept and how much crap they're going to have to get through to get it.

Casing a place you intend to rob is completely necessary, though there are certain precautions you should take. When entering an establishment ripe with security measures, a modest disguise is called for. It doesn't have to be anything along the lines of *Mission Impossible*. A hat will do to hide the color of one's hair, and it is easy enough to make sure your face doesn't get caught on camera. In most places, the security measures are out in the open. They're meant to deter the casual thief and, in the case of an art museum, to discourage patrons from getting too close to the masterworks. This open security is a big mistake when dealing with someone like me. It just lets me know exactly what I need to take out in order to get my prize.

I entered the Kimbell Art Museum, sweeping my hair forward in an attempt to partially cover my face. A throng of visiting tourists surrounded me and it was easy to get lost in the midst of art lovers, harried parents, and teens who paid way more attention to their cell phones than the masterpieces on the walls. The first floor held a portion of the standing collection and the offices of museum employees. Directly to the back, behind the front desk, were the stairs that led to the second floor and the primary exhibit spaces. Right now, the choice space was taken up with an exhibit of Italian Renaissance masters.

Glancing around, it was easy to see that the museum relied on cameras and human security. There was a small camera in every corner and, mounted slightly below it, a motion detector for nighttime security. Both would be so easy to take out it was ridiculous. Getting in would be the hard part. I glanced above me and was impressed by the thick concrete overhead. No ceiling access for this thief. If I wanted in, I would have to use a door, and those would be heavily guarded.

On the drive over in Marcus's rented BMW convertible, I decided that the best plan of action was to find out when the exhibit was being moved into its new home. Hijacking a truck might be easier than tackling the museum. I nodded at Marcus as we entered the building with its scalloped arches. He approached the front desk and knew exactly what to do.

"Hello, I'm Marcus Vorenus." Marcus didn't bother with an alias because after he was gone, no one would quite be able to remember what he looked like or exactly what he'd said. Vampire persuasion was a remarkable tool. "I believe you'll find I have an appointment with your director."

He didn't, but sure enough when Suzy Receptionist studied her empty schedule, it was right there for her eyes only. She smiled up at the immaculate Italian and promised her director would be with him in a moment.

"I don't get all this painting stuff," Lee said as he walked past some of the world's masterworks. He stopped at a Matisse. "I could do that."

"I doubt it." I studied the Gauguin next to the Matisse and found myself drawn into the self-portrait.

"Don't look too long, *cara*," Marcus warned, walking up behind me. "Paul was a bit of a wizard. He liked to place pieces of his soul in his self-portraits. See, he's winking at you."

Sure enough, those black eyes blinked. If Marcus hadn't pointed it out, I would have thought it was a trick of the light. Now I stepped back, slightly disturbed at the thought.

"Hello, Paul." Marcus waved at the painting. "I was never so happy to be a daywalker as the time I spent in Tahiti with Gauguin. He knew how to party, as you would say."

"See, that's just creepy." Lee studied the painting like it was something about to attack. "I always liked that one of the dogs playing poker though."

I sidestepped the issue of Lee's taste in art as I inspected the gallery and wondered what the other paintings were doing. There are times that knowledge isn't power, it's just scary.

"Mr. Vorenus." A small-statured man with a slight potbelly and wire-framed glasses came through the glass doors leading to the business offices. "I apologize, but I have no record of an appointment with you. Do you mind my asking what this is about?"

"Of course you remember, Stanley," Marcus said reassuringly, pushing his persuasion directly at the smaller man. We had tracked down the director's name on the Internet.

Stanley smiled widely and put his hand out for Marcus to shake. "How silly of me to have forgotten. It's good to see you, Marcus. Come on back to my office and we can catch up."

We were led through the corridors and into the cool confines of the museum director's office. I kept my face as forward as possible so no one would be able to remember me when we left. Once the door closed behind us, Marcus dropped the happy pretenses and got down to some serious persuasion. One minute our new friend was smiling and happy, and the next his face was a complete blank and the room was filled with pulsing talent.

I glanced up at Marcus, and his eyes were dark and large as he worked his magic. "You can ask him your questions now, *cara*. He'll answer honestly and forget you were ever here."

"Have you seen the Treasures of Ancient Rome exhibit?" It had already shown in New York and Chicago.

The director's voice held no emotion as he answered. "Yes. I saw it in Chicago. We had already negotiated to bring it here, and I wanted to get a team up there to figure out how to design the space for the exhibit. We spent several days with the artifacts."

"Was there anything at all unusual about the artifacts?"

"They're very old," he replied. "They date from the Roman Republic and the Empire periods. The collection consists of mostly statuary, sculptures, housewares, and jewelry. Some of the textiles are extremely fragile. We'll have to keep an eye on the humidity to preserve them."

I would have to be more specific. "Did anyone in your group notice any of the artifacts for odd reasons? Anything stand out as more intriguing than the rest? Did anyone mention that one of the artifacts made them uncomfortable or perhaps called to them in a way?"

Often with truly arcane objects, the item itself gives off a specific energy that even humans can feel. It can call to the human or repulse them, depending on what the object is supposed to do.

"There was one item. Brandy commented on it," he said in that monotone. "It was a sculpture. She didn't like it. I didn't understand because it was a wonderful example of the time period. She said the eyes bothered her. She refused to be in the room with it after a while."

"Was it of a wolf?" Marcus asked.

"Yes," came the reply. "It was a wolf in marble. The wolf is devouring a woman."

That was what I needed. Now I needed the wheres and hows. It took time to set up an exhibit, so the pieces were coming to Fort Worth weeks before the actual opening date. It was a simple thing to get the director to print off all the arrangements the museum had made with the security company that would transport the exhibit to Fort Worth. I knew all the contact information, the dates of transfer, the name of the driver who would be in charge, and the time the shipment was expected to arrive at each checkpoint. I would steal the artifact before it ever made it to the museum, long before Halfer had planned to get his hands on it.

I tucked the papers into my bag and thought about how much easier my career was with a vampire around. I could have gotten the information, but it would have taken me weeks to do it, and I would have had to hire a hacker which costs money and left me open to the perils of working with contractors.

I nodded to Marcus, letting him know I had everything I needed. "We thank you for your time, Stanley. You will take a rest now. The day's been long and you're tired. You'll awake in an hour or so and remember nothing that has happened."

The director sat down in his plush chair and was snoring almost immediately.

I was impressed. "Marcus, if Daniel ever decides to give up the game, you're welcome on my crew."

* * * *

Thirty minutes later, we sat on the lawn of the museum under the shade of the large oaks close to the fountains. Lee had crossed the street and bought a bag of burgers and fries of which I had one and he downed four.

Marcus had magnanimously sat beside me through it all, chatting about his life in ancient Rome. Lee lay back in the grass, his stomach finally full. He seemed so content lying there that I reached out a hand to rub his belly.

"Don't even think about it, sister." Lee growled, not bothering to open his eyes. "I bite."

"Neil used to let me rub his belly." Neil would make little sounds of complete contentment when Sarah or I would rub his belly. He always claimed it helped him sleep.

"I'm not Neil," Lee pointed out.

"He used to let me rub him behind his ears, too."

"No petting, Zoey," Lee ordered.

"I will let you pet me all you like, *cara*," Marcus announced with a smile.

"God, not another one." Lee looked up, his brown eyes wary. "I spent all day yesterday watching that faery try to get in her pants. I don't want to play chaperon again today. What the hell is it about you that has every man in a five-mile radius sniffing around you?"

"You're using the term 'man' lightly there," I pointed out. "It's not like I'm *The Bachelorette* with twenty guys fighting for my hand. Human guys are few and far between. I've seriously dated two, count them, two guys in my whole life and I live with both of them. Vampires shouldn't count. They're way more interested in my blood than my body. That leaves the pervert twins. Those are my choices."

"I'm extraordinarily interested in your body." Marcus gave me a sexy grin.

"How about you be extraordinarily interested in telling me everything you know about the Strong Arm of Remus." I deeply wanted to get off the subject of my love life.

"I told you, it's just a legend, Zoey," Lee said with a frown.

Marcus went from playful to serious in an instant. "I don't know about that. Romulus and Remus really existed. In mythology they were the children of Mars and a human female, but in truth they were werewolves, perhaps the first of their kind. Where they originally came from only the truly ancient ones know, and they no longer speak. As the wolves of my homeland told it, Romulus was smarter but Remus was the true alpha. Romulus wanted power and tricked his brother, managing to kill the faster, stronger wolf. He took his brother's right paw and through it he could control the pack. He founded Rome and became the king of the wolves. As long as he wielded his brother's power, he was the uncontested alpha, needing only to think an order and the pack would follow it."

"It isn't real." Lee seemed disturbed by the thought of it, and I didn't blame him. If something like that existed, it could change everything. Controlling the wolves meant winning any war you went into. "If it was, every wolf in the world would be hunting for the damn thing."

"Just because the artifact has been gone for thousands of years doesn't mean it's not real," Marcus told the wolf. "If it's real then we cannot allow it to fall into the hands of someone like Lucas Halfer. It's better that Zoey finds it and protects it from someone who would misuse such power."

I wasn't planning on protecting the artifact. If it was real, then there was only one thing to do with it. I would destroy it. Lee passed a long look at me and I chose not to mention my plan to Marcus. I knew without a doubt what the vampire would want me to do with it. He would want me to hand it to Daniel. It would be the scepter to his crown. Through the wolves, Daniel could control the vampires, and through the vampires, he could take the rest of the supernatural world.

"You're an interesting wolf, Mr. Owens," Marcus said, studying my bodyguard intently.

"I don't think so," Lee replied with his usual grumble.

Marcus sat back, more relaxed than he'd been before. "I'm an expert on wolves. I lived surrounded by them for many, many years. There was a time when wolves and vampires were allies."

"Then the vampires decided to make the wolves their animals." Lee took a long drink of his soda, never taking his eyes off the vampire.

"If you feel that way, then you can't possibly approve of your brother's decision to make his oath to Daniel."

Lee set the drink aside with a frown. "I guess as vampires go, Donovan's all right, though I think he could go really dark given the right circumstances. Zack's too eager to follow. He needs a strong leader, and he thinks he's found him."

Marcus went into professorial mode. "Zack is a normal wolf. The normal wolf seeks the safety of a strong pack and wants a dominant leader. It makes the wolf feel safe and protected." He looked back at Lee. "Your pack, it was weak?"

"Yeah," Lee admitted. "There were only twelve of us and the alpha probably wasn't a true alpha."

We'd found the Owens brothers in Vegas, but I didn't know a lot about their pack. "Why weren't you the alpha, Lee? I've seen you do some seriously amazing things. You're stronger than Neil and he was really strong. I don't think I've ever seen a wolf move the way you did yesterday, and your senses are off the chart."

Marcus shook his head. "Neil isn't an alpha, Zoey. Like Zack, he wanted a strong leader. It didn't matter that Daniel was fighting for good or right. Neil made his pledge to Daniel because he was the strongest. Lee is not an alpha, either."

"Damn straight," the wolf agreed. "The last thing I want is to have to deal with a bunch of politics and wolves whining about this or that."

"Mr. Owens here is something far more interesting. He's a true lone wolf. He has power and capabilities beyond a mere alpha, yet he has no instinct to take the reins of power. They're rare but necessary. The lone wolf serves as a balance to the powerful alphas. Consider him something of a sheriff. He's able to keep corrupt alphas in line because he has no need for a master. He might follow a leader he believes in, but it's not his primary instinct to lead or be led. I'm surprised, actually. Lone wolves aren't known for staying in one place for long. It's their deepest instinct to roam."

Lee let his eyes slide away and stared at the street in the distance. "Most loners don't have brothers."

It explained a lot about Lee. His only real loyalty was to his brother. He'd left his home and the pack he'd known since childhood without a backward glance. He didn't care a thing about what anyone thought of him and did nothing to try to fit in.

Marcus looked Lee over thoughtfully before asking his next question. "You show no desire to follow Daniel in his quest. You obviously have no great respect for Devinshea. Why would you agree to watch their queen?"

"It's a payday," Lee said, shrugging off the question. "Beer costs money."

"It didn't feel like a payday when you were going to kill me. You were willing to hunt down one of the oldest vampires in the world for a girl you seem to think very little of."

Lee sat up, an offended frown on his face. "I never said I didn't like Zoey. I just have no desire to jump her bones. She's a good kid." He thought for a moment and decided to press on. "She's important. Donovan and Quinn, they're ambitious. They might be doing this for the right reasons but men like that…power can change them. Donovan is a ruthless bastard. He loves the kill and if he takes power, he could be as bad or worse than anything the Council has ever offered."

"That's not true," I argued.

Lee moved on, choosing not to engage me. "Quinn is smart as hell and plays the game better than anyone I've ever seen. He might seem soft, but it's an act. He'd make the hard calls, the calls that cost people their lives without hesitating or regretting the loss as long as it paid out. There's one thing and one thing alone that keeps them in line."

"Zoey," Marcus said. He'd decided that was true a long time ago.

"Take her out of the equation and you get a bloodbath. Do you have any idea how terrifying it is that the safety of my whole world revolves around that?" Lee pointed at me.

I stuck my tongue out at him tartly. I don't think it made him feel any better about the situation.

It wasn't long after that Marcus needed to get back to Dallas to meet Marini for his flight to LA. He drove us back to Ether, and all the while my mind played the conversation over and over. It made me wonder what Danny would be like if I'd rejected him after he'd come back from Paris last year. It wasn't the most pleasant of thoughts. Dev had only gotten involved with Danny because of me. I had to admit that he relished his role. He liked the game. He liked the power and the politics and even the subterfuge.

I was still contemplating all that Lee had said when we dropped Marcus off. It was getting close to dusk when I told Lee I needed to go out to the farm. He herded me to his old beat-up Ford truck.

"I can drive if you like," I said, my humor returning. I'd watched him in the rearview mirror during our trip to Fort Worth. "If I drive, you can hang your head out the window."

"I make no apologies for that. It feels nice." Lee climbed into the cab, and I was forced into the passenger side where he apparently liked to keep his empty fast food bag collection. He had the good sense to look slightly embarrassed as he cleared off the seat. "I'll clean that out tonight. I don't have many passengers."

"You could let me drive." No one ever let me drive anymore.

"You're never driving my truck, Zoey." He turned the engine over with a twist of the key and then slapped my hand away from the console. "And don't you dare change my radio."

I sighed, thinking I would have to listen to George Strait for the next twenty miles.

"You want to tell me what you're going to do with that thing if you actually get ahold of it?"

"Oh, I'll get it, Lee. Don't doubt it for a minute." I rested my head on my knees. My feet were on the dashboard because there really wasn't room for them on the floor. "What I'll do with it from there is extremely simple. I'm going to destroy it."

"What if it works?"

"Then I'll make damn sure it never does again."

Lee grunted his agreement. "Those boys of yours are going to be damn upset about it."

I shrugged, the gesture much more negligent than I felt. "They'll live with the disappointment."

"All right then. You just tell me what to do." Just like that he went from bodyguard to accomplice.

I wasn't going to hide anything from Danny or Dev, I promised myself as the miles went by. I was going to tell them exactly what I was going to do. If I was their conscience, it was probably past time I got to work.

Chapter Sixteen

We arrived at the farm just as another car was pulling in. Justin Parker was getting out of an old Chevy Malibu, his hands full of grocery bags. I slammed the passenger door shut, my feet hitting the gravel with a satisfying crunch.

"Hey there, Justin." I gave the vampire a friendly smile. "How's it going?"

"Zoey, you're just in time. Angie's making empanadas." Justin waved a hand toward Lee. "Though I'll have to tell her to double the recipe now. Have you seen that guy eat?"

Lee scratched his stomach but made no comment as his eyes checked out the area. I had no doubt his senses were wide open, and he could give me a rundown of every living creature in a three-mile radius. He chose to follow me into the house, so I figured we were all right.

The heavenly scent of frying food wafted from the kitchen. Justin walked through the doors that separated the kitchen from the dining room.

"Thank god." Angelina Hernandez took the bag out of his hand. "I thought you were going to take forever, baby."

Justin shrugged, looking down at his girlfriend with great affection. "I wasn't sure which one you wanted, so I bought all three."

Angelina was contemplating the three pounds of cheese Justin had bought when her sister, Lisa, looked up from the conversation she was having with Zack. "Hey, Zoey. Good to see you, girl. Are you hungry? We're making plenty."

"I'm starving," I admitted, but a thought crossed my mind. "Please tell me that's chicken and not cat."

Angelina shook her dark hair. "No, honey. If you want good cat, there are some vendors on Good Latimer who make great tacos."

Everybody knew that but me. I really needed to start getting those memos. Maybe there was an underground Zagat's survey.

"I see you managed to survive the day." Zack congratulated his brother with a manly slap to his shoulder. He looked younger and happier now that his day was over. His tie was loose and his dress shirt was slightly rumpled, probably from making out with Lisa. I was never going to tell him I had made that happen. "Did she thrill you with endless rounds of shopping and salon services?"

"It was an interesting day." Lee's yawn didn't make the case for "interesting." "I got to watch another vamp try to seduce her, though he was strangely less annoying than that faery. On the plus side, it looks like we're going into the hijacking business, brother."

Zack held a hand up. "Nice. See, maybe if she'd tried something like that when I was around, I would have found her less obnoxious."

"I seriously doubt that, Zack. We're only getting into the hijacking business if I can convince the boys." Of course, I was going to convince the boys. I would ask until they said yes. "Where are they?"

I'd noticed Dev's Audi outside. Danny wouldn't have taken a car.

Justin was attempting to disentangle himself from his girl. "I have to go. I'm already late, baby. My master's going to be pissed."

"You tell your master if he has a problem he can just come and see me," Angelina said. It was the voice of a female who knew how to handle a man.

A couple of months before, I'd asked Angelina if she was happy with Justin. Most of the wolves I knew wanted to be with wolves. They weren't happy dating other species, but Angie always seemed glad to be with the vampire. She told me that Justin was sweet and so much easier to handle than a wolf. If he stepped out of line, and he never did, not only could she cut off his access to sex, she could deny him dinner.

Looking around the house, I wondered if any of the occupants realized just how odd their lives were compared to normal vampire society. The vampires here were trained with discipline but allowed to make their own decisions. Torture wasn't a part of their training. These men had chosen to turn and become a part of Daniel's army. The women here were all wolves or shifters. From what I could tell, their vampire boyfriends treated them like queens. They ran this household. It was the opposite of the relationship the vamps would have had with Council-trained companions.

"Come on, Zoey," Justin said. "I'll take you out to Daniel."

I followed the vampire out the back door. There was no real yard with a fence. The house sat on a couple of acres of land. The nearest neighbor was over a mile away and his name was Chad Thomas. As Chad was with Marini and Marcus flying to Los Angeles, there was no worry about prying eyes. This was the country and people for the most part left others alone.

Daniel stood, watching his small group of trainees as they fought each other using only hand-to-hand combat. He also trained the vamps in weapons, both handguns and heavier artillery. There were lessons in stealth and hunting.

Dev had taken to teaching the more academic pursuits. He taught the vamps about the creatures of the supernatural world. These men had grown up believing they were human and knowing nothing of the hidden world around them. Dev taught them how to deal with such things as weres, shifters, demons, and Fae creatures. Dev knew the cultures and how to get along. Daniel knew how to kill them if it became necessary.

Daniel's new vampires numbered seven, including Chad. Chad's year of training was almost up, and Daniel would be forced to send them another fledgling. I didn't recognize the new guy. Daniel had turned him two weeks ago. I knew his name was Joel and Daniel had found him in Oregon.

"Nice of you to join us, Justin." Daniel sent a glare to his fledgling as we entered the training field. The fighting stopped and the vampires moved back. "I believe we said nine o'clock. It's now nine fifteen."

"I'm sorry, master," Justin began, his head slightly down, not making eye contact with the man who'd guided him through his turn.

"Give him a break, Danny." I never liked watching the way all these vamps kissed Danny's ass just because his blood gave them power and strength and crap. "Angie's making dinner and she needed cheese. Cheese is a serious thing. You used to love cheese."

Daniel's blue eyes widened with sarcastic glee as he looked at Justin. "Well, don't let a little thing like training for a war stop you from some serious grocery shopping, buddy. Is there anything else you need to do for your girlfriend? Does Angie need new shoes?"

"No, master," Justin said, utterly chastened. He took his place next to the new guy.

I glared at Daniel, shocked at that attitude. This was not a man who told his wife no often. This was a man who said "sure thing, baby" and "right away" when I asked him to do something. He might put his foot down on occasion, but he could show Justin a little sympathy. "Daniel Donovan, is that any way to talk to Justin? He was just trying to be a good boyfriend."

Daniel made sure he turned his back on his men. He kept his voice low. "Hey, baby, don't do this now. I have to…you know, at least look tough. I have to keep these guys in line."

I moved around my husband because there was a more pressing problem than Daniel's unreasonable attitude. The new guy had just gotten a look at me.

"All right, Joel." I pointed at him with my best "do not mess with me" hand gesture. Joel's fangs were long and his eyes were focused on me, the iris bleeding out to fill his eyes with brown. It was a very scary thing that I no longer put up with from any vamp, much less a baby one. "Let's get some things straight right off the bat…"

"Zoey." Daniel tugged me behind him. He placed himself between me and the hungry baby vamp. Newbies aren't known for their rigid control, and I was a tasty treat.

Justin had a steadying hand on Joel's shoulder. He leaned into the new vamp, his voice filled with understanding. "Really man, I know she's pretty and all glowy and stuff, but you do not want to mess with that. If you try to get a bite of that, you better hope the master kills you first because he'll do it quick. If she gets ahold of you…"

Justin leaned in and whispered into Joel's ear. The new vampire's eyes got wide and I was surprised when his fangs detracted and his eyes went from scary to scared.

"Do those grow back, man?" Joel asked Justin, his voice slightly shaky.

"I think so, but it probably hurts," Justin replied sagely.

Now all the vamps were taking a short step back from me. Daniel turned to me with a shake of his head.

I grinned up at him. My reputation was secure in at least one venue. I went up on my toes and planted a kiss on his perfect lips. "You were worried about your tough-guy reputation? They're all impressed you're brave enough to risk your balls around me."

Danny's dimples came out in full force, and he gave my bottom a nice little slap. "After what you did to me last night, I'll risk a lot more than that. I'm a brave man."

One more little kiss and I pulled away. He was obviously busy and besides, I really wanted to break through the weakest link before I started in on Danny. "Where's Dev?"

Daniel's eyes narrowed. "He's in the weight room. What's this crap about him growing out his hair? We need to talk about that, Z. I already have to unclog all the drains in the condo twice a week because you shed everywhere."

I shrugged as I backed away. "I can't help it, Danny. That hair is hot. If I have to get a naval ring then Dev has to grow out his hair. I'm not sure what I want from you, yet. Maybe a sexy tat on your ass."

I heard his groan as I practically skipped back into the house. I loved being at the farm. I loved the chaos and the noise and the weirdness. I neatly sidestepped a lovely black wolf being pursued playfully by a larger chocolate brown one. Lisa was leading Zack on a merry chase into the woods. I would know exactly what those howls meant later on tonight. Angie handed me a perfect empanada as I sashayed through the kitchen. Gwen, a shifter involved with Jean-Marc, was mixing margaritas, and I promised to come back and share the pitcher.

I passed Lee, who had parked his butt in front of the TV and was already on his second beer. He grunted something as I went by. I told him Danny could take care of me for the rest of the evening, but he was already half asleep.

I was ready to greet my boyfriend with a happy hello on my lips when I looked into the weight room and my mouth dropped open. I left it there, helpless for a moment to do anything but drool. Dev was doing chin-ups, his body in nothing but a pair of cutoff sweats and sneakers. His back was to me and it glistened with sweat, making every muscle ripple as he pulled himself up. His legs were crossed at the ankles and he never paused to breathe, just kept pulling his body up and down, up and down. After a couple of minutes he dropped and stretched, pulling his muscles this way and that. He turned but didn't notice me. He had earbuds in. Despite the hip-hop and dance music he played in the club, I knew Dev was an emo boy at heart.

When I met Dev he was a gorgeous man, but the last few years had been damn good to him. He'd been gifted with excellent DNA and was stronger than a human without the aid of regular workouts. After our experiences in Vegas, Daniel had taken over his physical training and he was now extremely proficient in hand-to-hand and his body…athletes would envy that body.

He adjusted the weights on the bar and settled down on the bench, his long legs on either side. He smoothly started pressing the weights up and down. I sighed and watched him for a moment.

"Are you enjoying the show, my mistress?" Dev asked, replacing the weights and turning his head toward me with the sexiest smile on his face. He pulled the buds from his ears and let them dangle.

I giggled because sometimes just the sight of him makes me a little giddy. "Yeah, don't let me stop you."

"You're just in time," he said, his voice low. "There's one last muscle I need to exercise. I'm pretty sure I can press about one twenty-five with it."

I straddled the bench, putting myself right over that muscle he was interested in exercising. It was the one workout the man never avoided. I playfully squirmed a little and felt his interest rise. "Did you have a good time with your brother?"

"I did indeed have a fine interview with my brother, though I spent the entire time thinking about copulating with your luscious form, my lover. It is so distracting to be constantly assaulted by the mental vision of your body twisted in coitus," Dev said with a devilish smile, proving he could do a mean Declan impression.

"Yeah, what's up with the formal speech?" I asked. "It's weird talking to him."

"It's the way they talk at court." Dev's hands went to my waist. "It's a very formal place. I prefer our little court where I can just look at you and tell you to fuck me, baby." He pressed his hips up, letting me know he was ready to go now. I wondered just what he'd been thinking about during this workout of his.

"Did he order you to come home?" I asked, knowing that had been Declan's plan all along.

"He did, indeed." Dev rolled his green eyes. "He treated me like his snot-nosed little brother having a tantrum. He's generously offered to allow you to come with us, but I think he has ulterior motives. He thinks this plane is far too dangerous for one as gentle as me."

I laughed because he didn't feel gentle grinding his hips up against mine. As good as it felt, and my body was ready to go, too, I needed to have a little talk with my boy. "I had an interesting day, too. I have a job."

He pulled me down and his hands pressed our pelvises together. He rotated his core in a tantalizing fashion that made me groan and almost forget I was on a mission.

"Did you hear me, Dev?" I said, trying not to get lost in that feeling. "I'm taking a job. I'm going back to work."

"What are you planning on stealing, my mistress?" Dev asked as his hands started to find their way into my shorts. He sounded only vaguely interested.

"A little artifact, nothing big," I murmured, letting my hands run over his really perfect chest. His whole torso was cut. I thought seriously about locking the door and discussing the whole thing over a little oral sex.

"Is it privately held?" His fingers played at the edge of my pussy.

My answer came out a breathy little moan. "No, it's part of an exhibit, but I'm not going to rob the museum. Too much work."

"Then what are you going to rob, you pretty little thief?"

"I'm going to hijack the truck transporting the stuff to the museum," I explained, leaning down to run my tongue around his nipple. I was rewarded with a husky laugh.

"Is that all? Well, that seems reasonable. I look forward to the experience. How about you take off these shorts and let me play?"

I looked at his amused face, a little surprised he'd been so easy. This was Dev, so I shouldn't have been. He was the easiest person I'd ever met. Still, I expected a little push back. "You're saying yes?"

"Of course," he agreed.

Now I was a definitely suspicious. "I thought you would be worried."

"Oh, I am worried. I can say yes to you with a completely free conscience because I know beyond a shadow of a doubt that he—" Dev pointed to the doorway "—is going to say no."

My head whipped around to see Danny watching us. He leaned against the jamb and shook his head. "No, Zoey."

I sat straight up, my hand absently slapping Dev on the chest. "Now that's just rude, Danny. You haven't even heard my plan and you're arbitrarily telling me no."

"Oww," Dev groaned. "I said yes. Why am I getting hit?"

"I don't have to hear the plan, baby," Daniel replied. "It goes something like this. 'Hey, Danny. I'm going to go and steal this one little, tiny thing that won't mean anything to anyone. No one will even notice it's gone, baby. We'll make some easy money.' Then just when we get the damn thing in our hands—that's when the apocalypse starts."

I swung my legs over the bench and got toe-to-toe with my husband, who had just done a fairly good impression of my entire planned presentation with the exception of the money. We wouldn't make any cash on this one. "It's been a long time since I triggered an apocalypse, and I did a fine job of stopping the one I did start." It was true. It had been a really long time ago when Danny and I had started running jobs together. He was never going to let me live that down. "This is nothing like that."

Dev had turned on his side and was watching the byplay with his head in his hand. "Of course not, sweetheart. Like you told me a long time ago, you're only going to do easy jobs from now on. Simple smash and grabs, I think you called them. Then you ran a job on the Hell plane. That was not a simple job, Zoey, and I doubt robbing an armored car is simple either."

"It isn't," Daniel agreed shortly. "It's incredibly complex. You have to have some good intelligence. You have to know when and where that truck is going to be, which means placing a finger man at the security company. Who are you planning on using? I doubt Lee could get another job. Zack won't do your bidding, and Felix won't let Sarah do anything vaguely criminal. Face it, baby. Your crew is gone."

I smiled because I'd already solved that problem. "I don't need a finger man, Danny. I had Marcus. The director of the museum just printed out all the info I needed and handed it to me with a smile on his face."

That last part wasn't true. It had been more like a catatonic stare, but smile made it seem more like an accomplishment.

"You're bringing members of the Council into your heists?" Daniel asked, shocked.

"He was surprisingly good," I admitted. "I told him he could join my crew if you ever decide to give up the game. Besides, it's not like I have to hide my criminal endeavors from the Council. I'm their officially sanctioned thief."

"Don't remind me of that, Zoey," Dev said with a groan.

I frowned at him. "What's up with you? You said yes."

He sat up. "I always say yes. It's what I do. Situations like this are why we work as a threesome. If either Daniel or I were gone, you would most likely be dead, sweetheart."

Daniel laughed.

"Don't discount my input, Dan." Dev swung his legs around, sitting on the bench facing us. "If you were gone, I would always say yes and then Zoey and I would be dead. But if I were gone, you would have pushed her away for her own good and, bang, same result. Zoey's dead. Face it. If I hadn't come on the scene and swept her off her feet, you wouldn't have gotten jealous of all the sex we were having and you wouldn't have decided to join us."

"Well, I am here," Daniel stated implacably. "And I say no."

My eyes narrowed, and Daniel looked wary for the first time. "Say no all you like, Danny. I'm done asking permission. I'm informing you that I'm running a job. I'll find my own crew, thank you."

"Why is this so damn important, Z?" Daniel finally asked what he should have asked at the beginning of the conversation. "We have a whole lot going on. We need to concentrate on the wolf meeting and we need to find Halfer."

"If you want to find Halfer, maybe you should figure out what he's looking for."

"He's looking for you." A ferocious glare lit Daniel's face every time he mentioned that little fact.

I ignored his scowl. "He's also looking for an artifact called the Strong Arm of Remus. It's supposed to be able to control wolves. Sounds like Halfer might be planning to attend your little gathering, too."

"How the hell do you know this?" Danny asked.

It was time to shove the knife in. "I know because the aswang was hired by Halfer to kill me before the artifact comes to town. You remember that thing that was my alcoholic daydream? I got her to talk before I killed her."

Daniel moved to take a seat next to Dev on the bench. I softened immediately because a weary expression bore down on him. I walked over and ran my fingers through his thick, sandy hair. "I know you don't like it, Danny, but I need to do this. I'd rather have the two of you with me, but I'll do it myself if I have to."

"All right, Z," Daniel said, forcing the words from his mouth. "You handle the details and I'll be there. I have to deliver the new spy to the Council while they're still in LA. Dev, can you work with her?" I knew the inherent question behind that query was "can you keep her from killing herself?"

"I've never hijacked an armored car before," Dev said with a smile. "Sounds like fun. I'm in and so is Zack."

I hugged Danny, hoping affection would help. He held me for a moment, but when he looked up, there was a little light in his eyes. He glanced over at Dev.

A sly smile spread across his face. "I think this is one of those times, Dev. She's made me crazy, and I need to let off a little steam."

"I agree," Dev said because he always said yes.

Daniel's arms became a nice little cage around my waist. "We should get her back home. I feel the need to tie her up and play with her."

Dev shook his head. "Why wait? Just let me get my gym bag. I'm like a boy scout, Dan. I'm always prepared. I have a nice set of padded handcuffs for just such an occasion. I think you'll find after all the exercise last night, Zoey will probably be very sweet and obedient tonight."

I frowned at my naughty, naughty boyfriend. He was taking all the fun out of it. "I'll probably misbehave a little. If I don't, you won't have any reason to spank me."

Dev growled and kissed me just a little roughly. "God, she's perfect. Let's talk about discipline, sweetheart."

I smiled in anticipation because I was really becoming a glutton for punishment.

Chapter Seventeen

The night of the heist, I crawled in between Dev and Lee, taking my perch on a hill along the highway. Dev passed me the binoculars he was holding. I stared through the lens, the world shifting to that odd green and black that night vision gives you. At this time of night, there were very few people on the road, which made it the perfect time to transport an important load of priceless artifacts. It wouldn't do to get stuck in traffic, and I-35 could get seriously congested between Alliance Airport and the cultural district.

The shipment from Chicago had come into the airport on a specialized cargo plane built to handle the delicate artifacts, keeping them at the proper temperature and humidity. The plane had come in late and the transfer had been made in a hanger with some super security. The thought of grabbing the artifact at the airport had never entered my mind. Airports are a veritable field of land mines. There are so many layers of security at an airport a thief would have to be crazy to even try it. Stealing from the Hell plane had been easier. I wouldn't steal a Snickers bar from an airport.

From Alliance, the wooden crates had been loaded onto the truck. Due to the priceless nature of the collection, the museum had taken the added precaution of hiring three decoy trucks. Unfortunately, I had the insider information of knowing exactly which truck the artifact was actually on and the route it was going to take. One of the decoys had driven by not twenty minutes earlier, and I waved as it went on its merry way.

Hijacking a shipment from, say, your local Best Buy is a different proposition from the job I was doing. The mob long ago perfected the cargo hijack. It was made infinitely easier by the fact that the drivers were usually in on the hijacking. Had I had a longer time to prepare, I would've tried to get an inside man or woman at the security company. I preferred to have a member of my crew simply drive the truck with all its goodies to the drop. Since I'd had a week to plan, I was going to have to go a different route.

Unlike the above-mentioned shipment of LCD TVs and Blu-ray players, the truck containing my Roman artifacts wouldn't be tempted by the usual plays. This truck wouldn't stop at a local diner so the driver could get a cup of coffee and perhaps pick up a cute little redhead who so needed a ride to Fort Worth. I would have pulled out my Ruger and forced the now wide-awake driver to the drop where Danny and Dev would find my crate, and I would send the driver on his way. Scenario number two involved detouring the truck to the drop and then pulling my Ruger while the boys pillaged. It wouldn't work with this truck. On seeing the unscheduled detour, the truck carrying my item would simply turn around and head back to the airport until a team could figure out what was going on.

I needed shock and awe. I'd tried to get Danny to jump in front of the truck, set his shoulders, and just stop it with his body. It always worked in the comics, but Danny was a wimp and thought that would probably hurt like hell despite the coolness factor, so we were going with a greener method.

"Zoey, I have the package in sight," Zack said in my earpiece. "It's five minutes away. Has the big guy shown up?"

"Negative, Zack." Daniel was supposed to be here by now. I put the binoculars down and Dev frowned, the moonlight illuminating his tension.

"Where the hell is Donovan?" Lee asked, frowning.

Dev pulled out his cell and hit speed dial. "Dan, where the hell are you? This goes down in five minutes. Get your ass to the drop."

He clicked the *End Call* button and shoved the phone back into his black pants. I'd played stylist tonight. For the thief, black is the only color to go with. Dev and Lee were dressed in black from head to toe. They wore black turtlenecks, despite the ninety-five degree temperature. The ski masks they would put on sat on the ground. I knew they were both dreading it, but I had to insist. There were two armed drivers in that truck, and I wanted them both alive at the end of my job. If they were alive, then there was always the chance that they could remember something I would rather they forgot. I didn't want them thinking about things like hair or eye color. All they would know was there had been two men and one woman. If that was all they could offer, there would be no police sketches and no need to call in a cleaning crew.

Of course, if Daniel had shown up, I wouldn't have needed any of it. He could have just informed the drivers that they didn't remember and they wouldn't. I checked the rounds in the Ruger and Dev did the same in his new, shiny SIG Sauer. Neither of us said a word, but we were both worried. It wasn't like Danny to not show up.

He'd been quiet and contemplative the last week or so. I knew he was upset about sending another one of his soldiers to the Council, but it had to be done. He'd prepared a young vampire named Brian for the way his life would be during the training period. Brian had been with Daniel for over a year and he was unattached. Though Daniel had not once mentioned it, I knew he was avoiding breaking up another couple if he could. The situation with Neil had affected him more than he would ever admit.

Dev glanced at me, his eyes asking the question.

"We go now or we lose it, Dev." I wasn't willing to waste more than a week of planning and work because Daniel was late. In fifteen minutes the job would be over, and I could figure out what had kept him. I was certain it was Council business. He was supposed to fly back in from LA tonight and more than likely, he'd been delayed. It wouldn't be the first time the Council had forced Daniel to do their bidding on a moment's notice. The job would have been easier with Daniel, but I'd certainly run jobs without the aid of a vampire before.

"All right, sweetheart. I better get to work then." Dev gracefully pushed himself up and pulled our secret weapon out of his pocket. Seeds. Oak, he'd told me. He took the handful of seeds out to the road. He crossed the highway, strategically placing each seed for maximum coverage. When he was done, he jogged back to the side of the highway Lee and I were on and I watched as he took a deep breath. He held his hands to his sides, but his fingers splayed wide as he opened that place deep inside of him that called things to life. I felt the air around me pulse with energy. Even Lee sat up when he felt that power filling the air.

There was a rumble as the seeds popped open and life sprayed across the concrete. It was like watching a fast-forward nature video. Suddenly there was a burst of green as a grove of large oaks spread across the highway. It was a strange but beautiful sight.

185

"That's pretty damn impressive." Lee watched Dev work. "I thought he was just a walking, talking dose of Viagra."

I laughed out loud and had to remind myself we were running a job. "He's a fertility god, Lee. Most of his magic is about sex, but he also has some Green Man in his background, hence the expertise with plants. Don't underestimate Dev. Just because he's not as butch as you or Daniel doesn't mean he can't do some damage. He can pull you into the earth with those plants."

"I'll remember that," Lee said, staring at Dev with new respect.

Dev climbed back up the hill and held his hand out to help me up. "Is that satisfactory?"

I looked down on the small forest that now obstructed the roadway. It was better than any little detour sign. There was no way even a large truck was blasting through that thicket of strong trees. What took nature twenty years, Dev had managed in a minute. And he could reverse it at the end of the job. He would wave his hands and the whole grove would be back to seeds. The road—not so much. There were going to be some serious traffic jams in the morning.

"It's hard to remember you used to be crappy at magic." When we'd met, he'd struggled with control.

"That was before I found my goddess." He touched the place where the gold medallion rested under my shirt. "It means what it says. It will only be stronger once the ceremony is performed. Declan is meeting us at the Gathering. He hasn't said he'll give his consent yet, but he will act as witness. I have no doubt I'll convince him. I'll get the real one around your neck. You'll see."

I still didn't understand why we needed royal consent to perform a fertility ritual. It wasn't like it wouldn't work because Declan didn't give us his blessing. I'd started to notice the insane amount of pregnant females living in our building. I'd heard the women joking about something being in the water. It wasn't in the water, but he was living in the penthouse. Looking at those shiny green trees, it struck me that Dev's power had grown in leaps and bounds since he met me. If his power over plants had grown exponentially, then I had to figure his fertility powers had done the same. It made me want to up the strength of my birth control shots. I shook my head because that was just one of those problems I didn't like to think about. It seemed like something I would inevitably have to deal with, but I didn't want to borrow trouble.

"Truck's coming," Lee said, his hearing able to detect the advance of our prey far sooner than we could.

I touched my earpiece. "Zack, is anyone else coming?"

"That's a negative." Zack watched far too many movies. "It's all quiet here."

"Let me know if that changes," I replied.

There was the grinding sound of large brakes pumping furiously at the unexpected obstruction in the road. I pulled the ski mask over my face, getting ready for about ten uncomfortable minutes. Dev and Lee did the same. The three of us ran down to the road, weapons at the ready. The brakes groaned under the pressure and the truck started to jackknife, but finally the large vehicle came to a stop just as it bumped against the incomprehensible bit of nature in the middle of the highway.

"What the hell is that?" a male voice asked as one of the doors to the truck came open. He had an incredulous look on his face, and I knew I'd made the right call. If I'd tried anything vaguely normal, they would have attempted to turn around and gone into lock-down mode. There would have been no avoiding gunfire.

"I have no idea but I'm calling it in," the other voice said. This one came from the driver's seat.

"I'm going to have to ask you not to do that, gentlemen." I held the Ruger steady, the driver's head in my sights.

Lee moved quickly and before the driver had a chance to hit the call button, he was being hauled out the door. Lee pulled him by his shirt and held him a good two feet off the ground. "You ready?"

Dev nodded, not saying anything he didn't have to. He worked gloves over his hands and took out the plastic restraints we'd bought for just this occasion. The guy in my sights watched us, hands held in the air. He wasn't panicking, and I was grateful for that. Calm kept everyone alive.

I stepped up to my guy. "I'll need the gun, buddy. Reach one hand into the holster, carefully lay it on the ground and kick it over here, please. No heroics, okay? They can both move faster than you think, and they won't take kindly to you trying to shoot me."

"I have a wife and two kids," he stated quietly, looking at the ground rather than me. He knew what he was doing if he didn't want to get shot. He played at my humanity and made no move to be able to identify me later.

"I'll make sure you get back to them in one piece." I had zero desire to hurt some guy for doing his job. This is why I greatly prefer cracking safes. Safes don't tell me about all the people who'll miss them if they're suddenly dead. "My partner over there is going to tie up your friend. Then we'll get to you. Would we tie you up if we meant to shoot you? We're not even going to take the truck. We're interested in one item and then we'll be on our way. Now, I really need the gun."

He nodded and slowly, carefully slid his weapon from his holster and laid it on the ground. He used his foot to kick it my way and then dropped to his knees, assuming the proper position for turning oneself over. Dev had efficiently restrained the first guard and placed him on the side of the road facing away from us. I had given him this particular duty because he was damn good at it. Having been tied up by Dev on numerous occasions, I knew our victims would suffer no ill effects from his talents.

When both men were properly restrained, I started for the truck. Luckily, I knew what I was looking for. "It's in a wooden crate marked *fifty-seven*."

He nodded and we started toward the back of the truck. I could still feel the heat of the day on the asphalt and the quiet in the air around seemed slightly ominous. I shook off the feeling and tried to concentrate on the job, but I was still worried about Daniel. It wasn't like him to be late.

Heavy locks held the doors of the truck together. I could easily pick the locks or I could have brought some liquid nitrogen to freeze them and then break the offending material. Why bother when Lee could just pull it off? With one hand he easily broke through hundreds of dollars of security. The door came open, showing us the well-packed exhibit. In the moonlight, I could see the stacks of crates.

Dev jumped up and switched on his flashlight, illuminating the interior of the truck. There was enough room to maneuver through the rows of packages. He held his hand out and gave me a quick tug to bring me to his side. I glanced back at Lee, who had the strangest look on his face. He stayed back, which was odd because he always preferred to go before me. He typically shoved me back when I tried to go first and, despite the fact that Dev was here, I expected him to protest. He took his job seriously and probably wouldn't even trust Daniel to do it right.

"What's wrong, Lee?"

"I don't want to go in there, Zoey," he admitted, because Lee was nothing if not honest. If there was one thing I'd learned about Lee, it was that he followed his instincts. "Whatever is in there, I don't want it anywhere near me. There's something bad in that truck. My every instinct tells me to get the fuck away from that thing."

I nodded, not wanting to push him to do anything he didn't want to do. It gave me a great confidence that we were getting exactly what we wanted. The artifact must be powerful for Lee to be able to sense it through all the packing material. "It's all right. Dev and I can handle it. You watch our two guests. We'll be done in roughly two minutes. Give me the crowbar."

Lee handed me the metal tool, and Dev started to check the numbers on the crates surrounding us.

I was a bit startled when Zack spoke softly in my ear. "Zoey, you have a car coming. It's moving fast."

"Understood. We'll be out of here in five minutes tops. Get your furry ass here now. We'll pick you up on the way." I'd hoped to have more time, but it looked like our two drivers were going to be rescued pretty quickly. I had no doubt whoever came across them would call the police immediately.

"Got it, sweetheart." Dev picked up the wooden crate with a spray-painted fifty-seven on its side. He moved it to the middle of the truck and held his hand out for the crowbar. With a quick movement, he had the top cracked open and held the light over the crate, allowing me to peer inside. I moved to the side and started to push through the packing materials. "If that car wasn't coming, I would suggest we have a little fun. I've never had sex in a truck such as this. Come to think of it, we've never stopped in the middle of a job for a quickie."

I laughed as I sifted because Dev never let the tension of a situation force his mind from his favorite subject. I felt something that was just about the right size. "There's a pretty good reason we don't have sex on the job. Sorry, baby. You won't be checking anything off your list tonight."

"I wouldn't be so sure about that," Dev replied with a grin. "The night is still young."

I pulled the object free and brushed off the popcorn-style material they had packed the crate with. I gently unwound the item and was rewarded with my first glimpse of the Strong Arm of Remus. I found myself staring at the carved marble figure. The wolf emerged from the marble as though it was a part of the stone, taking form to devour its prey. The wolf held a woman in its sharp teeth, her face a mask of agony. There was no doubt in my mind that this was a werewolf. Whoever had created this piece had used a werewolf as a model. The violence in the stone was barely contained. As I stared at it, I knew that if I gave it a chance, that violence would spill out of the confines of the small sculpture and into our reality.

"Zoey," Dev said sharply, startling me out of my revelation. "We have to move, sweetheart."

Our time was up. I forced myself to hold the object against my chest, cradling it close so I wouldn't lose it, but I didn't like the way it felt against me. My stomach turned a little queasy. I followed Dev out of the truck. Even as we ran around the side, I could hear the sound of tires squealing.

"Lee, get the car!" I yelled as we rounded the corner.

Lee was on his knees in the middle of the road, his gun at his side. He held his stomach, and I could see he'd been violently ill. He shook with the force of his sickness. The closer I got to him, the more he shook.

"I'll get the car." Dev took off to where we had parked the sedan we purchased with cash and under an assumed name.

"Are you all right?" I asked my bodyguard.

"God, get that thing away from me." His eyes were tight as he pointed to the sculpture. "I can't...I can hardly breathe."

I took a couple of steps back and worried how I was going to get Lee home. I would lock the damn thing in the trunk and hope it helped. Surely Lee could handle it just until we got away. I hoped it didn't have the same effect on Zack.

Dev was climbing the hill and disappearing over it when I

realized that car had stopped seconds ago and yet no one had made a sound. There was no exclamation of surprise or the sound of a cell phone call being made. There was absolutely nothing from the other side of the truck.

"Zoey," Lee rasped, turning to me. He looked behind me and his eyes shifted to hold some part of his wolf. "You need to get out of here now."

"Dev will be here any minute."

If the people in the car got out to gawk at the strange sight in the middle of the road, all they would see was a robbery. It might freak them out, but for the most part, people stopped when they saw the gun. I was more worried about the fact that Lee had taken his mask off.

"Keep your head down," I ordered, holding the gun at my side again.

"I mean it, Zoey." He tried to get to his feet but faltered. His knees hit the pavement, and he groaned as the sickness hit again. "Get the fuck out of here."

"I don't think she's going anywhere, wolf," a voice said from behind me. "What happened to your last wolf? Looks like this one can't stand the heat."

Now I felt sick. I forced myself to turn around even though I damn well knew who was behind me.

Lucas Halfer smiled in the moonlight. "Hello, Zoey. I believe I made you a promise the last time we talked. Time for me to make good on it."

Chapter Eighteen

I raised my gun and had the former demon in my sights. I would have popped off a quick round, but he had me in his sights too, so I settled for a nice standoff. As Halfer looked at me, his self-satisfied smile told me everything I needed to know. I had walked into a trap. I could only hope I had a way out.

"So the aswang was a decoy," I began, trying to give myself time for one of three things to happen. I needed Dev to get back with the car, Lee to get back to himself, or Zack to show up with teeth and claws.

Halfer laughed, his eyes on the statue in my hand. "I like to think of her more like a herding mechanism. She got you right where I needed you to go. I doubt you would have responded if I'd sent you an e-mail politely asking you to steal that thing for me."

"Couldn't steal the thing yourself? Is the whole mortality thing difficult for you?"

He shrugged. "I probably could have, but why do all that work myself when I could get you to do it for me? Stay down, wolf."

I fought the urge to look at Lee. The minute my attention was drawn away, Halfer would make good on his threat to kill me. Where the hell was Dev?

Lee had crawled to my side. I heard him as he was trying to get up. His strength was being sapped by whatever magic was in the statue.

"Please just stay down, Lee." I begged, knowing how hard this was for him. "He will kill you."

"I really just want to kill Zoey, wolf," Halfer affirmed. "As long as you stay out of my way, I couldn't care less about some muscle her husband hired."

A sudden thought occurred to me. Just how carefully thought out was this plan of Halfer's?

"What did you do to Danny?" There was no way in hell my husband just forgot. He'd been worried about this night for days.

He'd made me go over and over the plan with him until he knew it better than I did. He forced Dev to prove he could perform his job three times before he grudgingly gave his approval. He would have found a way to leave LA on time even if it meant pissing off the Council.

Lucas Halfer no longer had fangs, but he smiled like they were still there, ready to take a chunk out of me. "I think you'll find I delayed your hubby with a little emergency. When I was cast out of Hell, I was informed that if I tried to interfere with Vampire affairs, I would face a trial. But they didn't say anything about firebombing a house containing a bunch of vamps the Council doesn't even know about."

It took everything I had not to shoot that bastard then and there. "Why? Why go to all that trouble? You have to know Danny is going to kill you. He wasn't in that house."

"I know," Halfer replied. "I just needed to make sure he was distracted. I gave him a heads up. I even sent him pictures. I love modern technology. He's pulling bodies out even as we speak."

I tried not to think about all the people I cared about who were in that house. I could only hope they'd been out. They were a nocturnal lot. Maybe they were out on dates or roaming the woods. They couldn't be dead. I wasn't even going to think about that possibility. Daniel would have gotten there, and he would have made sure everyone got out alive.

"I'll take that artifact now, Zoey." Halfer held out a hand.

"Why do you want it?" I asked, trying to come up with any way to keep him talking. "It just seems to make wolves sick."

"I've been around a long time. I know exactly what the Strong Arm of Remus does. It's been missing for millennia," Halfer explained. "I never gave a damn about the wolves until I found out Donovan wanted them. I would really do just about anything to fuck with that husband of yours. I'll make sure he gets caught by the Council even if I can't go to them myself."

One of Lucifer Morningstar's dictates to Halfer was to stay out of Council business. The king of Hell was interested in seeing where the vampires were going and didn't want his soldiers influencing the upcoming battle. I was sure it was the only reason Halfer hadn't called up Marini and laid out what he knew.

"So you're going to make the wolves sick? How exactly does that help you get back at Daniel?"

"That's not a normal wolf," he said, glancing down at Lee, who was moaning but refused to leave my side. I wasn't sure what he thought he could do except distract the ex-demon with his groans. "That's a loner. The Strong Arm calls to wolves both normal and alpha. It calls to their instincts to lead and be led, to follow the strong. That pitiful dog at your side doesn't have those instincts, so the object seeks to destroy that which will not follow it."

There was a sudden pop of gunfire behind me, and I couldn't help but look. I turned back around quickly and was surprised to find Halfer calmly standing there looking at me. He had a small smile on his face that let me know he wanted me alive, at least for now. He wanted something else from me.

"That would be my employees, Zoey," Halfer said softly as though intimating a secret to me. "I found I still had followers even without Hell's stamp of approval. I think you'll find that faery of yours is dead again. Too bad there are no vampires around to bring him back this time."

There was nothing to stop my finger from pulling the trigger now. I firmed my stance and shot. I preferred a two-fisted hold, but I couldn't put the prize down. The recoil kicked me back, but I was ready for it.

The shot managed to hit Halfer, his big body slamming back before he could return fire.

"Move it, Lee." I jumped back and used the front of the big truck as a shield.

"That fucking hurt, bitch," Halfer growled. He groaned a little as he moved the shoulder. He would bleed and hurt, but he was still as strong as a demon. It would take more than a single wound to even slow him down. "It won't work. Give me the damn artifact now or I'll blow your wolf all to hell."

I felt the hard rim of the tires against my back. I gazed to the hill where Dev had disappeared. My eyes filled with tears at the thought of him never coming back down. I sucked it up because I had to get myself and Lee out of here before I worried about avenging Dev. Besides, until I saw his body, I wasn't giving up hope. He had a gun, too, and he was no easy mark.

I moved to my knees and let myself look out from behind the tire. Halfer was positioned over Lee. He held my wolf's head by his curly hair and pointed the gun at his temple. Lee was too weak to even fight anymore.

"I'm serious, Zoey," Halfer called out, his voice hard as nails. "I'm going to blow this wolf's head off if you don't get your ass out here. You have ten seconds. Unless you've stopped giving a damn about your employees, and then please feel free to stay where you are. If you don't care, then I applaud you for finally growing a set."

He started his countdown, and I tried to see a way out. I was pretty sure he was still going to kill us both no matter what I did, but I knew I couldn't just stand back and let Lee die like that. I stood and took a deep breath. I forced myself to move away from my cover. "Okay. I'll trade you the statue for my wolf."

Halfer snorted. "You'll kick the gun over here first. I don't heal the way I used to and bullets hurt more now, thanks to you."

I kneeled down and carefully put the Ruger on the ground. I kicked it toward him and waited for him to shoot me now that I was an easy target. The sound of gunfire split the night around me, and I waited for the sting of the bullet hitting my body. I was surprised when Halfer cursed and jerked backward.

I turned my head and saw my green-eyed boy all healthy and whole, walking toward the scene, gun in hand, ready to take another shot.

"Your men are gone, Halfer," Dev shouted as he approached. "You're on your own."

There was a loud growl as Zack ran toward his brother. Halfer took one look at the big brown wolf who seemed to be suffering none of the effects his brother was and retreated. He took a dozen steps back. I could see his shirt was starting to get soaked in blood. I couldn't tell exactly where Dev had hit him, but it was definitely in the torso. Unfortunately, he'd been allowed to keep his demonic strength when he'd been cast from Hell. He could die, but he was one tough son of a bitch.

"I can still shoot her, Quinn," Halfer yelled, his face savage. The bullets had done some damage, but not anywhere close to enough. "You might get another shot off, but I swear I'll take her down if it's the last thing I do."

195

Zack growled, looking between his brother and the threat, unsure of what to do. I knew.

"Get Lee out of here." I used my best badass alpha voice. Zack was strictly a follower. He wanted to be told what to do. He could follow orders and would do so with great efficiency once someone stronger told him what to do.

Before Dev could countermand my order, Zack had his brother's shirt in his teeth and was pulling him away as fast as his four feet would carry them.

"Not the way I would have gone, Zoey." Dev frowned my way. "That was stupid. Zack could have killed him."

"Maybe, but he would have gotten either me or Lee," I shot back, wondering if I could get my gun back in my hands. It was between Dev and Halfer, just lying there in the road.

Dev read my face and shook his head sharply. "Get behind me now." I frowned but did what he told me to. Dev's eyes focused on the ex-demon. "I killed your little cohorts back there, Lucas. You're all alone. I can kill you here or you can run and let Daniel kill you later. It's your choice."

"Or I could find door number three." Halfer's face lit with a shit-eating grin. "Isn't that what you like to say, Mrs. Donovan?" He kept the gun trained but started walking backward. I hadn't even thought about what we had left sitting back there, all tied up and gagged. Halfer had noted them, though. He pulled one of the men from the truck out in front of him now and placed the gun at his temple. "Give up the statue or I'll kill this man."

"So kill him, Lucas," Dev replied, his tone flat. "You think I'm not ready for some collateral damage? This is war. People die. Innocent people die." Dev glanced back at me. "Zoey, get in the car. I'll follow you in a minute."

I heard him, but I just couldn't help but think about the fact that this was the guy with a wife and two kids. He'd been calm and done absolutely everything right. He should have survived this heist and been able to go home and crawl in bed with his wife and hold his children. Now, because I screwed up, he was going to die.

"I'm going to kill this one, Zoey," Halfer stated. "Then I'll kill the other one, too, just for kicks. Do you think he's just collateral damage? Are you going to be able to live with that?"

"She's going to go to the car," Dev said as though saying a thing with enough force of will could make it happen. Unfortunately, it didn't work that way with me.

I moved away from Dev, making sure to stay out of arm's reach. "I'm bringing it to you, Lucas. Don't hurt him."

I moved quickly before Dev could react and found myself taking the man's place with Halfer's gun at my head. I do stupid things sometimes, but Halfer was right. I don't believe in collateral damage. I couldn't live with it. Even in the dark I could see Dev's panic.

"Now, it's going to go like this, Quinn," Halfer started, firmly in control of the situation. "I'm going to take your lover and get in the car. You're going to watch and do absolutely nothing or I'll blow her head off. Is she collateral damage in your little war?"

"You'll kill her anyway," Dev said, and I saw the hatred in his eyes.

"Maybe, but I think that vampire is probably figuring out he should get his ass here, and I would love to not have him rip my heart out again," Lucas explained logically. "I'm going to get in my car with Zoey here and I'll leave her down the road. Her husband can come and save her. He likes to do that. Tell him to bring that blood of his because she's going to need it."

I felt the cold at my temple and then I was being herded toward a black Lincoln Navigator. I could see that Dev hadn't taken out all of Halfer's accomplices since there was a small man with beady eyes behind the wheel. Dev followed us, waiting for any slipup. I could see how angry he was in the way he held himself. His rage at being completely unable to save me was in every muscle of his body. I was pretty sure it wasn't just Halfer he was mad at.

Halfer opened the door to the back seat.

"Zoey," Dev yelled. "Don't you dare die. I'm planning on killing you myself."

"Love you, too," I shouted as Halfer shoved me in the car. The minute the door was closed, the driver hit the gas and plowed through the night.

"Let me have it," Halfer ordered, pulling the statue out of my hands. He groaned as he moved, but he forced himself to grip the artifact despite his obvious pain. He held it up and inspected it. He

197

didn't seem to have any of the same concerns I had about the piece. He admired it like it was a blessed object. "It's a shame, really. It's so lovely."

Halfer smashed the statue against the door with his good hand. It came apart under the strength of the impact, sending pieces of marble flying. I covered my eyes but when I looked up again, he was holding a petrified paw.

"I thank you, Zoey," he said with a self-satisfied smile. "I could never have gotten this without you. This is going to change the game. This gives me all the power in the world."

Suddenly there was a loud thump and the car swerved wildly.

"It's a wolf," the driver said, trying to get the car under control. "It's a big brown wolf."

Score one for Zack. I tried to look out the window to see if I could make him out. He seemed to be moving on the roof. Then there was a horrible screeching sound and a claw became visible through the top of the car.

Halfer cursed but held up the paw and intoned a spell in Latin. Demons love their Latin. I think it's pretentious and silly, but they don't really listen to me. Whatever it was, it wasn't working as Zack was doing a fine job of creating a sunroof where before there was none. I started looking at Halfer's gun, wondering if there was any way I could get it.

"Why isn't it working?" Frustration saturated his words.

"Guess you're out of luck," I said with that smile I was sure he hated. "It doesn't work on Zack. That's the name of the guy who's about to eat you. I'll introduce him properly when he gets through the roof."

With a howl of rage, Halfer slapped me across the face, and I felt my lip start to bleed. He reared back his fist and I waited for him to break my jaw. He stopped suddenly as Zack was almost through. I brought my hands up to try to protect my head.

"Time to see how well trained your wolf is." Halfer leaned over and opened the door on my side of the car. I took the opportunity to reach for the paw. The damn thing was mine.

"Uh uh," he said as the wind rushed in. We had to be going seventy. "Not going to happen, Zoey. Time to drop you off. It's been nice seeing you. Hope you enjoyed the ride."

He leaned back and with his expensive loafers, kicked me out of the car.

The world rushed by in a blur. I hit the pavement and rolled for a really long time. Without a doubt I would have been a dead girl if I hadn't been taking Daniel's blood on a regular basis. Even with that vampire blood, I felt every bone in my body. I wasn't sure how many were broken, but I was certain it was a bunch. I didn't even try to lift my head off the pavement. My whole body was a mass of pain. So much I couldn't really tell where it was coming from. It simply was. Pain. Utter agony blanketed me.

I heard a little whimper and felt the tentative lick of a warm tongue on my face. I opened my eyes, but everything was fuzzy and blurry. I tried to cry but that hurt, too. A low moan was all I could manage. Zack did the only thing he could. He stood beside me and let me know he was there. He threw back his head and howled to try to let the others know where we were.

My left arm was at an odd angle. I stared at it, trying to make sense of why it pointed the wrong way. I tried to move it but had no luck. My muscles seemed too concerned with pain to respond. I heard a car zooming along and then the screech of brakes. I would have turned to see if someone was going to call an ambulance or maybe animal control when they got a look at Zack, but then Dev was turning me over and I was moaning again. Every touch brought fresh agony.

"Oh, goddess. What did he do to you?" Dev asked quietly, looking me over.

"He pitched her out of a moving car." Zack was suddenly human again. He was naked, of course, and like most wolves, he didn't seem to care. "That bastard kicked her right out of the car without slowing down even a little. She should be dead."

Dev sighed. "She's not and we have more trouble than that. The vampire blood is going to start healing her soon."

I wasn't following the conversation well because Zack's face screwed up in horror at the thought. The vampire blood healing me seemed like a really good thing. I was pretty heinously broken and being whole again was a thing I'd like to achieve. Anything to make the pain go away.

Dev frowned down at me, his face tense. "Sweetheart, I'm not going to lie to you. This is going to hurt. I'm so sorry."

"It already hurts, Dev," I managed to get out. Tears stung my eyes. I really thought I couldn't take any more freaking pain. "Where is Danny?"

"I don't know," Dev said softly. "Hold her arm at the elbow, Zack. Don't let it move."

Zack kneeled beside me and held my elbow.

I got really nauseous at the sight of my bone sticking straight out of my arm. "Don't touch it!"

"Zoey, if we don't set that arm, it's going to heal like that," Zack pointed out.

My stomach rolled at the thought. I'd had a bunch of internal injuries healed with vampire blood, but this was my first broken bone. It was also apparently my second and third as Dev explained that both of my legs were broken. I just let the tears roll now as Zack held me firmly and Dev pulled. I couldn't help the scream that came but welcomed the blackness that followed shortly after.

"Hey, baby. You have to wake up, now." Daniel's voice broke through the darkness, and I moaned as I came right back into pain.

He was behind me, a smoky smell clinging to his clothes. He held his wrist to my mouth and the blood was flowing. I let it coat my tongue, wanting it more than I've ever wanted anything in my life. I lapped at it, praying it would start to work and I wouldn't feel every nerve in my body alight with agony. Relief washed over me as the blood started to warm my insides.

"That's right, baby. Take what you need," Daniel was saying as his free hand stroked my hair.

Dev stood over me, his expression grave, and I knew I was in for some kind of lecture when I was feeling better. Lee was sitting in the car, looking like he was getting over the worst of the sickness, but his eyes were guilty as he stared at me. Zack was dressed again, though in jeans and a T-shirt he resembled his brother more than normal.

"I'm so sorry," Daniel was saying quietly.

"Is everyone all right?" Dev asked, looking behind me at Daniel. I was sure Daniel had filled everyone in on Halfer's activities.

"Joel is dead." Daniel's voice was a flat monotone. "The house is gone. Justin worked fast or it would have been a whole lot worse. He got the girls out. Jean-Marc is burned pretty badly, but he'll recover. I moved everyone over to Chad's."

"We'll find a new place tomorrow," Dev assured him.

I let my head fall back against Daniel's chest. Exhaustion swamped me, but the blood was doing its work now. I could feel myself healing, and the pain was replaced with a warm sense of well-being.

"Take her, will you, Dev?" Daniel asked, and Dev picked me up and started toward the car.

I looked back at my husband. Danny's body was rigid with tension. He caught my eyes but there was nothing encouraging in his face, just a flat, hollow look.

Guilt pressed on me. I'd been reckless. I should have vetted the entire situation better, but I'd been eager to get ahead of Halfer, to prove that he couldn't best me in my own world. And Danny had paid the price. Joel had paid the price.

Daniel pulled his cell out of his back pocket and punched in a number. Dev was putting me in the car as Daniel began to speak.

"This is Donovan. My access number is 75502E45. Yeah, I'm going to need a cleaning crew. Send everyone you have to I-35 about three miles out of Fort Worth. You can't miss it." He paused and sighed. "It's not for me. Yes, it's my wife again. Just call Vorenus. He'll clear her. Hell, call Marini himself. I don't care, but if you don't get your ass out here, I can tell you what the front page of the *Star-Telegram* is going to be tomorrow morning."

Daniel snapped the phone shut. He frowned down at me. "I have to meet the crew at the drop sight. I'll see you at home."

I shook my head. "Dev has to go with you. He has to fix the oak grove." We couldn't leave it there. The mutilated road could be explained away, but not a bunch of trees.

"I did that while Zack chased you down. It took me thirty seconds, but I worry the drivers saw me. They need their memories wiped," Dev said.

Daniel nodded, and then he was gone again. Dev closed the door. He got around to the other side and joined me in the backseat. Zack and Lee were in the front, and Zack pulled away, driving us back toward Denton. We were going to take the long route home to avoid anyone remembering the car.

Lee looked back at me. "I'm sorry, Zoey."

"You couldn't help it." I'd gotten him into a bad situation, too.

"You should have left me," he said in a voice that told me he respected me because I hadn't. He turned back around and let his head rest against the seat.

"If you ever try anything like this again, I swear to the goddess I will lock you up," Dev started and I knew he was going to blow off some steam. "I'm going to be saying no a whole lot in the future, my mistress. I'm going to become the king of no. Do you understand me? Let me go over all the ways you tried to kill yourself tonight."

Dev yelled, letting all of his terror out in a torrent of words. The list of things I'd done was really long and went on for many miles, but I did one right thing as Dev was screaming.

I reached over and clicked my seat belt closed. I had learned that lesson.

Chapter Nineteen

I stared out the window of the large SUV, taking in the sights of the mountains, but I couldn't really concentrate. I leaned my head against the cool glass pane as the driver turned up what I hoped was the final road. John McKenzie's place was really isolated. Dev held my hand as he looked around as well. I could see he was satisfied with the beauty of the place. I, for one, was not looking forward to spending the next week in a tent.

Of course, it would probably be better than the last week. Dev had spent the entire night of my blown heist yelling at me and giving me all kinds of ultimatums I knew he would never follow through on. At one point, he was taking me to an unspecified location where he would keep me barefoot and pregnant for the rest of my days. He'd given me all kinds of guilt trips, but when the time had come to go to bed, he climbed in next to me and held me close. When morning had come, he woke me up in the sweetest way and was back to being Dev. I was coddled and cuddled and loved until I cried out all my tension.

Daniel was another story. Daniel was doing what he always did. Daniel was pulling away.

For the last week, he hadn't slept with us, preferring to use the interior room. He still fed and he still had sex with me. When he was making love to me, there was no question in my mind that it was love. He was passionate and said all the right things in the heat of the moment, but after, there was a coldness and a distance that left me feeling brutally alone. Danny had worked with Dev relentlessly to get ready for this meeting, but he wouldn't share a bed and he wouldn't go out with us when we took the night off.

He blamed me for what happened to Joel, or he blamed himself. Either way, I felt his absence and I was going to have to find a way to work through it.

Then there had been the unexpected nuisance of the purification ritual I'd been informed I had to follow for seven days prior to the fertility ritual.

Unlike the other rituals we performed, which I will admit have been informal and mostly for our own pleasure, this one had a few caveats. Ingrid had shown up four days ago with a box she said was for me.

When I opened it there was the most beautiful gauzy white gown. It could have been a nightgown, but it was more formal somehow. She'd made it for me and it fit perfectly. It was oddly old-fashioned for the ritual we were to perform, but it made my skin glow and showed off my breasts in a fashion I knew would make my faery prince's mouth water. When I gazed into the mirror, I thought I looked a little like a bride on her wedding night.

Then Ingrid explained all the things I couldn't do between then and the ritual. No meat. No alcohol. I was supposed to spend an hour a day in quiet contemplation. I have no idea what I was supposed to contemplate. I had to scrub my skin every day with some kind of exfoliant containing sand from Dev's *sithein*. I asked if I was to abstain from sex as well, but Ingrid glared at me like I was slightly off and told me there was nothing impure about sex. I was beginning to wonder what all the fuss was about and would have complained, but Dev was so enthusiastic I found myself unwilling to disappoint the only man who was happy with me.

"Wow, this place is beautiful," Sarah said from the third row of seats. She and Felix had come along as part of our retinue. We weren't allowed to bring vampires other than Daniel, so we had filled out our party with a small group of friends. In addition to Sarah and Felix, there was Lee and Zack. Declan would be along shortly, and I'd been informed that the organizers of the Gathering were honored to be hosting the future king of Faery. Unlike vampires, the *sidhe* tend to be welcomed wherever they go.

Albert had gone ahead of us to make sure everything was ready. The thought of our proper butler pitching tents made me giggle.

The car stopped in front of a magnificent cabin. I call it a cabin because of the materials used to make it, but it was a mansion really. McKenzie wasn't going to miss the million he was paying us.

Lee got out first. After a moment, he gave the signal for the rest of us to move. Dev rushed around to help me out and I waited patiently because it was important to him. There was a middle-aged wolf with a clipboard walking toward us, a wide smile on his face.

"Your Grace," he said to Dev, using the title bestowed on a high priest. In this case, his status as a high priest superseded his princely title. "It is such an honor to have you here. I am Matthew, Mr. McKenzie's assistant. He's waiting in the house and requests your company before you join the others."

"We would be honored." Dev threaded my arm through his and followed the assistant.

John McKenzie's home was a stunning combination of natural beauty and modern luxury. We were led into a great room with huge bay windows overlooking the valley. I glanced back at Sarah and bet she was wondering the same thing I was. She was wondering if Neil was out there in those lush forests.

"Devinshea." A man who could only be John McKenzie greeted us warmly.

He was an alpha, no doubt about it. There was a certain power that emanated from an alpha wolf that even a human could feel. He was a leader from his casual but expensive boots to the pearl snaps on his Western shirt. He was probably in his mid-thirties but could be older. He was in his prime, leading the largest wolf pack in the country.

"It's good to see you, John," Dev replied. "Your home is lovely. We're so pleased to be invited."

McKenzie shook Dev's hand. "And we're pleased you agreed to help us, Your Grace. I believe you'll find all has been made ready for you. We've been working on the altar for days. My wife's been having fun with it. She's handy with craft projects."

"Excellent. I'm sure it's lovely. My brother will bring a few things with him we will incorporate into the altar," Dev said and pulled my hand to his lips. "Let me introduce you to my goddess, Zoey Donovan."

"It is a pleasure to meet you," McKenzie said, tipping his head gallantly my way. "I thank you, in advance, for being willing to help us. Fertility has been an issue for many years now. It's been difficult on our females."

I nodded because put like that I was willing to overlook my embarrassment. "We'll do our best."

"If I understand correctly, you're also Donovan's queen,"

McKenzie said with an amused smile on his face.

I returned it because I was well aware ménages were not the norm on this plane. "I'm Daniel Donovan's companion, though I prefer the term wife. He's happy to have the opportunity to make his case to you, Mr. McKenzie. You'll find him a reasonable and fair man."

He looked slightly skeptical but seemed unwilling to argue with me. "I promise to listen to everything the vampire has to say. If he is correct, then I need to listen to him. But for now, please introduce me to the rest of your party."

The introductions went well. Everyone was polite and friendly right up to the point McKenzie and Lee got in each other's faces. One minute John McKenzie was a friendly host and the next he was growling at my wolf.

"What the hell do you think you're doing here?" McKenzie all but spat.

"My fucking job, Mac." Lee didn't move an inch.

"You know loners aren't welcome in my home," the alpha said.

A low snarl came from the back of Lee's throat. "I'm not going anywhere so you better get used to it. Are you hiding something you don't want the others to find out about? Can't stand anyone you can't push around?"

"Hey, what's up with the boy fight?" I put myself in between the growling wolves. I pushed Lee back and faced our host. They'd obviously met before, but I wasn't looking for that story yet. "Is there something wrong with my wolf?"

I placed a heavy emphasis on the "my" part.

"He's a loner," McKenzie said in an accusatory fashion, as if it was a horrible thing to be. "He's only here to cause chaos. He doesn't care about his own kind. He's a troublemaker." The alpha looked at Dev. "You didn't mention you were bringing a loner, Your Grace."

Dev held his hands up, taking himself out of this particular fight. "I didn't really know he was one until a few days ago. Don't look at me, John. I've fired him several times. My goddess has an incomprehensible affection for him."

"He's not going to cause trouble," I stated plainly. "He's entirely too lazy to cause trouble. He just wants to sleep and drink his beer and watch the occasional wrestling show, though I don't know why he likes that. I tried to explain to him that it's fake, but I don't think he believes me. He's completely harmless."

Lee snorted behind me. "I'm…"

I gave him that look I give men when I want them to shut up. He acted like he wanted to defend his manhood but made the smart play and closed his mouth. I turned back to McKenzie. "Lee promises to behave himself. He's just here to do his job which is to make sure no one kills me. I assure you, he'll be far too busy with that to cause a bunch of trouble. Tell him, Lee. Tell him that you'll try to play well with the other wolves."

I heard Zack snicker behind me and sent him a look too. Lee frowned at me, but after a moment nodded McKenzie's way. "I'm not here to cause trouble. I really am just here to do my job."

"Are people going to try to kill you, Mrs. Donovan?" McKenzie asked, a frown on his face.

"Oh, it's probably inevitable." Halfer was still out there. We had decided the possibility of him showing up here was very small. We'd talked endlessly about the fact that it hadn't worked on Zack. He'd felt absolutely nothing when close to the artifact. It had made Lee sick. The Strong Arm of Remus had been a bust so he couldn't use it on the wolves. He didn't have an army with him so we felt fairly safe from Halfer here among the werewolves. Of course, I had more problems than just him. "Is Mitchell Roberts here?"

"The Dallas alpha? Yes, I believe he's due to arrive here in the morning," the assistant replied, checking his clipboard.

I smiled. It was good to know exactly who would be coming after me. "Then yes, I expect at least one attempt on my life."

McKenzie's eyes got wide. "Do we need to supply you with extra security? Matthew, perhaps we should bar Roberts from the Gathering."

I shook my head, not at all worried. "Please, don't trouble yourself. It's nothing Lee can't handle if I don't kill him myself." I smiled brightly at the thought. The last week had been tension filled. A good fight might clear my head. I turned to my boyfriend. "Baby, this whole purging myself of impurities thing, does that include killing?"

"Well, murder is not the purest act, lover," Dev replied with a serene look on his face. "I would prefer you waited to kill Mitchell until after the ceremony is over."

I sighed. "Fine. If he needs killing before the ceremony then Lee can do it. See, Mr. McKenzie, there's nothing to worry about. You'll find we always try to handle our own problems. You won't even notice we're here."

McKenzie shook his head like he was having a hard time following the conversation. "You're an interesting group."

"You have no idea," Dev replied.

* * * *

It was almost nightfall when we finally made our way into the valley. This was all McKenzie's land and it went on for miles. It was completely isolated and the valley was filled with werewolves. They were everywhere. There were small tents, large tents, and simple setups with sleeping bags. Everywhere we went, the wolves smiled at us and shot Dev looks of great respect and gratitude. I wasn't used to being respected. People were wary around Daniel. When I played companion to Daniel's vampire, people tended to ignore me completely for the most part. That wasn't the case at this outing.

"Good evening, ma'am," a female wolf said as we walked through the valley.

"Hello," I replied, my arm still through Dev's. "Whatever you're cooking smells heavenly."

Her husband was behind her now and beamed down at his wife. "She's the best damn cook I know. Please join us. It's her legendary beef stew. We have more than enough."

Dev shook the man's hand. "It does indeed smell lovely. Unfortunately, my goddess and I are abstaining from animal flesh until after the ceremony. Purity of the body is important to the ritual."

The woman's eyes went wide with fear. "We didn't know. They didn't say anything about changing our diet."

"Not at all, dear lady," Dev said, charm oozing from his pores. "There's absolutely nothing you need to do but show up with your husband and desire in your heart. My goddess and I will handle the rest. Though be kind to her. She's been forced to give up burgers and cheese. It's made her cranky."

I punched him in the arm. "Has not. The lack of alcohol made me cranky. I need a beer."

The wolf couple laughed at our banter, and I was glad we would be able to help them. It was like that everywhere we went. We were offered food, drink, small gifts. A little boy welcomed me with a handful of wildflowers and I tried really hard not to cry because he was so sweet. He thanked me and said he wanted a baby brother.

By the time we made it to our tent, I was filled with a sweet sense of belonging. I stood beside the massive structure it must have taken several men days to erect and realized Dev's version of a tent was different than everyone else's.

"Seriously?" I asked because the damn thing had windows.

Smiling slyly, Dev pulled the flap open. "You didn't think I would have us in tents and sleeping bags, my lover? I thought you realized I don't camp."

I walked into our little movable palace and quickly found it had several rooms.

"Good evening, mistress." Albert greeted me as he was lighting a gas lamp. It gave the room a romantic air. "Dinner will be served in thirty minutes. It's a lovely spinach and strawberry salad with a saffron risotto."

"That sounds delicious, Albert," Sarah, the vegan, said. She'd been thrilled at my forced vegetarianism. She firmly believed that once I got used to it, I wouldn't go back.

"You know what would make it better? A side of beef," I groused lightly.

Albert smiled. "I've been informed to greet you with a pound of bacon three mornings hence."

"Now you're talking, Al." I was already looking forward to that little breakfast treat. Dev kissed my cheek and walked away to find our bedroom. I was left with our butler. "So did you pick out where you want to set up your 401k?"

He shook his horns and looked down at me, confusion in his blue eyes. "The master said you wished to free me. Have I done something improper? Has my work not been to your liking?"

Quickly I shook my head in the negative. "Not at all, Albert. You're the best butler anyone could ask for."

209

He pulled himself up to his impressive height, pride in every inch of his body. "Then why does my mistress wish to force me from my home?"

"Whoa, now, I never said anything about that. I just thought Dev should pay you," I quickly explained. Felix and Sarah laughed at my discomfort.

"It's insulting, mistress," Albert replied. "I could never show my face again if I accepted anything so vile as money for serving my master. I was hurt by the insinuation I would even want that."

"I'm sorry," I said quietly, hoping the slave would accept my apology.

Albert nodded in a superior, not at all slave-like fashion. "I will ignore the insult, mistress. I'm sure in your world it was a sweet gesture. I look forward to one day training your children in the ways of our world."

"Children?"

Albert smiled at the thought. "Yes, mistress. I'm also a well-trained nanny. The master made sure of it." With that little tidbit dropped, Albert went to the kitchens to make sure all was ready for dinner.

"I'm sure he'll be an interesting fixture at the playground, Z," Daniel said from the door. I turned to see a wry smile on his face. "Good evening, Sarah, Felix. I'm going to steal my wife for a moment. She'll join you for dinner shortly."

He took my hand and started to lead me away. Daniel took me down a corridor and I knew he, at least, hadn't been surprised by the opulence of the structure. He knew exactly where he was going.

"I will?" I asked, surprised I would be joining anyone shortly. Daniel usually took his time when he fed. He might not be willing to spend a ton of time with me talking lately, but he damn sure enjoyed himself in bed.

"I have to meet McKenzie in an hour," he explained. "You'll be dining with Felix and Sarah. Dev and I will be at the big house for most of the evening. It's just a preliminary meeting but it's important. If I can convince McKenzie, then he'll call in the other alphas."

He pulled me into a small room. There was no window here, and I drew in a startled breath at the sight of a coffin.

"I've got to sleep somewhere," Daniel said and pulled me to the couch which was the only other piece of furniture in the room. There was a single suitcase on the rug and a briefcase I was sure held his laptop.

"Why aren't you sleeping with us?" Dev would never have brought a small bed. There would be more than enough room.

"It's too dangerous," he said shortly, and I knew he was lying.

"Are you mad about the stuff Albert said?"

"The stuff about kids?"

I nodded. The worst fight Danny and Dev ever had revolved around the possibility of Dev knocking me up.

"You sleep with a fertility god, Z." Daniel's voice went low, his hand scrubbing through his hair. "He can be as careful as possible but someday… You don't want kids anymore? You always did before."

"I knew I wasn't going to have kids when you turned, Danny," I admitted. He couldn't have kids and I had accepted that a long time ago.

"And Dev? You just expect him to not have kids because I can't? That doesn't seem fair." Daniel took a long breath, his eyes turning weary. "You've already given up a hell of a lot for me, Zoey. I never meant for you to sacrifice so much."

He slumped down on the sofa, and I sat on his lap before he could stop me. I let my hands find his hair, smoothing it back. "I haven't given up much, Danny. I didn't finish college, but let's face facts. Was I ever going to get a nine-to-five job? We were fooling ourselves. The kids thing…we'll sort it out later. I just want to be happy for a while. I don't want you to pull away from me."

Danny sighed, his head falling back. "I watched you and Dev walk through the valley, Z. Man, everyone loved you. That had to feel good. They respected you."

"They respected the fact that Dev can help them have babies, Danny."

"They were happy to see you too, Z. You're his goddess. He doesn't do the whole 'get a bunch of wolves pregnant' thing if you aren't around."

I snorted at the thought. "I assure you if I weren't around, Dev would have another 'goddess.' He's a good boyfriend, but I doubt he would be celibate if he hadn't found me."

Daniel started to play with the collar of my shirt, his hand rubbing my throat. There was a little mischievous smile on his face. "Baby, what exactly do you think is happening two nights from now?"

I rolled my eyes. "We're performing a ritual, and I get to have sex with Dev in front of a bunch of horny wolves. Why are you laughing?"

Daniel leaned forward and kissed my neck. His hands tightened, and I felt his body begin to react. "I'm really looking forward to seeing you after that particular ceremony is over."

I frowned but let him continue because it was the happiest he'd been in days. If the thought of me embarrassing myself gave him some small measure of joy, then I would let him have it.

Daniel's magic flowed all around me. He pulled and pushed me until I straddled him, my knees cradling his hips. His big hands palmed my thighs, pushing up my skirt. I wanted to force him to talk to me. I wanted him to tell me what was wrong and let me help him solve it. I knew he wouldn't let me do any of that, so I took the only connection we had lately.

I kissed him, pulling his head to mine and licking lightly at his lips. He groaned and delved deeply into my mouth, his hands moving up until his fingers teased at my core. He didn't have to shove my undies aside since Dev hadn't packed me any. He'd decided they just complicated things.

My tongue slid along his, grazing his fangs as I unbuttoned the fly of his jeans. His cock was already long and thick, hot against my fingertips. I wrapped my hand around him, pumping him in my palm. Danny groaned and looked down, watching me work him.

I wanted to give to him, to take away his cares. The last week had been hard on both of us, and all I wanted was to see him relaxed and happy even if it was only for a few moments.

"God, Z, I don't have time for this," he said even as his hands gripped my ass and he pulled me tightly against him. "I need to get ready to meet McKenzie."

"Don't." This was the only way he would let me close. I couldn't lose it. I kissed him again, practically begging him to stay with me for a while. I felt him drifting and it hurt my heart. We'd been so happy all these months, but I'd screwed it up. I couldn't help but wonder where we would be if I hadn't gotten dragged back into Halfer's plans.

With a little growl, he lifted me. His lowered me onto his erection, filling me up. I held onto his shoulders, letting him control the penetration.

"You feel so good." This was what I needed. I needed him, but I was worried that the longer he stayed away from our bed, the further away he became.

But not now. Now he was inside me. He was with me, and I let time stop. I let the world shrink down until it was only the two of us. Everything else fell away. His magic blanketed us, a warm cocoon to keep out the rest of the world.

I shifted on his cock, pleasure vibrating through me.

Daniel gripped my ass, his hips slamming up. "I shouldn't be doing this. God, Zoey. I can't fucking help myself. You're going to be the death of me."

His words rang in my head, but his magic was stronger. The pleasure was stronger. I held on to him so tightly, praying it didn't have to end. I gave over to Daniel, letting him move me on his cock, his strong arms making a toy of me like I weighed nothing at all. Over and over he moved me, forcing his cock deep until there wasn't anything between us, no space, no time, nothing.

Daniel pulled my head back and suddenly sank his fangs in with a dominant strength that took my breath away. My fingers wound their way into his thick, sandy hair and held him as he drew heavily from my neck. His hips moved, thrusting his cock in time to the rhythm of his mouth. Every tug brought me closer to the edge until I finally let everything go and gave in to the powerful orgasm Danny was always able to draw out of me. It left me boneless and physically satisfied. I slumped over, wrapping myself around him.

Daniel released the vein and licked the side of my neck. A moment of pure peace flowed over me. I rubbed my nose over the strong muscles of Danny's neck, feeling smooth skin and breathing in his scent.

I felt his hands move, shifting me slightly so he could tuck himself back in. He stood, easily lifting me into his arms, and he stepped outside his small room. I didn't hate leaving that coffin behind. He seemed to know his way around Dev's little tent palace. He took a left and then strode into what had to be the master bedroom. Sure enough, there was a bed that was big enough for five, covered in sumptuous fabric. Gas lights lit the room. It was gauzy and romantic, and I knew how I wanted to spend the next couple of hours.

Daniel set me down on the bed, but he stepped back, not following me.

"I can make sure you're relaxed for your meeting." We could call Dev in and be together for a while. I stared up at him. His face had closed off. Those blue eyes were colder than before, utterly remote. "Danny," I whispered. "Please. I need you, baby."

I did. I needed him so much, and he was holding himself back.

He stood over me, his eyes staring, but I wasn't sure what he was seeing. His previous words came back to haunt me. I would be the death of him. I'd been the death of his charge. Daniel took those vamps seriously. They had a connection, a friendship that should have lasted for close to eternity, and because of me, one of them was dead.

I sat up, pushing my skirt down. "Can we talk about it?"

He was withdrawing, and I had to wonder if he was pulling back for the last time. I had to wonder if this was the time he left me for good.

After a long moment he smoothed his clothes out. "There's nothing to talk about, Z."

I didn't try to stop the tears forming in my eyes. "Please tell me what's wrong. I'll try to fix it. I didn't mean to get Joel killed. I didn't. I thought I was doing the right thing."

I saw the look of naked pain cross his face, but he banished it so quickly I almost believed I'd imagined it. "What are you talking about, Z? Everything's fine. I don't want to be late. This meeting is really important. It means a lot to me. If we don't get the wolves on our side…well, I have a plan for that, too. It doesn't matter now. Have a nice dinner. Don't wait up."

Daniel walked out without a second glance.

I sat there for the longest time wondering when he would tell me we were over.

Chapter Twenty

I gazed down at the beautiful meal Albert had prepared for us and questioned if I was just destined to make myself unhappy. I was sitting in a beautiful place surrounded by good friends. Dev had kissed me soundly before he left and told me he loved me. He'd enveloped me in his particular warmth. His joy in being in this place, preparing to do what he was born to do, should have been contagious. I really did love that he was happy. I just wished Danny could share in that, and that was the crux of my problem. I loved two men and I had begun to worry that having only one of them would never be enough for me.

"Z, what's wrong?" Sarah looked up from her meal, concern in her eyes. "I know it's not the food because the food is unbelievable, so I have to think it's Daniel."

I frowned at my friend. "Why would you say that?"

She smiled, but there was no humor to it. "When you're unhappy, Daniel is almost always the root cause, Zoey."

A little overdramatically stated, but Danny certainly had a strong effect on my moods. "I think he blames me for Joel's death."

Felix shook his head. "You're wrong about that. I think he blames himself, and he doesn't know how to deal with it. Daniel tends to push away the people he loves when he feels he's done something wrong."

"Yeah, well, he's pushing me pretty hard," I replied.

"He's been doing it for a long time. It's his default state. He's been happy since Vegas. What happened with Halfer just proved to him that everything in his life goes wrong in the end. If it helps you, I'm almost certain Devinshea feels as disconnected from Daniel as you do," Felix said sagely.

I studied the former angel for a moment before speaking. I always took what Felix said seriously. He had millennia of experience watching human behavior backing up his opinions. "He's spent every spare minute with Dev. I doubt Dev feels neglected."

"Daniel is no longer sharing a bed with the two of you," Felix pointed out. "Dev is a creature of physical affection. Though he and Daniel don't share their bodies, I assure you he feels his partner's loss."

"Partner?"

"What else would you call them, Zoey? Dev and Daniel have shared a business, a home, a quest, a female for almost a year now. Their lives have become intertwined in a way most people can't comprehend. They depend on each other. Daniel will never find another person who understands him the way Devinshea can, and I include you in that. You don't understand what it means to love you but Dev and Daniel do." Felix fixed me with a soft stare. "I believe Daniel has come to rely on Dev in a way he never imagined. But his past informs his future. Daniel learned at a young age what it means to lose the people he loved, the people who loved him. He lost his own human life. I'm sure he sees what happened with Halfer as a wake-up call. He imagines his life will always be filled with loss. In his head, it's a matter of time before he loses you and very likely Dev as well."

So we were right back where we started. "How do I fix it?"

"If you want Daniel to come back, you must stop thinking of it as a solo venture. You are a threesome. You must show a united front."

"You think I should talk to Dev about it?" I'd avoided talking to Dev, thinking it was my problem.

"I think you and Dev should talk to Daniel about it," Felix corrected. "It's far past time you got serious about your relationship. It's not just sex and pleasure. The three of you must care about each other. You must want to be together."

I smiled at Felix. "I do. I know Dev does, too. What if Daniel doesn't?"

Felix's head shook slightly. "No one has gained more from this relationship than Daniel. Daniel has gained power and the ability to walk in the daylight. Dev's magic gave him back that part of his life. More than this, Dev has given him a companionship he lacked before. If he wishes to end it then he's a fool. You move on with Dev. I think you'll find that Daniel is reacting, not thinking. Make it plain to him what the two of you need and what you deserve from him. He'll either come around or he'll leave. Either way, you'll have your answer."

"Aren't you supposed to be non-confrontational, cousin?" I didn't like the possible outcome of his scenario. I never like to face realities that don't suit me.

"I'm nonviolent," Felix amended. "Confrontation is unavoidable in a relationship. If you choose to hide, then Daniel will make the choice for all three of you."

Sarah patted her husband's hand. "He's right, you know."

"He's always right. It's disgusting."

"I know," Sarah confided. "It's really hard to live with him sometimes."

I heard the flap to the tent open and then the audible sound of not one but two safeties being clicked off. Sarah and I exchanged glances, both of us standing. I hoped she was armed because I'd left my Ruger in the bedroom and Felix would just try to talk whoever it was to death. I walked out of the dining room, Sarah and Felix hard on my heels.

"Stand down, lady." Lee stood in the middle of the front room, staring down the blonde women in the entryway. "Surrender that weapon and maybe I'll think about letting you live."

"Funny." Jane Nichols looked cool and comfortable in jeans and a tank top. I just knew there would be a whole lot of tank tops at a place like this. The private investigator gave my bodyguard the once-over. "I was just about to say the same thing to you."

The two wolves stared at each other, neither willing to give up the standoff. I had zero doubt that they would shoot if necessary. They were both hardened professionals who wouldn't back off. They were both being drama llamas, but then I seemed to be surrounded by them.

"It's fine, Lee. You remember Jane from Ether. She's the PI I hired to find Neil. Please don't shoot her before she tells me if she found him or not."

Lee lowered his gun with a grudging sigh, and Jane did the same.

"She should knock," Lee grumbled, but I noticed his eyes took in every inch of Jane Nichols, and not in a size-up-the-competition way. I was already thinking about how I could play the matchmaker.

It had worked really well with Zack. He was so much less obnoxious since he started dating Lisa. Maybe Lee would be less grumpy if he was getting laid.

"It's canvas," Jane pointed out, giving as good as she got. "I doubt a knock would have worked."

"I would have heard you," Lee replied misanthropically, but I noticed he tried to smooth down his wrinkled T-shirt. He kicked his empty beer bottle behind the chair he'd been dozing in.

Jane rolled her eyes and turned toward me. "I have some news for you."

"Please come in." I gestured toward the sofa in the large room we were in. It was set up like a parlor or sitting room. I assumed this was where Dev intended to have guests.

Albert walked out of the dining room. Jane gasped slightly at the sight of the demon, who ignored her, preferring to pin me with a disappointed stare. "Dinner was not to your liking, mistress?"

"It was delicious." I'd barely touched it, but I was sure it was good. Everything Albert did was spectacular.

"It was amazing, Albert." Felix patted his belly with a smile. "The risotto was divine. You have a delicate hand with it. We were merely interrupted with some business."

"I can set another place if that is your wish," Albert offered.

I shook my head, gesturing toward Jane. "I don't think she's the salad type."

Jane nodded. "I'm a carnivore."

Albert looked gravely disappointed in all of us, and I shifted uncomfortably. "Perhaps you will eat breakfast in the morning, mistress. You have to keep your strength up. If you faint, I assure you the master will blame me though I have spent every bit of my energy trying to please you. I'll serve dessert. It's a pineapple tart with a lovely dry wine."

Albert turned and disappeared into the kitchen.

Sarah couldn't stop the giggle now. "Man, no one can pull a guilt trip like a demon. You better think twice the next time you try to free him."

"I'm never mentioning it again," I assured her.

Jane walked around our shelter, shaking her head. "This is what passes for a tent with a vampire king?"

I had to correct that misunderstanding. "This isn't Daniel's doing. If it had been up to Danny, we'd be sleeping in the back of Lee's pickup. This is what passes for roughing it for royal faery kind. Devinshea doesn't believe in discomfort."

"Obviously," she muttered.

"It's one of the reasons he got along so well with Neil." It was time to bring the conversation around to the point.

Albert reentered with a tray. He passed everyone a small china dish with a perfectly presented tart in the center. The china was expensive and exquisite, and Lee clutched it uncomfortably, like he was terrified he was going to break it. The small plastic fork was incongruous against the wealth of the china, but one does not bring the good silver to a werewolf gathering. They get offended.

Everyone else got a glass of wine. I got handed a stupid bottle of water. I begrudgingly ate my tart.

"I believed the prince was as upset with Neil as the vampire." Jane got back to our conversation once the butler was gone.

"He was, but he'll come around. It's difficult for Dev to stay mad at people. He's infinitely more reasonable than Daniel."

"And why should I believe Neil will be safe or even welcomed into this home?" Jane asked. It was obvious she'd come to like Neil.

It made me trust her more that she could accept him. I'd been blatantly honest about Neil's past. I thought it necessary that Jane know as much about the situation as possible. She hadn't blinked when I talked about Neil's homosexuality. As the great majority of the wolf world was at least a little homophobic, it had bought big points with me that it didn't bother Jane.

"She doesn't know you very well, does she?" Sarah asked with a little laugh.

I had some guilt about not talking this over with Dev and Daniel. I'd tried, but they avoided the subject like the plague. Neil was in trouble, and I wasn't going to allow their stubbornness to cause him more pain. "Neil will be more than welcome here. If Daniel doesn't like it, then he can find somewhere else to sleep. It wouldn't be the first time he's burrowed into the ground for a daytime nap. When he decides to acquiesce, he can come home."

If he wanted to come home.

Jane leaned forward, her brows in a concerned *V*. "Those men

219

have reputations, Zoey. They're considered seriously dangerous. Donovan is a hardened killer. He's the freaking *Nex Apparatus*, for god's sake. It's said that the faery is more reasonable, but he's also the one who'll smile and make you feel comfortable and then shove a knife in your back."

"That sounds about right," Lee agreed.

I disagreed with all of those statements, but the boys had worked hard to build their reputations and I had to respect that. In my business, a ferocious reputation was as important as actual skill. My father's rep had been fierce even though he was a big old teddy bear at home. And Dev would never shove a knife in someone's back if he could avoid it. It would ruin his clothes. He would pay someone to do it for him.

"Neither Daniel or Dev would hurt Neil," Felix added.

Lee's amusement rumbled through his body. "They sure as hell wouldn't do it if they thought Zoey could ever find out. That wolf will be safe here. Trust me, she has her boys by the short hairs and she's not letting go."

"Eww. That's rude." Sometimes Lee's turns of phrases were a little vulgar.

"It's also true," Lee shot back.

Jane held up a hand. "All right, then, I'll work on the premise that Zoey is in charge of her household."

"Does all of this checking Z out mean you've convinced him to come home?" Sarah asked.

"He's willing to meet with you and Zoey," Jane affirmed, and my heart soared. "He'll meet with you tomorrow at noon. I'll guide you to the spot in the north woods. Just the two of you, though."

"Not a chance in hell, lady." Lee stood over the blonde, his face a grim mask. "You think I'm letting her run around the woods in the middle of a thousand freaking werewolves by herself?"

"I'll be with her." Jane stood as well, erasing Lee's height advantage. She didn't mind getting into his space either. "I'll make sure nothing happens to them."

"Over my dead body," Lee growled.

"That can be arranged," Jane growled right back.

Sarah and I exchanged a nervous look. I wasn't sure if this was going to be a fight or if I was watching some strange werewolf mating ritual.

"I think Jane can handle it, Lee," I said calmly, not certain I wanted to stop the fight. It might be interesting to see if Jane could handle Lee.

When Lee stared at me, I felt the full force of his will. He was one pissed-off wolf. "Look here, Zoey, have I done everything I promised? I let you kill that weird-ass thing with the bird. I let you fight the freaky zombies. I hijacked a damn truck with you and became an art thief. I let you castrate me in front of fucking John McKenzie who I hate. Foot's down now, Zoey."

I knew then that I'd hit Lee's brick wall. I smiled at Jane. "Lee will be accompanying us."

"Damn straight," he muttered under his breath.

"He might run." Jane backed down.

Lee shoved a hand through his hair. "He won't get far. I'm sick of Zoey being upset over this. He's being a stubborn idiot. If he runs, I'll chase him down and haul his ass home."

"That actually might be for the best," Jane said with a sigh. "I was going to recommend bringing him in whether he wants to come or not. He's very sick."

My stomach rolled at the thought. It was what I'd been really worried about. Though Neil was a werewolf, he'd lived in the city all of his life. He had all the instincts necessary to survive in the wild, but I worried about his will to live. Before he became Danny's servant, he'd had a rough life. The loss of Chad and Neil's whole support network would have taken a hard toll on my friend.

"Do I need to call in a doctor?" I was sure I would be able to find at least one doctor among all these wolves. It wasn't a profession known for a high werewolf population, but there had to be at least one.

"I won't know until we get him to change forms," Jane admitted. "As far as I can tell, he's been in wolf form for months with no physical contact at all."

Lee whistled at that. "None? No wonder he's sick."

"I don't understand," I said.

"When Neil was around, did he seem to require physical contact more than say a normal human would?" Jane asked.

I nodded vigorously. "Oh, yes. Neil was always holding my

hand. If we were watching TV, he would lay his head in my lap and I would rub his belly." I gave Lee a pointed stare because he had been serious about that no-petting rule. "And he didn't like to sleep alone. He had his own bed, but most of the time he ended up cuddled up with me. It surprised Dev the first time he turned over and Neil was in bed with us."

It had surprised him, but in true Dev fashion, he'd merely taken back his fair share of the covers, rolled over, and gone back to sleep.

"All wolves need that contact," Jane explained. "It's necessary for the wolf to be healthy. Without it they tend to fade. I think that's what's happening to Neil. I'm hoping he'll come out of it when he realizes he's still loved and wanted."

I reached out and held Sarah's hand. There was a sheen of tears in her eyes I knew mirrored my own. "He is wanted. And he is definitely loved."

And tomorrow, one way or another, he was coming home.

Chapter Twenty-One

It was difficult for me to fall asleep that night. I sat up for the longest time in the enormous bed Dev had managed to get hauled into the wilderness. It was so big I felt tiny as I sat in the center of it, wearing only a T-shirt of Dev's that hung down to my knees. The night air was slightly chilly even though it was June, so I pulled the quilt around me. I had convinced Lee that I could handle being in the room by myself. He seemed wary about the amount of wolves around. I'm not sure what he thought was going to happen, but my guard was just a little on edge. I think he would have slept at the foot of the bed if I'd let him.

I sat up and listened to the music playing in the distance. There was a big party going on somewhere, and I wondered if Danny and Dev were in the midst of it. I had considered forcing Lee to accompany me and checking out the rave that was going on, but I would have been thinking about my problems the whole time. I'd said good night to Sarah and Felix and sat in the dark, worried about Danny and Neil.

I spent more than my required contemplative hour thinking about what Felix had said. Was I being self-centered thinking that if Danny left, I was the only one it really affected? Would Dev miss Daniel? Then there was the question of whether Daniel could leave me at all. He needed my blood or he would go through some serious withdrawal pains. I was pretty sure Marini wouldn't just allow Daniel and me to split up without repercussions. If he thought Daniel had given up rights to me, I could only hope that Marcus had enough money to buy me if Marini even let me hit the auction house. I knew what Dev would do if he thought the Council was coming for me. I would be seeing a whole lot of Faeryland.

It was something to think about.

I still managed to fall asleep before the boys returned. My dreams were filled with visions of Daniel leaving and Neil dying because no one would touch him. Lucas Halfer showed up in there somewhere, holding that useless paw we had fought over, but I discounted him. He'd been the bogeyman in my nightmares for two years now. I doubted that would change anytime soon. You just don't forget the first man to show you the horrors of Hell.

Sometime in the night, Dev had crawled into the big bed beside me. Morning light filtered through as I saw his beautiful face through half-awake eyes. I reached out and rubbed that perfect jaw with the hint of a beard. He would ruthlessly get rid of the whiskers as soon as he woke, so I had to enjoy the sight now. I loved the roughness of his face in the morning when he rubbed it against me. I studied my lover in the early morning light. It had only been a few weeks, but his hair was already longer. Before too long, he would pull it back in a queue. It was so dark and soft. I let my fingers run through it, and he sighed in his sleep. I was just about to kiss him when I felt Danny move at my back.

I closed my eyes against the sweet warmth of his leg shifting over mine. I said a silent prayer of thanks to whoever listened to such things. His arm curled around my waist and pulled me firmly into his hard body. I wondered how late I'd slept because while Danny was able to handle some daylight, he usually didn't wake until after noon. I decided to relax though because Sarah would have awakened me. There was no way she was going to miss our meeting, and Felix was a morning person.

I sighed contentedly and wondered just how much time we had before I needed to get ready for the meeting with Neil. It would be nice to wake up Dev and let him and Danny have their wicked way with me. We could roll around together and then have breakfast in bed. It was one of Dev's favorite things to do. Maybe if we could remind Daniel how good it was between the three of us, he would think twice about whatever he was planning.

Danny's hand moved on my hip and I put mine over his, leading him under the T-shirt and up to my chest. His hand cupped my breast and played with the nipple, which hardened immediately. I stretched, filling his hand. His lips found the back of my neck, nuzzling the skin there softly and giving me sweet little goose bumps. I let my eyes close as he pressed his erection against my backside. This wouldn't be another quickie. No. I wasn't going to allow it. This would be long and lush and loving. Everything it should be between us.

My eyes flew open when I heard the sound of yet another gun being primed as I felt Dev shift in bed. My lover was suddenly on his knees, holding a gun pointed at Danny's head.

"Dev, what the hell are you doing?" I didn't move because I wasn't about to startle him and cause him to fire. What had happened last night between them?

"Take your hands off her, brother," Dev ordered, his face a tight mask of fury.

I stilled. "Please tell me you're talking about Danny."

He sometimes referred to Daniel as "my brother" especially in jest.

I knew I was wrong when I felt that strange energy that flashed through me whenever Padric showed up.

"Hello, Prince Devinshea." Padric was wearing that wicked-looking knife I'd gotten acquainted with weeks before. He didn't have it at Dev's throat yet, but the threat was there. He was calm, as though awaiting the outcome before acting. A leather tie held his long white hair back, and his light eyes studied the scene before him.

I sat up, pushing Declan's hands away from my body. I scrambled out of the way of the gun and sat back where I could see both Dev and his brother. Declan looked up at Dev, confusion plain on his face. Dev kept the SIG Sauer aimed at his brother's head. I hadn't realized he'd started sleeping with it. He'd likely picked up the habit after Marini's little visit.

"If you think you can take me out, Padric," Dev began, his voice cold, "I would point out that I can probably take off his head before you can slit my throat." He didn't actually look at the royal guard. Dev never took his eyes off the target when he had a gun in his hand. Daniel had trained him well.

"I am hoping to avoid that scenario." Padric sounded rather amused as he watched the brothers. "Your mother would have my balls if I allowed the two of you to die."

Dev brought the gun to his side. Clicking the safety back on, he sat down on the bed. He finally turned to Padric as he replaced the gun in a small cabinet by the bed. "Well, you're right about him anyway. I'm sure mother would kill me herself if anything happened to her heir." Dev slid his gaze back to Declan. "What the hell are you doing in my bed, Dec? I don't remember extending an invitation."

Declan sat up, rubbing his eyes. "I arrived late last night, brother. I was tired. I recognized the layout of this shelter immediately. It is the same as the one mother uses, so I knew where the nicest bed would be. Your servant tried to show me to a smaller room." Declan huffed as if anyone would try to give him a small room. "I do not understand your upset. This bed is huge. It is certainly made for at least three people, probably more. The vampire was not here so there was an opening. It is not as though we have never shared a bed before. We shared a bed for most of our lives, if you care to recall our childhood."

"It is not the bed I am upset about and you know it," Dev pointed out.

"That was not my fault." Declan managed a royal-looking pout. "She is very warm and soft. It is cold here at night, much colder than our *sithein*. Can I be blamed for cuddling up to her?"

"Yes," Dev and I managed to say in complete harmony.

"She cuddled back." Declan made no attempt to hide his nudity, but then again neither did Dev. I was thankful I'd slept in the T-shirt. It seemed like a bad idea to sleep naked in a strange place. The Quinn twins had no such fears.

"I thought you were Daniel," I shot back. I didn't need Dev getting all bent out of shape again. I'd learned my lesson and didn't even glance at Declan's hair this time. Or his penis. Which I kind of wished he would put away somewhere.

"I know you did, my lover," Dev said, his face softening. "He took advantage of you. Shall I thrash him?"

Declan rolled his eyes and lay back down, his body hitting the mattress with an audible thud. "The day my brother, the priest, can beat me in a fight is the day I cede the crown to him."

"I don't know, Your Highness." Padric took in Dev's form with a satisfied nod. "The little priest seems to have changed. His body does not look like a priest's anymore. He appears to be a warrior, and I think he might have used that weapon on you had you pushed him further."

Dev sat back against the headboard. "I probably would not have killed him. I would certainly have maimed him, though. I still might. I shall think on it for a while."

"What is the problem, brother?" Declan really didn't seem to see a problem with molesting his brother's steady. "It is not as though we never shared a woman before. She is a sexy, sweet little thing but nothing to fight your own brother over."

Dev's face flushed, and he stood up suddenly. He walked around to his brother's side of the bed, pulled him up by the hair, and smacked him brutally right across the face. I felt the force of it and I was several feet away. I was startled but Declan was shocked. Padric cursed in a foreign language.

Dev released the hold on his brother and walked calmly over to the dresser. He pulled on boxers and a pair of sweatpants and shoved a T-shirt over his head as Declan sat up and held his jaw.

Padric shook his head at the future king, his stance angry. He spoke to him as he would a wayward child. "I told you to take him more seriously. He has survived on his own for many years now. It has made him harder. I believe I also advised you that Prince Devinshea was serious about this one. He would not make the request for the Goddess Chain lightly. How do I explain this to Miria?"

"You can't be serious, Dev?" Declan asked, ignoring Padric. It was the first time I had heard him slip into informal speech. He sat on the bed looking at his brother and obviously wondering where the hell he'd gone wrong.

"Your choice of weapons, of course." Dev crossed his hands over his chest. He spoke casually as though they were planning a dinner meeting. "We can do it this evening. I believe I have time around five o'clock, though I will have to check my schedule."

"Weapons?" I didn't like where this was going.

Declan turned to look at me like I'd done something wrong. "Yes, weapons, Zoey. My own brother means to try to kill me in a duel because I touched your breasts. You're the one who pulled my hand up there. It would have been rude to not play with them. I hope you're happy."

I was so done with Declan. "So if I slap the shit out of him, do I get to fight him, too?"

"I am not fighting my brother and I am not fighting a girl," Declan shouted. He shook his head. "Fine. Just fine. I am sorry, brother. I apologize for cuddling with your goddess. Next time, I will just remain cold. I will freeze to death rather than touching your precious goddess. Zoey, I apologize for finding your body so luscious. Can we not fight now?"

"I will think on it," Dev replied magnanimously. I got the feeling that Declan Quinn didn't often offer apologies.

Albert appeared at the door. He looked over the chamber with a frown and a sad shake of his horns. "Breakfast is ready. If you're done shouting, you may all partake in the dining room. I shall, of course, set a few more places. Will you be eating this morning, mistress, or are you continuing to shun sustenance?"

"I'll eat."

"Very good," he said gravely, and I knew I better eat a lot. He would be monitoring my intake. God, I hoped there wasn't any tofu.

I watched as Albert exited with a formal nod. "You know, for a slave he is really bossy, Dev."

Declan got up and Padric handed him a robe from a satchel. "I will see that he is settled in the guest room."

Declan huffed and stormed out.

Padric picked up the luggage and gave Dev a slight smile. "It is good to see you, Prince Devinshea. Your brother has missed you greatly. Please take into account that it has only been a year and a half in our time. He still sees you as you were. It is difficult for him to think you have grown up because in many ways, he has not. He is still only twenty-two while you are now the older brother. It will be a hard change for him."

"I thank you for your guidance," Dev said formally, bowing his head.

Padric started out the door but stopped. "And Devinshea, your mother does indeed miss you. She is stubborn as well, but she deeply regrets what she did in fear. We will speak more at breakfast. Miria asked me to accompany Declan fully this time. I am to be here physically to act as her envoy. I fear he is going to push you away when he should bring you closer." The white-haired man turned and left.

Dev shoved a frustrated hand through his hair and sat back down on the bed. I crawled over to him and wrapped my arms around him. "Who exactly is this Padric person? I thought he was a guard, but he seemed like something more just now. I wouldn't have expected him to speak to Declan the way he did."

"He is a royal guard," Dev replied. "He's also my mother's lover and has been for a hundred years. Even when she was married to my father, it was Padric who held her heart. When I was younger, he was the man who forced my father away. Even when I left the *sithein*, I hated him. Now, looking back with older eyes, I can see that he tried to be a father. It was difficult for him to understand me. He's a warrior as Declan is a warrior. I was something different. Still, when some of the royal house suggested I be left to die for my impurities, it was Padric who threatened to kill any who touched me. I was unfair to him."

"You were a child in a difficult situation," I said, hugging him close. "Treat him fairly now. Show him the man you have become and give him credit for some of it. That will be enough for him."

Dev brought my hand to his lips. "Are you terribly angry at the way my brother treated you?"

I laughed a little. "Not really, baby. He didn't mean any harm. I doubt he'll try it again since he doesn't fight girls. I was just disappointed it wasn't Daniel. I thought he had come back. Is he in that coffin?"

"Yes," Dev replied solemnly. "I believe he intends to use it the entire trip. As you can see this is not a light-tight shelter."

"It's more than that and you know it. If he'd been sleeping with us and feeding off your magic, he could handle this light with no problem. Do you know what he's planning?"

"I believe I've figured out some of it," Dev confirmed.

"Is he going to leave us?"

Dev moved to face me and took my hands in his. "Would it be so bad if it was just the two of us?"

"I love you, Dev. If it were just the two of us, I would be content. Is that what you and Daniel have decided to do?" I measured my words carefully. It wouldn't be the first time the boys had made life-changing decisions without bothering to consult me. They always had their reasons. Usually it was about protecting me. I also tried not to let them get away with it.

"Keep me out of this fight," Dev said, shaking his head with a weary sigh. "I do not agree with him but when Daniel decides something, I'm certainly not the one who can dissuade him."

I felt his pain. He was in a relationship where he felt like the one who was expendable. It was an old wound but quite capable of reopening at the slightest provocation. If Danny walked out, Dev would worry that I would follow him. Dev would also worry that I would blame him for losing Danny. It was a difficult position for Dev to be in, always walking a fine line. The things Felix had said were all coming back now. It was far past time we all made some serious decisions that didn't involve what side of the bed the boys liked.

I cradled Dev's cheeks in my hands and stared into the face of my lover before kissing him sweetly. "What do you want, Devinshea?"

It was a question no one thought to ask him most of the time.

His face went still, but he didn't pull away. "I want you."

"Is that all?"

It took him the longest time to answer, as though he was deciding just how much to tell me. "I want us. I want the three of us. I want you and me and Daniel. Maybe Daniel doesn't feel the same way. He didn't grow up as I did. He didn't have a brother. I'm happier with one, though the one I have is a bit of an ass. I want you for love and Daniel for companionship. They're both intimate relationships. I've never been as happy as I am when we're truly together. Daniel doesn't feel the same way, and I cannot force him to care for me, Zoey."

We lay back on the bed together, Dev pressing his head to my chest. I let my fingers play in his hair. "I think he cares about you more than he lets on. He's not great about expressing himself. I don't know what he's planning and if you do then keep it to yourself. Confidences between the two of you are just that. I'm not going to ask you to betray him. But I want to fight for him, Dev. I want to let him know he can't just walk away from us."

He nodded. "I think you should let him know that. He needs to hear it from you. He loves you, Zoey. No matter what he says, no matter what he has planned, he loves you. He's being an idiot because he can't stand the thought of losing you."

"Dev, we need to fight for him together," I corrected him. "I want to go to Daniel together and let him know what we need. He owes both of us. We both owe him. I think the first thing we need from him is a promise to talk to us rather than arbitrarily deciding what's best."

"I don't know, Zoey. I might just confuse the issue."

I wasn't getting through to him. "Dev, how much do you and Daniel talk about that you never mention to me? How much do the two of you know about each other that I don't? I'm your lover and Daniel knows more about your background than I do. Does Daniel know how you feel about Padric?"

He hesitated before admitting, "It might have come up in conversation before. I'm not trying to hide things from you."

I stopped him. "I don't begrudge you your friendship with Daniel, and I don't require that I know everything he does. That's not my point, Dev. I want the two of you to talk. You need each other. That's why we go to him together. Begin as we mean to end— together."

"And if he still leaves?"

"Then we mourn his loss and move on with our lives," I said, hoping beyond hope it didn't come to that. I couldn't imagine not having Daniel with us. He was important. He completed us.

"You won't leave me?" Dev asked quietly, and I knew it was his greatest fear that I would leave and Danny would leave and he would be alone again. He'd had many lovers before me, but I knew that until Daniel and I had come into his life, he'd been lonely.

I forced him to look at me, to feel my will. "I will never leave you, Devinshea. I love you. I'm here for the long haul, baby. Just try to get rid of me and see what happens." I took a deep breath and decided to be honest with him. "Just so you know, though, I'm still going to make you crazy."

"I wouldn't have it any other way," he said, smiling and pulling me firmly under his body.

I frowned as I looked up at him, hoping he was going to take this little tidbit of information well. "I found Neil."

"Good," he replied. "It is past time for him to come home."

I let out a deep breath I hadn't realized I was holding. "I thought you would be mad."

"I can be angry with him and still want him home and safe. I always knew you would find him, sweetheart. I think you will find Daniel's anger has lessened as well. We both want to have it out

231

with Neil, but we want him safe. It's difficult to kick someone's ass when they're dead." Dev was grinning down at me. "I love you, Zoey. Those you love will always be welcome in our home."

I wrapped my arms around his neck, loving the feel of his weight pressing me into the mattress. "So I get to keep Neil and Lee?"

"I would never be so cruel as to force you to give up your pets. And we'll fight together to keep Daniel." Dev lowered his head and kissed me, softly at first but with the promise of more to come.

Albert was going to be so upset with me, I thought as I gave myself over, but breakfast was just going to have to wait.

Chapter Twenty-Two

It was almost eleven by the time breakfast was done. Declan had been quiet throughout, though his manners were back for the most part. He switched his stare from me to his brother often, as though contemplating his next move. I'd begun to suspect that Declan's pursuit of me had more to do with his brother than any mad desire for my body. If Dev had been willing to share me, it would prove I was just like the hundreds who had come before me.

Padric and Dev had spoken throughout the meal, discussing what had been happening in the *sithein* since Dev left. I noted that Dev didn't ask questions about a woman named Gilliana who might or might not be his wife. I wanted to ask about her and any possible child she might have but decided to leave it for a more private time.

After breakfast, I moved into the front room which was now crammed with crap Declan had brought. He really didn't travel light. There were a bunch of trunks, crates, and boxes. What the hell he needed with everything I had no idea.

"They are gifts to the wolves," Declan said quietly behind me, reading my mind. "And bribes."

"For Dev?" I asked, reading his just a little.

"I miss him," Declan said with a regal nod of his head. "I do apologize if I offended you this morning. I did not wish to recognize that my brother might be ready to take an important step in his life when up until a few weeks ago, I had no idea you existed."

"I know it seems sudden to you, but we've been together for almost two years." An ornate gold cage was among the gifts. I stared down into it. There was a small ball of fur sleeping peacefully, burrowed down in a nest.

"I was the leader. From the time we were small children, I was the leader and Devinshea followed me. His powers were small and soft. I was strong. I was ruthless. I could protect him. I was the favorite of our people, and the truth is Devinshea was only accepted by the royals because he was my brother."

"And the non-royals?"

Declan smiled slyly. "Yes, well, they did not really care he was mortal. He was the Green Man. He made their crops grow. Did you know that when Devinshea walks through the fields of our *sithein*, everywhere he touches turns green and fruitful? He could not hide when we played games because I just followed the footprints in the grass or plants that grew in his wake." He paused for a moment, his lips turning down. "We need him to come home, Zoey. No one realized how important he was. His pleasant nature made him beloved by the commons and even the bloody Unseelie. They requested him as my mother's ambassador during recent negotiations. It did not go well when I went instead."

"What did you do, brother?" Dev asked with a sigh as he entered the room followed by Padric.

"Well, they are not threatening war," Declan offered.

"Yet," Padric added.

Dev sent his brother an annoyed look. "Damn it. I told you how to handle them. You have to treat them with respect. You have to allow them their customs. They will try to push you into showing your distaste. You must never show them."

"It is hard because I find them very, very distasteful," Declan shot back.

They were off and arguing about politics which meant my mind was off and wandering. I don't much care for the politics that directly affect me, much less politics on some other plane. I was busy watching the little furry thing sleep. It was such a sweet little puff ball. It opened its eyes and they were large and blue.

"It is a jalibuit," Padric explained as Dev and Dec continued to argue. "It is a rare creature found in Faery. We brought two of them as gifts to the wolves. They are good to hunt."

I made no attempt to hide my outrage. "You're going to let the wolves hunt that tiny, sweet little rabbit thing? That's horrible. And it's rare? No wonder it's rare. You let wolves hunt them."

I started to reach through the bars of the cage to pet the poor little thing that would likely be some wolf's morning snack soon.

Padric's hand shot out just as the sweet little thing became a rabid fury filled with sharp teeth. It rattled the cage and tried hard to break free.

"It is rare, Zoey, because it is a ferocious predator," Padric said with a wry smile.

"Zoey." Dev pulled me away from the cage. "You will not be keeping it as a pet."

"I don't want to." It had gone back to its former sweet state, but all I could see were teeth.

Dev kissed me lightly. "I have to go now. Our ceremony is tomorrow night and there are rituals I must perform to ready myself."

"Does it involve scraping off half your skin with faery sand?" I asked grumpily because I was still a little raw from my last encounter with that sand.

"Yes, of course," he replied, not taking the bait. He picked up a bag he'd prepared and started out the door.

"Devinshea," Padric called. "I believe those rituals are for you and the male members of your family."

Dev shook his head. "Given the way Declan feels about it, I will be fine alone."

"I would offer my services, Devinshea," Padric said plainly.

Dev smiled slightly and inclined his head. "I would be honored if you would accompany me."

Declan was frowning at the two of them. "Well, if Padric is going I am, too. Besides, if I am left here, I doubt Zoey will be able to keep her hands off of me and then I will be forced to murder my brother in a duel. It is better I take the temptation away."

I rolled my eyes as Dev laughed and led the other men out of the door. He popped his head back in for one last instruction. "Be careful today, my goddess. That little predator is the second of two brought in for the hunts. The first hunt just began. Stay out of the woods to the north. It will be dangerous."

I nodded, promising to stay safe as he left with the men.

"Just another half hour," Sarah said as she walked up with a nervous smile on her face.

"God, I hope he's all right." It was going to be a long half hour. It seemed like I'd waited forever to see Neil again.

Sarah stared out the open flap of the tent. Dev had disappeared into the forests. Sarah and I walked outside and I enjoyed the sunshine and the way the aspens shook in the wind. It was a beautiful, peaceful place.

Sarah pointed to the woods in the distance. "Do you think he's already waiting out there?"

"I don't know. I hope so." The woods seemed far away. I hoped Neil wasn't far. Declan's words finally penetrated my brain. "Oh, shit, Sarah. Is that north?"

"Yes, silly." She laughed because I wasn't known for my spectacular sense of direction.

My heart practically stopped, and I shouted for the only person I was sure could help me. "Lee!"

Lee burst out of the tent, gun in hand. He quickly pulled me behind him and scanned for the threat. He wasn't happy when he turned around. "Damn it, Zoey. Don't scare me like that."

I was out of breath and just short of panic. "Lee, what happens if wolves are hunting and they come across a sick wolf?"

Sarah drew in a shocked breath, turning toward those woods. Sarah and I were both familiar enough with wolf society that we had an inkling of what could happen.

"They aren't going to take a sick wolf with them," Lee explained. "Hunts are always a part of gatherings like this. It's a part of wolf culture. It's nothing to worry about. From what I heard, they're hunting some weird-ass Faery beast. Only the strong will be on this hunt."

I pointed to the woods. "Neil is in those woods, Lee."

He went slightly pale. "Oh, god. They'll tear him apart. If he's weak and those wolves have their bloodlust up, they'll kill him without a thought."

Sarah bit back a cry. I ran into the tent and back to the master bedroom. I quickly located my suitcase and rifled through it until I found the lavender polo I'd brought along in case we needed Neil's scent. I'd packed away all of his things when I moved into the penthouse, but I kept a few items with me in hopes I would need them. I hadn't washed the shirt so it should still smell like him.

Time was of the essence so I opened the drawer and pulled out Dev's gun, shoving it into the pocket of my denim shorts after I checked the clip. I forced sneakers onto my feet and then raced back out to Lee.

I passed him the shirt and Lee put it straight to his face,

breathing in the scent. He let it wash over him, unwilling to hurry it even though I was impatiently pacing, waiting on him. He took one last long inhale and when he tossed the shirt at Sarah, his eyes were already wolflike.

"I can track him." He was looking toward the tree line, searching for something.

"Then let's go," I replied, starting to move toward the woods.

Lee pulled me back, his hand on my arm like a vise. "Zoey, it's dangerous out there. Those wolves are hunting. This is serious. You'll smell like food to them."

"If you go without me, I'll be right behind you." Neil didn't know Lee. He would run and hide. I had to be with him.

He growled at me, got right up in my face and tried to stare me down. He had a good half a foot on me, so I had to stare up at him. I didn't let the height difference intimidate me. I held my ground and refused to break eye contact. I did a fairly good growl right back at him to let him know I wasn't going anywhere. When he bared his teeth, I bared mine right back.

"You're the most frustrating woman I've ever met." He finally stepped back, throwing his hands up. "If you get your ass killed out there, it's not my fault. I'm going to move fast, so you better hang on."

Lee kneeled down and offered me his back. It was strange, but I was willing to go with it. I jumped on and wrapped my legs around his waist, locking my feet together. I steadied my hands on his shoulders as he stood up.

He used one hand to pull my arms around his neck. "Don't let go."

I glanced at Sarah. "I'll bring him back."

She nodded and then we were off.

I held on for dear life as Lee galloped through the valley toward the tree line. I had to close my eyes and bury my head in the back of his neck because watching the world go by at that pace made me dizzy. The wind whipped my hair and did crazy things to my hearing. It was like when a dancer twirls without a spot point. There's only so much the human senses can take, so I shoved my face into the flannel of Lee's shirt and prayed I could hold on.

Lee stopped on a dime and suddenly we were in the forest

surrounded by aspens. Despite the fact that we were on a steep incline moving up into the mountains, Lee was steady as a rock. He breathed in and then took off again without a word, veering sharply to the left and then the right. I could hear wolves growling now. We passed some small groups of wolves and they barked out warnings to others of their kind. Some took up pursuit, but none of them could begin to keep up with Lee even though he had a passenger.

Lee stopped again, and he slapped softly at my thigh, letting me know I could let go. I dropped to the ground, my feet crunching into leaves and dirt. A cascade of low growls pulled at my attention. Up ahead something was happening. Something menacing. Lee started climbing and I followed, pulling the gun out of my pocket, flipping the safety off.

As we moved closer, I caught the sight of a small group of wolves. They stalked in a circle, at least eight of them. They prowled, their four legs moving in time to some predatory instinct I couldn't understand, circling what I knew would be Neil. Lee's senses didn't lie. He wouldn't have brought us to this place if he hadn't known Neil was here. My heart caught at the thought of him sick and hurt and surrounded by ravenous wolves.

Picking up the pace, I followed Lee, leaving my fear behind.

One of the wolves stopped and in an instant he was back in his human form, a sneer on his familiar face. "Well, well, well, not so tough now, are you, Neil? Where's that fucking vampire you whore yourself out to? Did he get tired of you? It was inevitable. Everyone gets tired of you. No one wants you for long, you pathetic piece of trash."

Wyatt Roberts pulled back his foot and kicked the white wolf as hard as he could. I heard a low whimper and got my first good look at my best friend as he made a halfhearted attempt to get away. Blood covered his thin body, matting his normally gorgeous fur. The wolves had been playing with him for a while, taking small chunks out of him, making him their chew toy.

I saw the moment Neil caught my scent. His furry white head came up and those arctic blue eyes turned toward me. He whined with everything he had left and started to crawl my way. By this time, the other wolves knew we were coming as well. They shifted toward us, scenting the air and obviously liking the way I smelled.

More than one of the wolves licked their chops as though anticipating a nice meal.

I didn't really care. I was too blind with rage at the man who was still kicking his brother. Wyatt Roberts spat down at his younger brother, whose great crime in life had been his sexual preference. That one trick of biology had cost him a family, a home, and was about to cost him his life if his brother had anything to do with it.

I was close enough now to get off a good shot. Planting both feet on the ground, I aimed and fired. The kick was a little more than I was used to but nothing I couldn't handle. There was a satisfying thud as Wyatt's right side flew back when the round connected with his shoulder. I had promised Dev I wouldn't kill anyone. He'd said nothing at all about maiming. I was maiming for the purest reason I could think of, so I saw no reason it should be verboten.

"Zoey, let me handle this," Lee shouted my way. The small pack had switched their attention completely on me. Lee shook his head as he watched the pack prowl. "Damn it, I really liked this shirt."

"I'll buy you another one," I offered, knowing what he had to do. Werewolf bodyguards went through a lot of clothes. It was a hazard of the job.

I'd never seen anyone change as quickly or as fully as Lee Owens. One moment he was a curly haired, six-footish man and the next he was the biggest wolf I'd ever seen. I don't know how or why, but he seemed larger in wolf form than he did as a human, as though the wolf that inhabited his body could change mass as well as shape. Marcus had explained that Lee was different, and it was easy to see when he changed.

Lee's wolf was the same color as his hair. The wolf was all powerful muscle, and his body was reared back and ready for action. Lee growled, a sound that filled the woods with menace.

The other wolves stopped when faced with the biggest, baddest wolf in the woods. They backed away enough for me to take the chance and run to Neil. He crawled low to the ground, trying to get to me. I finally managed to put my hands on him, and he stopped and gave a great sigh. Neil's head was down on his front paws, and he looked up toward me, his glacial eyes asking the question.

I smiled down, hopefully with an assurance I wasn't feeling.

"It's all right, Neil. It's going to be okay."

I stroked his fur, offering comfort and loving the warm feel of him under my hands.

His body was so much thinner than I remembered. Slight and frail against my hands but even battered, he responded to a loving touch. His back arched into my palm as I ran it over his matted fur. I could see the places where the wolves had bitten him and scratched at his flesh. He would heal if I could just get some food into his stomach and some affection into his soul. I had to get him off the mountain first.

Lee was rumbling as the wolves started to turn their attentions back toward me. We were in a precarious position. Lee's threat might hold them off for a bit, but eventually one of those wolves was going to try to take a hunk out of me, and it would be mere luck as to whether or not I survived the experience.

Another group of wolves had joined the first, swelling their numbers and taking a position at Lee's back. We were completely surrounded and I leveled the pistol at the first wolf I could find, letting him know I would take his ass out.

Neil whinnied and I realized I'd forgotten something. Wyatt Roberts came up from behind me. There was a sharp, hard tug at my hair as he hauled me up.

"I thought we told you not to mess with pack business, bitch," he snarled in my ear, holding me far enough away that I couldn't get a shot off.

Lee growled, but if he attacked he could hurt me and Neil, who was at my feet unable to move any further.

"And I thought I explained that I don't like you or your dad, Wyatt." I wasn't willing to give an inch even when he could kill me. "How's it hanging for your dad?"

I'd shot Mitchell Roberts in the privates roughly a year before. With any luck, he should have managed to grow back his dick by now. If he gave me any trouble, I could always shoot it off again.

Wyatt's growl came from a place deep within him, and I heard Lee respond in kind. I got the feeling that Lee was going to pounce and take the chance on hurting me and losing Neil when suddenly a large black wolf changed forms and John McKenzie strode forward with Wyatt in his sights.

It was my lucky, lucky day since this was the third naked dude I'd seen since I'd woken up that I really didn't want to see naked.

"You let her go right now, Roberts," McKenzie commanded, his muscular presence leaving no doubt there was an alpha in the house. The other wolves put their heads down and averted their eyes to show their submission to the dominant male presence. Lee merely took the advantage, placing himself in an excellent position to kill Wyatt Roberts. He made no move to give McKenzie the dominant position, choosing to threaten Roberts himself.

Wyatt dropped his hand from my hair. I was shoved forward, forced to catch myself on my knees. I moved quickly to cover Neil's body with my own because if there was a fight, we would be in the middle of it, and I wasn't at all sure that he would survive much more. He whimpered beneath me and I stroked him, trying to let him know I wouldn't leave him. I would never let them take him from me without a hell of a fight.

"What do you think you're doing?" McKenzie asked, trying to ignore the fact that Lee wouldn't let him anywhere close to me. He was pointedly looking at Neil's brother.

"He's weak." Wyatt tried to hold his ground against the stronger wolf, but his eyes kept sliding away. "He's half dead, and we should put him out of his misery."

"I don't give a shit about the sick-ass wolf," McKenzie acknowledged with a sneer. "You were about to harm the priest's goddess. I invited Quinn here. I'm paying him handsomely to ensure our fertility. What is he going to do when we kill his goddess? I'm assuming you're completely ignorant, so let me make it clear to you. There's a god and a goddess. That's how the fertility ritual works. Kill the goddess and the god tends to get pissed off."

"She shot my father," Wyatt replied with a huff.

"I don't care," McKenzie shot back. He glared at Lee, who was still keeping him away from me. "Stand down, you freak of nature. Can't you see I'm trying to save her?"

Lee changed forms, but I kept my eyes on the ground because I didn't need naked dude number four ingrained on my brain. "You'll forgive me for not trusting you, Mac. She's my responsibility. I trust no one but her husbands with her. I don't think you're married to her, so I'll be sticking around."

"Would you like to explain why you interrupted our hunt, Your Grace?" McKenzie asked.

I pulled Neil firmly into my lap, no longer concerned that we were going to be torn apart. McKenzie had firm control of his pack. "I didn't know there was a hunt. I planned to meet with this wolf in this location. He's sick, so I came to find him."

"He belongs to my pack, sir," Wyatt said. "He's ours to dispense with as we please. He's weak. It's long past time to put him out of his misery."

I didn't understand pack law, but I knew that Neil belonged to me. "He hasn't belonged to your pack for a long time. He's mine. He belongs to Vampire. He made a blood oath to my husband."

McKenzie raised a questioning eyebrow as he contemplated what I said. "Which role do you speak from now, Your Grace? How do you claim this wolf? It seems you claim much that should belong to me."

I'd learned a lot about politics in the last two years. So much of politics is about sounding like you mean what you're saying. I looked John McKenzie straight in the eyes and said with every ounce of confidence I had, "Lee is mine. This wolf is mine. If you dispute my claim then I will be happy to meet you on the battlefield and we can decide it there."

McKenzie's eyes widened and he glanced at Lee, looking for confirmation.

Lee smiled, his hands crossed over his chest. "Oh, yes, she dares. You want to meet her, she'll be there. She is one crazy-ass bitch, and those two men love her to pieces. Take her on and you'll deal with a faery, a vampire, and me. I might not sleep with her, but I respect the hell out of her. She always means what she says."

"She says you belong to her," McKenzie said, looking at Lee with a questioning stare.

He shrugged a little. "There are worse things to be. You have no idea how far she'll go for someone she cares about. She's a fierce little thing. She loves that wolf. You better get them to back down or she'll rain down hell on your head and I swear to god, I'll help her."

Wyatt was still shaking with anger. He pointed down at Neil, revulsion in his eyes. "This is my brother. She can't have a bigger claim on him than that. He is a perversion. He's queer and an embarrassment to my father. He won't take a female to mate. He serves no purpose. I have the right to put him out of his misery."

"He has a mate, you piece of crap. I really can't wait to introduce you to him. Let me tell you something, Wyatt. He's going to have a few things to say to you, and I don't think you'll like how he says them." I firmly intended to let Chad know exactly how Neil had been treated. It was his responsibility to beat the crap out of the whole Roberts family if necessary.

McKenzie sighed impatiently. "So you take in gay wolves and loners. Would you like me to round up some runts for your collection, Your Grace?"

"If you're going to treat them like Neil, then bring 'em on, McKenzie."

McKenzie swore under his breath and shook his head. "Take him away from here, Owens. Take them both out of here. I can't vouch for their safety for long."

Lee walked over and picked up Neil, lifting him easily. I ceded my position to let him carry the white wolf in his arms. I stroked his head and assured him it was all right.

I glanced at McKenzie, who I was feeling magnanimous toward now. "Thank you."

He shook his head. "Why do you care about a sick-ass wolf? You have no ties to us. Why were you willing to risk your life for an outsider?"

It was an easy question to answer. "I love him. He's my friend. I would risk everything for him."

McKenzie appeared to think on this for a moment. He nodded gravely as he replied, "I think it might be a great thing to be your friend, Your Grace. I didn't expect you to care for one of us the way you do that wolf."

"I don't care that he's a wolf. He's Neil," I responded honestly. "I would do the same for Lee. I would do the same for any friend no matter what species they happen to be."

"Take your wolf home. Let me know if he needs anything. I'll make sure this one no longer troubles him." McKenzie stared pointedly at Wyatt, and I knew he was in for a bad hour or so. "And Mrs. Donovan, tell your husband I'll call together the alphas tonight. He has his meeting. Tell him to be at the big house at ten thirty this evening."

Lee started down the mountain, carrying his precious burden. I smiled back at the alpha. I was content with his judgment because everyone I loved was walking away healthy and whole.

I followed Lee and Neil down the mountain, trying not to stare at Lee's backside. I heard the howls of the wolves, marking the end of the hunt.

My hunt was over as well. Neil was coming home.

Chapter Twenty-Three

It's a testament to the tolerance of werewolf society that absolutely no one paid any attention to a naked man carrying an obviously wounded hundred and thirty-five pound wolf down the mountain. No one, that is, except Sarah, who had been pacing outside the tent, watching the tree line. The minute Lee and I walked into the valley, Sarah began sprinting toward us, her face a mixture of concern and joy. Other than Sarah, no one gave us a second glance, and I wondered if these hunts often resulted in injured hunters.

"Is he all right?" she asked as we headed into the tent.

"I don't know," I replied honestly. "We have to get him to change forms. I don't know how to do that, Sarah."

Lee walked straight into the living area. Albert stood up, a duster in his hands. He'd been making his daily rounds, giving everything a thorough cleaning. His dark eyes went right to Neil.

"Is that Master Neil?" Albert had never seen Neil's wolf, but his senses were sharp.

"Yes. He'll need food," Lee told the butler. "And a lot of it. I know Zoey is supposed to be some damn rabbit right now, but he needs meat. None of that spinach and riswhato crap."

Albert looked down at the wolf in Lee's arms, and his blue eyes held a wealth of compassion. "I'll find what he needs. Does my master…"

"He knows." I was able to answer honestly. "Dev knows I was looking for Neil. I told him this morning I'd found him. He said Neil was welcome here."

Albert nodded and went off to procure the much-needed food. I was glad he hadn't asked whether or not Daniel knew. I wouldn't have been able to be so honest with him on that question. I still wasn't sure how Daniel would react, but we had other problems, my vampire and me. Neil's presence was the least of my worries.

"Where do you want me to put him, Zoey?" Lee didn't show

any signs that the heavy wolf was taxing his strength in the slightest. Neil had been unconscious since McKenzie had first appeared and the wolves had been contained. The minute he'd realized he was safe, he allowed himself the comfort of oblivion. Unfortunately, I couldn't let him stay there.

"Take him to the big bed." What Neil really needed was human contact. It would be hard to give him that in the smaller beds. Neil needed to be surrounded by people who loved him. He needed warmth and love and, yes, likely he needed a big hunk of beef—but first the love.

Lee hurried past Daniel's room and into the room Dev and I shared. Laying Neil down on the quilt in the center of the bed, Lee turned back to me and Sarah. "You need to talk to him. He needs to change form and he needs to do it now. Some of those injuries are serious, and the best way to start the healing process is to change."

There's something about the process of changing from human form to wolf form and back that aids in the healing process. Staying in wolf form as long as Neil had was one of the reasons he was in the state he was in. It would have been harder to stay human. When the moon was full, the urge to change was almost impossible to resist. I'd never known Neil to miss a full moon change, but there was no lunar cycle that told the wolf it was time to take human form again and watch some TV with friends. The wolf had to will the change from wolf to human. When Neil was upset or threatened, he tended to revert to wolf form. He felt stronger and more in control when furry. I had to convince him it was all right to be human again.

I sat on the bed beside the white wolf and Sarah took the other side. We both started to stroke his fur. We stroked firmly to let him know that we were there.

"Neil," I said in a no-nonsense tone. "It's time for you to change."

"Neil," Sarah added, her voice just as firm as mine. "You're home now. It's all right. You can change."

The white wolf opened his eyes slowly, as though even that small action cost him immeasurably. He shifted his eyes from me to Sarah and back again, stopping briefly on Lee to contemplate the stranger who was looking through drawers and pulling out a pair of Dev's sweats. They were a little long but covered up what needed covering.

"His name is Lee and he carried you here," I explained, bending down and putting my head to his, wrapping my arms around his body. "He's a friend, Neil. You're in Colorado. We came looking for you, Sarah and I. Remember the nice lady wolf who found you? I hired her. I've been looking for you since the minute you left. I wanted you to come home because I love you, Neil. I missed you."

"Please come back," Sarah begged quietly.

Lee watched in silence, waiting to see if our pleading worked. I didn't really want to know what he would try if it failed. It didn't matter because I felt the change start under my fingertips, a little sizzle that let me know Neil was trying. It was slow and painful, utterly different from what usually happened. Normally Neil just was. One minute he was Neil and the next he was the beautiful snow-white wolf I'd seen so often at my side. On the flip side, he changed as quickly from that wolf to my little club boy with curly blonde hair and a male-model body to die for. Now the transition was hesitant. He seemed to get stuck in places, and Sarah and I were both terrified at what would happen if he couldn't get back to the boy we knew and loved. If he was incapable of returning to form, he would fade and die and there was nothing we could do about it.

"Neil Roberts, you change now!" Lee's voice boomed through the space, filling it with his will. He crossed his arms over his burly chest and yelled in his best drill sergeant voice. "Get up off your fucking lazy ass and change."

Sarah turned on the lone wolf, fury plain in her eyes. "Don't you talk to him like that!"

Lee growled at her, either not caring or completely ignorant that she could hex his privates. "Talking sweet ain't working, darling. He needs to follow orders. It's in his blood." He focused his attention back on the wolf. "You'll change or I'll take you right back out to those woods and give you back to that brother of yours. I'll let him put you out of your misery if you don't have the guts to change now. That girl risked everything for your sorry ass and you can't be bothered to change form? Hell, I'll take you out myself. Change!"

That last bit was said in a roar that might have blown my hair back if I'd been in front of Lee. It startled me, and I was just about to have it out with my bodyguard when Neil growled stubbornly and forced himself into human form.

I sighed as I looked over his body. If I thought his wolf was thin, the gaunt human who lay miserable and shaking in the middle of the big, comfy bed shocked me. His whole body shook, and his eyes were pale and sunken as they stared up at me, pleading.

Lee sighed, satisfied he'd been able to get him to this point. His gaze went from me to Sarah. "He needs contact even more than he needs food."

Lee walked toward the door. Sarah and I knew exactly what Neil needed and we didn't hesitate. We shucked our clothes off as quickly as possible. I kicked off my sneakers, dropped my shorts, tossed my T-shirt aside and unclasped my bra because warm, naked skin was needed. Sarah did the same. In quick time we were down to nothing but warm skin.

Lee turned, speaking again. "I'll go and find some wolves who won't mind getting naked with…whoa!" Lee turned quickly, startled at the sight of Sarah and me naked and starting to pull back the covers. "I did not need to see that, Zoey. You are two married ladies. You shouldn't be all undressed and stuff."

I was slightly amused because I'd never known a wolf to be hesitant when it came to nudity. It was normal and natural for the wolf. In most cases, they didn't even see it as sexual. Lee was prudish for a wolf.

"I saw you naked. Well, I saw your butt," I pointed out as I climbed into bed with Neil and Sarah.

"That was different." Lee didn't turn around, probably because he was afraid he would catch a glimpse of something he didn't want to see. "I don't have boobs. I can see the two of you have the body-contact thing down, so I'll go help the big red guy hustle up some grub. Please don't get naked around me again."

Lee left the room and Sarah and I shook our heads. It was a little insulting, but I would make sure I was always covered around Lee. I pulled the quilt over us and sank down beside Neil.

"How long?" Neil's voice came out in a little croak as he shivered and shifted toward me. The wolf sometimes lost track of time, especially when in animal form for long periods. He'd wandered, not caring about the turning of the clock or paying attention to what month it was.

I opened my arms to him and pulled him into the heat of my body. Sarah wrapped herself around his back, and I felt a great shudder of relief go through him. He buried his head against my chest and we held him close.

"It's been seven months," I replied, letting him nuzzle my neck affectionately.

He nodded. "Is that all? It felt like longer. It felt like forever."

Sarah rested her head against the back of his neck. "You've been gone too long. You missed a lot. I got married."

"Really? To the hot angel guy?" Neil asked, though his throat sounded like he had gravel in it.

"Yep," Sarah replied.

"That's good." Neil took a deep inhale through his nose, letting the scents of the place wash over him. "Zoey's still having sex with Dev. I can smell him all over you. It's good to know some things never change." Neil laughed a little, and there was that light in his eyes he always had when he teased me.

Sarah chuckled. "He doesn't know about that, Z. He really is out of the loop."

"Well, for god's sake, Sarah, fill him in. It might give him the will to live knowing he can watch the strange soap opera that is my life," I replied good-naturedly because I'd been waiting to fill him in on my love life for seven long months.

"Z's living with Dev and Daniel," Sarah said, her voice taking on the tone of salacious gossip.

Neil managed to lift his head to show me his shocked face. "Like Vegas living together?"

Neil had been the first one to find out the boys and I had been experimenting sexually.

"I'm afraid so but it's kind of going to hell," I admitted. "Danny's going to leave us."

Neil's face fell, and he sank his head back to my heart, placing his ear right over the sound of it beating. "Like I said, some things never change." He was quiet now. "Is he still mad at me?"

"I don't know." I lied just a little. "I didn't ask him his opinion."

"He doesn't know I'm here?"

I petted his curly head, trying to calm him. "It doesn't matter. Devinshea knows and while I think he's planning on giving you a

249

stern talking to, he also said it would be good to have you home. Crap, we don't have a home anymore."

"What's that supposed to mean?" Neil had lived with me in my house in the country before I moved to the penthouse with the boys.

Sarah answered for me. "Her house got blown up. Halfer torched the place, and Daniel lost one of his baby vamps. Zoey was busy hijacking a truck."

I frowned. "Halfer showed up there, too. He took my prize and shoved me out of a car going seventy miles an hour. I broke three bones. Dev had to set them. It was really heinous. Don't worry about it. There's plenty of room in the penthouse."

Neil shook his head. "No wonder you came looking for me, honey. You've been working with amateurs. Well, I'm back now. You just set up some jobs. I think I'll like living in the penthouse. It'll look good on me. God, I want to go shopping. I missed seven months of TV."

Albert walked in, a plate filled with a savory brisket balanced in his hands. It made my mouth water. Neil sat straight up in bed, and I could hear his tummy rumbling.

"I had been preparing this for our non-vegetarian friends, but I can always find another. It's not as done as I believe it should be," Albert said with the frown of a chef who likes things to be perfect.

"Oh, it's fine, Al." Neil's eyes glazed a little as Albert passed the plate to him. "Hello, meat I didn't have to hunt down. I missed you. I missed you so much." Neil turned his light eyes back up to the butler. "This is a good start. If you have anything sweet, I would be so grateful. They don't have cupcakes you can chase down and eat in the woods. It's a real oversight."

Albert nodded and went off to round up some sweets. Neil was downing the meat quickly when Zack entered the room. He had a gun in his hand, and I realized we hadn't informed the bodyguard of our guest.

Zack took in the sight and quickly lowered his gun. He rolled his eyes and his sigh was one of great impatience. "Do you ever just sleep by yourself? Most of us just sleep alone or with a single partner but no, Zoey's got to have a cast of rotating players. Lee's going to be disappointed. Hell, I have to go find my boss and tell him his precious goddess is shacked up with some random dude and her best friend. How do I explain that to him? He's out there making himself pretty for you and you just jump into bed with the first wolf you see."

"Who the hell is he?" Neil asked, forgetting his manners as he talked around a mouthful of beef.

This was going to be awkward. I hadn't even considered the fact that I would have to introduce Neil to the man who had effectively replaced him. "Well, he's Dev's bodyguard."

Zack couldn't let it sit. He stared down at me, letting me feel the full weight of his disapproval. He holstered the weapon and shook a finger at me. "What am I supposed to tell my master, Zoey? If you felt the need to cheat, why couldn't you have at least had the decency to hide it from me? Now I have to get involved and I don't want to be. And you." He pointed at Sarah. "How could you after everything Felix gave up for you?"

Sarah's eyes lit with mischief. "Couldn't help it, Zack. Have you seen her boobs?"

Neil picked up on the one thing I was hoping he'd miss. "Master?"

The question was asked with that controlled voice one tends to get just before one blows one's top.

Zack sneered at him. "Yes, my master. Daniel Donovan is my master, and I'm not ashamed of it. Look down your nose at me all you like, but he's a great man. He's trying to save all of us. You should be so lucky to call him master." Zack was used to wolves not approving of his job and had started to confront the prejudice head on. Of course, he had no way of knowing Neil wouldn't be judging him for serving Daniel. He would be upset for other reasons.

"Daniel took another servant?" Neil growled out the question.

"Sweetie, you need to eat and concentrate on feeling better," Sarah said, hugging him from behind.

Understanding lit Zack's brown eyes. "Oh, this is the first wolf. The one who ran away from his duties." Zack nodded, finally satisfied I wasn't doing something dirty that would break his precious boss's tender heart. "He was gay. Carry on then, Zoey. He probably needs body contact."

"Nice to know you approve, Zack," I muttered because I could feel Neil's tension.

"Ran away from my duties?" Neil spat the question. "It was pretty hard to run away from my duties when Daniel decided to take over my freaking body. Did you know he can do that, Zack?"

Zack rolled his eyes at the question. "Of course I did. I know my master. Everything was explained to me before I made my oath."

"How does it feel knowing he can just take over your body the minute you disobey him?"

"I don't intend to disobey him," Zack replied smugly. "I don't intend to disagree with him. He knows what's best. That's why he's my master."

"You just wait," Neil said bitterly. "Wait until he sends your lover off to the Council."

"I don't think they'd take Lisa. If they did, they'd probably send her back. She's bossy," Zack said, shaking his head. "From what I understand, Chad was eager to go. He enjoys playing the spy and he's good at it. Did you try to talk him out of it?"

Neil handed me the now empty plate, and I put it on the side table.

"He didn't tell me," Neil admitted.

"Then perhaps you should be upset with your lover rather than your master," Zack said obnoxiously. "She died, you know."

"Zack, he doesn't need to hear about that." Zack needed to keep his damn mouth shut. I didn't intend to ever tell Neil that story.

"What?" Neil asked, not letting it drop.

Zack walked to the end of the bed. "Halfer killed her because she didn't have a bodyguard. He killed Dev, too. He sliced them up with a knife. Marcus and Daniel had to save them. From what I understand, Zoey almost didn't make it. They hired me and Lee the next day."

The shaking was back now as Neil let his head fall into his hands, and he started to cry.

I shot Zack the dirtiest look I had. He shrugged but seemed a bit more sympathetic. "He would have found out sooner or later. He needed to know what he cost you. I'm going to find my boss and let him know what's going on."

Zack strode out of the room and Sarah and I were left with a devastated Neil. I pulled him back into my arms, and Sarah did the same, wrapping him in our body heat and letting him cry.

"I'm fine, Neil," I assured him. "Dev's fine. Everything worked out."

"I got lost, Zoey," he whispered. "I got so lost. I'm sorry."

I sighed when he finally fell asleep. He snuggled down between our bodies and slept even while I worried that Daniel was about to be lost to me. If he chose to get lost, I knew beyond a shadow of a doubt I wouldn't find him again. Sarah and I passed a worried look between us, but after a while we closed our eyes and let sleep take us as well.

Chapter Twenty-Four

I hadn't gotten much sleep the night before so it wasn't terribly surprising that it was just after dark when I woke up again. It was easy to sleep with Neil's warmth pressed against me, but I heard voices whispering and was pulled from sweet oblivion. I knew it was after dark because someone had come in and lit the gas lamps. Sarah stirred on the other side of Neil. She'd obviously fallen asleep, too.

"It is normal, Felix," Dev was saying.

"Are you sure?" Felix asked. "Shouldn't I be more possessive? We're married. We made very specific vows. I'm pretty sure those vows precluded stuff like this."

"Dude, your vows were read by a guy in an Elvis costume," Dev replied.

"They still count."

I heard Dev sigh. "I don't understand human marriages."

"Obviously," the former angel returned with a chuckle. "Otherwise tomorrow night might not be happening. I'm looking forward to it, by the way."

"I'm glad to have you there, but you should know that it's the most natural thing in the world to get turned on by two hot naked chicks in bed together," Dev protested. "If one of those hot naked chicks just happens to be your wife then good for you, man. It means you chose wisely."

"I'll admit that it's harder to retain pure thoughts with an actual functioning penis," Felix confided. "It seems to make decisions for me at times."

Dev laughed. "Welcome to my whole fucking world, Felix. Little Dev is in charge, man, and guess who's in charge of Little Dev. Little is a misnomer. I'm actually quite large."

I turned, letting my eyes find the men standing at the end of the bed. I shook my head at Dev. "Don't you go and corrupt him, you pervert."

Sarah sat up and gave her husband a surprised look. "Felix, how long have you been standing there?"

He flushed guiltily. "Awhile."

Dev pointed. "He was here way before I was."

"I thought you were supposed to be preparing yourself." I shifted to make sure I was properly covered. Neil was still asleep between us.

"I was, sweetheart," Dev replied. "I was reaching a state of contemplation when Zack showed up and announced that you and Sarah were beginning a lesbian relationship."

I rolled my eyes. "That's not what he said."

"Well, that is what I heard, my mistress." He had a sweetly salacious grin on his face. "I quickly finished my rituals and got here as fast as I could." He shifted his attention to the other girl in the bed. "Sarah, I will pay one million dollars if you'll just kiss on her a little, maybe slip her some tongue and" —his fingers twitched— "play with her nipples. You won't have to do much. They're sensitive. Seriously, I can get it in cash."

I laughed and shook my head because Dev would really do it.

Sarah looked at her husband, obviously expecting a little bit of outrage. "Felix? Are you just going to take that from him?"

"The money, no," Felix said with a frown. "But if you wanted to do...all the things he said, I'm fine with it, really."

"Zoey, I need to talk to...holy crap, are they naked?" Daniel asked, walking into the room. His blue eyes went wide.

Males are males whether they happen to be humans, vampires, faeries, or fallen angels. They all have penises and that means they have certain common reactions. They stop at the sight of two unclothed women in any type of close physical contact. Daniel stared for a minute, his jaw slack. I let my eyes roam over his body. He was in soft, well-worn jeans and a T-shirt that showed off those big arms of his. I couldn't help but remember how good it felt to be held by him, to have him deep inside my body. I wasn't sure I could handle another sexual encounter where he walked away like it meant nothing to him.

"Is that Neil?" Daniel asked shortly, his lust turning to anger just like that.

I tensed at his tone. "Yes, it is. He was sick."

He made no comment on that. "I need to talk to you." He said it in a flat, no-nonsense tone that made me think this was it. This was the fight I'd been waiting to have since the night of the heist when he'd turned away from me. He was going to do this here and now.

"All right," I said, my voice shaking only a little. "I'll get dressed." I turned to Sarah. I didn't want to do this in front of everyone. "Can you stay with him?"

"Of course. I wouldn't be anywhere else. Felix can take your place." She nodded to her husband.

"I can?" Felix repeated as though he would never have thought of it himself. His wife's eyes were narrow with irritation. "I can take your place," he said, now with utter confidence.

The men left the room and I slipped into a robe, not wanting to take too much time. I'd been worrying about this for weeks now and I wanted to get it over with, no matter the outcome.

I belted the robe around my waist and gave Sarah a little smile that came nowhere near my eyes. "Take care of him. I'll be back one way or another."

I walked out of the bedroom and Felix passed me on his way back in. Dev and Daniel were standing in front of the room Daniel had been using. The minute he saw me, Daniel entered. It seemed like he wanted to get it over with as well.

Dev gave me a tight smile and led me in. It was lit from the inside by a camp lantern. The atmosphere was ruined by the coffin and the look on Daniel's face. He was frowning as I walked to him.

"What do you need, Danny?" My heart pounded in my chest. I already had tears threatening. *Don't let him leave me. Don't let him leave me. Please, please don't leave me.*

He sighed. "Dev, do you mind? I'd like to talk to my wife alone."

"I do actually," Dev replied. "If you're going to have this conversation with her, then I would like to be there. It affects me as much as it does Zoey."

Daniel's eyebrows came together in the little *V* they always got when he was concerned. "Fine," Daniel said, his gruff tone belying his words. "Fine. I suppose it does concern you."

Daniel's arms crossed defensively across his chest. "I'm going to head out. McKenzie wasn't interested in listening last night, and I just don't see a way to get him to trust me. It's a bust. You two are going to stay on and complete the ritual."

I knew something he didn't, but I really wanted to see where he was going so I held that ace in my pocket for the moment. "You don't think it's worth it to stay and try, Danny? He might be more reasonable after the ritual."

Daniel shook his head. "No, I think it's useless. Besides, I have to get back to Dallas. I have to meet someone there."

I didn't like the sound of that.

I also didn't like the way Dev tensed beside me. He knew what was coming next, and he thought it would hurt me. "Don't do this, Dan. We can find another way."

Daniel's jaw tightened. "There is no other way. You're the one who taught me to use the cards I have, Dev. That's what I'm doing."

I took a deep breath. "All right, Danny, I'll bite. Who do you have to meet, baby? Who's so important that you would leave us behind here?"

He didn't even flinch. He just looked me straight in the eyes and replied. "Her name is Tamara. I found her in Oregon when I found Joel. She should be at the penthouse by now, but I need to make sure she's comfortable."

Getting punched in the gut hurt a hell of a lot less than hearing those words come from his mouth. I could guess just what Tamara was. Danny had solved one of his problems, no doubt. But he was going to have to say it. "And who is Tamara, Danny?"

"She's a companion, Zoey," he said, making my fear a real thing. "She's my companion."

I quickly searched Dev's face. It was tight and his mouth twisted down. That told me this woman actually existed rather than being a lie to get me to run away. Maybe he wasn't trying to get me to run, I acknowledged for the first time. Maybe he was just sick of me. I let myself sink onto the sofa because my legs didn't want to work anymore. I knew my face was red, and the tears were already filling my eyes when I looked back up at him.

"Did you already perform the ceremony?" I forced the words out of my throat.

"Does it matter, Z?" he asked quietly, his mouth a thin line.

"It matters to me," I replied.

He nodded, accepting my answer. "No, I haven't yet. I didn't actually make contact with her until a few weeks ago. I intended to bring her in for one of the baby vamps. To make them strong. I changed my mind."

"After the heist." After I managed to screw everything up and get his vamps torched, I added silently.

He hesitated, but finally acknowledged the timeline. "Look, Z, this hasn't been working for a long time. It's obvious to me that it's best for everyone if I just let you go with Dev. He'll make you happy and Tamara can give me what I need. I need an easier companion. I need a companion who I never have to call a cleaning crew in for. You can see why I'm anxious to get home. I need to perform that ceremony."

I was trouble. I was a whole lot of trouble. I didn't follow directions. I didn't always do the best thing. I tried to do what was right, but I often screwed up more things than I solved. I had to accept the fact that he might be telling the truth, that he really wanted someone other than me.

I knew suddenly that it didn't matter. His not loving me didn't change the way I felt about him. It just made my heart break.

"All right, Danny." I wiped the tears from my eyes. Fighting wouldn't change anything. Yelling at him would only make me look like a fool. "If that's what you want, I can't stop you. I'm really sorry about Joel, though. I didn't mean…I never thought trying to steal that artifact would hurt anyone like that. I thought I was helping."

"You always do, Z," Danny said with a sigh.

I stood back up. I was going to leave, but stopped because something he'd said finally penetrated the haze of pain the conversation had caused. "Why is she in my house?"

Daniel frowned, turning to Dev. "You haven't told her what we decided?"

Dev shook his head. "You decided this, and you told me what I was going to do. Don't you dare pin this on me."

"I thought we were in agreement that this was the best course." Daniel had that hard edge to his voice that told me he was getting angry because things weren't going the way he planned. He was more emotional than he was letting on. His eyes found mine. "You're going to the *sithein* with Dev the day after tomorrow."

Son of a bitch. Bastard. I laughed, a humorless sound, because now I knew his game. "No, I'm not. I'm going home the day after tomorrow, and she better not be there, Danny. I won't take it well. You should fly back and get her settled into your place because I'll be damned if I let you toss me out of my home. If we're getting a divorce, I'm keeping Dev and Dev's keeping Ether."

I wouldn't be relegated to a prison because Daniel found me inconvenient.

"Dev, would you like to explain this to her?" Danny's every word was clipped and hard.

Dev stopped stooping over and raised himself to his full height. He walked over to me and slipped his hand into mine. "We need to go to the *sithein*, Zoey. There are some things I need to do. I'll explain it all to you later, but I have obligations I need to fulfill. If the ritual goes as I hope it goes, I'll be a true high priest, honored in every way after I make the rounds in Faery. It won't take more than a month," he explained and I heard Daniel sigh impatiently, unhappy with what Dev was saying. "But, sweetheart, we have to face certain realities."

"Finally," Daniel said under his breath.

"The minute Daniel takes another companion, you become fair game." Dev neatly explained the impossible situation Daniel was trying to maneuver us into. "I assume he's going to make a big announcement."

"I'm required to inform the Council," Daniel said casually, as though he wasn't changing my entire life. "It'll be all right, Zoey. As long as you're in Faery no vampire is going to touch you."

Dev ignored him completely. "So when we get back from Faery, I think our best option is Marcus. He'll let us stay together. We'll get back from Faery and head immediately to Venice. I already contacted Marcus earlier today and informed him of what's going on. He'll have everything ready, and he'll perform the ceremony the night we arrive. Marini won't take you away from Marcus. We'll be safe."

"You wouldn't dare." Daniel's face was stark white and his hands gathered in fists at his sides.

"Give him a call, Dan," Dev replied, his eyes giving nothing away. "You'll find everything is ready. I never bluff about a good plan. You should know that. Marcus is more than happy to accommodate us. He's quite eager to take a new companion. I also find myself unwilling to throw my mistress out of the only home she has left. You'll remove your new wife from the penthouse. You have a perfectly good apartment. I suggest you use it. I set up an account in your name. It has ten million in it. I think that's fair. We'll need the penthouse. Marcus has agreed to split our time between Venice, Paris, and Dallas. Zoey will want to spend time with her friends and family. We'll keep ourselves out of your life and your line of fire, but we won't leave our home."

"Why? Why the hell would you do this? Why would you give her to Marcus?" Daniel practically roared the question.

Dev stood his ground. "She won't be happy in the *sithein* forever. I won't be happy there, either. I like this plane. I've made it my home. Marcus is offering us a way to stay together and be safe. He cares for Zoey, and he's promised to allow us all the freedom we have now. I believe that he'll be kind to her and tolerant with me. It's our only option if we don't want to run for the rest of our lives or be held in a cage. That's what this little plan of yours leaves us with. We must remain on this plane. She has obligations here."

"What obligations does she have here?" Daniel asked, confused.

"I have to work for Marini or he'll kill you," I responded quietly. "I have to go to Faery and do the job, and then I'll do the job after that and so on and so on. I'll do what I have to. Dev is right, though. Marcus can keep us safe."

"That's the stupidest plan I ever heard," Daniel said, stalking toward us.

"Don't," Dev warned. "Don't you dare question my judgment when you're leaving me all alone to take care of her. You're leaving both of us. You have no right or say in anything we do after this, Daniel. We'll be on our own, and we'll make our own way."

"Why, Zoey? Why would you work for Marini after I leave you for another woman? Why would you let her, Dev?" Daniel's face was filled with emotion now. He couldn't stop it.

I stared up at my soon-to-be ex-husband and knew I was blotchy and red because I looked like hell when I cried. It didn't matter. "I'll do it because I love you, Daniel. I always have and I always will. I'll love you until the day I die. I'll stand by you even if you don't love me anymore."

Love didn't have to be returned. It only had to be honored. I wouldn't allow Daniel to turn me into something I wasn't. I loved him. I would fight for him. I would be kind to him. Even when he wasn't kind to me.

Now it was Dev's turn. "I love Zoey and I believe in you, Daniel. I believe in the man you are. I haven't had many friends in my life. I'm going to miss you. I really am. You talked to me yesterday about how you watched us walk through the valley and how different our reception would have been had you been by our side. I would have walked with you anyway. You mistake respect and need for love, Daniel. I would take my friend over a thousand affectionate strangers. Zoey and I would walk anywhere with you. Leave us if you must. We won't abandon you. If you ever need anything, just come to Venice."

Dev pulled me close to him and started to lead me out of the room and down the hall toward the front door. We needed fresh air. I needed to be away from Daniel. I needed to cry for a really long time.

"What's going on, Zoey?" Lee asked as we walked toward the outer door. I was sure he heard more than I would have wanted as he sat in his chair in the front room.

I shook my head, but he was a brick wall. "I'll be fine, Lee. Danny is leaving us. Could you please let Albert know that he's leaving tonight? Albert doesn't like surprises."

"I don't either," Lee replied, looking behind me with a stern frown. "I don't like them at all."

"I don't think I'll be leaving until we clear a few things up, Zoey," Daniel said, following us out into the parlor.

I ignored him. He'd said everything I needed him to say. He'd brought another woman in. She was waiting at my house. I had to stifle a cry because of all the things he could do to me, I hadn't expected that. I suppose it wasn't fair. I had Dev. I wasn't exactly pure, but Dev was part of us. I thought we'd gotten past that.

Dev walked up to Lee. "Zack will be going with Daniel. I hope you'll stay on with us. Zoey is comfortable with you and she's going to need your help more than ever. We'll be doing a bit of traveling, though."

Lee's gaze shifted between us and Daniel. "I'll follow Zoey. I said I would. I'll take care of her."

Daniel shook his head. "What the fuck are you doing, Dev? This isn't what we talked about. You know why I'm doing this, and you're fucking everything up. You promised me if everything went to hell that you would take care of her."

Dev turned back and acknowledged Daniel's presence. "It hasn't gone to hell, but you obviously have made up your mind. I talked to McKenzie earlier. He found me during my ritual. He was very intent on making sure I knew he'd changed his mind. You have your meeting. The alphas will be gathered at ten thirty this evening in the main house."

His blue eyes wide, Daniel stared at us. "How? He was extremely negative last night. It's why I decided to do this now. You said so yourself."

"He told me he was impressed with Zoey. She saved Neil earlier today from a pack of wolves. She stood up to all of them, McKenzie included. He said any man with a woman like that could probably be trusted," Dev explained. "Good luck, Daniel."

I heard Daniel curse as we left the tent.

Dev pulled me into his arms, carrying me as we fled the tent. Even as I started to cry into his shoulder, I heard Lee and Daniel screaming at each other. I lifted my head and turned back toward the sound.

"Don't, Zoey," Dev commanded as he walked into the forest. "Lee can handle himself. I think your big brother is giving Daniel a much-needed lecture. I take back everything I said about that wolf, by the way. He's a perfect guard for you. He's welcome in our household."

I held onto Dev for dear life as he walked through the quiet forest until he found the spot he was looking for. It was a clearing near a pond, and he sat down, shifting me in his arms so I sat in his lap as he relaxed on a huge rock. He stroked my hair and let me cry for the longest time.

I finally looked up at him, wiping the tears from my face with the back of my sleeve. "She better not touch my shoes."

Dev chuckled, holding me close. "I promise you, my love, she cannot fit in your shoes. Her feet are enormous. They're not sweet and dainty like yours."

"So she's really big?" I asked hopefully. "The only answer here is she's an awful person and she's horribly unattractive and she'll make Daniel miserable."

He smiled faintly. "All of those things, lover. She's quite mercenary, actually. I've only spoken with her briefly on the phone, but Daniel described her to me. He really did think to bring her in for his vamps at first. He's been negotiating with her. Obviously he would never bring in an unwilling companion. He was going to bring her in and allow her to choose." He took a deep breath. "Zoey, I'll take care of you."

"And I'll take care of you. So we're going to Venice, huh? I've never been out of the country." I held on to him so tight. I knew what Marcus was going to want. It made me uncomfortable, but Dev was right. I didn't see another way to go. I didn't want to end up on the auction block. Marcus was strong enough to defend a companion, and I knew he cared for me. He would never give me a platonic, marriage-in-name-only arrangement though. He would want blood and sex in exchange for that protection. I steeled myself. If that was what it took to protect Dev, myself, and my dumbass husband, then I could handle it. Even now, when he'd broken my heart so completely I wondered if it would ever be whole again, I knew I couldn't leave him to fate.

Dev pulled my face to his. His green eyes were serious. "Zoey, I will never share you with Marcus. I would kill him first. I have no intention of selling your body for our protection."

"But, Dev, it makes sense," I argued.

"No, Zoey." His expression was the tiniest bit savage. "I will not have it. That was just a bluff to break Daniel's game. You wanted me to fight, sweetheart. Well, I don't fight fair. That's the way to lose. It still might work. Daniel seemed perplexed that things didn't go the way he wanted. If it doesn't work, then I have another plan."

I shook my head in amazement. "You always do, Dev."

"It certainly doesn't involve marrying you off to another damn vampire," Dev said under his breath. "I've enjoyed our relationship with Daniel, but that's the extent of our experimentation. After tomorrow night, there will be no more threesomes, lover, not if

Daniel proves too stubborn. It will be you and me. Daniel said something about using his assets. Well, I intend to use mine. I'll be making a deal with the Unseelie. When we return to this plane, you'll be tied tightly to Faery. You'll have Lee and apparently Neil, and you'll have an Unseelie guard. I assure you, lover, that I can find some nightmares to protect us. Literally. They're actual mares, though they have some really nasty teeth. Please, don't try to give them carrots."

I nodded. My trip to Faery was going to be educational. There was a certain comfort in Dev's planning. It left me feeling less bereft. It gave me something to hold on to.

"If all goes as planned tomorrow night, when we get back from Faery, Declan and Padric will return with us and we'll meet with Marini. We'll set down all the rules and regulations regarding your employment. He can agree or he'll have a war on his hands. And, Zoey, if anything ever happens to me…"

I knew what he wanted, and I was willing to promise him anything. "I'll go to Faery and find Declan."

"Not Marcus," Dev reiterated.

I wound my arms around his neck. "Not Marcus."

Dev pulled me into the warmth of his body and kissed me passionately. There was a lot of emotion between us in that moment. There was love and sadness and an overwhelming sense of commitment. My heart ached at the thought that Daniel wasn't with us, didn't want that commitment from us.

There was a rustle in the forest, and Dev shot straight up, shoving me behind him. He cursed as he reached for the gun that should have been in a holster at the small of his back. In the chaos, he'd forgotten it. The SIG Sauer was still in the nightstand where I'd replaced it earlier. We hadn't thought about safety or weapons when we were fleeing the scene with Daniel. Lee had stayed behind because he trusted me with Dev. He wouldn't be prowling around.

"I thought I smelled you," Mitchell Roberts spat as he walked out of the woods. "Are you going to try to shoot me again, bitch? I won't give you a second chance."

He snapped his fingers and two large wolves prowled out of the trees, baring their teeth. One of the wolves was a sandy blond, and I knew beyond a shadow of a doubt it was Wyatt Roberts. He'd healed from the gunshot wound I'd given him and anything McKenzie had done to him earlier in the day. The other wolf was gray. The fur on their backs was standing straight up. They were ready for blood.

I took a deep breath and held on to Dev's waist. It was time for us to take care of ourselves, and I had the sudden feeling we weren't anywhere close to being ready for the task.

Chapter Twenty-Five

"Quinn," Mitchell addressed Dev, "my fight is with the girl. We've been kicked out. My place as alpha has been challenged. McKenzie is sending in three strong candidates to replace me. I have to fight and kill all three if I want to keep my spot."

"You won't survive." Dev looked around for anything that might help us.

"You think I don't know that? That's the point. They're going to kill me, my son, and my second in command," Mitchell spat. "McKenzie wants all of us out because of her. I'm going to kill her, Quinn. Walk away now and I'll let you live. I don't have a fight with you."

"Walk away from my mate?" Dev laughed, using terms the wolves would understand. "That's not going to happen and you know it."

"It's your funeral," Mitchell replied.

"And how will McKenzie handle it when you kill me?" Dev asked suddenly, trying to keep the werewolf talking. "He's going to know it's you, Mitchell. No one else wants me dead. The rest of the wolves need me alive. McKenzie will hunt you down. For that matter so will my brother."

Mitchell smiled, a pale imitation of joy. "You seem to think I got something to live for, Quinn. You don't understand. The alphas are just a legal way to kill me. If I run, McKenzie will have me assassinated. He's done with my family and all because we won't have a queer in it. You should have stayed out of this."

Mitchell changed. His wolf was a large black thing with powerful muscles and a set of razor-sharp teeth.

In my experience with wolves, they rarely just up and attack. They greatly prefer to elicit a maximum dose of fear from their victims. I've never had it confirmed, but I often suspected some wolves feed just a little from the raw emotion that courses through you when realizing that you're about to be eaten alive. I would have used my speed dial—because this was one of those times I'd promised to give Lee a little call—but I was underdressed for the occasion. I was the dumbass who wore a short cotton robe and no shoes to a wolf fight. My cell phone, like Dev's shiny, would-have-been-really-helpful gun, was sitting on the nightstand.

Unlike a regular, plain old doesn't-turn-into-anything else wolf, the werewolf will split their targets. A normal wolf pack will choose the weakest target and all of the pack will attack, leaving a Darwinian shot for the stronger animal to flee. This would not be the case with us. If Dev or I tried to run to increase the chance of the other surviving, they would simply split up and run us down separately. I tried to remember just how far we had come into the woods. How far away were we from the tent and the range of Lee's supersensitive ears?

"Stay behind me, Zoey," Dev said quietly as the wolves growled.

"So they can eat me second?" I didn't see how that was going to help.

I didn't need to see his face to know he was rolling his eyes. "Yes, my sarcastic love. I want them to eat you second. Have a little faith."

Dev hands were at his sides and now his fingers spread apart, splaying wide. I felt his skin get hot as his magic grew. The wolves reared back and as they attacked, vines shot out from the ground, thick shiny roots and glorious arms of green pulling at the wolves' limbs, carrying them to the ground. The wolves struggled mightily, using their teeth and claws to chew at the ties that bound them.

Dev moved quickly. "Time to get up, sweetheart."

He held his hands out to give me a boost up the nearest pine. I planted my foot in his interlaced palms, hurrying because I could hear the wolves struggling to break free. Dev used his strength to shove me up. My hands gripped the lowest branch and it almost felt like it was going to break under my weight. Miraculously, it held and I climbed up to the second, much more stable branch above it. I leaned down, reaching for Dev.

"Not going to happen, lover," he said, shaking his head. "I've got a good seventy pounds on you." He turned back to the wolves, two of whom had gotten free. "Stay where you are no matter what

267

happens. Declan will look for us. Go with him, Zoey."

"Dev," I yelled as the first wolf pounced. I saw blood and just started screaming.

The black wolf was at Dev's throat. He managed to kick up with his legs, pushing the wolf back. There was a deep scratch across his cheek and the wolf had taken a bite out of his arm. Blood began to well up. God, I couldn't lose them both in one night.

Dev kicked his legs up and was suddenly on his feet again. He picked up a heavy branch that had fallen from one of the trees and wielded it like a baseball bat. The other wolf was kicking and biting his way free.

I screamed for Lee, praying he could hear me with those freaky sensitive ears of his. The wolves circled Dev now, and he didn't dare throw down the only weapon he had. They would be on top of him before he could call anything else. I had one option.

Dev needed a diversion.

I looked at the forest floor below me. It was a good twelve feet away. I needed to hit the forest floor running as fast as I could. It was instinctive for a wolf to chase something that was running. It might give Dev a chance to try something else, and if it didn't then we would both be dead anyway and he wouldn't have a chance to yell at me. I leapt, but before I could reach the ground, two strong arms caught me. Daniel looked at me with a frown.

"Not on your life, baby," he said before he shoved me back into the tree. "Stay there, Z."

Dev brought the stick he held down on the yellow wolf's head with a satisfying crack. The wolf howled but was back up and snarling as the black wolf was leaping onto Dev.

Daniel pulled the black wolf by the tail and swung its heavy frame through the air in a circle until it crunched against the trunk of a tree.

I heard the wolf's spine break. Daniel let Mitchell Roberts drop as he changed forms, his human body hitting the ground. Daniel pulled the gray wolf off Dev, who had fallen down. The wolf tried to take Dev's leg with him but Daniel reached down, putting a hand on the top and bottom of the wolf's jaw and just pulling.

It didn't take much before the jaw split and the wolf whimpered. Daniel, now with a nice coating of blood, had his fangs out. He pulled the injured wolf up and twisted his slack-jawed head around until it broke and the wolf fell silent.

Dev sat up and pulled himself out of the line of fire as Daniel turned to the last wolf standing.

The wolf whinnied and backed away, realizing it was facing a bigger, badder predator. He tried to avert his eyes, to give Daniel his submission. I could have told him that was never going to save him. He'd tried to kill me, and Daniel wasn't going to accept an apology.

Daniel can call wolves. It was a talent he used rarely, but he now called on it to force Wyatt Roberts to change. Daniel held out his hand and his magic spoke to Wyatt's power. Unwilling, Wyatt fought the change, and the pain was apparent from the way he screamed.

Daniel showed no mercy.

I dropped out of the tree, perfectly safe now that Daniel had made sure none of the wolves could move of their own volition, and I made my way to Dev. I grimaced at his wounds as Daniel and Wyatt fought to gain control of Wyatt's body. There was no doubt in my mind about the outcome, so I focused on Dev. His leg was the worst. It was bloody, and I could see a chunk of flesh had been torn out. I ran my fingers through his hair and kissed his forehead. He sat there, completely exhausted, but watching the scene before him with rapt intensity.

Daniel had come for us. Dev's fingers threaded through mine. There was still hope.

Wyatt was finally in human form, and his whole body shook, terror on his face.

"It was my father's idea," Wyatt said, practically pleading.

"Was it your father's idea to try to kill my wife?" Daniel asked. It was his beast talking. His eyes were glowing a sapphire blue, and he pinned Wyatt with his will. The wolf tried to run but found his feet wouldn't move. This was vampire persuasion at its finest. "You will tell me the truth. What would you have done with my wife had you caught her?"

"I would have raped her." Forced by Daniel's persuasion, Wyatt's mouth spoke the truth. "I would have raped her and gutted her with my claws. I would have bathed in her blood."

Daniel crossed the space between himself and Wyatt in one of those quicker-than-my-eye-can-see moves. One moment Wyatt was standing and the next he crumpled like a broken doll, but not before I saw a gap open in his chest and blood bloom across his white skin. Daniel turned back, and I saw a heart in his hands.

Daniel crossed the ground to where Mitchell Roberts was lying, his spine shattered and unable to move.

Daniel dropped the heart in front of him and knelt beside the man. "Your line dies now. The only one left to carry your name is the only one you denied. He won't weep for you."

"Kill me, Donovan." Mitchell could barely speak.

Dev forced himself up.

"What are you doing?" I asked, scrambling to help him stand.

Daniel pulled a wicked knife out of his boot, offering it to Dev. I stilled my surprise. It went against Daniel's nature to offer Dev a piece of his kill when it came to revenge. Daniel was a killer, but a quick, efficient one for the most part. He was only brutal when those he cared about were threatened, and then he acted ruthlessly and always in a singular fashion. Offering Dev that knife was a sign of respect. It said Dev had as much to lose as Daniel. Daniel was acknowledging Dev had the right to defend me. "Would you like the honors? You suffered more."

"He's hurt," I objected because a good portion of his calf was missing and I didn't care who killed Mitchell Roberts as long as he was dead.

Dev ignored me and took the knife. He went to his knees in front of Wyatt and held the knife over his head.

"Take the heart," Daniel said, directing Dev. "It's tradition."

I watched as Dev brought the knife down and ended Mitchell Roberts's life. He carved up the chest with brute strength, and his hands were covered in blood by the time it was over.

"I don't have to eat it or anything?" Dev asked, and I could tell he really was interested in the answer.

"I wouldn't advise it." Daniel walked toward me, and I thought he was going to go to the pond behind us.

Daniel always tried to hide that savage part of himself. He would wash off the blood and change his clothes and pretend he hadn't ripped someone's heart out. He would walk back to me and tell me he didn't love me and order me into a *sithein* for my own protection. I waited for him to walk past me like I didn't matter.

Covered in blood, fangs out and eyes gone to blue, Daniel walked up and went to his knees before me. Shaking, he put his arms around my waist and pulled me to him. Daniel buried his head in the valley of my chest and listened to my heart beat.

If I backed up for even an instant, I knew I would lose him. He was offering me all of himself—Daniel, the good, the bad, and the beast within.

If I hesitated, he would walk away and never open himself to me again. He would go to this Tamara person, and he would love me from afar because he wouldn't feel worthy.

There wasn't even a tiny piece of me that hesitated. I threw my arms around him, holding him close. I didn't care that he was covered in blood or that his fangs grazed my skin. I wrapped my arms around his neck and held him to me like he would disappear if I didn't. He held me tight but finally his head turned toward me and I leaned down and kissed him, tasting blood and feeling fangs. I kissed him with all the love I had.

"I don't blame you for Joel, Zoey," he said quietly. "He was twenty-three years old and I talked him into following me. He should have been in grad school, drinking beer and trying to figure out how to spend the rest of his life. I killed him, Z. I did it."

"Danny, you didn't mean for him to die," I replied, aching with his pain. "This is war and people are going to die. All we can do is fight and try to make their deaths mean something."

"I tried that line of reasoning on him," Dev said tiredly.

"What if I get you killed, Z?" Daniel asked, stating finally which fear was pressing him now.

I looked down at him and sighed. "Daniel, you either love me enough to take that risk or you don't. I'm going to die someday. I can take your blood every day and I'll still die on you. Are you willing to throw away the hundred and fifty years we could have together because one day it's going to end? If you are then walk away now, baby. If you love me, be brave enough to risk losing me."

"I'm not going to hide myself anymore," Daniel said. "I'm tired of it and I think that it's more for me than it is for you. Can you love me, Zoey? Can you be with me as I am now?"

"I don't want you any other way," I said fiercely, meaning it. I

271

wouldn't change him.

"I'm sorry, Z," Daniel said. "Please forgive me. I was being a coward. I won't do it again. I promise."

I kissed him soundly in reply.

Daniel got to his feet and his face was back to normal. He walked to Dev and gave him a hand up. "Dev, I promise I won't try to leave again. I'm sorry." He was even more hesitant with Dev than he'd been with me.

"See that you don't." Dev limped over to my other side.

"Daniel," I said, my voice going hard. "I want that woman out of my house."

Daniel nodded, and now he was the one avoiding eye contact with me. "She'll be gone in the morning. You should know I would never have really performed the ritual with her. She was for Joel. I won't…would never take another companion. I meant to send you to the *sithein* and never let Marini know you weren't with me." He looked at Dev. His mouth was a flat line. "You'll tell Marcus he can take his offer and go to hell."

Dev shrugged. "It will be like it never happened."

Relief flooded me, but now I was worried about something else. "I really expected Lee to show up. I thought he would be able to hear me."

Daniel suddenly seemed deeply interested in his feet. His head moved in that "little boy caught with his hands in the cookie jar" fashion. "We kinda got into a fight after you left. I'm sure he'll wake up soon."

"You beat up my bodyguard?"

"Well, he was acting like he was your dad or something. He was bossing me around and telling me what to do. Dev, sit your ass down so I can fix your leg," Daniel said. Dev sat down and pulled the fabric of his pants apart, giving Danny access to the complete horror that was his leg. "He was worse than your dad, actually. He called me all kinds of names and threatened to stake me if I didn't follow his advice."

"What did he tell you to do?" I asked, wondering what Lee considered love advice.

Daniel bit a chunk out of his wrist and spat it on the ground. He wasn't discreet. He wasn't gentle. He was seemingly making good on the promise of not hiding anymore. "He told me I should go find you and get down on my hands and knees and beg your forgiveness."

Daniel dripped the blood over Dev's leg, and my faery prince sighed as the pain receded.

"Which you did," I pointed out.

"I'm sure he'll be thrilled. Once he wakes up," Daniel shot back, satisfied Dev's leg was healing. "Flex your foot. It'll be fine. You need more to heal your back and that face of yours. Zoey will cry if you have a scar."

"Maybe she'll think I'm tough," Dev offered.

I shook my head. Dev didn't need scars to prove his manhood. "No, I won't. Fix his face."

"We'll need to go back to the tent," Dev replied. "We don't have a cup here." When Dev took Daniel's blood, it was passed to him in a cup or a thermos.

Daniel took a deep breath and came to a decision. "That's not how I prefer it, Devinshea. I would prefer you took it from me, unless you find that distasteful."

Dev went still and just for a moment, there was a weirdly vibrant tension that went through my men. "I find very little distasteful, Dan, and you know that."

Daniel sat behind Dev and offered him his wrist. Dev put his mouth to it and took that precious blood. Danny's eyes closed. It's pleasurable for a vampire to share blood. It was a big step forward. I watched my boys and couldn't help but think it was really kind of hot. Neil would love this. It would feed his fantasies for a month. I was having a few fantasies of my own.

"Zoey?" Daniel asked, his blue eyes lit with mischief. I could never hide when I was turned on from him. "Don't get that in your head, baby."

Dev released Daniel's wrist, having drunk his fill. He looked between the two of us, figuring out what Daniel was talking about. "Not going to happen, Zoey."

I shrugged. We had a hundred and fifty years or so. Lots could happen especially now that Daniel wasn't going to hide anymore. I was willing to wait. "Fine. Can we go back to the camp now? I need to get cleaned up."

"No," Daniel said firmly. "We have a meeting with McKenzie."

"Daniel, I'm half naked, more than half, actually." I didn't want to walk around the forest covered in blood. It was usually a bad idea.

Daniel strode to me and picked me up, cradling me in his arms. "We're closer to the big house than the tent. Dev, can you follow? Is your leg fine?"

Dev took a couple of tentative steps. "More than fine."

Daniel nodded and began to stride through the woods. "You're coming with me to the meeting. You look sweet and vulnerable. Any alpha male worth his salt will look at you and be outraged at the thought of someone trying to hurt something so soft and pretty."

Dev smiled, a savage light in his eyes. "Yes, it will put McKenzie in a bad position. His wolves attacked the ones trying to help him. He can't take the high moral ground. We'll walk into the meeting with the advantage."

"That was my thought," Daniel affirmed.

"Excellent play, Your Highness." Dev tipped his head as the big house came into view.

"I learned from the best," Daniel returned.

"Your Grace?" A voice called out. "Is that you?" John McKenzie stepped out onto his huge wraparound porch, a fierce frown on his face.

Daniel strode forward. "Yes, His Grace is here, though he's alive no thanks to your wolves. My wife nearly died as well. Can I trust you enough that we can clean up here before we leave?"

I kept my mouth shut because Daniel obviously had a plan.

"Leave?" McKenzie shook his head. "The ritual is tomorrow. We have the meeting tonight." He gasped a little as Daniel stepped up and he caught his first real sight of me. "What the hell? Zack called and said there might be trouble. What happened?"

"Your wolves happened. And there will be no ritual tomorrow."

McKenzie's face hardened. "I think His Grace might have something to say about that."

Dev inclined his head toward Daniel. "His Grace defers to his partner, His Highness. I follow my king and my partner in all things. We've allowed you to think that I'm an equal partner in our endeavors, but the truth is I serve at the leisure of my king and queen, as all royal advisors do."

Daniel let me settle on the floor, still holding me close but reaching out to Dev, pulling him into our circle. "You're more than my advisor. You're my partner, Dev."

"I am content to allow you to make the decisions, Daniel." Dev practically radiated peace and serenity. "So long as they are the right ones."

Daniel chuckled ruefully, his arms tightening around us. He was back to serious when he looked to McKenzie. "I will not allow my precious blood to be harmed. We'll leave in the morning."

McKenzie's hands immediately came up. "Your Highness, I'll find out what happened."

It was the first time he used Daniel's title with what sounded like respect.

"Mitchell Roberts and his betas happened," Daniel replied.

McKenzie cursed under his breath. "Just come inside, Your Highness. You'll be safe here. I assume you killed Roberts."

"And his son and beta."

The alpha nodded, walking to his door. "I should have killed them myself. Please, Your Highness. Come inside and clean up. Let's talk. I'm ready to listen."

Daniel finally relented. Everything had gone exactly as he'd hoped.

McKenzie showed us to the guest suite and promised that we were safe here and a meal would be ready for us when we were finished cleaning up.

The minute the door was closed, Dev sent a satisfied smile Daniel's way. "That went well."

Daniel's hands were in fists at his sides, but his voice remained steady. "Yes, it did. Go and clean up. We need to move fast. The alphas will be here soon."

Dev pulled his shirt over his head, dropping it aside. "Come on, Zoey. We can shower together."

Daniel's arm went around my waist. "Not tonight, Dev. Tomorrow, she's yours. Tonight, I'll take care of her."

With a short nod, Dev disappeared into the bathroom. The moment he heard the shower come on, Daniel pulled the robe off my shoulders.

"Can you forgive me, Z?" He shifted me around and his fangs

were out. "Really forgive me? You have to know I wouldn't have touched her. I will never touch another woman. All of my life, past and future, is for you. You only."

"I forgive you. Always." Even when I'd worried he was going to leave me, I couldn't leave him. "We're your family, Danny. We won't leave you. We want to face all of this together."

Daniel sank to his knees in front of me. His hands went to my breasts, and I was pretty sure I was about to get slammed on the bed, but instead he leaned forward and I shivered a little as he licked a long path along my breasts. I couldn't help it. I tried to move away. I had blood all over me.

Daniel held me firmly, his eyes still glowing.

"Don't move, Z," he commanded in a low growl. His beast was close to the surface, but he wasn't fighting it. "I'm not going to hurt you. The blood's still good and it tastes like your skin now. It tastes really fucking good."

He dragged his tongue across my chest with a sensual groan.

"Okay." I'd promised him I could handle the vampire stuff. I stopped moving and let him surround me, holding me in place while he seemed to devour me.

He gripped my ass as he started licking a path down my torso. "You want a vampire? I can give you one, baby. I sent Dev away because he's covered in his own blood and I really like his blood, Z. I really wanted to lick that off, too."

It was an admission he would never have made before tonight, though I knew it. I'd watched him feed from Dev and while he held himself back, I saw the way he closed his eyes and savored the blood. Daniel was a vampire. What had he expected? He was going to be a connoisseur. He generally preferred female blood, but faery blood was different. It was unique, and I had a feeling Daniel wasn't going to hold back in his appreciation any more. I looked forward to his next session. Daniel was going to prove to be every bit the hedonist Dev was. I seemed to attract them.

Daniel continued his long slow cleansing of my flesh and I gave over to my vampire.

Chapter Twenty-Six

The day of the fertility ritual, I woke up with a smile on my face because I was in bed with every man I loved. I snuggled down in the soft mattress with Danny's hand wrapped around my waist, perfectly confident that it wasn't Declan this time.

After the successful meeting with the alpha wolves, we returned home and relieved Sarah and Felix of their body-warming duties. Dev slid in on one side of Neil and I took the other. Daniel slipped in behind me and curled his body around mine.

While Dev immediately fell asleep, Danny had spent the hour before dawn cuddling and paying particular attention to my neck. He ran his nose around it, sniffing and breathing in deeply. He kissed and licked it with long strokes of his tongue. His fangs grazed it, drawing little lines of blood he lapped up. He'd sighed contentedly before he dropped off to sleep, and I knew he'd wanted to play like that for a long time. It was weird, but nothing about it wasn't pleasant, so I figured I would just have to get used to the fact that Danny had a perfectly normal-for-a-vampire preoccupation with my neck.

Neil opened his eyes a little and smiled at me, his face soft. "Morning, Z."

My heart skipped a beat because I was so happy. "Good morning, Neil. How are you feeling?"

His lips curved up in a naughty little smile. "I think I'm in heaven. I'm so sorry to tell you this, Z, but it's what I suspected all along. Dev's gay. He's really in love with me. He was using you all this time to get to me. Hope you're not too upset."

"Is he cuddling you?" I tried not to giggle too loud. Dev couldn't help it. He was a cuddler. He almost always ended up wrapped around me. If there was something warm in bed with him, he was going to be pressed against it by the end of the night. Today Neil was the lucky one.

"He's spooning me," Neil admitted with a happy sigh. "Oh, and he suddenly seems happy to be doing it."

"Did he just get his morning friend?" I asked, and Neil confirmed it with a grin. It was right on time. If Dev followed his usual morning routine, I was in for a good laugh.

Dev sighed and cuddled closer to Neil.

"Hey, baby," Dev said, his voice sleepy and his eyes still closed. He ran his hand down Neil's side and then sat straight up in bed, probably realizing I wasn't as muscular as Neil. "Shit. I thought...I'm going to take a shower."

Dev stalked out of the bedroom as Neil and I dissolved into laughter.

"Stop being mean to Dev." Daniel pulled me firmly against his thighs. Dev wasn't the only one with a morning friend. "He can't help it. He's a pervert."

"How do you explain this, then?" I asked, wriggling my butt against that glorious vampire cock of his.

"That's a perfectly normal reaction to waking up next to my superhot wife," Daniel replied. "I would use that on you, too, if we didn't have guests."

"Don't mind me," Neil offered.

"Maybe you can call Tamara." That was now my go to whenever I wanted him to feel guilty.

"And just like that, it's gone," Daniel grumbled, sitting up. "Great, Z, now I have an off switch."

I gave him a tart look because if he hadn't wanted me to lob that grenade his way, he shouldn't have given me such awesome ammunition. He did look mighty fine in his boxers, though. God, I loved that six-pack of his. I gave him a grin to let him know I was only teasing. I forgave him and hoped he'd finally learned that Dev and I wanted to share whatever fate had in mind for him.

He leaned down and kissed me, nuzzling my neck. "I'm going to sleep in the coffin. It's too loud out here. Too many damn people. If I put in earplugs and close the coffin, I think I can get some sleep. Wake me up before you leave for the ritual. I don't want to miss that."

Danny walked to the door and gave it a cautious look.

"What's wrong?" I asked, hoping we weren't about to be attacked again.

"I'm just pretty sure Lee's going to jump me sometime in the near future. Tell him about the begging, Z. You tell him I begged politely and maybe we can avoid another fight." Daniel turned and I heard him say, "Morning, Sarah," as he left the room.

Sarah did a double take as she entered. She was carrying a bag and a large picnic basket. "Great, Daniel can daywalk now and nobody told me."

"I knew," Neil said.

I threw my hands up. "Well, it's supposed to be a secret. We won't be keeping it for long if Danny just walks around the house in his underwear, scratching his belly in the middle of the morning."

"It's afternoon." Sarah held up her items. "It's also time to start getting ready for tonight. I was fully instructed on all the rituals we have to perform to prepare you. It's just supposed to be the girls today so Neil can come, too."

Neil sat up, his eyes wide with curiosity. "What are we supposed to be getting ready for?"

"Z's performing a fertility ritual with Dev tonight," Sarah confided.

Neil snorted. "She does that every night and probably twice during the day."

"It's public, Neil," Sarah said as I flushed, my cheeks flaming. "You should see the altar. It's on a hill so everyone will have a nice view."

Neil's eyes closed and he sighed in pleasure. "I missed you guys soooo much." A cloud passed over his face and he sank back into the bed. "I'm not going. It'll only cause trouble. My brother's here which means my dad isn't far behind. If they see me…"

My heart fell as I realized I hadn't told Neil about last night. He'd been asleep when we got in and we'd been so happy this morning.

"If they come anywhere close to you, I'll hex them," Sarah promised.

"Not really necessary. You don't have to worry about them anymore, Neil." I watched him cautiously because they were his family after all. Just because they were assholes didn't mean Neil wouldn't have a reaction to the news of their deaths.

Neil sat back up and took me by the shoulders. "What did they do to you?"

I shook my head. "They didn't get a chance. Danny and Dev took care of them."

"They're dead then." Neil nodded as though it wasn't even a question.

"Yes." I didn't think I needed to mention the heart pulling out stuff.

"He would have killed you, you know," Neil said, searching my face. "You embarrassed Wyatt and he would have killed you. I meant to warn you this morning. I guess it was too late. Don't feel any guilt, Zoey. They raped their way through my pack. They killed anyone who disagreed with them. They deserved whatever Daniel and Dev gave them."

"You're not upset?"

He shook his head and hugged me. "No, I just wish I could have been there." He turned back to Sarah, clearly putting his biological family in the past, concentrating on the family he'd built for himself. "No more of that. It's a relief to tell you the truth. So how do we get Zoey ready for her big performance?"

"Well," Sarah said brightly, holding up a familiar canister, "I was told this sand is important."

I groaned and fell back on the bed. I hated that sand.

* * * *

After we got up and found Neil some clothes, we started to head out when Lee scowled at us. "Where do you think you're going?"

I stopped and stared at him because he was sporting two serious black eyes. Lee had some amazing healing powers, so I would have hated to see him when the injury was fresh. "What happened to you?"

Lee growled and his swollen eyes narrowed. "Your cheating, good for nothing husband happened. Son of a bitch got a couple of lucky punches in."

"Looks like more than that," Neil said, his eyes wide. "What did he do to your ear?"

Lee's hand shot to his left ear. "It's still on, right?"

"He pulled your ear off?" My voice hit that pitch I got when I couldn't believe what I was hearing.

"He bit it off," Lee said. "I'll admit though, I had just kicked him in the balls and I was trying to claw out his eyes at the time. It's okay because Zack held it on until the skin grew back together. Of course he was telling me the whole time how I should stay out of the master's business and I needed to not upset the master. I'm going to kick Zack's ass, too. But not until I kill that vampire."

"Lee, you can't kill Danny," I protested. "After he knocked you out, he totally followed your advice and I was damn lucky he did. He killed three wolves who were trying to murder me and then he begged my forgiveness. He was trying to protect me. He thought he could get Dev to take me to Faery and I would be safe from Marini."

Lee gave that a moment's thought before finally speaking again. "Did he get on his knees?"

I nodded and Lee seemed somewhat satisfied. I still wasn't sure he wouldn't get Danny back, but at least he wasn't going to try to kill him.

Sarah, Neil, and I spent the rest of the day wandering among the wolves with Lee trailing along. Lee hadn't been pleased with Neil's strength and followed us around, frowning the entire time. I tried to ignore his pessimistic attitude because I was feeling good today. Daniel was with us and it felt like forever this time. We'd broken through that barrier and he was going to be himself. Dev and I were going to do his little ritual thingee, and both my boys were going to be happy with me. When the boys were happy, I tended to be happy.

It was the first time since we'd gotten to Colorado that I had a chance to really enjoy the Gathering. We walked through a massive flea market where all sorts of artists sold their wares, from paintings to ceramics to wood carvings.

A portion of the valley was celebrating the festival of Litha. It wasn't a holiday the werewolves usually observed, but they made accommodations for their Fae guests. Tonight was the solstice. At midnight, we would celebrate the rites of fertility promised to all on Midsummer Night. I watched Dev and Declan teaching a group of children how to dance around the maypole. I smiled but didn't approach as we were forbidden to speak until the ceremony and I was trying to take it seriously. Dev had given me a look that told me he was anticipating the evening.

I had a surprise for him, too. We'd managed to find a little tattoo booth offering piercings as well. Wolves are big on piercings. The artist had several lovely rings with jewels on either side. I found an emerald one and one with sapphires and I knew just what I wanted. Once I bought both, the proprietor was more than happy to change them out so I had one emerald and one sapphire. They matched my boys' eyes and I loved the way it looked.

The wolves had decorated their tents and shelters with wildflowers, paying particular attention to sunflowers, marigolds, and St. John's Wort. Sarah explained these were the flowers associated with Litha and were said to aid fertility. I found the entire thing fascinating while Lee groused the whole time.

The sun was starting to set as we finally made our way to the stream Dev had directed Sarah to take me to for our final preparations. Sarah spread the blanket on the ground and stripped down to her bikini. There were several torches around the space that I supposed Dev and Declan had prepared. Sarah went around lighting them. It gave the whole place an intimate feel.

"You should probably turn around now," Sarah said Lee's way. "I know how you don't think you should see naked married ladies."

"Damn it. Why does all the faery crap have to be naked?" He found a tree and sat with his back to us.

Sarah laughed and got out all the products she'd been told to use. "Okay, Z, take it off, honey. You're seriously supposed to get this stuff everywhere."

Neil looked up from his place on the blanket where he was unwrapping the ham Albert had sent. "Do you need any help? I can eat this really fast."

"We have to wash her hair," Sarah explained. "But we're not allowed to use anything modern on it afterward, so when I'm done here, she'll dry off and you can comb her hair out."

"Nice," Neil replied. "It's curly when we don't use a blow-dryer and a flatiron."

"Then we have to weave St. John's Wort all through her hair," Sarah continued, referring to the little yellow flowers she'd brought with us.

"I can wash my own hair," I grumbled as I shed my clothes for what seemed like the thousandth time since Dev decided to go all formal on me. I didn't see why we couldn't just get it on. It had worked fine before.

Sarah and I walked into the stream and had to get all the way in the middle before it got deep enough to bathe in. Even in the mountains it was a hot summer, and the water was a respite from the heat. It was cool against my skin and felt a little delicious. I sighed and let myself sink in. Dev had done this yesterday. He'd bathed in the same pond, thinking about me. I wondered if Declan had washed his hair for him. I would have paid to watch that.

"So, I think I've waited long enough to ask," Neil said, knocking back a bottle of soda and starting in on some cookies. "Who's Tamara?"

I rolled my eyes and Sarah simply stared at me expectantly. I knew she'd heard some of the fight. I sighed and answered honestly. "Tamara is the companion Danny brought in to replace me."

"No, he didn't," Neil said, his jaw dropping open.

"That's why I kicked his ass." Lee threw in his two cents from behind the tree.

I shook my head at Neil because Lee really hadn't kicked Danny's anything. I would let him think that, though. I didn't have many people willing to go up against Daniel for me so I was going to let Lee think whatever he wanted.

"OMG, Zoey, I can so handle this for you." Sarah's eyes went a little dark. "By the time I'm done with him, his dick will wish it was just a pretzel. I have a hex that will make it turn in on itself."

"The witch is making sense." Lee yelled from behind the tree.

I took the soap from Sarah's hand and started the first part of my well-orchestrated bath. "He's upset because it's getting serious. He's just realizing that what we're doing is dangerous. People are going to die. People we know and love are probably going to die."

"So Danny gets all freaked out about you dying and tries to get Dev to take you someplace safe before you can die." Neil neatly summed up the story with a shrug. "Well, I was his servant for years. I heard many a dumbass plan to force Z into a cage where she would be safe, and she would never have to know all the creepy stuff he wanted to do to her."

I smiled, thinking about the night before. "Well, he's decided to do all the creepy stuff to me now. Once I got it through his thick skull that I wasn't playing that game, he suddenly wasn't so hot for Tamara, who better get herself out of my house."

"Yeah," Sarah said, starting to soap up my hair. "I've got a hex for that bitch, too."

"We might be using that one," I said under my breath. "Okay, Neil, so you've been around Vampire Daniel for a long time. Explain to me why he thought I couldn't handle the freaky vamp stuff?"

"Do you want his reasoning or the actual truth?"

"Hit me with both."

"In Daniel's mind you're far too sweet and innocent to ever handle his darker impulses," Neil offered. Lee snorted because he'd seen some of my own dark impulses. "He has you on a pedestal. You're his darling, beloved princess who shouldn't be bothered with the bad crap the world has to offer."

"But I seek that crap out," I replied because god knew I did.

"I didn't say it made sense. Think of it this way, Z," Neil offered, trying to make me understand. "Daniel died. That in and of itself is horrible and traumatic. Then he rises and figures out he's this monstrous thing. He finds the girl he loves and all of a sudden she glows like an angel and when he tastes her blood for the first time, it's so sweet and makes him feel so good and then she's gone. He spent the next three years being tortured and made into a death machine. All he wanted that whole time was to get back to you. You were this perfect light for him. He would have done anything to keep you safe. Then you run off with Dev."

I groaned because put like that, it seemed like a crappy thing to do.

Neil shook his head. "I can see now that Dev is necessary, Z. Daniel would never have accepted you as a partner without Dev. He would have taken you as a companion and hidden you away from everything, but he wouldn't have been able to handle the real you. Dev forced that issue."

"It doesn't hurt that he trusts Dev to take care of you." Sarah opened the dreaded canister and started to rub that sand into my back. "Daniel can do what he needs to do without being worried you're on your own."

"All right." I accepted his explanation. "And what's the real reason?"

"So if Daniel thinks you can't handle the truth then the real reason is this—Daniel can't handle the truth," Neil stated bluntly. "The things he wants to do, he's afraid you'll never forgive him for."

Sarah laughed, a sweet sound. "Yeah, I'm living, breathing, not in Hell being tortured proof of Z's ability to forgive."

"He's fighting his nature," Neil said. "He's going to lose."

I thought about the look on his face last night when he cleaned the blood off of me. He enjoyed killing the wolves and he'd definitely enjoyed playing with me afterward. "I think he lost that battle last night."

"It's the best thing for all of you," Neil said. "You and Dev can handle Danny's freaky stuff. If any two people in the world can embrace the sexual dark side, it's you and Dev."

I turned to look at Neil as Sarah scrubbed my scalp. "So, Neil, when you and Chad used to…"

"Make mad, passionate, earth-shattering, award-winning love?"

"Yes," I allowed. "Did he do weird things to your neck?"

Neil threw back his head and laughed. "Daniel's coming out of his shell, girlfriend. You have no idea. Chad would just sit and lick my neck for hours. I think it's their version of TV. He would do this thing where he scraped his fangs…"

"…and drew a little blood and licked it up?"

"Yup. He got a hard-on every time I got a paper cut. I got a whole lot of paper cuts while we were together." Neil sniffed the air deeply. "God, Z, sometimes I can still smell him."

I heard Lee growl deep in his throat, and despite his promise to himself to never see me naked again, he came out from his hiding place. He started to circle around something as he scented the air and growled.

Neil joined Lee, though his senses were not as good now that he was weakened.

I frowned as I watched the wolves circle something that wasn't there. Sarah stood beside me, waiting to see if we were about to be attacked, but I knew our visitor just liked to show off. I would have covered myself up, but this visitor didn't care about boobs and hell, he'd seen them in action. "Chad, you might as well come out. Lee won't care that he can't see you. He'll tear a hunk out of your invisible flesh just as fast."

Chad appeared between the two wolves. Lee still growled but Neil took a startled step back. I could guess what he was thinking. The Chad who stood before him was a completely different person than the one he'd loved. Chad had been a straightlaced lawyer who tended toward slacks and button-downs. His hair had been stylish but conservative. The vampire who looked at Neil like he was going to eat him alive was a dominant sexual being in leather, his hair running long.

"Lee, it's all right," I said quietly. "He belongs to Daniel."

Chad bowed to the wolf. "Daniel Donovan is my master, wolf. If you protect that which is his, you'll have a care with me."

"Yeah, I only give a shit about Zoey," Lee replied, letting Chad know he wasn't impressed. "I couldn't care less about Donovan or his property."

Chad arched a dark eyebrow curiously. "Interesting." He bowed to me. "Good job finding him, Zoey. I knew you would do it."

"I didn't do it for you." I went back to washing my hair. I had a ritual to get to and Dev would have my ass if I was late. "Did you bring the stuff from Marini?"

"I did," Chad replied. "I gave it directly to my master."

"That was for me."

"It's for my master to decide," Chad said solemnly. "I serve him, Zoey. I follow his orders." He turned to Neil, who was still staring at his boyfriend. "Hello, my lover. You're far too thin."

Neil rolled his eyes, his expression bitter. "You walk out on me and the first words out of your mouth after you get business out of the way are to complain about my looks. Nice. That's makes everything so much easier."

Chad pinned Neil with his gaze. "I wasn't complaining. I was worried, Neil. I told Zoey to find you for me."

"If there is one thing on this planet that I am certain of, Chad, it is that Zoey loves me," Neil said quietly. "She would have found me whether you gave a damn or not. She wouldn't have stopped."

Chad seemed unsettled by that announcement. "I had a job to do. I'm doing this for you, Neil. I haven't sacrificed myself for my own pleasure. I did this to protect you."

Neil glanced my way and we had a moment of pure sympathetic

connection. He looked back at Chad. "You love me enough to sacrifice a year of your life, but not enough to take five minutes to discuss the decision with me. Perhaps we'll speak on it further when you return from the Council." Neil turned his back on Chad and walked to the water's edge, picking up a big fluffy towel on his way. "Come on, Z. We need to start on that hair now. We only have until midnight and it'll probably still be damp."

Sarah had scraped off the top layer of my skin, so I supposed I was ready. I let Neil wrap the towel around my body and rub the soft material over me. Chad watched his lover help me through angry, slitted eyes.

It was now me under the glare of Chad's dark stare. "You think to take him from me?"

There was that good old vampire jealousy. I folded the towel under my arms. "I'm not taking anything from you, Chad. This is totally your fault. You should have talked to him. You should have treated him like a partner and not some piece of property that would just sit at home and wait for you."

Suddenly Chad was in my face, his fangs twin threats. "He is mine. I will not allow you to take him."

Lee was ready to pounce, but I held him off with a wave. If I couldn't handle one vampire who was blood oathed to my husband then I didn't deserve my title. I stared Chad directly in his dark, scary eyes. "You will back off now, Chad Thomas. You forget yourself. Neil belongs to me as you belong to me. My husband is king and I'm your queen, or do you deny me?"

Put like that, he could do one of two things. He could back his ass down or he could break from his master. Chad wisely chose to back his ass down.

Chad took a smart step back, lowering his head in a deferential gesture. "Forgive me, Your Highness. It's easy to forget. You don't hold yourself apart. Of course, I don't deny you. I've merely missed my lover. Please accept my apologies. We do belong to you."

I sat down on the blanket, that particular crisis averted. Sarah came in behind me and started working the comb through my hair because Neil had other things to worry about. Chad stood there looking at his feet, unwilling to leave. I took pity on him. "You should have told him that. You could also try begging. It works for

Daniel."

Neil looked at me, and it was easy to see that he wanted to be with Chad. I knew how he felt because I'd been there before so many times. He felt backed into a corner and his pride wouldn't let him out. He was angry with his lover, but there wasn't time for such useless emotions if he wanted to get to the good stuff. Chad would be gone again tomorrow night. They shouldn't waste time on rage. Danny and I had done enough of that for all of us.

"Neil," I said as Sarah fought with a tangle. "Could you escort Chad back to the tent? If you get lost on the way, I'll understand."

"I can do that for you." He walked over and took Chad's hand. "Just because I let you do some nasty stuff to me, don't you dare think this fight is over. I won't be in a relationship where you treat me like a piece of ass even though I'm a really sweet piece of ass."

"Oh, the fight is over," Chad corrected him. "You win. Let's find some private place and I'll do a little begging."

Sarah and I watched as they walked into the forest, and I knew they were going to do some serious making up.

Lee sighed heavily and threw me an accusatory stare. "Gay werewolves, gay vampires, public sex, and naked women all over the place. What the hell have you gotten me into, Your Highness? I want a raise."

Lee stalked back to his tree and tried not to see anything.

I let Sarah work her magic on my hair. In the distance, I heard music being played. The festival was starting. The bonfires would be lit and the dancing would begin. It was almost time for me to play the goddess. I'd seen how many wolves were counting on us and I hoped I was enough for them.

Chapter Twenty-Seven

"God, you look so beautiful, Z." Daniel held my hand as we walked from the tent toward the east field where the festival of Litha was in full party mode. It had been a distant music when I dressed in my bedroom, but now it was starting to sound like a roar. I was grateful for the strong feel of Daniel's hand in mine.

"I look like a virgin sacrifice." Between the gauzy, white dress, the garland in my hair, and my freshly scrubbed face, I looked younger than my years. I also looked much more innocent than I had ever been.

"I wish…" he started wistfully.

"What?" I asked because the look on his face was so sad. I wanted to wipe away that sorrow.

"I just wish we'd had a better wedding, that's all," he admitted quietly, looking straight forward.

I squeezed his hand. Our wedding had been a covert thing. I hadn't known I was married until someone—a nasty old demon—had pointed it out. It was also an old wound that had healed for me, and I didn't want to reopen it. "It was fine, Danny. If I recall there was more honeymoon than wedding, but it worked out. I'm still wearing the ring."

Daniel stared down at my left hand, his eyes widening as he took in the ring. "Z, baby, you can't wear that to this ritual. It wouldn't be right."

"Dev told me to." Dev had been casual about it. "He said it was the only jewelry I was allowed to wear." He didn't know about the navel ring, but I suspected he would be all right with it.

Danny stopped and some unnamed emotion crossed his face. He shook his head and continued down the path. "That sounds like him. He's a good friend. Listen, Z. He's really nervous about this."

"Dev has performance anxiety?" Dev had never had a problem performing, ever. Dev could perform drunk, stoned, or injured. Whatever a person could be, Dev could probably keep an erection through it.

Daniel laughed at that thought. "He's not worried about the sex, baby. He's worried about the magic. This is a big deal to him. Though he's mortal, if he proves he can do this, the Fae will treat him as a true fertility god because of the ascension. You're not afraid of the ascension, are you?"

I remembered the word ascension being mentioned in all the stuff Ingrid had said. I wasn't sure why I was supposed to be afraid of it. "I'm fine, Danny."

"Because you should know I've checked everything out. Dev will always be in control. That's the way it works. If it works. We're hopeful and that's why he's got so much pressure on him. If he can handle this magic then his place as a high priest is more than just a name thing. They'll have to respect him if manages to do this."

"Is that why Declan has to be here?" I asked because I was still waiting for a good explanation on why I had to get my freak on with Declan Quinn watching.

"Yes," Daniel replied acerbically. "I swear, Z. Did you listen to a word Ingrid said to you? She explained everything. If I know Ingrid, she explained it in great detail. Declan is there as a royal witness. If he gives his consent, then you will be respected as the one woman who can bring out Dev's magic. You'll be his goddess."

"So I have to bring his magic out?" I asked, for the first time really nervous about something other than the public nature of this thing. The truth was I really hadn't listened to Ingrid. I'd been planning a hijacking, and it had kind of crowded out everything else. Now I wished I'd skipped the stupid heist altogether and listened better in class.

"You have to bring his passion out," Daniel corrected. "The passion brings out the magic. He's just worried about the magic and his control of it. He might not show it or admit it, but he wants his brother's respect. He wants Padric's respect. The more aroused he is, the stronger the magic is going to be, and the more likely his ascension is. From the looks of it, you really need to turn him on."

Daniel was referring to the massive crowd that filled the field. Couples were everywhere as we approached Padric, who was waiting for me at the edge of the gathering. The night was lit up by enormous bonfires. In the distance, I could see the hill and the altar above it. Dev was waiting at the bottom of the hill, but I could see Declan was putting the finishing touches on the altar. Padric would take me to Dev and then take his place beside Declan as witnesses.

"Wow." It was a lot of people and a lot of formal ceremony. They would all be watching. I was having some performance anxiety of my own.

"You can do it, Z," Daniel said encouragingly, a grin on his lips and his dimples on display. "I happen to have great faith in your ability to turn a man on. Well, at least two specific men."

We reached Padric, who looked regal in his white pants and flowy white shirt.

Daniel pulled me back at the last moment. He took my face in his hands and he was suddenly serious. "I love you, Zoey Donovan. I would never allow you to do this with another man. I only allow this because he belongs to me, too. Don't think this lessens my possessiveness or makes you any less my wife."

I searched his face, trying to understand. "I know, Danny. I didn't think it did. I love you, too."

Daniel smiled a secret little grin. "I'm looking forward to after the ritual, baby. I'll leave the two of you alone for this, but I intend to share the rest of the night with you. Don't let him completely tire you out because I have plans for you. I'll see that Neil has different arrangements."

Daniel kissed me one last time, gave Padric a forbidding look, and turned back toward our tent.

"That vampire is very unpleasant," Padric said, watching him walk away. He was probably remembering the thrashing Daniel had given him. His face softened as he threaded my arm through his. "You, on the other hand, look quite lovely."

"Not too short?" I pushed my bare feet forward and they peeked out of the hem of my gown. I was completely without the armor of stilettos.

He looked down at me with a regal smile. He towered over me. "You are that. It can't be helped, I suppose. You make a beautiful goddess despite the height disadvantage. I think Devinshea will find a way to make it work."

"He always does." The crowd became less noisy as we began to walk through and they cleared a path. They watched respectfully as we walked the full length of the field. I noticed the children were missing. This was an adults-only evening.

"Zoey, I would ask you a favor," Padric began. "Devinshea is determined to treat you with great love and respect on this night. He believes you deserve tenderness and love."

I shot Padric a look that told him I didn't see the problem with that.

"I worry Dev's magic will require more than tenderness," the guard confided. "He's never attempted anything as big as this gathering. He would never have thought to attempt it when he was in the *sithein*. He is a different man now. He's surer of himself and more powerful, but I worry. If he fails, he will not get another chance. He will always be a priest, but he will be considered a lesser thing, Zoey. I would not see him fail. If it comes to it, I expect you to do what needs to be done, whether he likes it or not. He might say he doesn't need Declan's approval, but I assure you, he desires it greatly."

I wasn't sure what Padric expected me to do, but I was willing to try. My heart stopped as the crowd parted and I saw Dev standing before a smaller fire. He was dressed only in white pants, his glorious hair crowned with a garland of small yellow flowers like the ones that adorned mine. He was so beautiful I wanted to run to him, but Padric held me back.

"Follow the rules for now," he chided me. He walked slowly to Dev, who smiled down at me. I could feel his tension as Padric put my hand in his.

Padric stood in front of the boy he'd helped to raise, smiling at him with great affection. "As the Oak King gives way to the Holly King this night, so I give this woman to you. Do you accept her as your goddess?"

Litha marked the midpoint of the year when the waning sun took over from the waxing sun. The Oak King, who ruled from Yule to midsummer, gave up his throne to the Holly King in ancient pagan lore.

"I do." Dev took my hand firmly in his.

"Then go forth and prove your godhood," Padric challenged. Padric started up the hill to join Declan. Dev pulled me into his arms. He held me for a long moment before lifting my chin and dropping a sweet kiss on my lips.

"Thank you for saying yes to me, my mistress," Dev said solemnly. "I will not call you that again after this night."

I was kind of fond of being his mistress, but I could settle for goddess. His body was tense despite the smile on his face.

"Devinshea, is everything all right?"

"It's fine," he replied, kissing my forehead. "Everything will be fine." He leaned over and picked me up, cradling me in his arms. The crowd cheered as Dev turned and in one graceful move, leapt over the small fire. He landed on the other side and winked down at me. "It's tradition. It ensures wealth and fertility for the couple."

I didn't think I needed anything but Dev to ensure my future fertility, and he had the wealth thing down, but I was being a good goddess so I made no comment on the subject. I wrapped my arms around his neck as he climbed up the hill. His long legs ate the distance and before I knew it, he placed me on the ground before the altar, my feet nestling in the soft grass. The altar itself was made from stone and covered in a soft white pillowy fabric. The coverlet was strewn with yellow and gold marigolds and handfuls of shamrock.

Declan came forward with a golden goblet in his hand. It was large and carried the same symbol he wore on his crown. He was dressed in all white for the occasion and looked more serious than I'd ever seen him. He offered his brother the cup with all due formality. Dev picked up the goblet and brought it to his lips, drinking deeply. He passed the cup to me.

"You'll like it," he said when I hesitated because I'd been offered some pretty freaky stuff before. "It's honey mead."

"Alcohol, nice." I took a long drink of the sweet beer-like liquor. It was good to become reacquainted with booze.

"Zoey," Declan began as I handed him back the cup. "You are here of your own free will."

"Is that supposed to be a question?" Because it hadn't sounded like one.

Declan groaned impatiently. "Fine. Are you performing this ritual with the priest of your own free will? Do you take him as god to your goddess?"

"I do," I replied.

"Carry on," Declan said with a royal wave of his hand as he returned to his place.

Dev leaned over and kissed me. He put his hands around my waist and lifted me up on the altar. Gently he parted my knees and made a place for himself. He laid delicate kisses across my face as his hands stroked up and down my arms.

"It's going to be all right, Zoey," he whispered. "I know you're worried about being embarrassed. I'll be discreet. I'll treat you with the utmost respect."

He took my mouth, kissing me deeply, his tongue lazily playing with mine. My hands found that gloriously cut chest of his and moved against it, loving the feel of those hard muscles. I moved forward to get my legs around his hips and pull him closer. He found the bottom of my skirt and lifted it to my knees, his left hand starting to work on the tie at his waist. I knew he was hard, but he was almost always hard the minute he kissed me.

What he wasn't was ready to go.

I pulled away because his skin, while warm, wasn't even beginning to get that hot sweat that covered him when his magic started flowing. When we made love, I always felt a pulse of energy roll from his body to mine. It had been that way ever since that night in Vegas when his magic had come roaring back to life. Now I was getting nothing, and it scared the hell out of me. I touched his arm, trying to find the connection, the crazy, intimate, I'll-do-anything-for-him connection I felt when his magic got rolling. There was nothing coming off him.

This was what Danny and Padric had warned me about.

"Dev, what's going on?" I wasn't quite able to keep the panic out of my voice as I stared into his eyes. They were his normal green, not the dark, deep emerald they should be by now.

"Nothing's wrong," he insisted, but I heard the doubt in his voice. He was getting flustered. "We'll just keep the dress on and no one will be able to see you. We can make this work. Just follow my lead."

Normally, in all sexual situations, following the sex god's lead is a really good and potentially mind-blowing idea. But this time the sex god was trying to please too many people. He had to please the wolves who were counting on him. He had to please his brother and de facto stepfather or he would be considered weak for the rest of his life. He had to please me, and he was trying to please me on a non-sexual level by treating me like a china doll so no one thought less of me. All of this pressure was resulting in one thing and that was complete failure on the magical front. Dev would be perfectly able to push my skirt up, shove his way inside me and get off. None of that would result in the pulse-pounding lust that he needed to get his magic started.

Dev needed to start thinking about pleasing Dev.

Even from high on the hill I could feel the confusion of the crowd below. They were expecting something to happen and it just wasn't. Dev was starting to panic as he tried his damnedest to solve every one of his problems.

"I told you this would happen," I heard Declan saying. "He required six women to get him into this state before. He is not that strong."

I knew Dev heard it, too, when I saw his face fall and his concentration falter.

"I should never have let him try this," the future—if I let him live—king of Faery was saying.

Maybe I was going about this the wrong way. I was trying so hard to be a good goddess when what Dev needed was a bad one. Dev needed to get turned on, and soft, sweet, gentle lovemaking just didn't do it for him. Dev liked it dirty—the dirtier the better. Unfortunately, he liked it a certain way, too. He would fight me if I tried to take the lead. Dev liked to be in control, but more than that, Dev liked to dominate. He even struggled to give up control to Daniel in the bedroom. We played at those little fantasies with padded handcuffs and gentle submission.

Tonight, we were going to have to go a little further because those priestesses needed to know who was in charge, and so did Declan.

Sometimes, a girl has to be a little cruel to be kind.

I pulled away from Dev, and his head shot up. "What's wrong, Zoey? Are you afraid, sweetheart?"

I winced inwardly because I'd really done a number on my lover when I refused him the first time. I needed to make up for it, but he wasn't going to like how I had to do it, at least not at first.

"No, I'm not afraid," I said in a sarcastic voice. "I'm bored. What's wrong with you tonight? Those wolves are waiting and I'm pretty sure they're not going to hang around forever."

His jaw clenched, frustration apparent in his every muscle. "Zoey, I'm trying. I just need a little more time."

I needed to push him and I needed to push the hell out of him quickly or we would lose this crowd. I looked to where Declan and Padric were standing looking worried. I knew just what to do to force the dominant sexual god out of my hesitant boy. I pushed Dev away and jumped off the altar. He had to get it through his head that I was serious about this.

"If you can't do the job tonight, lover, I'll find someone who can." With every ounce of bravado I had, I slipped that gorgeous gown off my shoulders, gave my lover a naughty smile, and walked straight to his brother.

Declan's eyes grew wide as I walked to him. He started to say something, but I took his open mouth as a perfect opportunity to slip my tongue in. Declan, being a Quinn, wasn't about to pass up a naked female trying to shove her tongue down his throat. His hands were on my back, sliding downward when I heard Dev roar.

I tensed, knowing what was going to happen, and I just hoped I wasn't too damn sore in the morning.

The things we do for love…

I was jerked away from Declan as Dev pulled me back, his strong fingers tangling in my hair. He whipped me around to face him, but not before I saw a look of relief pass onto Padric's face.

"I believe I gave you specific orders concerning my brother, lover," Dev said, his face filled with masculine outrage. "Was I not clear enough? Do you need me to remind you to keep your hands off him?"

"If you wanted me to stay away from him, you should have taken care of me yourself." I taunted him because even now I could feel that heat on my skin where his hands touched me.

He panted, trying to get his anger under control. "I was trying to be thoughtful, to take into account your tender feelings but, my lover, if I have miscalculated then I can make amends. You want to get fucked in front of an audience? I'll make sure they all see you."

His hand was a manacle around my arm, and I gave a good

show of protesting. I pulled against him, but my weak-ass fight
didn't make a dent in his intent. Even as I tried to pretend I wasn't
interested, that magic, that will of his, was starting to pour off of
him. It was stronger than I'd ever felt, and it sapped me of any desire
to tell him no. This was the true danger of Dev's magic. In the hands
of a different man, it could be used against someone. When he
wanted to, he could make me willing to do anything.

"On your knees, my goddess," he commanded harshly. "I will
remind you who you belong to. You're going to worship me
tonight."

I went down to my knees, my hands shaking with the need to
touch him. He shoved the white pants off his hips and tossed them
aside, standing proudly naked in the moonlight. I licked my lips at
the sight of that magnificent cock of his. It was the biggest, thickest
thing I'd ever seen, and it was gloriously hard as he pushed it toward
my face.

He shoved one hand back in my hair, controlling me with
ruthless strength as he guided his cock to my mouth. I licked at him,
needing to taste him. Things were different this night. The magic
was so much stronger. Even his taste was sweeter. I licked at the
head where there was already a drop of pearly fluid leaking. I forgot
about everything else and followed my instincts. I let my tongue roll
over the head of his cock, teasing at his slit, wanting more of his
salty sweetness.

The wolves were getting restless now. I heard them beginning to
howl, and lust and magic thickened the air around us all. I breathed it
in, smelling him. The salty scent of his arousal mixed with my own,
so heady I knew I would never forget it. The air felt heavy on my
skin.

"Take me, my goddess." His deep voice was a command not to
be denied. "Stop playing and take me."

His hand tightened just to the point of pain. He held my hair and
pushed his cock past my lips and fully onto my tongue, into my
mouth. I whirled my tongue around his velvety head, loving how he
groaned as I moved over his cock.

"More," he demanded. "Suck harder, Zoey."

I took another inch but my mouth was getting full and I hadn't
taken half of him yet. I sucked him deep, tasting salty liquid on my

tongue. I let my hands run up his thighs to cup his tight balls, rolling them against my palms.

"Fuck, that feels good," Dev said in a guttural moan. "More. You have to take more. Relax, sweetheart. You can take it all. Breathe through your nose. You can do it. You will do it."

I'd never taken him this deep. I was pretty sure he was wrong. Despite my ability to yell really loud, my mouth is actually pretty small, especially compared to Super Cock. I tried to take a little more, but I seemed stuck. He was filling me to the point of ridiculousness.

Another wave of magic hit me and I felt it in my womb as it rippled through me, the pleasure making me shudder. It had never been this strong before. Dev's magic made orgasms feel like heaven, but it had never just been an orgasm rolling over my every nerve ending. It was like each cell in my body was experiencing the orgasm individually, creating a symphony of pleasure.

I wasn't the only one feeling it. I could hear the howls from below. My jaw relaxed and Dev took advantage, shoving another inch in. He was lost now. His head fell forward as he shoved his cock into my mouth, blindly seeking the release he knew he would get. He fucked my mouth, pushing his cock in while pulling my head forward in a fierce rhythm. I rolled his balls, feeling them draw up tightly, preparing to shoot off.

If I hadn't been riding that wicked magic, I would have gagged. I would have begged him to stop because he was too big. My jaw ached from taking the whole of him in. But those waves of lust rolled off my lover and made me beg for more even as the head of his dick hit the back of my throat and tried to press down. I sucked as hard as I could, wanting and waiting for him to explode. I wanted everything he could give me. I wanted to be filled with him.

"I'm gonna come, lover," he warned me, picking up the pace. "Oh, goddess, am I gonna come. You will swallow me. You will swallow everything I give you."

He gritted his teeth as the orgasm hit him. He cried out my name and moaned something in Gaelic. His hands tightened on my hair, holding me still as he pumped his come straight down my throat. I sucked furiously, desperate to take all of it. I felt the wetness dripping from my pussy now, I was so aroused. I needed for him to toss me on that altar again, shove his face in my pussy, and lick me until I came.

A wave of strong magic hit as he pumped into me one last time and released his hold on me. I fell backward to the soft grass and lay there panting, trying to breathe because that last bit had hit me like a tidal wave, and I shook with the force of it. I cried out as I came again, and he hadn't touched me below my shoulders.

I lay back, listening to the sounds of the wolves crying their pleasure below me and thought about trying to get up, but nothing was working. My whole body was limp, every muscle exhausted. I didn't care that I was naked or that I'd just done something really dirty to my boyfriend while his family watched. I was just happy. They wouldn't be able to deny him now.

Suddenly there were strong arms lifting me back to the altar. I smiled as I looked up at my Devinshea, who had beyond a doubt proven his godhood. He would be accepted as the fertility god he was, his mortality meaningless now.

"I'm not done with you, my beautiful goddess," a voice said. "Do you know how long I've waited for you?"

Now my muscles were working and I pushed away because I was looking into eyes and hearing a voice that did not belong to my lover.

Chapter Twenty-Eight

"**I**t worked," Declan said with wonder in his voice. He'd stepped forward but not too close, as though he was unsure he should get too near whatever had taken over Dev's body.

Good to know he was a little scared.

"Zoey, it's fine." Padric kept his voice calm, trying to reassure me. "He won't hurt you."

I wasn't so damn sure about that. Dev sported completely green eyes and spoke with a voice that didn't sound like him. His eyes had no white at all, a bit like Daniel's when his beast was off the leash. His hair had grown, too, as though all that magic pouring off him had to change him in some way. It had been at the top of his neck just past his ears before, but now it was thicker and hit past his shoulders. He was a gorgeous god of a man. If he was still a man at all. He studied me with great curiosity, and I knew it wasn't my Dev who stared at me. I used my feet to push away from him, thinking to go off the other side of the altar. When I got to the ground, I could run.

His hand shot out, catching my ankle and pulling me back to him.

"Do not run," he said, his voice deep and dark. "This one's instincts are to chase you, to bend you to his will. They're quite powerful. I don't know if I can resist them. I'm stronger than he is, but I'm not sure how to use this body yet. I do not wish to harm you."

"Zoey," Declan was speaking now. "Relax, it is Dev. This is the ascension. He did it."

I shook my head because it wasn't Dev. And I really didn't give a shit about the ascension.

"I am Devinshea," the man above me said with a thick Irish brogue. "I'm Dev and something more." He was looking at my body, his eyes more than curious now. They were hot and his body was aroused, the cock I knew so well swelling again.

"Yeah, well, it's the 'more' part I'm scared of." I tried to fight my instinct to run. I wished like hell I had some damn clothes on. It hadn't bothered me before, but now I felt so vulnerable.

"She was not prepared for this?" The god in my lover asked, his mouth curling down as he frowned back at Padric and Declan. "You sent her into this unaware and ignorant. Perhaps you were looking to bond this one with another god. I do not take advantage of mortals. If she does not consent, then I will leave this bonding."

Padric shook his head. "Please don't. I do not understand, My Lord. My...the prince is very thorough. I assure you he followed every rule and tradition of this ritual. He would never have allowed her to come into it ignorant."

"I might not have been listening," I admitted even as I tried to gently pull away. "I don't always do as I'm told."

"No goddess worth her salt would," he said with a chuckle, relaxing again. "I believe you about the priest." His hand slid from my chest to my naval, where the little ring I'd put in glinted in the light. He seemed fascinated by it. He gazed at the two gems on either side of the ring. "The emerald is for this one, for Devinshea. Who is the sapphire for? Ahh. Very intriguing. A vampire? You have interesting tastes. And he's your partner? No, I do not mind. I do not mind at all. You are in control. I am merely a guest, priest."

I was pretty sure he wasn't talking to me. It's odd to have a conversation with someone who has two people in their body.

He smiled fondly down at me and pulled me close, wrapping my legs around his waist. I could feel his release had done nothing to curb his appetite. He was huge and pressed against my core, though he made no moves to impale me yet. "The priest loves the ring. He's very aroused by it. He says your vampire will enjoy it as well."

"I'm glad he likes it." I tried to relax because it didn't look like I would be going anywhere soon.

He seemed content for the moment to run his hands along my skin and rub his face in my hair. The magic was softer now, warming my skin and making me the slightest bit drunk. "Do not fight me, sweet goddess. It's been so long since I held soft flesh in my arms. It feels so good to have a body again. Your lover is here. I would not shut him out." His eyes were thoughtful for a moment as though he was listening for something. "He wants to know where you were when someone named Ingrid told you this could happen.

He wants to know what you were daydreaming about. I don't know what that means exactly."

I laughed because Dev was definitely in there. I did remember now she had said something about ancient gods and taking their aspects, but it had seemed like one of those non-literal things at the time, like calling Dev a fertility god because his magic came from sex. He was actually mortal, but now I wondered about the god part.

This particular ancient god smiled down at me as he played with my hair, his fingers stroking lightly. "He's so grateful to you, Zoey. He knows you did not want that…what is a brat?"

"He's talking about his brother," I replied.

Dev's lips kissed my forehead and while I wasn't sure about the whole "god taking over his body" thing, it felt really good. He was being so gentle and loving, and I needed that after the brutal pleasure of before. I needed to be reminded he loved me. I could play all the parts he required and I enjoyed it, but after I wanted his sweetness and care.

I felt something tickle my hands, and when I looked down I saw the marigolds had exploded as though they had multiplied. They were rich, perfect blooms that should have been planted in fertile ground. They weren't dying flowers. The magic was gentler now, but it still filled my lungs and hummed along my skin.

"Yes, he is pleased to have proven him wrong. It is often like that with brothers," he said. "Devinshea wants you to know he understands why you went to him. He was faltering and you pulled him back. He couldn't have done this without you. He also wants you to never do it again. He's possessive for a priest. I find him an interesting host."

"May we know your name, My Lord?" Padric asked carefully, as though the answer would tell him something important.

"I am Bris," he replied absently, kissing my ear. He ran his tongue along the shell, and I shuddered in response. His hands found their way to my breasts, and he cupped them as he sighed in appreciation. I felt my nipples harden as he brushed his thumbs across the tips.

My female parts were all warming right back up again.

"Yes," Padric said with satisfaction. "We hoped it would be you. It seemed a good match because you are right. The prince is not an ordinary priest. Zoey, Bris is a revered Irish god of fertility and agriculture. He is also known to be gentle. My Lord, I hope you find our prince a good match."

He turned to the two Fae watching the scene with rapt intensity. I felt the loss of his attention and my head fell forward against his chest. His arms went around me to support me, cradling me close, surrounding me with his tenderness. "He is worthy. He's mortal but strong, and his goddess is certainly most worthy. She's lovely and feminine and so fertile. I've been dormant for a long time. I feel the world has changed. This language I'm speaking is odd. I've not heard it before. Am I not in my homeland? The land looks strange."

"You're in a country called America," Declan explained. "It did not exist before."

The god laughed and pulled me closer, as though he enjoyed the warmth of my body against his skin. His hands moved on me constantly, petting my hair, stroking down my back, caressing my breasts, as though he couldn't get enough of me. "Perhaps its name didn't exist, but the land did. You're arrogant, but you're a royal so it's to be expected. Why has it taken so long for a host to appear? Is my magic no longer needed?"

"We left this plane." Padric's voice was sad as though he missed his former home. "The world changed too much for the Fae, and we sought refuge elsewhere. Our numbers are few now and your magic is needed more than ever. We lost the only one of our kind with fertility magic. Devinshea is the first in many generations to show an aptitude. We feared his mortality would displease you."

"Nothing about this displeases me," the man in Dev's body said as he leaned down and kissed my lips. His tongue licked along the seam of my mouth, pouring magic into me. I was drowsy with that magic. Any urge I had to fight him was gone completely. "I've always preferred mortals. His mortality enhances his passions. Immortals tend to be less fiery. This one knows he must live while he can, and it makes him vital. He loves this female so much. It flows through him. I enjoy the feeling, the emotion."

His fingers touched my chin, tipping my face up to gaze at him. "Please do not be afraid, little one. He is here. I'm staying, but I won't take his place. I'll strengthen him and he'll share his passions with me. I'm lonely. I have been for millennia. Do not deny us. I can help you all. I can make this one strong for the fight. Yes, he is explaining everything to me and you should know that I will stand with you and with the vampire. I will be your truest friend."

I was thinking it would be impossible to deny him anything right now because I needed. I needed so much. The magic was draining me of everything including my strength and certainly my will. It was leaving me with one thing and one thing only, the urge to meld with him, to be one with him.

"Zoey," Dev's voice cajoled. I sighed because now I knew he was with me. His voice was smooth. Maybe he wasn't alone, but he was here and I trusted him to take care of me. "Zoey, relax. The hard part is over. The rest is pleasure. Let me thank you, my beautiful goddess. I would have failed without you."

Dev lowered me to the altar and got to his knees, pulling my feet onto his shoulders and kissing me where I needed it the most. He pressed my knees apart, giving himself full access. His tongue licked all along my pussy, eagerly lapping up the cream of my arousal. I looked down between my legs where he was worshipping me now and saw his eyes were still not his own. This was Dev and something more, but I no longer cared as his tongue pressed against my clitoris, delicately at first and then with sweet, firm pressure. I moaned as my juices began to flow, coating his tongue and causing me to press against his mouth.

"You are sweeter than the mead," he said, his voice deeper than usual, and I knew Bris was back in control. "And so much more intoxicating."

He slid a long finger into my pussy, expertly finding my sweet spot and rubbing it. He slid a second finger in and stretched me gently. Those fingers scissored inside me and I shook with arousal. His tongue whirled around my clit, making it swell and beg for release. My back arched as his tongue and finger found a perfect rhythm, and I exploded against his mouth.

The magic was in full effect again and the wolves began to howl. Declan stepped back—or rather Padric pulled him back.

Before I could recover from the orgasm, he was climbing on top of me, spreading my knees and guiding his cock into me. As he worked himself into my slick pussy, he leaned over and kissed me, letting me taste myself on his mouth.

He thrust in as far as he could go. His body covered mine, chest to chest, my legs around his waist, arms holding him close. His tongue came out, licking along my lips before delving deep. But this was sweet, soft, in a way it had never been before.

I was being worshipped, and it felt so good.

"You are my goddess," he whispered in my ear as his hips set a soft rhythm. I lay back, completely unwilling to fight him. I let him do whatever he wanted to me. I was his slave in that moment. "You are our goddess."

The god in Dev's body went up on his knees, pulling my legs around his waist, and began fucking me in earnest now. His hands were on my hips, holding me where he wanted me. He pounded himself in, his head thrown back, and the magic started to pulse against me.

I wanted to cry that it was too much, that my every nerve ending was raw and I couldn't take another minute of this pleasure, but I could. I gave myself over to it and moaned as the man over me ground himself against my clit and released his semen with a shout. He pressed against me even as his need waned, trying to keep the connection, but he finally let his body rest against mine. Dev looked at me with a happy, tired smile.

"I love you," he said as he let his head fall against my neck.

His heavy weight pushed my body into the cushion beneath me. I was sleepy as I let my arms wind around his neck. Everything seemed so far away now as his heart beat against mine. It was almost easy to forget that we'd done anything but make love. I didn't think about the fact that there had been an audience or that Dev now had a deity living inside him. While his heart pounded against mine, it was easy to believe we were just two people who loved each other and needed each other.

Declan pulled me out of that fantasy.

"He could have done it with any female," Declan was saying to Padric. "This proves nothing except that he had fantasies I never dreamed he would have."

"Are you insane, Declan?" Padric shot back, his voice proving his annoyance with the younger man. "He would have failed had it not been for Zoey's intervention. Did you see the way Bris reacted to her? He was completely enamored. He couldn't resist her."

"Well, after what she did to my brother, can you blame him?" Declan said. "I'm enamored, too."

"I saw the way you reacted. Did you forget to wear the charm that kept us safe from the lust magic, Your Highness?"

"I am wearing the charm, Padric, but it did not make me blind," Declan declared. "She was filthy. She was truly disgusting. It was beautiful. She is so small, but she managed to take all of him. I would never have imagined she could do that. He had to be halfway down her throat. I take back what I said. Any woman who can do that is worth fighting your brother over."

"But you don't think she is a proper goddess?"

Declan sighed. "I think my brother is still young. Why should he be tied to one woman? She will expect that from him. She will expect him to be faithful. He should be with a Fae girl who will be more realistic. He is a priest of the old ways. What will it be like for her when we go home? Our people will be shocked when she is unwilling to allow him sexual freedom. Bris is not going anywhere. Dev can keep the god and his freedom."

Dev raised his head wearily from my body and shook his head at his brother. "Stop fighting, the two of you. Padric, give it up. He won't give consent, and I no longer give a damn." Dev kissed my lips and pushed up. He got to his knees and grinned down at me. "Are you all right, my goddess?"

I nodded, feeling a little more energetic now that the magic was gone. "Is Bris still there?"

At least now I understood what Daniel had been talking about.

Dev's smile was wide and let me know he was thrilled with the outcome of the evening. "He's with me. He's content to stay with us. Zoey, he's here, but I'm in control. I'm here with you. I can call on his strength but still be myself." He chuckled as he leaned down and dropped a kiss on the ring in my belly button. "This is ridiculously sexy. Tell me Daniel hasn't seen it."

"Not yet," I admitted.

"He will lose his mind," Dev said, obviously looking forward to it.

"You aren't mad?" I asked, thinking about Declan, who was being a complete ass.

Dev didn't bother to feign misunderstanding. "It doesn't matter.

He can pretend, but I know what I am. I no longer need his approval." He pushed himself off the altar and reached down. When he came back up, he was wearing his white pants and had my dress in his hands.

"Come along, my goddess," he commanded, pulling me up. When I was in a seated position, he drew the gown over my head and arranged it properly on my body. He had to reach into the gown to draw my breasts into the right position. "I wish I had a camera. It's not traditional in Fae culture to take pictures on a night such as this, but I wish we had them. You're so beautiful. My beautiful goddess."

Padric was scowling at Declan. "You are seriously going to deny what you have seen tonight?"

"Padric, stop," Dev commanded, not taking his eyes off me. "It doesn't matter. He can deny it all he likes. It changes not a whit of what happened tonight. It merely means I will not be returning to Faery with him. I do not need to. Look at how the lesser Fae have embraced her."

Padric stepped closer, and I heard his startled intake of breath.

Dev grinned down at me. "Don't be startled, my goddess, but the pixies have come to welcome you."

"What?" I didn't understand until I glanced out of the corner of my eye.

Butterflies were everywhere. They clung to me. They landed on my dress and my skin and in my hair. They were startlingly glorious shades of blue and green and yellow. I lifted my hand close to my face. A huge butterfly with sapphire and amethyst wings rested there. When it was close enough for me to see the details of the insect's face, I realized Dev was correct. These were not butterflies. The winged creature stared back at me with an almost human face. He bowed his head to me and I turned to Dev, not knowing what to think of the action.

The pixies had landed on him as well, paying close attention to the midnight waterfall of his hair. "Say hello, Zoey. They're welcoming their goddess." He lifted his hand and greeted the smaller Fae. "It's good to see you, pixies. I promise I will bring you fertility. I will be your good priest."

Their wings fluttered in anticipation.

Wonder filled me as I took in the sight of pixies flying all around, a cloud of colors. "They're so beautiful, Dev."

"Yes, they are, my goddess, and they're ours," he replied with a satisfied voice. "I wish you luck, Declan. The pixies have made their choice. I'll be staying on this plane with my true goddess, and I don't doubt that others shall follow the pixies' lead." He breathed in the night air and let it out as he helped me from the altar. His smile was only for me now. "We'll have to do some renovations or perhaps change our residence. I expect the pixies will follow us and the brownies not long after that. Once the *sidhe* realize my brother has denied a true fertility god, they'll seek us out as well. He can be the king of an empty *sithein*."

Padric had had enough. "By rights given me by the queen, I am taking over the ceremony. Queen Miria gives her royal consent to these proceedings. She welcomes your goddess as she would a daughter. Will you allow me to finish the ceremony so it can be made legal?"

Dev inclined his head, giving his consent.

"Zoey, take his arm," Padric commanded as he unwound a long length of golden rope.

"No, sweetheart, like this," Dev corrected gently and he moved my hand from his palm up to his elbow, aligning them. Our arms lay against each other, and Padric wound the gold chain around us, binding our arms together.

"Zoey, do you wish to be this priest's goddess? You will be the maker of his magic, the keeper of his spirit, and the protector of his heart. You will hold nothing back from him and give him every piece of you, the good and the bad, the light and the darkness. You will be mother to his children. You will be his partner, his love, his goddess in all things. Are these vows you enter willingly and with an open heart?"

The only part that worried me was the part about the children, but that might have already been decided for me. I answered Padric solemnly. "I do."

Padric turned to Dev. "High Priest, this is your true goddess. Do you take her? You will be her provider, her defender, her lover. You will pour your magic into her and be grateful for that magic flows only from her. You will hold nothing back from her but give her every piece of you, the good and the bad, the light and the darkness. You will be father to her children. You will be her partner, her love, her god in all things. Are these vows you make willingly and with an open heart?"

"I do," Dev replied, looking down on me with a satisfied smile.

Padric shifted his attention to Declan who had watched the proceedings with a sort of weary resignation. "Do I have to fight you for the chain?"

He shook his head. "No, I will do it."

He pulled a golden chain from his pocket. It glowed in the soft light from the torches. The pixies had landed on our joined hands and their wings fluttered at the sight of the Goddess Chain. Declan let the medallion drop so all could see it hanging from his hand. While the jeweler who had made the copy might have had all the surface elements right, that copy didn't shine the way the real one did. It was stunning, and I knew the minute I saw it that it was mine.

Declan crossed to me and put the chain over my head. He gently arranged my hair around it and pulled the medallion into the proper place.

"Welcome, my sister." He kissed me lightly on the cheek. "I welcome you to our family and wish you every happiness in your union."

My eyes shot to Dev, who looked like a man who had just gotten everything he wanted. It all fell into place for me, and I was going to kill Daniel because he knew I had completely misunderstood the situation and he let me walk into it anyway.

I tried to make my question soft and merely academic because it wasn't like Devinshea had tried to hide anything. I was just that stupid. I was really, really stupid. "Baby, did I just get married again?"

He stared at me for a moment, confusion plain on his face. "You have got to be kidding me."

I winced as he unwound the rope and let go of my hand. "Unbelievable," he muttered under his breath. "Padric, take care of my wife. I need a moment."

Declan gave me a "told you so" smile. "I knew there would be trouble."

I ignored him and ran off after my husband.

Chapter Twenty-Nine

I called out after him, but his long legs carried him quickly away from me. I got only halfway down the hill when my own legs gave out, and I forced myself to sit before I fell and went tumbling down the hill. It would be the perfect way to end the night. I could fall in a graceless heap and perhaps break my neck.

I was tired, so tired. I was sore. I was feeling intensely stupid. They tried to tell me, every single one of them. They'd tried to explain about the possibility of Bris and now I recalled that the word union had been mentioned several times when Ingrid spoke of the ritual. Did I listen? No. Zoey Wharton Donovan…god, Quinn. I was practically a soap opera character and I didn't listen to anyone.

I needed a shower and I had no idea how I was going to face these wolves in the morning. Our entire party was supposed to have brunch at the big house with McKenzie tomorrow and I just wanted to hide. It had been easy in the heat of the moment, but I felt the full weight of everything hitting me now.

The leftover magic had me shaking. I didn't think I could make it back to the tent. I was going to have to sit here until Dev came back or Padric took pity on me and carried me home. I hated feeling so weak but more than that, I hated feeling so stupid. I should have known there was more to this. Now I realized all the signs had been there and beyond that, I knew why Dev had done it.

I could still hear Dev and Daniel in the limo after the night at the club. Daniel was going to get the wolves and Dev was going to get Faery. This had all been one huge power play. Dev needed to go back to Faeryland in a position of power. He needed a tool to force his mother to our side, and his ascent to godhood was just what the doctor, or the vampire, ordered.

I knew what their reasoning would be. They were just protecting me. Tied to Faery, Marini would have to think twice about messing with me. I was now a high priest's wife. I was a member of the royal family. They would be obligated to defend me should anything happen. It would satisfy Daniel's need to see me safe.

It would be nice just once to be married because some man just loved me rather than needed to protect me.

The pixies landed on me again, and I watched as they perched on my hands and lapped up the tears that had fallen there.

I also had to deal with the fact that I might be pregnant. Apparently ancient fertility gods didn't do safe sex. There had been condoms on the altar, but they hadn't been used. Tonight had been the first time Dev had taken me without protection. Up to now, we always used two forms of birth control. I took a shot four times a year and he used a rubber. I had to hope the shot worked, but that magic had been so strong and I had taken the brunt of it. It might work out just fine for the boys. I would be pregnant and confined to the safety of a *sithein* for the rest of my life. They could have their war knowing the wife was safely left behind.

"Zoey," Padric's voice called from behind me. "Allow me to take you back to the shelter."

I shook my head, unable to face anyone just yet. "I'll just stay here for a while, thank you." I glanced back at the man who was for all intents and purposes my new father-in-law. "If you could please ask Neil to come for me in an hour or so, I would be grateful." I could get the crying out of the way and then I could tell Neil about it.

"Devinshea would have my head if I left you alone."

"Oh, Dev has had everything he could want from me this evening," I replied unfairly, but I couldn't help but be a little bitter.

"I wanted a happy wedding night and a happy bride," Dev said quietly as he walked my way. "I did not get everything I wanted, Zoey." He nodded to the royal guard. "Please leave us. I'll take care of my wife. I'll start acting like her husband rather than a spoiled child." He reached down and picked me up, lifting me into his strong arms. "Let us go and join Daniel. Perhaps he can bring back your smile."

I slumped in his arms because I was almost boneless in my exhaustion. He carried me through the pasture where the wolves were breaking up and returning to their tents. They seemed happy and hopeful. They stopped and watched as we passed them. It was no wonder they gawked a bit. Dev was a god carrying his goddess with a trail of pixies following. It wasn't a scene they normally saw every day.

"You didn't wish to be married to me?" Dev carried me toward our tent. I noticed the field was filled with wildflowers that had been absent before the ceremony. Life had sprung up everywhere. "I was to remain the third in your marriage to Daniel?"

"I didn't understand, Dev. I didn't listen to you or Ingrid or anyone else. I was thinking about the heist and then I was thinking about finding Neil and losing Daniel. I thought of everyone but you."

He stopped. "You didn't answer my question. If you don't want this marriage then I can annul it."

"I didn't say that," I practically cried. "I love you. I've acted as your wife for a long time. Why would I not want to marry you? I told you last night I would never leave you. I was ready to marry Marcus if it meant keeping you safe. Don't question my love. Answer me this. Did you marry me because you love me or did you and Daniel see it as a convenient way to tie me to Faery? Our marriage makes this fight Faery's fight. Tell me that didn't occur to you."

I saw from the flush on his face that I was right. He began walking again. "I love you. Why is it wrong to want you safe? I want this marriage. I want it more than anything. I'll annul it and when you are ready, we can try again. Perhaps we can marry as is customary on this plane. It won't be recognized by Faery. It will be just for the two of us. I'm sorry. I thought it would please you. You've said in the past that you wanted a real ceremony. I was being selfish in giving you a ceremony from my culture that you didn't even recognize as a wedding."

"Dev, I should have…" I started but he was talking over me.

"I suppose public proof of sexual compatibility is not a part of human ceremonies," he said with a shake of his head. "I also bet that non-corporeal gods don't fuck the bride at a human wedding."

"We also don't have pixies and I really like the pixies. I don't want to annul our marriage. I love you. Can we just forget about the last twenty minutes and have a happy wedding night?" There was nothing to be had from annulling our marriage. There was nothing good that could come from us fighting. He'd had good intentions.

"I would have married you even if Padric had declined to

intercede," Dev explained quietly. "I would have counted myself your husband without my family's consent and I would have cut ties with them. I love you, my wife. I love you more than you can know."

I nodded and rested against him. "Then understand this, my husband. I might never blow you again. My jaw is never going to be the same."

Dev threw his head back and laughed. "Well, if that was my last blow job, at least I got to go out with a bang. You have Declan's everlasting respect, my wife. Good evening, Zack." Dev greeted the wolf who was standing guard outside the tent.

"All went well, sir?" Zack asked, politely not commenting on what I was sure he could smell.

"It was rocky, but we got it done," Dev admitted.

Zack threw back the door flap and we entered the tent. The front room was full. Neil and Chad sat in a chair, Neil on Chad's lap, and it was obvious they had made up. Chad had his face buried in Neil's neck doing that thing Danny had done last night. Sarah and Felix were sitting together on the sofa and Daniel was pacing.

Dev looked straight at Daniel. "You're a bastard, Donovan."

Daniel slapped Chad on the shoulder. "I told you. You owe me twenty bucks."

Chad turned his eyes to me, humor forcing his lips up. "You were surprised at being married? When did you realize it was a wedding, Your Highness? If the white dress didn't clue you in surely the handfasting ritual did it, right?"

I frowned as Chad laughed.

"Zoey," Sarah said with sympathy, "Goddess is what they call the wife of a high priest."

"Yeah, well you might have mentioned that to me," I shot back.

Dev lowered us into a chair but kept me in his arms, which I appreciated. I cuddled against his chest because I still had the shakes.

"You've dated a faery prince for almost two years, sweetie," Sarah pointed out. "You've lived with the man for over six months. I just thought you would know."

Daniel was laughing, and I sent him a forbidding look. "Don't you even say it, Daniel Donovan. I know what you're thinking.

You're thinking no one could be that stupid, but we both know damn well I can."

"I'm sorry, Z." He knelt down in front of me. "It was mean of me. I was just jealous because our wedding was so crappy and Dev got to plan out his dream wedding."

"Yes, it was a dream, Daniel. She didn't even realize it was a wedding until Declan welcomed her to the family," Dev said. "You should have mentioned it to me."

"Wow," Felix said, looking around the room with a light in his eyes. "That's a lot of pixies. That was some strong magic."

"I felt it from here," Sarah acknowledged. "I'm not surprised you have the shakes. You were the closest one to it. I have Albert heating up a tonic that should work."

I couldn't help but notice Neil, who was being strangely quiet. He moved off Chad's lap, and his eyes were following the pixies. He watched the sweet little butterflies with the sharp gaze of a predator. He moved suddenly, so quick a person not paying close attention would have missed it.

"Neil Roberts," I yelled, finding some energy at last. "You let that poor little pixie go!"

Neil garbled something incomprehensible around his mouthful of pixie.

Sarah got up, stalked over to Neil, and slapped him firmly on the back of the head. He coughed and spat the little red pixie out. She flew out in a fury of wings and saliva. As fast as her wings could carry her, she flew to my hair. I couldn't understand her, but she seemed to be giving Neil an earful. I offered my hand and she landed on it, trying to shake the spit from her and regain her dignity.

"He's really sorry," I said.

She said something tiny that sounded a little like "hummpff."

"He won't do it again." I would have to have a long talk with all the wolves.

"They look like they'll taste good, Zoey," Neil protested. "It's a food chain thing. You gotta respect the food chain."

Dev stared down at the outraged pixie. "When you seek your revenge, please try to remember that the wolf belongs to our goddess. She will have to clean up after you. You might show some mercy."

She didn't seem to care much about that and flew back to land on my hair. Neil was going to get pixed and then we'd see what he thought of the food chain. Pixies are lovely and known to be mean when angered.

Albert walked in carrying a large tray. He walked straight to me with a smile on his ferocious face. "Good evening, Your Grace. I offer my congratulations on your marriage to my master."

"Thank you, Albert," I replied as he offered me Sarah's tonic. My hands were shaking so Dev took it instead and held it to my lips. Albert had reminded me that I'd picked up another title. Yay, me.

"It should stop your shaking, Z," Sarah explained. "It's a restorative."

"Mistress," Albert began. "I have drawn a bath for you and the masters. It is at the ridiculously hot temperature you prefer. If you and the masters will retire to the bath, you will find I have laid out a repast of traditional honey cakes and nontraditional vodka. I'm sure the three of you will want to enjoy your private time together, to celebrate the final bonding of your marriage."

"Thank you, Albert." I sighed at the thought of hot water. I drank down the rest of Sarah's tonic and Dev picked me back up.

"Good night, mistress," Albert bade me. "I'll be leaving in the morning to return to our home. I must make preparations for our trip to Faery. I understand we'll be staying at the palace. More than likely I shall have to set the place to rights."

I told everyone good night and minutes later I was settling against Dev's chest as we let the hot water start to work its magic.

"Damn," Dev cursed as he sat back. "Has she always needed the water to scald off the top two layers of skin?"

Daniel laughed because it had been a point of contention before. I didn't care if Dev didn't like the water. I had earned his small discomfort.

"So, what's it like?" Daniel asked, pouring two shots of vodka. "I'm talking about the whole ancient deity taking up residence, not being married to Z. I know what that's like. First there's the hot sex, and then she's pissed off because she didn't mean to get married, and then she runs off with some other guy. I think it's my turn to be the guy she runs off with."

I growled at my first husband. God, I had to keep them straight in my head now.

Dev chuckled. "I think she's learned her lesson." He knocked back the vodka and passed it back to Daniel for more. "His name is Bris. He's Irish. He's a fertility god with agricultural powers. He's an excellent match. He's powerful. I think the wolves will be having a lot of puppies come early spring. It should make them willing to back us up."

Daniel nodded. "And Faery?"

Dev shrugged. "We'll see. We have to deal with my mother now. She's formidable. She'll be much harder to deal with than Declan, but in some ways she'll also be more reasonable. Having Padric on our side doesn't hurt."

Oh, god, I had to meet Dev's mom. I never had to meet Danny's mom because she died long before I met Daniel. I didn't know how well I would go over with the in-laws. What happened when she asked about my career? Did I proudly tell her I didn't have a criminal record despite the fact that I richly deserved one? I was going to have to explain Danny, too. Or would I? Vampires weren't allowed in Faery.

"She's freaking out." Daniel had a little smile on his face.

"What's wrong, sweetheart?" Dev asked. "Do you need a drink?"

I nodded because I figured it wouldn't hurt. It was how many humans had been conceived, so I took the shot and let the vodka start warming me from within. "How long are we going to be in Faery?"

Daniel poured me another drink and kneeled at the edge of the tub. He was wearing jeans and a T-shirt and let his hand sink into the water to play with my naval ring. "God, this is so hot, Z. I'm going to have to get that tat, aren't I?" he said absently before answering my question. "We think it will take at least a month, no more than three."

"But a month in the *sithein* is much longer out here." I sat up and moved to the other end of the tub where I could face them both. "Who's going to feed Danny? There isn't enough in the backup supply for that long."

Dev let his toes play with mine. "It won't matter because I plan to shove Dan in his coffin and take his ass with us. Mother can either accept our ménage or we can turn around and leave. I have no intention of separating us for so long. We're all going. I've already informed Padric I'm bringing my entire retinue including the wolves, Sarah and Felix, and most certainly my partner, the vampire. He's agreed to allow us to bring Daniel in if we use certain precautions."

"I get to travel wrapped in silver chains in a coffin," Daniel said with a frown. "I hate traveling in the coffin. It's cramped and it gets hot after a while."

"I'm sorry, baby," I said, feeling a little friendlier now with the vodka getting to work. I got up on my knees and leaned over to kiss him. "I'll make it up to you."

Daniel growled and his fangs came out. "I'll make sure you do. Maybe we can play around in the coffin before we go. It'll make it more pleasant if it smells like you." His eyes were starting to glow, and I could tell he was tired of being the third wheel.

"I can handle that." I'd never made out in a coffin before and considering who I was married to, it was a real omission.

"Tell me about the fertility god." Daniel ran his hand possessively down Dev's neck, fingering the thick vein there.

Dev stilled, his whole body stopping, but I watched as he finally leaned into the hand on his neck. "What do you want to know, Daniel?"

Daniel stared at Dev's hair. "I want to know if I'm going to have to exorcise the fucker. I allowed this only if you stayed in control, Devinshea. I won't let some ancient god to take over your body and shove you to the side. I explained that to you. I'm willing to try it to make you strong for the coming fight, but if it doesn't work, I'll need to make arrangements."

I could make a guess what those arrangements would be. I would have lots of company in whatever safe house Danny was planning on shoving me in when the war started. And that would kill Dev.

Dev turned slightly. "It's fine, Daniel. I'm in control. I will admit, our bonding threw me for a little bit of a loop. I don't remember everything, but he's talking in my head now. I've seen his soul. He wants to help us. He's been alone for so long. He wants a family. He's willing to give me his power, his strength, if I'll just allow him to share my emotions."

"And what about me?" Daniel's hands threaded through all that silky hair of Dev's and pulled his head back, a show of pure vampire possession and dominance.

"What?" Dev asked, sounding completely shocked.

It was fun to not be the only one on the receiving end of the jealous vampire. "Hey, we wanted him to stop pretending. You feed him regularly. It was inevitable he would get possessive. It's his nature. He likes your blood, Dev. It turns him on."

"I don't know if I'd go that far." Daniel pulled back, chuckling a bit as though he was amused with himself. "I do like the taste. It's different from yours, but gives me the same boost. I like the contrast. You're sweet but he's savory. Z is right. I am possessive and it's bothering me that I don't know if we just brought someone into our lives who might try to push me out."

Dev smiled, letting Daniel know he didn't mind at all. "I wouldn't allow it. Bris can accept our relationship or find another host. As it happens, he finds the thought of living with a vampire intriguing. He knows little about your species and is curious. And he definitely wants to get our hands on Zoey again."

"I'll have to get used to that, too." Daniel turned my way. "So I suppose you didn't really understand the whole ascension thing, either."

Did he have to bring up my idiocy again? "No, of course not."

"Then I have to ask you the question I thought I'd already asked. Are you all right with this, Z?" Daniel spoke, but both men were staring at me. "If it scares you, there are rituals to dispense with the god."

Dev put a hand on his heart as though it suddenly hurt him, but his mouth remained closed. I could only imagine the voice in his head. It wouldn't be shouting. I knew that instinctively. Bris was gentle, tender even. He wouldn't fight Dev. He would be hurt and alone.

"It's okay. He seems nice." And I might be pregnant with his baby. Go me. Except it would be Dev's child. If I was pregnant. Which I probably wasn't. I'd had unprotected sex with someone who had live sperm once in my life. What were the odds I would actually get pregnant?

"He wants to talk to you, Daniel," Dev said quietly.

"Why doesn't he then?" Daniel stared at him as though a bit ill at ease.

"Because he won't take over the body unless you give him permission. I've already said yes, but he believes he understands our relationship now and he wishes for your approval, Your Highness."

"I don't require that you obey me, Dev."

Dev's lips curled up. "He's a little old school when it comes to kings. You should be a shock to him, Dan."

Daniel nodded. "All right. I've never met a god before. Z seems to think he's okay. Let's have it. Or should we, like, get you dressed?"

"I'm perfectly comfortable naked, Your Highness. And I believe you've seen this body more than once." The change was startling. One minute Dev was speaking and the next a lyrical Irish accent was flowing from his mouth and his eyes had gone a solid green, twin emeralds staring from his familiar face.

Daniel tensed. "I can't sense a difference. I thought...I guess I thought I would be able to tell."

"The eyes and the accent don't give him away?" I asked. I gave the fertility god a little smile. It's probably not a good thing, but I was starting to get comfortable being naked around everyone, too. "Hi, Bris."

His face went from slightly alien to infinitely warm. "Hello, my goddess. You are well? The magic of the ritual hasn't made you overtired? This one and I will take care of you if you need to rest."

"I can take care of my wife." Daniel crossed his arms over his chest.

"I am sorry, Your Highness," Bris said. "Perhaps I should go because I am incapable of not forming an attachment to her. It's already there. I feel what Devinshea feels. It's why I waited millennia to bond again."

"What's special about Dev?" Daniel asked. "As a priest, I mean. You bond to a priest from what I understand. You waited in the ether for a thousand years? Surely there have been more than a handful of priests in that time."

"Yes, but they didn't match my needs. You have to understand that Fae priests aren't trained to love. To care certainly, but for many people. Priests are not monogamous. They don't take lovers in that fashion. Sex is a thing to share with many."

319

"And for you?"

"I loved my goddess and when she was gone, I went to the ether on my own. I went until I found someone who loved as strongly as I did. Your Highness, if my regard for your wife is going to cause trouble, then I should go because loving her, caring for her, and quite frankly for you, are the reasons I bonded with this priest in the first place. He thinks you want me to strengthen him for the fight that is to come, but I think something different."

"And what's that?"

"I believe you want me to keep him alive. I think you would prefer he didn't fight at all, but you know it's his nature. I can be helpful, Your Highness. I can bring him strength that you can't imagine. And I can keep him safe. It will be my highest priority to protect all of you."

"You're a fertility god...what should I call you?"

"Bris is fine. I feel this world is less formal than the one I last lived in. More open, as well. You have progressed. In my world, I would have been called My Lord, but I want a friendship with you, Your Highness."

"Daniel, please." I could see he was softening.

Bris smiled and it lit up the room. "Yes, Daniel. I don't want you to worry that I mean to cut you out. I could no more do it than cut out my own heart. I share a soul space with Devinshea. I feel what he feels. I am empty without him. You have to understand that his emotions rule me. It is why if you don't wish me to touch your wife, I should end the bonding. For that matter Devinshea loves..."

Bris suddenly stopped, his eyes sealing shut, and when he opened them again, he was Dev. "See." His smile was a bit unsteady. "I can take control when I want to. Do you understand better now, Dan?"

I stayed perfectly quiet because this seemed to be a moment between them. Nothing Bris had said made me wary. And I trusted Dev. He was sharing a body with this god person.

Bris had touched me, kissed me, worshipped me. I'd been in the middle of his magic. If I had to make a bet, he was one of the good guys.

Daniel's hands went straight to Dev's face, cupping his cheeks and looking deep into his eyes. "Tell me you're okay. Tell me he's being truthful because he sounds too good to be true."

Dev's hands went up, covering Daniel's. They were so beautiful together I felt my heart nearly stop. "He's with me. He's part of me. He wants so badly to be part of us. We're good, Daniel."

Daniel stood up suddenly and shucked his shirt, the tension rushing out of the room. "All right, then. You two hurry up. I'm hungry and I didn't like being left here alone."

"You weren't exactly alone." I shifted back to Dev, reveling in his warmth. "You had everyone else here."

"I'm alone if I'm not with you two," he said quietly.

"We can't have that, Daniel," Dev replied. "What should we do with our wife? Our wife. I like the sound of that."

Daniel's dimples came out as he stood over us. "It does sound good. I thought I'd give you the night off, Z, since he already did god knows what to you. I'm sure it was filthy."

"Oh, it was more about what Zoey did to me," Dev said with a salacious grin. "Do you want me to tell you, Daniel?"

"Oh, yes," Daniel replied, a little shudder in his voice. "The two of you meet me in bed and give me every detail about how Zoey misbehaved tonight. I think it would be fun if I bit Dev while Zoey took care of Little Dev there. We were both bad. We should be punished." Daniel winked at us as he left the room.

"I think I created a monster," Dev observed as Daniel left. He hugged me tight and I could feel his satisfaction. "Looks like we're not through tonight, my goddess. I think my wedding night is going to be happy after all. I like being in the middle."

I shook my head and laughed, avoiding several questions I would really like to ask. The boys weren't ready to go there so I let go of the whole thing. "You're going to have to settle for a hand job, buddy."

Dev nodded. "I can handle that."

When we joined Daniel, he welcomed us. Our threesome was finally blessed in both of their worlds.

Daniel pulled me into his arms and the magic began all over again.

Chapter Thirty

"Zoey." Neil jumped onto the bed the next morning. His weight made the mattress shift underneath me and shoved me further into Dev's arms. "Zoey, wake up."

I groaned and opened an eye. I could already tell it was way too early. Dev grumbled in his sleep and disentangled himself from me so he could turn over and shove his head under a pillow to try to escape the noise. I wasn't allowed such retreat as Neil was insistent.

"God, Neil, what time is it?" I moaned the question.

"It's time for you to help me." Neil's voice was a little desperate and whiny. "If you want to make that brunch we're supposed to go to before we head home tonight, you'll get up and fix this."

I sighed and pushed myself up. I really couldn't miss the brunch with McKenzie. We were still negotiating the alliance, and after last night, we were coming in from a position of power. I just wished I could have slept the day away. My husbands had taken the idea of a wedding night seriously. Danny had kept me up until right before dawn, reminding me I was married to him as well as Dev.

My vampire couldn't seem to stop indulging in the new freedom he was giving himself. When I told him I couldn't take anymore, he just cuddled against me, playing with my neck or pressing his ear against my chest because he said he loved the sound of my heartbeat. Dev passed out after our little feeding session, the events of the night having exhausted him completely. As I drifted off to sleep, Danny had kissed me and promised that when we got home, he would sleep beside us again. The noise of so many people kept him awake, so he slipped off into his coffin for the day. Now I was kind of wishing I'd gone with him because I would still be asleep.

"What's the problem, sweetie?" There was no getting around it now. I was awake.

Neil scratched his head and his eyes had a desperate look to them. "I think it was the pixie." Tears welled as his voice quivered so slightly. "I think she gave me fleas."

I tried really hard not to laugh but Dev didn't bother. He just shook with the force of his amusement.

He tossed the pillow aside and pushed up on his elbows to regard Neil with sparkling green eyes. "I told you she would get you back, wolf. Pixies may be small, but they're great believers in revenge. Hope, no pray, she's satisfied with this or it will only be the beginning."

A horrible thought hit me. The ramifications could be truly terrible. "Dev, this isn't funny. If Neil has fleas, then they could move over to Lee and Zack. All of our wolves are going to end up like this. I have to flea dip Neil or they'll be all over the house."

Dev thought that was just the funniest thing he'd ever heard. He let his head fall back as he laughed loudly. "I assure you Zack would never let himself be flea dipped, but you should probably check out Lee. I heard he went hunting last night so he wouldn't have to listen to the sounds of our wedding night."

Neil was still scratching his hair furiously, trying to stop that itch. "It's making me crazy, Z. Please tell me I won't have to wear a flea collar. They don't go with anything. I promise I won't eat the pixies anymore."

I shot a look around the room where the pixies were glaring at Neil. I pulled the sheet around me even as Dev protested the loss of it. I rolled out of bed and addressed my new tiny retinue. "He'll leave you be from now on. You've had your revenge and he's sorry. All the wolves will know the rules. You have to get along with them because they're not going anywhere. Now, I have to go delouse my wolf. Try to stay out of trouble."

I swear those little butterflies were laughing their asses off and their priest was right there with them.

"Come on, Neil," I said, giving the entire Fae contingent my most forbidding look before holding out my hand to him. "We'll wake up Sarah. I'm sure she knows something that will get rid of the fleas."

An hour later, Neil sighed as I used a scrub brush on his hair. He sat in the tub looking a little like a drowned puppy with his blonde curls flat against his face. Sarah had whipped up something with orange, yarrow root, and a bunch of flowers that seemed to be working. At the very least, Neil had stopped trying to peel his scalp off. Sarah wielded a pitcher of warm water and poured it over his head.

Lee walked in and frowned at the scene in front of him. "You do know he's human too, right? You two girls treat that boy like he's one of those yippie dogs debutantes buy. I bet you'd carry him around in your purse if you could."

Neil's hand shot up, and he scratched behind his ear. "Missed a spot, Z."

He probably wouldn't have cared if we did carry him around in an oversized handbag as long as it was Louis Vuitton.

I rubbed some more of the paste into his scalp and frowned at Lee. "Well, you better stay away from the pixies or I'll have you in this tub too, mister. Neil tried to eat one and she gave him fleas."

Lee's face lost all color. "Are you talking about the little butterfly things that are suddenly everywhere?"

"Tell me you didn't eat one," I begged.

"It got away." Lee sighed a little. "They're really fast."

Sarah shook her head. "I'll make up some more."

"Actually, I was looking for you, Sarah. I don't feel so hot. My stomach is upset. Nothing too bad, but I was hoping you could give me something."

I gave Neil one more thorough rubdown as I cast a glance at Lee. He'd been running around in the woods all night. "Well, it was probably something you ate. Have you been eating strange birds again? I told you that would give you a tummy ache."

"I have just the thing." Like the good little healer she was, she declined to give Lee a lecture on not eating nasty things. "Ginger will take care of it. You'll feel better in no time. I swear, Z. I'm going to have to pack up my garden when we go to Faery."

"Oh, Sarah," Dev said from the door. "You haven't seen gardens until you've been to Faery. I assure you, you'll find everything you need and many things you never thought you would ever see. I'm truly glad you and Felix have agreed to journey with us. Zoey will need her friends around her. It's a strange place but very beautiful."

Dev was going home for the first time in seven years, and he would be returning with more power than anyone could have imagined. He would be returning with a wife and his friend. He'd left alone, but he was going home with an entirely new family at his back.

"I wouldn't miss it," Sarah said, her eyes filled with anticipation.

Dev was dressed in his version of casual, expensive but comfortable slacks and a T-shirt that hugged his chest. His long black hair was pulled back at the nape of his neck, but I remembered the way it hung down when he was on top of me. I smiled up at him, my breath catching a little because I was so happy. Danny was happy, really happy, for the first time in a long time. He was finally relaxing and learning to be comfortable with who he was. Dev was happy. They had promised to stay with me forever. Our relationship, the three of us, finally felt settled. There would be more changes. I knew that for sure, but it felt like forever this time.

"Sweetheart, Declan and Padric are here. We'll be going over to the big house together." Dev looked at me, amused with my activity. "When you finish scrubbing your wolf, get him dressed because we need to leave in twenty minutes if we want to be on time." He turned back around with a superior look on his face. "I managed to catch Zack before he chased down a pixie. I explained the rules to him and he'll follow them. You won't have to worry about him. My wolf is much better trained than yours."

I wrinkled my nose as he laughed and went to join his brother. I tried not to think about the fact that Lee chose that moment to scratch fiercely behind his ear. He tried really hard to stop, but he was suddenly scratching his head all over.

"I'll heat up some more water," Sarah said with a frown. "And maybe I'll get a couple of the guys because I don't think he's going into the tub willingly, Z."

I gave Lee my most ferocious stare. "We'll see about that."

* * * *

"Your Grace." McKenzie greeted me as we entered the big house. He had a large smile on his face and the look of a man whose plan had worked out well. "I'm so pleased that we were able to host the marriage of a priest to his goddess. It was truly an honor. The magic associated with the ceremony was beyond our wildest dreams. My own wife is certain that it worked. She's hopeful for the first time in a long time, and I can't tell you how grateful I am for that."

"We were happy to have the ceremony here." Dev gave the alpha a courtly bow. "It was beautiful. Everything was perfect. My goddess and I thank you for making our wedding a memorable one."

"It should have been performed in Faery," Declan pointed out just a little sourly. "It is traditional. It should have been performed at Devinshea's temple. My brother has an inexplicable fondness for this plane."

"If it hadn't been performed on this plane, I could never have received Bris." Dev didn't look at his brother as he spoke.

"I meant the marriage, brother, not your ascent," Declan shot back. "Obviously your ascent had to be performed on this plane. The marriage could have waited until we returned. Mother will be upset you ran off to another plane and married without ever bringing your goddess home to meet your family."

A servant was passing around champagne glasses with mimosas. I sipped mine while watching Dev and Declan bicker. It was going to be a long trip if this is what they did the entire time.

"Besides, mother should have been here to witness the act itself," Declan said with a sigh of pure regret. "She will never believe anyone as small as Zoey could swallow you whole."

I coughed up just a little of my drink while John McKenzie couldn't stop his laugh. There were four other alphas who stared at Declan, shocked but amused. They'd all been there last night so I was sure it had already been discussed, probably at great length and in ridiculously graphic detail. Everyone else ignored him because they were used to Declan's outrageous comments by now.

"I am simply saying that you might be asked to prove my tale, Zoey," Declan continued. "Mother is a great believer in seeing proof before she accepts truths."

I shot a desperate look at my husband, hoping he would tell me his brother was just teasing me. He simply shrugged and downed his drink before seeking out another one.

Padric patted my back soothingly. "I am certain she will accept my version of the tale, Your Grace. Declan is trying to scare you. I would point out that when he chooses to marry, you have every right to be one of the witnesses at his ceremony."

"Damn straight," I shot back at my brother-in-law. "I'm going to watch and comment on everything, Dec. You'll be lucky if you can perform over my incredibly loud commentary."

"Dev, you would not allow that." Declan sent his brother a pleading look.

"There's a saying on this plane, brother," Dev replied. "Turnabout is fair play. I look forward to your ceremony."

"You have just given me another good reason to not get married at all," Declan admitted. "And I had a list before."

McKenzie introduced us to the alpha wolves joining us this morning. They were the four most powerful in the country and important to Daniel's plans. Each had been impressed with the magic Dev had performed and commented on the rare nature of what they had witnessed. Dev talked to them smoothly, working in certain points and making them laugh. He played the politician with ease, and I knew he enjoyed having the wolves right where he wanted them. I only caught them looking at me a few times, obviously remembering what they had seen the night before. They had each been there with their mates.

"Relax, Your Grace." Padric guided me slightly away from the crowd.

"Really, I prefer Zoey." I had to crane my neck up to get a good look at him. I'd brought mostly flats in deference to the fact that we were in the woods, but I would be taking my good heels to Faery with me. I would need them.

"What you did last night was a great act of love and nothing to be ashamed of, Zoey," Padric said softly, looking down on me with affection. "Devinshea is lucky to have you for a wife."

"Thank you." I was happy I had at least one faery on my side. Now that we were as close to alone as we seemed fated to get, I decided to ask the question I'd waited to ask for almost a year. "So am I really his wife? Am I his only wife?"

Padric blinked a couple of times in obvious surprise. "He told you about Gilliana?"

I nodded. He'd told me the tale when we'd gotten serious about our relationship. Gilliana was the woman his mother had wanted Dev to mate with, despite the fact that he hated her. His mother had used magic to force her will on him. "Of course he did. I know what happened. Did he get her pregnant?"

Padric frowned, and his eyes strayed over to where Dev was talking to the wolves. He seemed to wonder just how much to tell me. I was sure he would rather talk to Dev first and find out what Dev wanted me to know.

"I'll find out, Padric," I warned the royal guard. "You can tell me now or I'll find out later and it will be worse."

He sighed. "The short answer is yes. Gilliana did get pregnant from the night she spent with the prince."

I felt my eyes well up immediately at the thought of some other woman having his child. It made my stomach roll.

"Zoey, don't cry," he said quickly. "She was foolish and lost the child. She acted as though she wasn't even pregnant. She got drunk and fell down her own stairs. She lost the child in her fourth month. I believe she was with another man at the time of the accident."

"I am sorry for her." I hated the fact there was a part of me that was relieved. It was horrible, but I couldn't stand the thought of that woman who wanted to leave Dev to die when he was proven mortal having his baby.

"Don't be. She's vile, Zoey. I don't know what Miria was thinking except that she's been obsessed with Devinshea reproducing. She fears he will die and leave her with nothing. He would never believe it, but he's her favorite child. She died a little the day she discovered his mortality. It's been difficult for her to deal with the fact that she will lose him."

My eyes narrowed in suspicion because that wasn't the way Dev told the tale.

"There are always two sides to every story," Padric pointed out, sensing my disbelief. "I'm sure you've heard Devinshea's, but I ask that you hear Miria's side as well. Devinshea was young. The filter he viewed the world through was self-centered. I think he'll see it differently as he ages and has young of his own. You will meet the woman and I ask that you judge her worth based on your experiences with her, not Devinshea's childhood struggles. You remind me a little of her, actually."

I doubted that, but I was willing to give my mother-in-law a chance since this journey meant so much to Dev. Walking in and punching his mother might cause him trouble. It seemed like it was going to be hard on me, though. "So I'm a second wife?"

Dev would have been married to the witch when she came up pregnant. The fact that they were compatible would have ensured the marriage. Being a second wife limited my rights once we got to Faery, the way I understood it. I wouldn't be running Dev's household and I would be relegated to second class status, given only the rights his first wife was willing to give me.

"Miria annulled the marriage herself when Declan and I returned and told her Devinshea was taking a goddess," Padric explained.

I let out a breath I hadn't realized I'd been holding. I wasn't sure how Dev would have reacted to being forced to live with a wife he hated. I was certain he wouldn't be happy that she would have had authority over me.

Padric smiled at my relief. "She loves her son, Zoey. It was her right to annul the marriage because there were no children. You're Devinshea's only wife and a full member of the royal family. You should take it as a great sign of her love for her son that she consented to the marriage with no proof of your fertility."

I was choosing to ignore that. I didn't wish to be married for my fertility, but I knew it would be highly prized in Faery. "And Gilliana is all right with this?"

"She realized how much she angered the queen when she lost the child." Padric frowned. "You will have trouble with her. She's been petitioning the queen to be allowed to leave the *sithein* to join her husband on this plane in the hopes she would get pregnant again. She wasn't happy when Miria denied her and then annulled the marriage. She's vowing vengeance on you, Your Grace. I fear she won't go down without a fight."

So I'd be packing my Manolos and my Ruger. I'd take some knives with me too, I decided. Cold steel. I smiled up at Padric. "She won't find me an easy mark."

"I do not doubt that. I believe she is expecting a sweet little flower like Devinshea's priestesses. You'll be a shock. She will also not be expecting your vampire. I've already discussed the situation with him. I thought it best that he understand the position you're in. Devinshea must act the royal and the priest. Daniel's position is freer. He can protect you without worrying about any consequences."

"So you think the queen will allow Daniel to stay with us?"

"If it means her son comes home then yes, she will most likely make allowances." Padric gestured to my left. "I think something is wrong with your wolf, Your Grace."

I turned to see Lee as he fell to the floor, clutching his stomach. Zack and I got to him at the same time.

"What's going on, brother?" Zack took a knee beside him.

I got down on the floor with the wolf, who seemed weak all of a sudden.

Lee was sweating and his face had lost its color. "I hate this. What the hell is wrong with me? I don't get sick, damn it."

Dev left his conversation and looked down at us now with great concern in his eyes. "What's happening?"

"I don't know." I put my palm against Lee's forehead. It was cold and clammy, not warm as it should have been. Wolves tend to be warmer than humans. Even as I touched him, his muscles began to shake. "He said he was feeling bad this morning. Sarah gave him some ginger for nausea."

"It's like before." Lee ground out the words between clenched teeth.

I started to have a very bad feeling because I had an inkling of what he was talking about. I remembered well the last time Lee had gotten this ill.

I looked around the room. All of the humans and the wolves associated with us were watching Lee with concern on their faces.

The crash of glass breaking forced my attention away from Lee. And then another, and then there was the sound of a plate smashing. The other wolves in the room dropped whatever they were holding and blank looks came across their faces. They dropped their drinks or the plates they'd been holding and no one made a move to clean up the mess. Almost as though they were one, their heads turned toward the front of the house and without a word to anyone, they began walking.

I stood, terror starting to creep across my heart. One moment they were laughing and joking together and the next all those alphas were zombie-like, moving as though someone else controlled them.

John McKenzie was the only wolf left with us, and he was sweating and shaking. "What the hell is going on?"

"I don't know," Dev replied, his eyes tight. "Are you feeling ill?"

McKenzie shook his head. "I feel a great urge to leave this house and join the crowd in the field. I didn't even know there was a crowd in the field. He's calling to me, but I won't answer, damn it. I am the alpha. I submit to no one."

Just as Dev shot me a look of sudden understanding, my cell phone rang. I took a deep breath, praying it was a wrong number. I was pretty sure if I looked down the number would be *1-800-YOU'RE FUCKED*. I slid my finger across the phone to connect the call.

"Hello, Zoey," Lucas Halfer's smooth voice said, not bothering to wait for me to say hello. "I finally figured out why our little prize didn't work on old Zack that night. You had me worried there. I thought this whole Strong Arm of Remus thing was just a bunch of bullshit."

"Why didn't it work on Zack?" I kept him talking while I tried to take inventory of exactly what our assets were. I hoped McKenzie had an armory somewhere because my little war with Halfer was heating up again. Dev already had his SIG out, checking the clip and flicking the safety off.

Halfer chuckled in my ear. "You neglected to tell me Donovan had found another idiot wolf willing to take his blood. It doesn't work on loners or wolves who are dumb enough to oath themselves to vampires. So I guess you'll at least have Zack to defend you. I'm sure your faery is there, too. Loved the show last night, by the way. You're a woman of many talents. I would have been envied by all the demons if I'd managed to get you into Hell with me."

"What do you want, Halfer?" I finally asked and heard Dev curse beside me the minute he heard that name.

"I want you to come to the window. Come see what I have planned for you."

"I think I'll pass," I replied flatly. "You probably have a rocket launcher planned for me. I'll stay out of sight where it's nice and cozy and you're not precisely certain of my position."

"No rocket launcher, though I like the way you think," he said with a chuckle that froze my insides. "You can come to the window and see my impressive display or I can start killing these wolves. I

331

think I'll start with the kiddos."

There was a click that told me Halfer had said all he was going to for the moment. I cursed vilely and got my ass up to do what he told me to.

"What are you doing?" Dev asked, pulling me back.

I took his hand in mine and dragged him along. Padric and Declan followed close behind. "I'm seeing just how screwed we are, my husband. This might be one of the shorter marriages on record."

All the breath in my body seemed to flee as I stared through the huge bay windows that looked over the valley below McKenzie's house. I saw Lucas Halfer, ex-demon but still full-time asshole. He stood in the middle of the field with a shit-eating grin on his face and the Strong Arm of Remus in his hand.

All around him a massive army of wolves twitched and growled, waiting for their new master to give the command. They were all in wolf form, clothes ripped from their sudden and unexpected change and strewn throughout the valley. The wolves had been called and they answered, dropping everything they'd been doing to heed the siren's call.

Halfer said something, raising that paw high above his head, and the wolves turned as one enormous pack, their teeth bared and the need for blood howling through them. Though I hadn't heard the command, I knew what it was.

Kill.

Chapter Thirty-One

I felt the magic pouring off my husband before the wolves had taken more than two steps toward the house. It wasn't lust magic this time, but something a bit more helpful in this situation. Dev stood beside me, his hands splayed wide as he slowly brought them up, raising them with the greatest of intent from his legs to his chest. His arms moved slowly as though they were pressing against a great weight.

The ground outside the house rumbled as the dirt split open and spat out life. Flowing grass and vines and all manner of things green and vibrant flew up from the earth and formed a tangled mass roughly twelve feet high. Even from where I stood, I could plainly see the thorns that wove their way through the wall of green. It was a barrier as far as I could see either way.

"Goddess, brother," Declan breathed as he watched the field outside. "When did you learn to do that?"

Dev took my hand and spun on his heels. "They will still get through. We have a little time though. Padric, do you have a guard with you?"

"Always, Your Grace," Padric responded.

"When the time is right, you will call them," Dev commanded, his voice all steely determination. I probably shouldn't have found it irresistibly sexy given the situation, but I did. "They will protect my goddess. Is that understood?"

"Yes, sir." Padric didn't try to hide the small smile he had. I could guess what he was thinking. He was proud of the man Dev had become. He was proving cool in a crisis and capable of making the right decisions. Declan was the warrior, but Padric was looking to Dev for his orders.

McKenzie seemed a little better as we hurried back into the great room. "What the hell is going on?"

"I'm afraid we've brought some of our problems with us, John," Dev admitted calmly. "You find yourself in the middle of a small war."

"It did not look small, brother." Declan didn't seem terribly concerned, but rather intrigued by the prospect of a good fight. "That was a large army of wolves."

"Wolves?" McKenzie spat. "Those are my wolves. Why would they be attacking me?"

"The Strong Arm of Remus," I said and watched McKenzie blanch.

The alpha shook his head. "That's a myth."

Lee managed to sit up. The barrier of plants seemed to be helping him a little too. He was still shaky, but some of the color was coming back to his face. "It's not a myth, Mac. Zoey tracked it down a couple of weeks ago with the full intention to destroy it. Just being near the damn thing made me violently ill. We got blindsided by that fucking demon and lost it. We thought it didn't work. It didn't affect Zack at all."

Zack was one of two wolves on whom it had absolutely no effect. "I don't see what the big deal is. It's a petrified paw. It didn't stop me from trying to kill that bastard and I don't feel anything right now except regret that I didn't tear his throat out the first time."

"It's not having any effect on Neil, either," I pointed out.

"Are you telling me Halfer is out there and he has control of all the other wolves in the valley?" Neil asked, his eyes wide. He knew the story. All wolves knew the story of the Strong Arm of Remus. They had thought it was just that—a story. I now had irrefutable proof that it was more than a myth.

"Daniel's blood is protecting you," I told Neil and Zack. "You both took a blood oath to Daniel."

"But Neil hasn't taken Daniel's blood in over seven months," Sarah pointed out logically.

"Yeah, it's some good shit," Dev said, his face losing all its smoothness. His eyes were dark and he was ready to fight. Dev had been ready for this fight for a long time. "Tell me where your armory is, McKenzie. Please tell me you're well equipped. We need guns, preferably semiautomatics at the very least, and silver rounds. Grenades or flash bangs would be helpful."

"I have some guns, but I'm not running an army here. Why would I have silver rounds?" McKenzie still didn't seem to believe what was going on. "I have a few in case of emergencies, but it's just a single box. These are my people. I don't shoot them full of silver."

Declan rolled his eyes at what he clearly considered the naiveté of the alpha's statement. "Certainly no one's people ever rose up against their good leader. You wouldn't last a day in Faery, McKenzie. The good news, brother, is my entire guard is excellently equipped."

"With bows, arrows, swords, and knives." Dev shook his head. "I wasn't planning on doing close-combat fighting with a bunch of werewolves. It tends to be best to keep out of the range of claws and teeth."

"Yes, it is traditional weaponry, but it is all reinforced with silver." Declan sounded pleased with himself. "I changed all the tips on our arrows to silver and the knives and swords are all silver as well. I was serious about taking that vampire out, Zoey. Then there will be an opening in your bed."

I ignored my obnoxious brother-in-law in favor of freaking out about another obvious problem. "Daniel's out there, Dev."

"Yes, he is," Dev acknowledged as McKenzie began to lead our party toward the armory. "The good news is Halfer won't consider him any kind of a threat and probably won't even look for his resting place until after he kills all of us. The bad news is Daniel can't hear a damn thing in that coffin. He's wearing an advanced set of earplugs. I bought them because he's such a grump when he doesn't get enough sleep and Zoey snores."

"I do not," I protested as Dev drug me alongside him.

"Yes, you do, my goddess," Dev shot back. "I think your little snuffles are sweet and they don't bother me at all, but Daniel struggles because his hearing is so much better. He says you sometimes sound like a water buffalo trying to mate. His words, not mine, my love."

I huffed, offended because I was quite certain I didn't snore. Danny, on the other hand, had been known to blow the roof off from time to time when he was human. I was pretty sure vampires didn't snore at all.

McKenzie stopped and opened a door. The armory was small and full of mostly shotguns and rifles. Dev would use his SIG as his primary weapon, but he took a shotgun and shoved a .38 in his pocket as well.

He sighed over the tiny armory. "I spend a fortune, deal with the most unsavory of arms dealers, and when I finally get my little war, I'm stuck with this. I hoped to finally get to use the P90s. Well, perhaps when we fight Marini." He handed me two pistols and a box of bullets.

Felix stepped forward, his hand out.

Dev looked at him sympathetically. "Felix, we all know you're a pacifist. You don't have to do this. Just stay at the back of the group and we'll protect you."

Felix gave Dev a hard look and kept his hand out, waiting for his weapon. "Give me a gun, Dev. If you think for one moment I'm going to let a bunch of wolves tear my wife apart, then you're wrong. I took vows. I took vows of nonviolence, but I took deeper vows, too. I vowed to protect her. It takes precedence over everything else."

Dev passed Felix a shotgun and quickly showed him how to load it. Sarah had never been a pacifist and knew better than Felix how to use a gun. She shoved a .38 in her pocket and kissed her husband passionately.

"It's going to be all right, Felix," she said quietly. She would do whatever she could to protect the man she loved. She'd been off the black magic for a long time, but I was sure she would use it if she had to.

"Zack," Dev called to his bodyguard. Zack ran forward from the back of the group. "I need you to change."

Zack changed with zero hesitation. His suit ripped around him, falling in pieces to the floor. He sat back on his haunches, waiting for further instructions.

Dev focused on his well-trained wolf. "You will find a way out of here. Those wolves out there are trying to kill us. They will likely ignore another wolf, especially if you don't cause them trouble. Get to Daniel. Wake him up and tell him to get off his ass. It's time for us to kill Halfer. Tell him I'll be waiting. You must be sneaky, though. I don't want Halfer to suspect Daniel isn't in the ground as he should be. Watch and wait for the time when Halfer won't see you slip into the tent. Join with the others if you have to in order to bide your time. Be patient, Zack. This is our only shot."

The big brown wolf thumped his tail once and then took off.

"So we're supposed to stay alive until sundown?" McKenzie asked, sarcasm dripping. "I don't think that's going to happen, Your Grace. There are at least a thousand wolves out there and many of them are stone-cold killers."

"Under the influence of that artifact, we have to consider them all stone-cold killers. They'll do Halfer's will, and he wants us dead. We have a secret weapon that Halfer isn't counting on. Trust me, McKenzie," Dev assured him. "My partner is a king. Daylight will not stop him. We have to stay alive until Daniel is awake then he and I will take care of Halfer. How do we get out of here?"

McKenzie moved down the hallway and we followed. "I have a secret tunnel that leads from the house to a cave in the mountains to the north. We'll be able to see the field so at least we'll know what's coming."

He led us to the back of the house. Even now I could hear the wolves beginning to howl. The sound was far closer than I was comfortable with. At least some of the wolves had made their way around the barrier. We found ourselves in a narrow hallway. McKenzie came to a dead end and we stopped, giving him space to do what he needed to do. The walls in the hallway were paneled in rich wood. The alpha pushed against a seam in the paneling and a small door slid open. McKenzie pulled on a pair of heavy gloves that had been hanging from a hook near the door.

Neil had taken up position at the rear. He listened, his senses wide open. "Dev, we're about to have incoming."

Even as he shouted the warning, I heard the crack of glass shattering as the strongest and fastest of the wolves made their way through, over, or around the barrier Dev had created. McKenzie opened the door with his gloved hands and ushered Felix and Sarah through. Declan stood beside his brother, sword drawn, and Neil ran to stand in front of me.

"Come with me, Your Grace," Padric demanded, taking me by the arm.

"Dev," I yelled out as Padric tried to manhandle me into the passage.

Dev turned briefly to look at me. "Go with Padric. I will follow you, my goddess. Padric, if you have to carry her out of here, you will do it."

I didn't understand why he couldn't just come with me now, but he was being a control freak with Daniel out of action. He would never allow anyone else to control the battle besides Daniel. I saw Lee trying to stay by Dev's side, but he faltered and fell to his knees.

"Lee!" I couldn't leave him behind. Even if he changed, he was different. The wolves would sense his difference and he would be at their mercy. I struggled against the royal guard, trying to get back to my wolf.

McKenzie cursed as Padric shoved me into the small passage. He pushed us through as quickly as he could, directing us to move through the darkness. I looked at John McKenzie and attempted to play to anything soft inside him.

"Please," I begged the alpha who was more than strong enough to bring Lee with us. All he had to do was drag him a few feet. "Please, don't leave him behind."

The alpha shook his head and started toward the sick loner. "Damn it, Owens," McKenzie said under his breath. He picked Lee up in a fireman's hold and walked through the doorway. "Get through that gate and we should have a shot at getting out of here."

"We're through," Padric called out as he hauled me past a large gated doorway. It ran from the top to the bottom of the tunnel and created a complete barrier. Even in the gloom of darkness, I could see the silver shine of that tightly barred gate. I shivered as I realized if we got stuck in this tunnel, Daniel wouldn't be able to get through the gate. He would be helpless to get to us.

Dev, Declan, and Neil ran through, though Dev was now laying down suppressive fire. Neil and Declan scrambled into the tunnel while Dev backed into the space, not letting up on his firing position. I held my breath as a huge black wolf reared back and leapt toward my husband. The wolf was in midair, snarling with fury as Dev took his shot. The wolf hit the floor and Dev fired through the gate as Declan slammed it shut behind him. I heard the satisfying sound of the bolt sliding home.

Dev pulled me close as the first wolf hit the gate and his flesh began to sizzle. We all turned back toward McKenzie.

"Well I don't shoot them full of silver, but I'm not a complete idiot," he explained. "Everyone needs an escape hatch when the going gets tough."

I shrank back as another wolf joined the first. They shoved their bodies against the silver, not seeming to care that their flesh was burning. They snarled and howled their frustration at being so close to their prey but unable to take it down. The two wolves shoved their paws through, trying desperately to get their claws on anything.

I didn't recognize them in this form but I knew these were people I'd probably met during our stay here. These were men and women who asked us for help and offered their hospitality in return. They weren't raging killers. They were just pawns. They had children and lives to go back to.

Dev raised his gun and leveled it at the wolves trying to claw their way through the silver bars to get to us. His eyes held no mercy, and I knew he was ready to kill every wolf that came our way. I wasn't quite so ready as my husband.

I put a hand on his shoulder. "Dev, they're victims, too."

"Victims who are trying to kill you," he growled at me. "You'll forgive me if I don't feel a lot of sympathy."

"Please." I forced him to look me in the eyes. "They're contained. Let's go and wait on Danny. If we can get out of this without killing our allies, won't it be best for all concerned?"

He shook his head but lowered his weapon. "We'll go, my goddess, but there will be no mercy for Halfer. Understand that now. I will not be swayed."

I rolled my eyes. I wasn't about to plead for that bastard's life. "I won't try to sway you. Kill Halfer, please, and use a painful method."

McKenzie found a flashlight on a shelf built into the side of the tunnel. He clicked it on, and I watched as he stared back with the greatest of regret. There were more wolves at the gate now but it seemed like it would hold. I was sure McKenzie was looking back at those wolves, recognizing them and wondering if he was going to have to kill them before the day was through. I wondered if it wouldn't have been easier on him to give in to that initial urge to join the pack, to follow the Strong Arm of Remus. McKenzie had fought so hard to remain in control, to maintain his alpha status, but now it was costing him as he was on the other side from everyone he knew and loved.

"I'll do everything I can to keep your wolves safe," I promised him.

He gave me a sad half-smile, not showing any sign that Lee's weight was bothering him. "I believe you, Your Grace. I'm not so sure about your husband though."

He started to guide us down the tunnel, leaving the wailing of the angry wolves behind.

"I won't kill for pleasure, John," Dev explained flatly as though he didn't care what the other man thought. "I will also not allow my wife to be killed."

"My wife is out there too, Quinn," McKenzie snarled, his temper fraying. "She's out there and for the first time she has a real shot at getting what she's always wanted—a baby. We've tried for years and she finally believes it's going to happen. She's a strong bitch. She won't stand at the back of the crowd. She'll be fierce. She'll kill or be killed, and I don't want either of those options for her."

I needed to bring down the testosterone level a bit or my husband and the alpha would be at each other's throats. "None of the wolves want to attack us. They're being used, and we have to remember that. The rounds aren't silver so more than likely they won't kill if we don't use too many or hit vital organs. We just have to hold them off until Zack wakes up Danny."

"Well, I can certainly kill the wolves." Declan held his sword in hand, walking with an arrogant swagger. "I assure you with my weaponry, when I fight them, I can kill them."

"I'm asking you not to, Declan," I said between clenched teeth.

He simply shrugged and kept walking. "I promise you nothing, Zoey. I am a prince of Faery. I will defend that which belongs to Faery. I will agree to allow the wolves to consume the others if that is your wish, but I will kill them if they lay a single paw on anything that belongs to me or mine."

I drew in a frustrated breath and followed McKenzie as we walked through the dimly lit tunnels. It was cold here, deep within the mountains. The chill seemed to come from the tunnel itself. We were down to single file at one point. The faeries had to duck down to get through the shortened ceiling in part of the passage. Every now and then we came to another gate and McKenzie opened it and locked it again, a wall between us and the wolves. We walked for what seemed like hours, but I knew it couldn't have been more than twenty minutes. I wondered if Zack had done his job and Danny was awake or if he was still out there, waiting for his chance.

We came out of the smaller portion of the tunnel into a wide room, and I could hear Dev sigh as he could finally stand up straight again. McKenzie let Lee drop to the ground as he felt around in the darkness. He lit a match and then the room started to fill with the glow of torches.

"This is a way station. There's food and water. We rest here for a minute and then push on." The alpha pointed to a group of metal shelves containing bottled water. He took one for himself and started to pass them around.

I cracked open a bottle and went to where my bodyguard was resting.

Lee was a little better now that we were farther from the artifact. He lay against the floor, but even in the gloom I could see his color was coming back. I sat down beside him and shifted his head into my lap. I twisted the cap off the water and held it to his lips. He drank for a moment and then let his head rest back down. Without thinking really, I stroked his head.

"I said no petting," Lee growled.

I pulled my hand back. "Sorry." But I was happy that he was growling again.

He sighed deep in his chest. "Just this once, Zoey. But it doesn't make me your lapdog."

I grinned down at him and let my hands rub his head and scratch lightly behind his ears. I was glad he let me do it because I knew he felt bad and the contact would help. I stroked his now flea-free scalp and he tried not to show me how nice it felt. I gave him another drink and thought briefly how much nicer he smelled after his time in the tub. If we survived, my bodyguard and I were going to have a long fight about grooming.

Before I could mention it, my brother-in-law was standing over me.

"If you do not mind, I would like a word with my sister-in-law before we move on." Declan held his hand out, and Lee managed to get himself into a sitting position. I took Declan's hand and allowed

341

him to haul me up.

The prince glanced behind him and when he was certain his brother was engrossed in the conversation with Padric, he pulled me to a place where there was no way Dev would hear our conversation.

I didn't like the proprietary way he clutched my arm. I also didn't like the fact that he didn't want his brother to know what he was going to say to me.

"What do you want, Declan?" I practically hissed the question.

"There are many things I want, dear sister, but I have to put those things aside and think of my position," Declan whispered bitterly. "Several things have become clear to me over the last twenty-four hours. The first and foremost being my brother loves you. He will not be swayed away from you."

"Well, he is my husband." I wondered where he was going with this. I held my tongue, waiting for the threats to start.

"Yes, and you aren't going to let him be the priest he should be. At this point, I do not think he would do it even if you let him. I do not know what you did to my brother to ensnare him so much he will not even look at another woman."

"Why is it so bad, Declan?" I didn't understand his point at all. We were in love. That couldn't be a bad thing. "If your brother is happy with me, then what's so wrong with that?"

His eyes took on an angry sheen. "What is wrong with that? He is the only one of our kind with this magic. We are not a fertile people. We need his magic or we will die. We may be immortal, but even immortals need a reason to live. Without children to love and care for, many of our kind have faded. Dev is a mortal. When he dies, that magic dies with him. The best and most reasonable course of action is for Dev and his new friend, Bris, to impregnate as many women as possible in order to pass on their magic. You have made that impossible."

I tried to step back, but his hand gripped my arm like a chain keeping me where he wanted me.

"I thought about killing you myself. I believed he would mourn you for a while, but then go about his business. Then last night happened and I now think he would lay down somewhere and allow himself to fade if you were to die."

"Why are you telling me this, Your Highness?" I kept my voice low because here and now wasn't the place for a brotherly throw down.

Declan raised himself to his full, intimidating height. "I am telling you this because I need you to understand me. Your womb is now the most important thing in my life. Devinshea has been too happy with his brand new marriage to think about the consequences of last night's activities. I am well aware of what happened."

I didn't pretend to misunderstand him. "I'm not pregnant. You don't understand how medicine works on this plane. I take this shot and it chemically stops me from getting pregnant until Dev and Daniel and I all agree to it."

Declan had the nerve to laugh. "I assure you, Your Grace, that even if your womb had been removed, after that magic Bris pumped through your body last night you would merely find you had grown a new one and it would be full. He said it himself. You are very fertile. He knows what he is talking about. I do not doubt that even now his child is starting to grow inside you. I want that child. Faery needs that child."

Lee growled behind Declan. He'd gotten to his feet and even now his eyes were changing to hold his wolf. He was quiet about it, not wanting to attract attention, but he wanted Declan to know he was there and he'd heard everything. I noticed the others were still resting or talking. Only Neil was making his way from Sarah's side, moving toward me.

Declan let my arm go. His voice was perfectly steady now, all brotherly caring. "I am concerned for your safety, sister. You should understand I now count your safety as my highest priority. I would sacrifice anyone to save you. I request that you not make that necessary. I would prefer to not have to make hard choices."

The ramifications of what he was saying washed over me. I should watch myself because if it came down to it, he would take the child in my womb over his brother. I felt sick to my stomach and suddenly Neil was there holding me up. He didn't understand what was going on. He only knew I needed him.

Declan turned to go but I had one more question and I needed to know. "If I am...is it Dev's?"

"No, Zoey," Declan replied remorselessly. "Though I have no doubt he will consider the babe his. The child would look like Dev's, but it would be a magical child. He would be a fertility god. That baby in your belly could save all of Faery. I will kill to protect it."

I heard Neil breathing behind me and knew what Declan said shocked him, but he held his tongue.

Declan looked down on me and sighed. "I like you, Zoey. I am sorry it must come to this. I told you before. I am to be king one day. I must think of my kingdom. The needs of a single person must be pushed aside for the safety of all my people."

"What is going on, brother?" Dev asked, finally noticing our little gathering.

Declan sent his brother a smooth smile. "I was just telling my new sister how things work in Faery. I would not wish for her to go into her new kingdom ignorant. She should be well aware of her duties. All of this is, of course, dependent on our surviving this current experience."

Dev pulled me to him and kissed me. "Her only duties are to be my sweet wife and to drive me and Daniel as crazy as possible." He cradled my face with his hands. "Don't let him scare you, sweetheart. I will take as good care of you in Faery as I do in our world."

I plastered a smile I didn't feel on my face. "I have no doubt."

"It's time to go," McKenzie said. "We have another mile and a half to cover. I hope your wolf has done his job."

Dev nodded as he took my hand firmly in his. "He will do his job as Lee and Neil will do theirs and protect my wife."

"I assure you, I'll protect her. From everyone," Lee said in a low growl, but he was looking at Declan when he said it.

McKenzie's flashlight was joined with several more and now we could move more freely through the tunnels. The opening was larger, and Dev was able to hold my hand as we made our way toward the cave.

"It's going to be all right, Zoey," Dev promised. "I would never let anything happen to you."

I knew he meant that, but I suspected something had already happened to me, and I had no idea how I was going to deal with it.

Chapter Thirty-Two

"Let me kill him, Zoey," Lee growled in my ear as I sat toward the back of the cave we were hiding in. I'd been informed by Padric that I should sit at the back of the cave, far away from the entrance. I had no doubt Padric was protecting my womb from any possible long-range weapon.

"Yes," Neil said in my other ear. He sent a hard look to the front of the cave where Declan was sitting with his brother. "Let Lee kill him."

I shot Neil a look.

"Well, I'm still weak. I don't dare change forms," Neil replied. "I promise to help Lee eat him once he's done with the killing part."

"I'm thinking about killing Dev, too," Lee admitted. "And the vampire."

"You have to stop that." I couldn't have Lee threatening to kill my husbands at every turn.

"Daniel has to know that there's a freaky-ass god in Dev now and that he apparently wants to knock you up," Lee replied.

"It's not like that. You weren't there and yes, Daniel knew. He's trying to make Dev strong for the fight." When I really thought about it, it was a testament to how far Danny had come that he even considered allowing Dev into the fight. As possessive as Danny had become, he should have been plotting to hide Dev away with me. But he'd allowed him to take the risk to ascend. It would kill a part of Dev to not be involved. He'd spent his life being thought of as a lesser being. "And Bris was sweet. Almost like a different side to Dev."

"I don't know about that, and I'm going to watch him like a hawk, but from what the brother said, Dev doesn't even realize what happened yet," Lee shot back. "We should tell him that his brother plans on taking Zoey's baby from her."

"We don't even know there is a baby, yet." We had more urgent problems. "Can we not borrow trouble? We need to get out of this situation before we deal with any possible babies. And we are not telling Dev or Daniel anything. This stays between the three of us until I am certain there is a problem."

"Zoey, I have to tell Daniel." Neil laced his hands together, a nervous habit.

"Why?" The truth was I needed people on my side who didn't feel the need to run to my husbands and gossip. "Are you his wolf or mine? That goes for you too, Lee. Make the decision now."

"You know my answer, Your Highness," Lee replied, breathing deeply as he sat back. He was letting the situation go for now, but I knew we would revisit it in the future.

Neil seemed to struggle. He'd been Daniel's servant for many years. Breaking with him was hard. It was still his instinct to serve Daniel first. "I belong to you now, Zoey. The truth is I always belonged to you. I'll follow Lee's lead. If you want to keep this quiet, I will. But I'm never going to let that bastard take your baby. I don't care if it's Dev's or some asshole god's. It's yours and I won't let him take it."

"That goes double for me," Lee proclaimed. "I'll kill him twice if he tries it."

I let that settle in as I watched Dev on his belly, trying to see down the mountain. He was attempting to get some idea whether or not Daniel was awake. I thought not. It was awfully quiet even this far away. If Daniel was awake then he would be making some noise. I let my head fall against Neil's shoulder. The air in the cave was cool against my skin, and the light had been a shock after spending so much time in the darkness. What was taking Zack so long?

Dev crawled backward, keeping his head down. Padric, Declan, and McKenzie joined him in the back of the cave.

"He has people around him," Dev said. "I count four men, all armed with high-powered rifles."

"Well, we knew he still had followers." I kept my voice down even though we were far from where Halfer could hear. "Where the hell is Zack?"

Dev shook his head. "Zack is following the pack. There's a man stationed outside our tent. Halfer has been talking to him for a while. Zack keeps circling, but he can't get in without Halfer seeing. He's going to keep trying, Zoey. Don't give up hope. So far, they don't know where we are."

"How long is that going to last?" I wondered out loud.

"How many people know about the tunnels?" Dev asked McKenzie.

"Just my wife and my second in command," he replied. "Both of whom are down there waiting for the chance to kill us."

"I think it only works when the victims are in wolf form. Otherwise, why wouldn't he just have them switch forms and tell him where we are?" I had a sudden idea. "Dev, I need to check on Halfer's location."

Dev's eyes closed briefly, and I thought he might reject my request. He took a long breath and his hand slipped into mine. "Stay low and close to me."

"Dev," Declan started. He sent a pointed stare in my direction.

"She's my wife and she's good at things like this," Dev shot back to his brother. "She's an asset. I will not allow her to come to harm, but I'm not going to stow her away in the background when she can help, either."

I gave Declan a "go to hell in a handbasket" smile and crawled low to the ground along the cave floor, following my husband. We reached the edge of the opening, and I could see both the valley below and the field where we'd spent last night. He shook his head in the direction of the valley. "There's Halfer."

My nemesis stood in the middle of the wolves, who twitched and growled around him, waiting for something to kill. He was talking to a young man with a rifle in his hands. Halfer gestured around the valley, obviously telling the man to find us no matter what it took. Everything about him screamed frustration, from the frown on his face to his bunched up, bulky shoulders.

There was no way we were getting out of this cave without someone noticing, and I doubted it would be long before some wolf got our scent. The best werewolves in the country were down there in that pack. They would eventually catch something in the air and it would lead them back to us. We would be caught. We could run back into the tunnels, but we would have to face the wolves at the gate. This was what it meant to be caught between a rock and a hard place. I was just grateful the artifact didn't work on Lee because while the gate might have stopped him, he could have tracked my scent through the ground. If Lee had been tracking me, he would have been waiting when I emerged from the caves.

"See, sweetheart," Dev breathed into my ear as he pointed. "There's Zack."

A brown wolf prowled the edges of the massive pack, circling around. His gaze would stray to the tent every now and then, waiting and watching for his chance to get past the guard. We were damn lucky the guard hadn't gone in there or he might have discovered Daniel's coffin and the small army of pixies we'd ordered to stay behind so the wolves didn't try to eat them.

Halfer suddenly held the paw up. Behind me, Lee groaned. The wolves stopped what they were doing and all focused on their new master. After a moment, I watched as four small groups of wolves took off in various directions, no doubt trying to figure out where we'd gone. Even worse, one of the men was now walking up toward the house, toting his rifle behind him. He was going to search the house and eventually he would find the door we had been forced to leave open. We'd bolted the gate from the inside but I was certain Halfer had come prepared.

"Damn it. I hope he doesn't have any C-4." Dev didn't sound too hopeful because I was sure if he was running this, he would have come prepared. "Screw our contracts, Zoey. From now on I'm bringing in weapons whether our allies like it or not."

This was the second time our playing by the rules had cost us with Halfer.

"Do you see the way he has to hold up the paw when he wants the wolves to do something other than prowl?" I pointed out.

He nodded. "He's been doing it a lot. I think he has to do it to maintain such a large group. And he obviously has to remain in direct contact with it."

"How good is your brother with that bow of his?" I wished I didn't have to rely on that bastard, but we were running out of time.

Dev got still as he followed my line of thought. He shook his head because he knew I was right. "He's the best archer in generations. It's like the weapon is a part of his body. Even so, it's a small target and we're a long way away."

Declan snorted behind us where he had crawled forward to listen in like the sneaky bitch he was. "I could hit that with my eyes closed and the rest of my body engaged in a bit of fornication."

It was time for my brother-in-law to stop talking and do a little walking because the minute they got that gate open, we were going to be surrounded.

"I am going to need a better perch than this, however." Declan craned his neck to look around. "I would have a much better spot if I climb up a bit, but then I would be exposed."

The three of us moved back in the cave so we could speak more freely and the others could hear us.

"If the prince climbs out of the cave, they will shoot him," Padric pointed out because guarding the royal was his chief occupation in life.

"We need a diversion." Dev ran his fingers through his hair. "This is where the grenades would have been helpful, John."

"You really like blowing shit up, don't you, Quinn?" McKenzie asked, rolling his eyes. He looked like a man who'd had to blow up too many things to think it was cool anymore.

He did, I acknowledged silently. Daniel had forced Dev to watch far too many action movies in the last couple of months. After exploring the oeuvre of Michael Bay, Dev had started buying all kinds of exotic explosives. He was now obsessed with big bangs. He sometimes forgot that small diversions could work just as well.

I suddenly had one of those awful ideas in my head. I get really dumb ideas from time to time. They usually end with me dying or getting my ass handed to me.

"So you want the faery to shoot the damn paw out of Halfer's hand?" Lee asked, leaning against the cave wall. "What's to stop Halfer from running back to get it?"

"Uhmm, the wolves who suddenly get their free will back," I explained. "I think they might be pissed off and not at us."

"This is a terrible plan," Padric said, shaking his head.

"It's the only one we have." I really hated this rule-by-committee thing. It was easier when I was running my own damn crew. I just had to deal with Daniel's objections because everyone else knew I was the boss. I hated having to justify everything. It was just about time to act and let the others follow my lead.

"The fact that everyone's attention would suddenly be on Declan could give Zack the shot he needs at taking out the guard and getting to Daniel." Dev stared out the cave, thinking.

"Nice, brother," Declan said but even as he groused, he was snapping those imperious fingers. "So I am to be bait. That is a loving way to describe the man who shared a womb with you." Reality twisted around a tall Fae with long blond hair. He handed Declan his bow and arrow with a deferential bow and gave Padric a long silver sword.

"Are we needed, Your Highness?" The guard asked the question with an academic tone.

Declan waved him off. "Not yet, Geary. The cave is too small for all of us. You may go."

Neil's eyes were wide as the Fae disappeared again. "That was cool."

"Well," Declan said with a small smile. "I suppose we will see now if I am faster than those bullets Zoey is so impressed with."

But I had no intention of letting our only hope of getting out of this alive be a target. If they shot Declan, we had no one else who could do what we needed. If they saw him moving, then the wolves would be all over the cave and we were done.

Declan would need to move into position, set up his shot, and take it. He wouldn't do that in one easy, fluid move no matter how good he was. The truth of the matter was we still needed bait. While I wasn't sure exactly what Halfer's orders were to the wolves, I did know I was his prime target. If we sent someone else out, say a McKenzie, there was no way to know if the wolves would go for him. I thought they would follow him until they got my scent and then chase me down in the cave, taking everyone out in the process. I had no doubt Halfer would let the wolves kill everyone, but he would make damn sure I went first.

When it comes to bait, shouldn't you always go with the choicest morsel when trying to hook a big fish?

Dev sighed beside me and suddenly his hand was in mine. He leaned down and spoke quietly in my ear. "You're the most obnoxious woman I've ever met. You are certain this is the path you want to take?"

My mouth was hanging open, and Dev laughed lightly. "How did you…?"

"I've been through enough of these little adventures to know what you will do, my wife," Dev replied, a sparkle in his eyes. "I also know I can't stop you. Besides, it really is the only thing that makes sense. Those wolves want you, sweetheart. They'll come after you no matter where you are. But this time, I think, I will let them eat you first."

I grinned up at him, the adrenaline already pumping through my system. Declan was at the edge of the cave now. He reached up and pulled himself over the cave ledge. Without a word to the others, Dev and I took off, leaping in the opposite direction, going down. I heard Padric yell behind me and Declan curse righteously from above, but there was nothing he could do now except the job.

Dev and I tumbled down a short hill. My husband pulled me to his chest and shielded me from the worst of the rocks and sticks with his big body. When we stopped, he was on his feet quickly, lifting me up with him.

Just in case the fuckers missed our little trip, Dev held up his gun and blasted two rounds in the air. The sound split the silence, cracking through the valley.

Every wolf in the area turned toward the sound, and Halfer's head snapped around. Even from the distance, I could see the triumphant gleam in his eyes as he raised the paw over his head and the pack shifted as one great predator toward us.

"Shit, that's a lot of wolves," Dev said, shaking his head. "If we get out of this alive, I will be expecting payback for all the terror. I plan to take it out on your soft, sweet body."

"I have no doubt." I took his hand and began to run, but not before I saw that brown wolf taking his shot. As I turned, Zack was leaping onto the guard, his teeth at the man's throat.

I ran as hard as I could, trying to keep up with my husband's long legs. It wouldn't be long before Daniel was awake. We just had to stay alive long enough for Declan to do his job or Danny to wrestle the paw away from Halfer.

"Follow me," Dev yelled as he started to run even faster but not in a straight line.

He zigged and zagged across the field because the wolves were not our only problem. Already one of the humans with Halfer was beginning to take shots at us. He was at a disadvantage. We had rolled down the hill and into the valley so we were on flat ground.

The man with the rifle needed a sniper position and he just didn't have one. Dev was making us a hard-to-hit target by constantly changing our path.

My lungs started to hurt as we ran because I've lived most of my life at sea level and my body was sadly human. Dev wasn't even breathing hard yet, but my chest was burning and I could hear the wolves behind us, thundering through the valley, desperate to finally get their teeth into me.

I made the mistake of looking behind me and they were eating the distance between us like a single ravenous beast. They were going to catch us before Declan or Danny could save us.

Dev scooped me into his arms in a graceful move. He never stopped running, simply held me to him and ran as fast as his long legs would carry him. I looked into his eyes and saw Bris there. He winked at me and Dev's body started to move faster than I had ever seen him. He'd told me he could strengthen Dev. I thought he meant strengthening his magic. Now I understood he made Dev stronger in every way. He was faster, stronger, more capable.

I locked my arms around his neck and turned so I could see behind us. Declan had his bow taut, waiting for that perfect shot. We only needed a moment more. I watched Declan, so focused on his target and then suddenly, we were falling and blood bloomed across Dev's shoulder.

We tumbled, Dev falling first to his knees, trying so hard to keep me safe even as the bullet lodged in his bones. Dev or Bris, I wasn't sure which, seemed unsure of what had happened.

"Goddess?" he asked, and now I was pretty damn sure who it was. "What is this thing?"

"It's a bullet," I told the fertility god who probably had never been shot before. More than likely he'd never seen a gun. From what I understood, he'd been dormant since long before someone decided to use gunpowder as a propellant.

"It hurts," he said. "I do not like it."

It wasn't going to hurt as much as being torn apart by wolves. I tried to scramble up and pull Dev with me. They were close now, too close to run from. They would catch us with no trouble. I could run as fast as possible and get pulled down anyway, or I could spend the last minute I had in his arms.

"I love you," I said, throwing myself around him. I held him close not caring about the blood. I really wanted to get eaten first. I didn't want to watch it happen to him.

"I am sorry, goddess," Bris's voice said sadly. "It doesn't seem fair. I wanted more time with you. I don't want to go back to the darkness."

"Give me Dev," I ordered as the wolves reached us. Like the wolves they were, they circled us, not content to just rip and tear. They liked the terror. "I want my husband."

Bris closed his eyes, acquiescing to my wishes, and when they opened again, Dev was there.

"Help me up, sweetheart," Dev ordered.

I shook my head. "There's nothing we can do now."

He was looking, searching for anything he could use. The wolves were too close to throw up a barrier. We would get caught in it, too, and be torn apart by the vines and thorns. There were no trees within reach for Dev to command. His arm hung useless at his side anyway. Dev always used his hands when he called forth his magic. We were caught, and there was no way out.

I thought about Dev and Danny and the baby that might or might not be in my body. Could we have made it work? Could we have had that odd little family?

It didn't matter now because the biggest wolf in the pack had broken from the circle. He charged forward, a locomotive of power and muscle and killing rage. I was in front of my husband, my back to his chest, and he wrapped his arms around me, an instinctive move, nothing that would stop the wolf. Dev shrank back from the teeth and claws, trying to take me with him.

I felt hot breath on my face and knew this was my last moment. I felt Dev's warmth at my back and was glad that would be one of the last sensations I would feel. The wolf growled his triumph and opened his mouth to tear out my throat.

And stopped.

The enormous black wolf sat back on his haunches and surveyed the space around him as though trying to figure out just where he was and why he was about to eat these two people. He was calm now, and the confusion was obvious in his dark eyes. All around us the wolves were coming out of the artifact's control. They stumbled and shook their mighty heads as though trying to clear the magic from their systems.

My eyes flew to the cave, and I watched as Declan swung down from his perch, a look of enormous superiority on his face. I watched as he called his guard, and ten Fae appeared at the cave's entrance. Almost as one unit they turned to where Dev and I sat among the confused wolves. Declan pointed and I had no doubt it was me he wanted brought to him. If I let that guard take me, I would be held far from this fight and perhaps taken to Faery against my will. They were surely being ordered to stop me from doing something stupid.

The trouble was I still had stupid things to do, and I wasn't about to let some royal guards stop me. I still had a job to do. I stood up and helped Dev. "We have to get that paw before Halfer takes it again."

He nodded and despite what had to be the agonizing pain in his shoulder, he took my hand and started to run toward the camp where Halfer and that artifact lay.

Even as we ran, I could hear the gunfire and the screams of men.

I smiled fiercely because I knew beyond a shadow of a doubt my Danny was awake.

Chapter Thirty-Three

I looked at Dev who was struggling now, his body so strong but he'd lost blood and the bullet was still lodged in his shoulder. Even as I watched, his body was trying to heal itself. Dev took Daniel's blood, too, and the vampire blood didn't think about the fact that no one had taken the bullet out. It simply healed. I wanted to wait, but that guard was making its way across the field and they weren't heading into the important fight. They made a beeline for me.

"Dev," I said, breathless as I ran back to help him.

"Go," he said. "Get that paw. Daniel will keep Halfer busy. Take my gun." He pressed the SIG Sauer into my hand. "It's better than anything McKenzie had. Zoey, kill those followers of his. They would kill you. The guard is coming. They will aid me. Go."

I didn't think that was going to go the way Dev expected. He seemed to think they were coming to help us, and I knew for a fact that they weren't. I kissed him with all my might and ran toward the gunfire.

I heard the shouting coming from across the field. Declan was screaming as I ran into the line of fire. The guard quickly changed course and they were moving to intercept me. Forcing my legs to pump as fast as I could, I broke for the valley. Even at a distance, I could hear Zack growl and then a mighty roar nearly shook the ground beneath me.

Daniel's beast could be really loud. Daniel was calling to me. There was a burst of gunfire, but I wasn't going to make it. The guard was so fast. I glanced to my right and they were rushing across the field to cut me off from the fight.

It was me versus ten big strong warriors of the *sidhe*. They had trained all of their lives to guard, protect, and hunt. I was a thief who almost never made it to the gym. What made me think I could win against that army? It was arrogant to even try, but I kept running.

Daniel needed me. It was Danny against Halfer and three men with high-powered rifles. Normally that wasn't even the beginnings of a fair fight, but it was full daylight and no matter how much he fed on Dev's powerful magic, daylight cut his strength way back. If Halfer or one of his men got that paw back in their grubby little hands, the balance would shift firmly into their corner. Right now, the wolves seemed to not know what to do. I wanted to keep it that way, but it looked like the royal guard was going to fuck up my plans.

The one Declan had called Geary broke from the rest, and it seemed like he was going to win the fastest asshole guard competition. His hands stretched out toward me, ready to pull me down to the ground. I had no doubt I was about to be taken into custody, hauled back to Declan and held against my will. If I was lucky, he might let me watch as Daniel was taken apart by the wolves. Perhaps he would try to save his brother, but I couldn't be sure of that. The baby that might be in my belly was the only thing he cared about. Angry tears flooded my eyes as I tried to evade Geary's arms. Just an inch more and he would have me. Just another step and I wouldn't be able to help Danny. I wouldn't be able to save Dev.

Alone. I was so alone as he reached for me to pull me down and take me out.

Just as his hand was about to touch my arm, Geary hit an invisible wall and flew back. I did a double take, looked to the caves, and I knew I wasn't alone anymore.

Sarah stood behind Declan, who screamed at his guard. He and Padric watched in confusion, and Felix stood beside them doing his best to keep their eyes on the field. Declan yelled, but he didn't turn around because he had no idea Sarah was a witch. It would never occur to him that the cute, funny girl with the electric blue bob and ready smile could render his guards completely useless. Neil stood behind her and I saw him put a hand on her shoulder, lending her his strength.

I smiled up at my friends as I gave Geary my happy middle finger and went about my business because my crew had my back.

I ran hard, getting a second wind from the adrenaline of winning that particular battle. I broke through the tree line that separated me from the campsite, and the first thing I saw was Daniel. He was standing among the tents and campsites, his body already covered in blood and unfortunately I was pretty sure a lot of it was his. He was dressed in nothing but a pair of jeans, his boots, and a jacket he seemed to have slung on in lieu of a shirt. The jacket gaped open and blood covered his chest.

He'd taken several bullets, but two of Halfer's men were down. They wouldn't be getting back up again. Zack was at his master's side. He didn't have trouble with the daylight. He was at full power and on vampire blood.

I stopped at the edge of the valley before it ran into the field where Dev and I had been married. I flipped the safety off my gun and peered from behind a tree. Halfer shot Daniel again and he fell backward. I had to stifle a scream and force myself not to run for him. I had no doubt those were silver rounds. Halfer would use nothing less, but running in a panic wouldn't help Danny.

Zack attacked, going for Halfer's legs. Halfer screamed and used the butt of his rifle to hit the wolf squarely in the head. Now was the time to act. I took careful aim and squeezed the trigger, hitting Halfer in the back before he could shoot Daniel again.

It wasn't enough. Halfer's body tensed, but he didn't go down. Halfer turned, looking for me. He yelled something at the last of his men and the henchman started searching the ground. I had no doubt we were looking for the same thing.

Halfer fired in my direction and I quickly shielded my back with a tree. I was about to try to move when the air was filled with pixies. They landed on me and I could tell from their fluttering wings that they were concerned. I remembered what Dev had told me about these tiny members of Faery. They were small but tough. They didn't back off from a fight.

But what the hell could my army of butterflies do against an ex-demon and a bunch of AR-15s?

Though I didn't actually need them to fight.

I held out my hand, hoping whoever was their leader would understand. A sapphire and amethyst pixie quickly landed in my palm. He, I thought of him as a he but I could be wrong, bowed and seemed to wait for me to speak.

"Do you know what a paw is?" I asked, cutting directly to the chase because I had no idea how much time I had. Declan could discover Sarah was working against him any minute. Halfer could come looking for me or his henchman could find the artifact.

The little pixie nodded his head vigorously.

"I need you to find a gray paw for me. It was being held by that man with the dark hair. The prince shot it out of his hand from the cave. It probably has an arrow in it." I gave them all the information I had. "Please find it. It's so important. I would be in your debt."

The pixie bowed again and then the whole group took off. I watched as they spread out but no one paid any attention to them. I looked from behind my safe little perch and what I saw made my heart stop.

Daniel was on the ground, blood pouring from his chest, and Halfer aimed at him ready to pump more silver into his body. Zack had been hit, too, but he stood over his master's body, faithful to the end. If we got out of this, I was going to be nicer to Zack. I was going to carry around some treats in my pocket for when he did well.

I took a deep breath and did the only thing I could do. I did something crazy.

I walked from behind my nice, safe tree and strode toward the big-ass, high-powered demon with the rifle. I held the SIG with both hands and fired straight into that asshole's body. I didn't let up. I didn't waver. I kept on course, ignoring everything else. When I felt my left arm burn as a bullet passed through it, I simply switched to a one-handed hold. It was harder, but nothing was harder than giving up Daniel for dead.

I hit Halfer over and over because I might not be a fixture at the gym, but I did go to the shooting range.

Lucas Halfer's body bucked with the force of the bullets hitting him. His head turned my way and I saw the hate there. He forgot about the vampire on the ground and focused every ounce of his fading will on me. He raised the rifle and even as his chest became a mottled mess, he pointed that gun straight at me.

Unfortunately, he also forgot about Zack, who took the opportunity to leap onto his back and throw off his aim. Halfer's bullet went astray. Daniel got to his feet, struggling and fighting for every step.

I had enough time now to turn and catch the jerk who had shot me. He was taking aim again, but obviously he hadn't had as much practice as I had. His eyes were a little wild and it looked like this was his first rodeo. It wasn't mine. He was panicking, and calm in these situations always wins the day. I didn't hesitate. I aimed at his head and pulled the trigger. Before I could see the neat hole in his forehead start to bleed, I was back to my main target.

Halfer hit Zack again and gained his feet. He looked down, shot Zack, and swung around to fire at me. I squeezed again, completely unwilling to give up my position just because the bastard was about to kill me, not when I was so close to getting him on the ground where Zack could finish him off. Even as we exchanged fire, that wolf was getting off the grass, preparing to take another hunk out of Halfer.

I fired again and Halfer moved, throwing off my aim. He went down on one knee and aimed for my chest. Just as he was about to fire, I tripped and the blasted bullet missed, grazing my shoulder when it should have hit my heart.

I glanced down and saw the vine that had tripped me up. It waved at me, and I turned to see Dev, bloody and battered but using his good hand to call all things green to our aid. He was limping but he'd made it to us.

"Stay down," he shouted as he lifted his hand and the earth began to rumble.

I rolled out of his line of fire as the grass grew around Halfer's feet and caught him in an embrace. He struggled against the tight binding, but it was useless.

Daniel staggered up behind him. He shared a look with Dev across the field. Dev nodded and then Daniel's hand became a wicked claw. He held Halfer's head up by the hair and the former demon's howl drew the eyes of everyone. Even Sarah's concentration slipped and the Fae started to run across the field again.

Halfer screamed his rage. Even as Daniel drew his hand back to deliver the final blow, Lucas Halfer, Brixalnax, the ancient lord of Hell, sought my eyes. I met them and I knew in that moment that if he could reach past death, if he could open that doorway, he would come for me.

He would never stop.

Daniel drew his claws across Lucas Halfer's throat and it split. At first it was a simple, neat line, but then it gushed with life. His long life, his blood, his soul, spilled across the field.

The green bindings that held him vanished back into the ground and my greatest enemy fell, never to rise again.

I forced myself to my feet. The guards were almost on me, and Declan followed close behind. I moved toward Daniel, who was stumbling, making his way to me.

I met him in the middle and took his shaking body into my arms. I knew what he needed and pulled his head toward my neck. His eyes were filled will love and gratitude as his fangs sought my vein. This was one of those times when I usually dealt with his beast, but that beast was quiet now because Daniel knew I would help. Daniel knew we could handle this.

We sank to the ground and I held his head in place as he fed.

Suddenly Dev was at my back. As I fed Daniel, he rested his head against my shoulder on the opposite side from Danny. The three of us were together and connected again. I let my hand pull Daniel close as the other drifted behind me to cup Dev's face. Daniel's hand reached around me to rest on Dev's good arm, letting him know how happy he was we were all alive. I breathed in the sweetness of the moment.

"Let her go, vampire," the one called Geary commanded, breaking up my happy moment. The asshole.

"Stand down." Dev shifted away from us, looking to the guard, his voice firm even as his body showed his weariness.

"Those are not my orders, Your Grace." Geary was backed up by the rest of the guard. They surrounded us and all brandished weapons covered in silver. The last thing Danny needed was a silver arrow. "I am to take your wife into custody. I am to deliver her to the prince. I will say it again. Let her go, vampire." He notched his arrow and aimed it at Daniel's back. "Let her go or we will kill you."

"Daniel," Dev said cautiously. "I believe they are serious. Please let Zoey go. If you need more blood, I will be more than happy to provide it."

Daniel took one last drag from my neck and released the vein. He didn't release me. He struggled to his feet, though his strength was coming back now. He helped me up and pushed me behind him, keeping me between him and Dev. We were surrounded by the guards, each brandishing a weapon that could take my vampire's life in his weakened condition.

"Dev, why is your brother's guard trying to take our wife from us?" His question was hard and made no attempt to hide the fact that he would fight. Broken, bruised, and bloody, he wouldn't let them take me.

"I do not know," Dev admitted. He was somewhere between shocked and enraged. "But I will find out."

Declan finally made it across the field with Padric hard behind him. "Stand down!"

I let out a sigh of relief as they lowered their weapons.

I waited to see just which way the prince was going to play this. He finally relaxed. "It is obvious the threat has passed. You may go."

Like the well-trained boys they were, the guard disappeared one by one to wait for the prince to call upon them again.

Declan looked at his brother. His green eyes were deceptively innocent as he regarded us. "I was merely protecting your goddess, brother. That is what you requested. Was I wrong?"

He was manipulating events, but I wasn't about to point that out now. We needed to tend to our wounded and find that paw.

Dev gave his brother a tired smile. "Of course I wanted her safe. You were only doing what you thought best. You do not know her as I do. She's capable. And she needs no rescue from Daniel."

"The guard did not understand your ménage," Declan lied smoothly. "They only knew a vampire was biting your goddess. I will, of course, bring them up to date."

"Zoey," Neil said as he and Felix helped Lee across the field.

Zack changed and immediately went to his brother's aid. Despite the fact that Zack had been hit several times, his human body was back to perfect.

Neil pointed behind me. "Look."

I turned and saw a cluster of brightly colored wings fluttering over the ground. They flew around and I could see they were trying their best to lift something out of the earth. Smart little pixies. They had achieved the goal I set.

"Neil," I yelled as I took off toward them. "Come with me."

Neil was at my back by the time I made it to the pixies. There in the ground a hundred yards from where Lucas Halfer had stood and wielded it against us, lay the Strong Arm of Remus, bisected by Declan's silver arrow. It had buried itself in the ground but came out easily when I pulled it.

"Thank you," I said to the pixies. "You did a wonderful job. I couldn't have asked for more." I held the paw in my hand, the arrow springing from either side, and I could feel the magic pulsing through it. Even now, it sought a master. It wanted someone to wield it.

I turned around and found an army of wolves staring at me. They had come from the field and now sat silently, waiting for my orders. It was a massive army of teeth and claws. This pack could ravage the world and all it needed was a single command. The artifact in my hand whispered seductively.

They are yours. All those wolves are yours to command.

"Zoey," Dev said quietly as he walked forward. His emerald eyes were on the paw, and I realized it was talking to him, too. It spoke directly to the ambition in my husband. It told him all his plans could come to fruition if I gave up that one little paw. "That's important. It could turn the tide of this war. Give it to Daniel, please. It belongs to Daniel."

I looked to Danny, who stood under the shade of a tree and was already looking battle-ready again. He glanced down at the corpse of his former enemy, and his face was lit with triumph. He strangely didn't look at the artifact in my hands, but rather directly at me. His voice was oddly casual for so important a moment. "It would be helpful, Z. No one would threaten us ever again if we had this army at our backs."

"That belongs to me," McKenzie yelled as he crossed quickly toward where I stood. Everything that was alpha in him wanted that paw. I lifted the gun with one hand and he stopped. "I am the alpha. It should go to me. They're my wolves, and I'll decide their fate."

Padric and Declan restrained the alpha. Declan had a silver knife at his throat. He struggled, but the threat kept him from breaking free.

"Danny," I started because I needed a little guidance and Daniel seemed like the only one not under the artifact's sway. It was playing to my wants and needs, too. Now it was trying a different tactic with me. It whispered that I could keep the wolves safe. If I kept the paw, I could take care of them all. I needed someone to pull me out. "Would you use it?"

His blue eyes caught mine and he smiled. "You know I would, Z. I would use it and I can't promise you I would always use it for good. I'll take it if you give it to me. If you don't then we'll find another way. This is your call, baby. Follow your heart. Do what Dev and I can't do."

Dev's face fell but he walked over to join Daniel. "It's all right, Zoey. Do what you think is best."

This little object in my hand could save us so much trouble down the line. We needed the wolves and here they were, in my grasp and ripe for the taking. If I gave it to Danny, no wolf would ever deny he was their king. Daniel's crown would be set and taking the Council down would be a silly little afterthought.

And all these wolves would be mindless slaves. I looked across the crowd and saw Lee watching me silently. He was sick standing so close to it but his eyes implored me. *Do the right thing.*

What did power or even safety mean if we lost sight of everything we fought for?

The voice still whispered to me, but I consigned it to the background, unwilling to listen any longer. I found a small fire that was still burning in front of one of the tents. Neil and I walked over to it and he picked up a can of lighter fluid. He grinned at me as I tossed that ancient artifact on the fire. He poured the propellant on it and I swear the thing howled as it was consumed.

The wolves came completely out of their daze now. Some changed and walked around, finding loved ones. Some ran, trying to make sense of what had happened to them. A small group circled Halfer's corpse. The largest of the wolves grabbed the corpse's leg and pulled it into the woods. I could hear the wolves howl as they took apart the man who had made them slaves.

I ran to my husbands. I threw myself into Danny's arms and they closed around me.

"You did the right thing, Z," he whispered.

"Right is not always expedient," Dev pointed out but kissed me anyway. He frowned at Daniel. "You're going to have to dig this bullet out of my arm. The skin has healed around it and my poor faery body doesn't spit out foreign objects the way yours does."

Daniel laughed and there was a little revenge in his eyes. "Well, now, I seem to remember an incident with some arrows a couple of weeks back. What did you say? Oh, yes, you told me to stop my whining as you carved them from my body. I would be delighted to help you with your current problem."

"I will do more than whine," Dev promised. He would. He hated pain. He would whine and pout and beg me to distract him. He would probably have some creative ways for me to take his mind off the agony. I remembered something from earlier and turned to Daniel about my snoring. It had gotten lost in all the blood and fighting, but it was something we needed to clear up.

"Water buffalo?" I asked, every bit of offended femininity in my accusation.

Daniel glared at Dev. "You bastard. You told."

Dev shrugged. "That's for ruining my wedding."

John McKenzie made his way toward us and I braced myself, waiting for his vitriol. He'd wanted that power, too. He stared at me for a moment as he held a woman in his arms. His mate, I guessed. She was shivering and wearing only her husband's shirt.

"You destroyed it," he said, disbelief in his voice.

"Yes." Had he believed I would keep it?

McKenzie's brown eyes searched mine. "Why? You would have had everything you wanted. These wolves would have done your bidding without question, without a fight. Why would you throw it all away?"

"I don't want to win that way. We can't win that way," I explained as I amended my statement, bringing my husbands in. "It wouldn't be a win at all, John. It would just be exchanging one bad guy for another. We're not the Council. Daniel won't grind you under his boot. When he says he wants a fair system, he means it. No one should have that much power. Not you, not Daniel, and certainly not me."

Lee pushed past McKenzie, his focus on one thing. He moved to me and when I thought he was going to hug me or something, he fell to his knees. I leaned down, worried he was still sick, but his eyes were on Daniel now.

"I told you when I found someone I believed in, I would make my oath," Lee stated, his voice strong. His face was passionate and I knew he was filled with emotion and ready to pledge himself to the cause. I was going to miss having him to myself. "I'm ready now."

I looked at Daniel, prepared for him to start the small ritual that would make Lee his servant. He stared back.

"He isn't talking about me, Z." Danny stepped forward and popped out his claws. He held my arm in his hand gently. "It'll only hurt for a second."

I shook my head, not quite understanding. "My blood doesn't do anything. It doesn't mean anything."

"It does to him," Daniel said quietly.

"I will follow you, Your Highness. I will be your faithful guard," Lee promised. "Your fight is my fight. Your fate is my fate. And your blood is my bond."

I nodded, not quite able to stop my eyes from welling with tears. Daniel drew his claw across my arm, drawing a thin line of blood. Lee took my arm in his hands and lowered his head to take the blood that was only a formality. It wouldn't hold him to me. His own strong heart and loyalty would do that. Just before his mouth fastened on the small cut, his eyes stared up at me and my Lee was back.

"This doesn't mean you can pet me," he growled and took the blood that made him my wolf.

I laughed and promised to keep my hands off of him.

"You have your army, Donovan." McKenzie held his hand out to shake Daniel's and make the deal. "When you're ready, we'll fight. When you take your crown, we'll be at the table to help you form this new government of yours."

Lee moved to my side, and Daniel shook the alpha's hand. I saw something in him release as those wolves started to look at him with respect.

"Can we go home now?" Neil asked with a tired smile.

I reached out and grabbed his hand. "Yes. It's time to go home."

Chapter Thirty-Four

"**S**he looks perfect, Declan." Dev slapped his brother's hands away from my dress.

"Well, she had better," Declan replied, looking uncertain. "Everyone is waiting to see her. All of Faery is waiting for your return."

We stood in front of what my Fae husband assured me was the opening to his *sithein*. We were in Hill Country, deep in the rolling barrens of Texas. It wasn't the place one would expect to find an entrance to a magical plane.

I felt odd and vulnerable in the traditional dress Declan insisted I wear. It was rich and sumptuous. It made my skin glow and offered up my breasts in a way that made Dev's breath hitch when he stared at them. All of that would be fine if we were in our home playing some sexy game. But we were going to Declan's kingdom, and I felt like I was walking into a gilded prison.

The two weeks we'd spent at home after leaving Colorado had been hectic and filled with excitement for everyone else. Even Daniel had been upbeat about this trip to Faery. It was the last little piece to his puzzle, and he was looking forward to tackling it.

After taking a thorough inventory of my shoes and discovering Tamara hadn't gotten away with a single pair, I'd spent the time reading over the material Marini had given me. There wasn't much to it. He wanted me to steal a jewel. The blood stone. He reminded me in a phone call that he could kill Daniel with the flip of a switch. We still had to solve that little problem. We could have the wolves and all of Faery behind us, but if Marini killed Daniel it didn't mean a damn thing.

And then there was my small trouble.

I told myself it was too early to know if I was pregnant. I told myself I should just wait and nature would take its course. I couldn't be having a child. I used birth control and then it was only the once when we hadn't used backup. Surely that one slip wasn't enough. I told myself any story to stem the tide of panic. The one thing I didn't do was tell my husbands of my fear. I was hoping I never had to do that.

"Are you ready, my beautiful goddess?" Dev was so happy to be going home that I pushed all of my fears and worries down deep where he wouldn't know them.

I simply smiled and said yes.

I glanced back at the long train of friends and servants behind us. This was a parade in honor of the newly ascended fertility god. All of Faery would welcome us. Devinshea and Declan would lead me in and behind us was Padric. Neil, Lee, and Zack came next, carrying that coffin between them where Daniel lay. I had kissed him as Dev closed the lid and promised to see him soon. Sarah and Felix walked behind the casket, leading the train of luggage we were bringing.

Dev took my hand and squeezed it encouragingly as the door to the *sithein* shimmered and faded. There, in the hill, was another world. I could see mountains in the distance and a palace of shimmering white. My mother-in-law waited there to greet us. It was stunning and the people lined the streets leading to the great city. A shout went up as the door opened.

Declan took my other hand and held it firmly. "It's tradition," he explained with a smile as I was caught. "I want everyone to know how much I care for my new sister. I want everyone to know how important she is."

We moved forward and the twins helped me walk gracefully down the road as our train began moving into Faery. Dev's face was alight with excitement as his people greeted him. Declan smiled as he nodded my way. I could practically feel his satisfaction.

I was in his world now.

I glanced back and saw the door that separated the worlds shimmer and close and wondered if I would ever see my home again.

Zoey, Daniel, and Dev will return in *Steal the Sun*, coming March 2014!

Author's Note

I'm often asked by generous readers how they can help get the word out about a book they enjoyed. There are so many ways to help an author you like. Leave a review. If your e-reader allows you to lend a book to a friend, please share it. Go to Goodreads and connect with others. Recommend the books you love because stories are meant to be shared. Thank you so much for reading this book and for supporting all the authors you love!

Steal the Sun
Thieves, Book 4
By Lexi Blake
Coming March 2014!

Zoey thought she would never have to choose, but to save one husband, she will have to betray the other...

As Zoey Donovan-Quinn first sets foot in the faery homeland of her beloved Devinshea, life is perfect. Her enemy is defeated, her heart is full, and Neil and Sarah are at her side. Daniel and Dev are happy, so their visit to the *sithein* should be a pleasant honeymoon full of wonder and joy. Well, except for the part where Zoey needs to steal an ancient gem from the Queen of Faery in order to prevent Louis Marini from killing Daniel.

Reunited with her whole crew, stealing the magical artifact should be relatively easy, but unknown to Zoey, Dev, and Daniel, there are dark forces gathering against them. As her search for the Blood Stone gets underway, Zoey makes a startling discovery that will change her life, and Dev and Daniel's forever.

When her new enemy finally strikes at Zoey from the shadows, her newfound happiness is shattered, and to avenge the horrific attack, Dev prepares his mother's kingdom for war. Recovering from the attempt on her life, Zoey and Daniel desperately search for the stone and in the process unmask the real monster behind the assault.

Stopping the real threat, and saving Daniel, will force Zoey to choose sides in an epic war between the Seelie and Unseelie Fae, even if it means betraying Dev and his people.

* * * *

Dev nodded that we were ready to be announced and then we walked down a magnificent marble staircase. Twenty steps lead us into a huge ballroom that had been set for the royal banquet.

I held on firmly to both their arms because the last thing I needed was to tumble down the stairs and break a limb. I looked out over the crowd and realized Dev had been right. Everyone was hoping for a big scene. They were whispering behind their hands and gawking. They moved their attention between the three of us and the woman at the end of the hall.

I glanced up and got my first glimpse of my mother-in-law.

Miria, Queen of Faery, sat upon her throne before me. There was a raised platform with three chairs. Miria sat on the largest of the three in between two slightly smaller thrones. All three were carved from oak and elaborate in their design. Declan sat in one to her right, a look of aloof superiority on his face. I suspected the seat to her left was the one Dev used. There were several people standing around the queen and I suspected they were counselors and high nobles. Padric stood closest to the queen. It was fitting as he was both the head of security for the royal family and the queen's lover.

Miria, Queen of Faery, was gloriously lovely. I was surprised to find she had long strawberry-blonde hair. I guessed the twins got their dark good looks from their father. Miria was very fair but by no means bland. Her face was delicately sculpted with high cheek bones and a lush mouth. Her eyes marked her as the twins' relative. They were emerald green and sparkled with the same intelligence Dev had.

"Dude," Daniel said as we approached the throne. "That's your mom?"

I knew what he was thinking. She didn't look old enough to be his mom, but that was the way it was with the Fae. They reached their prime and just stopped aging. Miria looked to be about twenty-five. Dev was twenty-seven now and would look older than his mother or brother had he not been taking Daniel's blood regularly. Daniel's blood stopped the aging process in humans when taken on a regular basis. I'd begun noticing that for Dev, it seemed to actually reverse aging a little. The fine lines around his eyes he got when he laughed had disappeared.

Miria tried to maintain her cool composure but the closer we got the more her eyes ate up the sight of her son. I saw her eyes get glossy with unshed tears, and she reached out to Declan. He patted his mother's hand and for a moment looked less like a brat prince.

"Good evening, mother," Dev said formally as we reached the throne. He bowed deeply.

I could see her son's formal tone was not what the queen had been hoping for. "Devinshea, it is good to see you."

Dev didn't give her anything. He nodded but chose to introduce us rather than reply. "Mother, this is my goddess, Zoey. And this is my partner, Daniel Donovan. I assume Declan brought you up to speed on my living arrangements."

That last was said coolly and with just a hint of challenge. He was just begging for his mother to say something disparaging about his lifestyle.

Miria was having none of that. She smiled broadly and stood, causing Declan to quickly get his butt up as well. She wore a lovely white gown and a crown that sparkled in the candlelight. "Yes, of course. Declan and Padric both spoke very highly of your wife and partner."

Declan snorted at that. He didn't like Danny. It probably had something to do with the fact that Daniel had kicked his ass the first time they met. "I certainly did not. I spoke very poorly of him."

Miria ignored her elder son. She stepped off the platform and walked to us. She stood before me. "It is so good to meet you, daughter," she said with what seemed like complete sincerity. She kissed my cheek and gave me a long look. She laughed brightly. "Well, Devinshea, you certainly brought a beauty home. You are lovely, dear."

"She is beautiful but not very obedient," Declan noted. "That is not the dress I told her to wear."

"Hush," she admonished. "The dress is stunning and suits her far more than anything in our style. Our styles would swallow her beautiful body. Declan, you were right about her breasts. They are delicious looking."

The last bit was said with a slight breathless appreciation. I felt Danny tense beside me as he tried really hard not to laugh at my sudden discomfort. My mother-in-law was looking me over with a sensual smile.

"I told you," Declan said with a lecherous grin.

Dev leaned over and whispered in my ear. "Mother swings both ways. Sorry I didn't mention that before."

I gave him a "what the hell" look but Miria was moving on to Daniel.

"I should be upset with your presence, Mr. Donovan," Miria said, looking him over. "Devinshea was supposed to keep you under

371

control until I decided if you were dangerous or not."

Dev started to argue but Daniel stepped up to the plate.

"I assure you, Your Highness, I am perfectly harmless," he said with more charm than I'd heard him use on any woman but me. Dev was rubbing off on my vampire. Daniel was imitating his smooth tones.

Miria looked Daniel up and down, from his Ferragamo loafers to his perfectly cropped blond hair. "I doubt that, Mr. Donovan. I think you could do some serious damage."

I saw Padric roll his eyes and mutter, "Not again."

"How about I promise to be a very good boy?" Daniel offered, his voice a dark seduction. I stopped myself from giggling because Danny was getting good at this.

"Please don't," Miria said, her lips curling up. "Where would be the fun in that?"

"Mother!" Dev said sounding completely prudish for the first time in my relationship with him.

Declan snickered beside his brother.

Miria turned her attention back to her son. "Well, Devinshea, when you bring such lovely bodies home, what do you expect? They are very exotic and look like they would be excellent bedmates. It would be rude not to admire them."

Yes, she was definitely Declan's mom.

"The Earth plane has changed my brother," Declan complained. "It has turned him into a squeamish old woman. He refuses to even think about sharing Zoey with me. He pulled a gun on me just for cuddling with her."

"I would have done worse," Daniel growled. He looked at Declan and his fangs were long suddenly. "And I don't need a gun."

The rest of the room was startled and seemed to take a big step back, but Miria stood her ground. She went toe to toe with Daniel. She was definitely interested in those fangs.

She spoke to her son but her eyes were on Daniel. "Declan, you should know vampires are possessive creatures. It is impressive that Devinshea was able to forge a ménage with such a powerful creature and his companion. It makes a statement about his prowess. I am very proud of you, son. You have done well. Tell me, Mr. Donovan, do you bite my son?"

372

"As often as possible," Daniel replied with no hint of self-consciousness. "I find faery blood to be quite the treat."

"Yes," she returned with regret. "Unfortunately, it is why I was forced to close the mounds to your kind. Your kind likes our blood, and we tend to like your bite, Mr. Donovan. I found it to be a combustible mix."

"Please call me Daniel," my vampire offered smoothly.

"I will," Miria promised. "And you and your companion may refer to me as Miria or mother if you like. I am your mother-in-law. Formally, of course, for Zoey, but I completely recognize your relationship and approve. I am pleased to welcome you. You will be treated as a member of this family, Daniel."

"Good," Dev said between clenched teeth. "Then you can stop hitting on him. And for the record, while I feed my partner, we are not lovers beyond the fact that we share Zoey."

Miria looked startled. "Why ever not, son? He is very attractive. I did not raise you to be so close minded. You should really…what is that human term you told me about, Declan?"

"Hit that," Declan supplied helpfully.

"Yes, Devinshea, you should hit that," Miria said seriously.

Daniel finally lost it and there were tears in his eyes as he laughed. He looked at Dev. "Shit, man, we should have come here earlier. This is awesome."

Dev leaned in. "My goddess, what are the chances of the floor opening up and swallowing me whole, sending me to a blissful oblivion?"

"Not so good. Sorry." Miria made me feel better about my dad.

"I think we should begin dinner now," Padric said sourly, looking at Daniel with a shake of his head. He took Miria's arm and began to lead her to the head table. Already servants were rushing to action.

Danny just couldn't help it. "Dev, your mom's a total cougar, man."

I grinned as Dev blushed for the first time in…ever. "My mother is five hundred thirty-two years old. Cougar does not apply."

"Sabertooth, then." Daniel just had to rub it in.

Yes, it was time for dinner since we'd already put on a show.

373

Unconditional: A Masters and Mercenaries Novella
Masters and Mercenaries, Book 5.5
By Lexi Blake
Coming January 28, 2014

A curious woman

Ashley Paxon understands responsibility. After her fiancé left her alone and pregnant, she forged a new life for herself and her daughter. Moving to Dallas, she went back to school and found a job at a club called Sanctum. As one of the BDSM club's waitresses, she watches the Doms and their submissives every night. She yearns to explore their lifestyle of discipline and power exchange, but she knows she wouldn't belong.

A wounded man

Keith Langston believes in living in the moment. Haunted by the past, he moves from one casual relationship to the next and never looks back. But the moment he lays eyes on Ashley, something primal and possessive takes over. He can't stop thinking about her and yet he knows he can't offer her what she needs. Having her seems impossible until Sanctum's owner, the mysterious Ian Taggart, makes him an offer he can't refuse.

The perfect contract

Offered the chance to train Ashley and initiate her into the D/s lifestyle, Keith is delighted to accept. Under the guidelines of a carefully crafted contract, they lose themselves in the pleasures and intimacies of being Master and submissive. But when Ashley and her daughter are threatened, Keith realizes she needs much more than a part-time Dom. To protect her, he will have to break through the barriers of their contract and finally face the demons haunting his heart.

* * * *

"Hey, calm down. Are you afraid?" His hands changed to soothing strokes down her legs.

Afraid? Yes and no. "I'm worried you won't like me when you

realize I'm not one of those girls who can…"

"Come?"

It seemed so easy for him to say it. "Yes. I read somewhere that not every woman can."

His hands were dangerously close to the junction of her thighs. "Turn over again. I need to see something."

Why did they have to talk about this? She'd been so happy. He was insistent, his hands moving her. She finally rolled over. He'd been kind to her. Maybe it was for the best they get this out of the way. She'd been looking forward to the next couple of weeks of their contract, but if he was thinking she was going to be some kind of sex kitten, then he should find out the truth about her sooner rather than later.

Her skirt was around her waist. A moment ago she hadn't minded. Hell, she hadn't even thought about it when he was spanking her. When she'd realized that twenty or so people had watched the whole thing, she'd merely wondered if a curtsy would get her spanked again.

Now the tone changed, and she could feel all of her insecurities creeping back.

He was looking at her pussy. He was just staring at it. God, she'd never really looked at it. She wasn't the kind of girl who looked at herself in the mirror for long periods of time, much less one who inspected her own pussy. And he could see her C-section scar, though he seemed to be avoiding that.

"You look like you have all the right parts."

Sure she did. They just didn't work properly. "Keith, it's all right. You don't have to try to prove anything to me."

His face suddenly loomed over hers. "If you don't stop talking, I'm going to put a ball gag in your mouth."

She almost protested and then thought better of it. He'd made good on all of his promises up until now. She was pretty sure if there was ever a place to randomly find a ball gag sitting around, it was Sanctum.

He nodded, obviously satisfied that she intended to comply. "Very good. Now, when I ask a direct question, you can answer me, but other than that, I want silence. Oh, unless you feel the need to moan. Moaning, screaming in pleasure, and calling out my name are perfectly acceptable. Look at that. You just got your first lesson in protocol. We're moving along quite nicely."

Wow. Not being able to reply really sucked. She was forced to stay where she was.

"Now, like I was saying before I was rudely interrupted, you have all the right parts for an orgasm. Do you masturbate often?"

She felt her skin flush.

"That was a direct question, sweetheart. You can answer."

Where was the ball gag when she needed it? "What if I don't want to answer?"

He shrugged a little. "If you don't answer, I'll decide you don't like to talk and would prefer to spend the time I would devote to conversations learning which type of nipple clamps you like."

"I don't masturbate," she said as quickly as she could because she would really prefer to embarrass herself over testing out nipple clamps.

He frowned down at her, his hand over her belly. "Never?"

He seemed really intent on making her blush as often as possible. "I've tried a couple of times but it doesn't work."

"Vibrator?"

"Where would I find a vibrator? I was raised in a tiny town in Texas. Those old biddies came down hard on us for yawning in church. Do you honestly think they would let an adult store in?"

His hand was moving down her body, tickling her skin where it touched and making her wish she wasn't wearing the small amount of clothing she was wearing because she really liked having his hands on her. Heat seemed to follow everywhere those fingers skimmed.

"There's this new thing called the Internet. I might be an old man, but I think you youngsters are pretty good with it."

She opened her mouth to refute that statement and then realized it had been a land mine.

Keith chuckled. "Very good. Not a direct question. You're getting the hang of it. Why didn't you use the Internet?"

"Because my mom watched me like hawk. After Dad left, she was really hard on us about everything. And then she died and after Jill made sure I got through high school, she left and everyone was watching me. I worked in a local church, saving money for college.

There aren't a lot of choices where I was raised. If you want to get a job there, you better have a good reputation. There isn't even a fast food place to work in."

A single finger slid across her clitoris.

Holy hell.

"I'm sorry to hear that, sweetheart. I was raised in the godless city so I masturbate a lot. Give me your hand. I want to teach you."

It wouldn't work, of course, but she'd already felt more from him than she had in all the tries before.

"The key is to relax." His hand covered hers, fingers sliding over to guide her.

Dungeon Royale
Masters and Mercenaries, Book 6
By Lexi Blake
Coming February 18, 2014

An agent broken

MI6 agent Damon Knight prided himself on always being in control. His missions were executed with cold, calculating precision. His club, The Garden, was run with an equally ordered and detached decadence. But his perfect world was shattered by one bullet, fired from the gun of his former partner. That betrayal almost cost him his life and ruined his career. His handlers want him to retire, threatening to revoke his license to kill if he doesn't drop his obsession with a shadowy organization called The Collective. To earn their trust, he has to prove himself on a unique assignment with an equally unusual partner.

A woman tempted

Penelope Cash has spent her whole life wanting more. More passion. More adventure. But duty has forced her to live a quiet life. Her only excitement is watching the agents of MI6 as they save England and the world. Despite her training, she's only an analyst. The closest she is allowed to danger and intrigue is in her dreams, which are often filled with one Damon Knight. But everything changes when the woman assigned to pose as Damon's submissive on his latest mission is incapacitated. Penny is suddenly faced with a decision. Stay in her safe little world or risk her life, and her heart, for Queen and country.

An enemy revealed

With the McKay-Taggart team at their side, Damon and Penny hunt an international terrorist across the great cities of Northern Europe. Playing the part of her Master, Damon begins to learn that under Penny's mousy exterior is a passionate submissive, one who just might lay claim to his cold heart. But when Damon's true enemy is brought out of the shadows, it might be Penny who pays the ultimate price.

About Lexi Blake

Lexi Blake lives in North Texas with her husband, three kids, and the laziest rescue dog in the world. She began writing at a young age, concentrating on plays and journalism. It wasn't until she started writing romance that she found success. She likes to find humor in the strangest places. Lexi believes in happy endings no matter how odd the couple, threesome or foursome may seem. She also writes contemporary Western ménage as Sophie Oak.

Connect with Lexi online:

Facebook: Lexi Blake
Twitter: www.twitter.com/@authorlexiblake
Website: www.LexiBlake.net

Sign up for Lexi's free newsletter at
http://lexiblake.net/contact.html#newsletter

CPSIA information can be obtained
at www.ICGtesting.com
Printed in the USA
LVOW11s1755250917

549974LV00003B/573/P